a novel of slasher horror
by CAMERON ROUBIQUE

ISBN 9781790360154

This book is for my wife Darla.

Contents:

Chapter One: The Dance . . . 1

Chapter Two: Confidentiality Agreement . . . 17

Chapter Three: Job Search . . . 37

Chapter Four: Good News and Bad News . . . 55

Chapter Five: Job Orientation . . . 67

Chapter Six: Opening Day at Countryside Pool . . . 74

Chapter Seven: After Hours . . . 85

Chapter Eight: Opening Day at Thrill River . . . 94

Chapter Nine: The Wave Pool . . . 117

Chapter Ten: The Rocky River and The Falls . . . 130

Chapter Eleven: Stronger Than Déjà Vu . . . 156

Chapter Twelve: Can't Talk About It . . . 179

Chapter Thirteen: This Party Is Dead . . . 199

Chapter Fourteen: The Last Ones Left in the Park . . . 213

Chapter Fifteen: Runnin' With the Devil . . . 239

Chapter Sixteen: The Screamin' Demon . . . 254

Chapter Seventeen: Beach Party . . . 274

Chapter Eighteen: A Call For Help . . . 289

Chapter Nineteen: Survivors . . . 303

Epilogue . . . 322

Afterword . . . 329

Chapter One:

The Dance

Murder and death were the furthest things from Cyndi's mind as she stood in front of her vanity mirror getting ready for the dance. She often thought about the horrors she had experienced last summer, but tonight her mind was blessedly preoccupied. She glanced away from the hot crimping iron in her hand to check the time on the pink, old-fashioned alarm clock sitting on her night table. It was 4:26.

How can it already be after four? she thought. Johnny wouldn't be picking her up until seven. She still had plenty of time, but the entire day had flown by in what felt like only three or four mindless, forgettable hours. If she wasn't careful, the time would *really* get away from her.

"Calm down, calm down. Plenty of time," she said to herself. She took a deep breath and tried to focus on her hair.

Cyndi had come a long way from the silent, antisocial girl that she had been just a year ago. She had a boyfriend, Johnny, who was almost two years older than she was. He went to DeAngelo High School, where she would be going this upcoming fall. Through Johnny, she had met a new group of friends. She was still a quiet girl by most teenage standards, and she still listened to her Walkman too much, but she no longer used her music as an excuse to shut out the rest of the world. Now she listened to music simply because she loved music.

The new Go-Go's record, *Talk Show*, (she considered it another instant classic) played in her room as she worked on her hair, but she wasn't really listening to it. In her mind, she went over and over the fact that Johnny would be picking her up in just over two hours to go to her very first high school dance, a thought that made her more nervous than she had been since...well, best not to think about those things anymore.

*   *   *

Little did Cyndi realize, Johnny was almost as nervous about the dance as she was. He didn't know how to dance and had never even been to a dance before. The thought of looking like a complete idiot, dancing in front of all his classmates, hung over his head like a dark cloud. Now that he finally had a girlfriend to take to the Spring Dance at school, he couldn't just sit this one out at home like he did last year.

He had woken up that Saturday in early May to an overcast sky and drizzling rain, not the kind of weather he had expected. He had no nice clothes for the dance, and had put off buying new ones until today. With his savings almost totally depleted, and a extra forty bucks on loan from his mom, he drove his rusty old Seafoam Green '58 Chevy Bel Air out to the Westview Mall. Finally, after awkwardly scouring the racks at JC Penney, he bought a light tan sport coat, a nice black shirt, and a white skinny tie that was squared off at the bottom.

If this is what adults have to deal with everyday, I'm not sure I want to finish growing up, he thought to himself as a cranky middle aged lady with long, fake, dark red nails rang up the clothes.

Now, at 5:30, the sky had cleared, opening up to a nice sunset. He stood in the bathroom in a wife beater and combed mousse into his sandy blonde hair. He flipped his hair over to the side and carefully pulled a few strands down over his forehead in a haphazard, but fashionable way. The trick was to make those strands look perfect without making them look like you tried to make them look perfect.

Once he was dressed, he stood in front of the mirror and sighed. *Better at least give it a try.* He tried his best to dance. To his horror, he looked totally stiff and gangly. He looked like a total dweeb.

"God, I'm in trouble," he sighed to himself.

"I'll say," a high-pitched, giggly voice chimed in from outside the bathroom. Johnny's thirteen-year-old sister, Christie, stood outside the bathroom door, looking smug in her comfortable, everyday street clothes. She giggled at him with her hand over her mouth, then began imitating his practice dance.

"Get out!" he shouted at Christie and slammed the door.

*   *   *

Cyndi sat in her window, watching the sunset and waiting for Johnny's old clunker to pull up out front. She was all made-up with her thick eyeliner and light blue eye-shadow. She had spent two meticulous hours on her hair and it looked as good as it was going to get. A light smile came to her lips as she remembered that she had been sitting right here at the window the first time she and Johnny had smiled and waved to each other. It had been last summer after she came back home from camp. She remembered how her heart had jumped into her throat with excitement. Now sitting here in her light blue dress and full makeup, she felt that same nervous excitement, only it was more intense.

After what felt like a full hour of sitting on her windowsill and looking at the alarm clock every thirty seconds, Johnny's old Bel Air finally pulled up to the curb out front. Cyndi immediately jumped up and stood in the middle of her room waiting for the sound of the doorbell and her parent's voices calling for her to come downstairs.

Johnny stood on the front step and braced himself before ringing the doorbell. It was no secret to Johnny that Cyndi's parents didn't like him. Her parents had no problems with him at the beginning of last summer when they hired him to mow their lawn, but ever since he and Cyndi started dating last September, they had seemed cold and uneasy toward him. He had never given them any reason not to trust him. He always came to the door and talked with them before picking Cyndi up, and had always gotten her home by their specified curfew times. There had never been any big arguments between he and Cyndi, and he'd always been polite and friendly without trying to seem like he was kissing her parents' asses. It was simply the two year age difference. Technically, Johnny was only one year and six months older than Cyndi, but it wasn't the calendar year that bugged them. They just didn't want their eighth-grade daughter dating a sophomore in high school. Johnny and Cyndi were crazy about each other though, and polite as he was, he wasn't about to back down and break things off with her just because of a slight age difference.

He rang the doorbell and listened to the faint shuffling sounds from inside. Cyndi's mother opened the door and gave him a polite smile.

"Hello, Johnny. My, you look nice." Johnny noticed, and ignored, the brief hesitation before the word *nice*. Apparently she didn't quite approve of his thin sport coat with the rolled up sleeves, or maybe it was the skinny tie. From what Cyndi told him, her mother didn't approve of her fashion sense either, and Cyndi dressed in much wilder outfits than Johnny ever did. Johnny usually wore acid washed jeans and T-shirts or loose Hawaiian shirts. He dressed in a kind of modest surfer dude style even though he had never surfed in his life.

"Thanks, Mrs. Stevens," he replied without missing a beat.

"Well, come on in, she'll be right down. CYNDI, HONEY!"

Cyndi's dad got up from his armchair in the living room and held out a hand.

"Johnny," he said curtly. Johnny had been through this routine before. Cyndi's dad always tried to look somewhat intimidating and stern, but with his big glasses, mustache, and skinny build, Johnny was never very afraid of him. Johnny looked him in the eye and gave him a firm handshake.

"How are you, Mr. Stevens?"

"Oh, fine. Just fine."

"There she is. Oh! Look at you, honey," Cyndi's mom gasped in adoration.

Johnny looked up and saw her standing at the top of the stairs. Cyndi looked like a goddess to him as she slowly came down. Her blonde, crimped hair looked flawless, cascading down one side of her face and almost covering her right eye. It bounced lightly with each step she took. Perched on the left side of her head was her usual matching bow. She wore a low cut light blue dress that fanned out at her waist. He thought she looked a little strange without her usual orange headphones dangling around her neck and dozens of bracelets around her wrists and forearms, but there was still enough of her usual fashion sense left over to seem familiar.

Cyndi's eyes caught his and she gave him a quick embarrassed smile as she descended the stairs.

"You look incredible," he told her as she reached the bottom landing. The words sounded geeky and poorly chosen as they left his mouth. *Jeez, you couldn't think of a better word than 'incredible?'* She didn't seem to notice and smiled at him.

"Okay, I gotta get a picture of you two on your big night," Cyndi's mom said excitedly. In one hand she held her nice Nikon camera, and with the other she began herding them toward the front door.

"Mom," Cyndi grumbled impatiently.

"Come on, come on." As usual, her mother was unflinching in her need to take lots of pictures at every big moment. They put on their best smiles as Cyndi's mom clicked off shot after shot, directing them into various poses. After a dozen pictures, Cyndi slumped her shoulders in irritation.

"Mom, you're wasting film again."

"Oh, just one more, Cyndi. For goodness sakes."

"Now I want you kids back here no later than twelve, you got that?" Cyndi's dad chimed in.

"Sure. Noon tomorrow," Johnny grinned. Mr. Stevens was not amused. "Kidding. No sweat, Mr. Stevens. We'll be back by midnight."

"All right have a good time, you kids." Mr. Stevens walked over to his wife and held her arm down as she was about to raise the camera again and ask for one more shot. Johnny opened the door for Cyndi and he followed her out.

Watching them go down the front walk, Cyndi's mom felt an immediate sense of loss and fear.

"Be careful," she called out to them.

"We will," they both said as Johnny opened the dinged and dented passenger door for Cyndi.

Once they were both inside the car and the engine started up, Cyndi's mom said, "Oh God, did that just happen? I'm worried already."

Mr. Stevens shook his head. "Come on, honey. Let's go inside." He knew he was in for a long night with his wife.

*   *   *

Johnny clicked on the radio and tuned it to Cyndi's favorite pop station as they drove toward the school.

"Sorry about them," she said.

"No, no. Nothin' to be sorry about," he laughed. Cyndi was always so embarrassed by her parents. Johnny had seen worse, his best friend Eddie's parents were far more embarrassing than Cyndi's.

They drove on in silence for the next five minutes, each lost in their own nervous thoughts. Then Johnny glanced over and caught Cyndi staring at him. Trying to keep his eyes on the road, he smiled at her.

"What?" he asked.

"Nothing." She turned and looked out the passenger window again.

"You're *too* quiet."

Cyndi turned back to him. She hated being called quiet. It was something she had heard much too often over the last few years of her life. Ever since last summer, she had made a conscious effort to not be so "quiet," whatever that meant.

"I could say the same thing about you," she countered playfully.

"Well, I've got a confession to make." She

7

raised her eyebrows in anticipation as he considered how to put his thoughts into words. He finally decided to just come right out with it. "I...can't dance." Cyndi burst out laughing, and Johnny couldn't help but join her. "I know, I know. It's stupid, but I look like a total geek."

"Maybe we'll look like a couple of geeks together. I can't dance either."

"Get outta here. You? The queen of music? Can't dance?" he asked incredulously.

"I like to *listen* to music, not dance to it. I never learned how."

"Well, I guess we'll just have to learn how to dance together then."

"Guess so." Cyndi smiled at him. Both of their nerves about the dance settled a little.

*   *   *

The doors to the DeAngelo High School gym swung open, and the driving beat of "The Safety Dance" by Men Without Hats pounded out at them. The gym floor was thick with kids dancing, laughing, and shouting excitedly over the ear shattering music. Crazy colored lights illuminated the gym all over, some swirling in random patterns. Along the walls were more lights at floor level, casting illuminated pillars of light up walls and bleachers. A disco ball spun lazily from one of the metal rafters overhead, adding a spinning sparkle to the huge gym. Cyndi held Johnny's hand as they walked in, and she was immediately overwhelmed at the sight of everything.

My God, these kids all look so adult and so...tall, Cyndi thought with panic. She stood only five feet tall, and had a cute, youthful face with round cheeks and thick, pouty lips. She noticed that some of the boys here had patchy mustaches. All the girls seemed to be so

8

curvy and well developed, making her feel small and young and inadequate.

Before Cyndi had time to notice much of anything else, Johnny began pulling her along into the crowd. He had spotted Eddie and his date Jodie. Eddie was in a blue sport coat with the sleeves rolled up, just like the one Johnny was wearing. Cyndi also noticed he was wearing one of those goofy piano-key neckties.

"Uh-oh, the party's here!" Eddie screamed as Cyndi and Johnny walked over to where he and Jodie were dancing wildly.

Brief introductions were made. Cyndi and Eddie knew each other, but neither she nor Johnny had ever met Eddie's date. Cyndi had to yell her own name three times to her, she still wasn't comfortable yelling. Eddie joked with Johnny quickly then went back to dancing. He was a lanky, scrawny guy with curly auburn hair and geeky, exaggerated facial features. He looked and acted like a class clown, and had a slight Jersey accent when he talked. His dancing was like some strange version of The Robot. Cyndi and Johnny stood uncomfortably next to Eddie for a moment, wanting to dance but not quite having enough courage to start.

"What? Are you two just gonna stand there in the middle of the dance floor like a couple of scarecrows? Lighten up, will ya?" Eddie yelled at Johnny, giving him a playful shove. Johnny looked at Cyndi for approval and shrugged. She gave him a shy, hesitant look.

"We can't look any worse than him," Johnny shouted, pointing to Eddie with his thumb.

"Hey, I heard that!" Eddie chimed in.

Johnny started to sway back and forth to the beat of the music. He attempted nothing fancy, only an extremely modest dance.

Here goes nothing, Cyndi thought and joined

him.

As they began to dance, both Cyndi and Johnny thought, *this isn't nearly as bad as I thought it was going to be.* It took a little while to get used to letting go of their own inhibitions, but they each found that the longer they danced, the easier it became. Johnny looked around at the other kids and discovered that no one was staring or making fun of them.

Somehow, they had lost Eddie and Jodie in the crowd and stood dancing in the middle of a bunch of kids that Johnny only knew in passing. Cyndi looked around for Eddie and couldn't spot him. Johnny was the only person she knew in a sea of dancing high schoolers. He smiled that cute crooked smile of his and her racing heart sped up even faster.

"Havin' fun?" he shouted to her. She nodded and grinned at him.

"Are you?" she asked. He didn't hear her quiet voice over the music, but easily read her lips and guessed what she asked.

"I'm having a great time!"

Cyndi bumped into another girl and glanced apologetically in her direction, but the girl seemed to take no notice of her. She looked around the room and realized that she had lost her bearings. They were surrounded by strangers. Somehow they had drifted out to the middle of the dance floor. She tried to look for the walls or the main doors that they had walked in through, but found it hard to see over the shoulders of the other kids. Everyone here seemed so much taller than she was.

She looked off to the left across the gym. A few rows of bleachers had been pulled out to give the kids somewhere to sit and socialize between dances. Through gaps between dancing kids, she saw a dark corner behind those bleachers where there were no decorations or lights. Something white caught her eye deep in the darkness. She peered between the other kids to get a better look.

A gap formed between the dancing couples and Cyndi could make out the dark figure of a tall man standing back in the corner. He hung back in the darkness staring directly at Cyndi. His chest heaved with each heavy panting breath, as if he were in a red rage. He wore a familiar faded white grinning mask with tangles of greasy black hair.

Cyndi's heart dropped and she gasped deeply. She immediately stopped dancing and her eyes went wide with terror.

The masked man stepped into the crowd of dancers, walking briskly. He bumped into a kid who looked at him in annoyance. The man didn't look down, he kept his gaze focused directly on Cyndi. He bumped into a girl, grabbed her by the shoulders, and rudely shoved her out of the way. She flew like a rag doll into the other kids. He grabbed another kid by the shoulders with his powerful, fish-white hands, ripped the kid off his feet, and sent him spinning away.

"Cyndi, what's wrong?" Johnny asked, noticing the look of terror on her face.

Kids began to scream from somewhere off in the corner near the bleachers at the back of the gym. Johnny turned to look in the direction of where the screams were coming from. He thought he saw a flash of white as it ducked down into the crowd. Kids immediately began shoving and pushing in Johnny's direction. He turned to grab Cyndi and protect her from the wave of chaos that was stampeding toward them, but he only grabbed an armful of empty air. Cyndi was gone.

*   *   *

Cyndi saw the killer coming for her and instinctively sprinted for the doors. She forgot all about Johnny as her worst fears had been realized.

Shit! Shit! Shit! He wasn't dead after all! He came back for me! He found me!

She slammed into the catch on the gym door and sprinted out into the dim white glow of the fluorescent emergency lights in the school hallway. There were a few groups of kids loitering outside the doors who stared at her with alarm. She ignored them and sprinted down the hallway past rows of green lockers.

She reached the end of the hall and turned the corner. This part of the hallway was deserted. Her low heels clacked on the checkered black and white linoleum, echoing loudly. The muffled boom of the speakers in the gym continued to pound and vibrate from behind the lockers and the painted cinder block wall on her right. She faintly heard screams from somewhere behind her and a great panicky commotion. Then a heavy, thudding set of footsteps echoed behind her from somewhere down at the end of the hall. She felt like screaming in terror but didn't dare give herself away in case the killer was searching for her.

Up ahead there was a closed metal gate blocking off the rest of the hallway from the floor to the ceiling. She looked around frantically for a side hallway or a classroom to duck into, but there was only an endless stretch of lockers. If she didn't find anything soon, she would be caught like a rat in a trap, easy prey for the killer that had somehow tracked her down after all this time.

High up above the lockers on the wall to her left, she spotted a sign that pointed to the ladies bathroom. She skidded to a stop and turned, slamming into the bathroom door. As she ran into the bathroom, she was immediately swallowed in darkness. The janitors had turned off the lights in here and it was pitch black.

Cyndi turned back to the door and groped blindly for a light switch. Her fingers jammed painfully into something hard and metal, and all at once there was an intense whirring. She had hit the hand dryer.

"Shit!" Cyndi cried out, clutching her fingers as they started to throb. Too late now, the killer would know exactly where she was. The light switch had to be near the hand dryer somewhere. Using her other hand to slide against the wall, she found the light switches only two feet past the hand dryer. She flicked on the first of the switches and a fluorescent bulb flickered to life above the mirrors and sinks on her left. She caught a glimpse of herself in one of those mirrors. Her face looked pale and there was a sheen of cold sweat on her forehead. Her blonde crimped hair was all disheveled and out of place. *I spent hours on it this afternoon.*

No time for looking at yourself. Just get in one of the stalls and hide! Or better yet, jump out a window! No such luck, there were no windows in this bathroom. Five stalls lined the wall on the right with their doors neatly closed. Which stall would the maniac check first? Most likely one on either end. The middle would also be an obvious choice. She picked the second closest stall and went in, hoping she could out-think him.

Once inside, she closed the stall door and turned the lock. Lifting up her blue dress, she climbed onto the toilet seat and sat there with nothing to do but wait.

Now that she could catch her breath, she realized she was breathing too heavily and would give herself away. That loud whirring hand dryer was still on and would drown out the sound of her own breath for now, but she would have to get her breathing under control as quick as possible. She covered her mouth and nose with her hands and struggled to slow her breathing down.

Just then the hand dryer shut down. Cyndi held her breath as the silence flooded back into the bathroom. It was *almost* completely silent. He was in here with her, she could feel his presence. He was holding his breath too.

There was an almost inaudible swish of clothing, then a click as the light switch flicked off and the bathroom was plunged into total darkness once again. The killer allowed himself to breathe again, the darkness was his element. His breath rasped in that same muffled animal pant behind the mask. Cyndi hadn't heard that sound outside of her nightmares since last summer. Heavy boots clunked as the killer slowly walked across the bathroom tiles. He examined the bathroom stalls in the darkness, listening for any sounds or signs of movement. Cyndi's heart pounded madly in her chest. She took only the shallowest breaths behind the cup of her hands.

He stopped dangerously close in front of a stall door. Was he in front of her door or the one next to her? She couldn't tell. The man stopped breathing and Cyndi wondered if he had moved. It was too hard to sense anything in the dark with her heart hammering in her ears.

Suddenly the maniac kicked in the door of the first stall, the one right next to hers. She flinched at the crashing sound and the shuddering stall walls around her. He lunged into the dark stall and wrapped his arms around empty air. His ragged breathing slowed in disappointment as he discovered that his prey had still eluded him.

An idea popped into Cyndi's mind. It was a long shot, but there was a chance she could get out of this. She prepared herself to move quickly, desperately

14

wishing she were wearing something more comfortable than this stupid clumsy dress and these awkward shoes. She listened as the killer regained his footing and left the stall he had kicked in. He took a few soft steps forward until he stood directly outside the stall where Cyndi hid in terrified anticipation. He stood quietly outside the stall contemplating, trying to guess which door might pay off.

Cyndi listened to his shallow breathing against the rubber grinning mask that had haunted her dreams all these months. The same dread, the same hollow sickness in the pit of her stomach came rushing back. Her heart was pounding too hard, too loud. Could he hear it?

He took a step forward, apparently deciding to move on to one of the other stalls farther down the line.

Thank God, she thought. *Now maybe I can--*

The killer kicked out at her stall door, faking her out and catching her off guard. She let out a short scream that was as much surprise as it was fear. The door bucked and rattled, but the lock held. She heard a splintery crack from the stall door's hinges.

Stepping down off the toilet, Cyndi lowered herself to the floor. The killer launched another powerful thundering kick at the stall door. It crashed open and he lunged forward just as Cyndi dropped to the cold floor tiles and slid underneath the partition into the next stall. The killer groped around blindly for her in the dark and to his surprise he felt only the toilet and the wall behind it. Then he heard the shuffling of her dress and the click of her short heels on the tile behind him.

Cyndi got to her feet, hiked up her skirt, and sprinted for the door. She flung herself at the door, sensing that he was right behind her.

The light in the hallway blinded her eyes, and she shrieked as a man caught her in his arms.

"Whoa, whoa, hey, Cyndi. It's me," Johnny

said.

Cyndi struggled and lashed out at Johnny for a second before her eyes adjusted and she realized who was holding her. She looked into his earnest eyes and began yanking him by the arm.

"We have to get out of here!" she cried.

"Whoa, hold it. Cyndi, slow down," he pleaded.

"Come on! Come on!" She tugged at his arms and pulled him down the hallway. Her eyes frantically darted back and forth between Johnny and the closed bathroom door.

"Cyndi, what's going on? Was someone in there with you?" Johnny had noticed her eyes glancing back at the bathroom and he looked back himself. Nothing about the bathroom seemed out of the ordinary to him.

Cyndi suddenly let go of Johnny's arms. He turned away from the bathroom in time to see Cyndi go sprinting back down the hallway toward the gym and the front doors of the school.

"Cyndi, wait up!" he called out and ran after her.

If Johnny had waited another second to watch the bathroom door he might have noticed that it wasn't quite closed. He might have noticed the crack between the door and the frame, and the white grinning mask peering out at him from the darkness.

Chapter Two:

Confidentiality Agreement

At Cyndi's urgent, almost hysterical pleas, Johnny fired up the Bel Air's engine and tore out of the high school's parking lot. His tires squealed loudly on the pavement and left long black streaks.

"You wanna tell me what this is all about?" he asked, somewhat annoyed.

Cyndi only stared out at the shadowy frame of the school, watching for signs of the killer. She expected to see him come shambling out of one of the side exits any second, chasing after the car.

"Cyndi! Hey! What happened in there?" He raised his voice loud, trying to turn his shout into a verbal slap on her face to break her out of her hysteria. She ignored him. He glanced over and saw her staring intently back at the school as if searching the grounds for someone. Her shoulders were tense and she was breathing in short wheezing gasps. Whatever she had seen had freaked her out big time.

"Cyndi, talk to me. What the hell is go--"

"Just *drive!*" Cyndi snapped. To Johnny, she

didn't sound like herself at all. It was a like she had taken on a strange voice that Johnny had never heard come out of her mouth. She always seemed so meek and mild, but this voice was aggressive and almost...God, was she actually *angry?*

"Where?"

"Take me home."

Oh shit, here we go, he thought. *Her parents are just gonna love this.*

They drove in silence. Cyndi kept turning and looking out the back window. Johnny checked in his rear view mirror once or twice to see what she was looking at, but saw only darkness and the red glow of his own taillights. Once they were about a mile away from the school, Cyndi finally relaxed a little and slumped back in her seat. Johnny could see that her mind was still racing. He didn't press her for answers, but he was dying to know what had happened to make her freak out like that.

Her neighborhood came into view. Johnny pulled over underneath a streetlight in front of a random house that looked like it was nearly the same style as Cyndi's house.

"What are you doing?" Cyndi asked.

Johnny kept the engine running, shifted into neutral, and took his foot off the clutch. "Listen, if I take you home now, your parents are gonna freak and think I did something to you. Now you gotta tell me what happened. Did I do something wrong, or what? I mean... Was it that fight in the gym? Or was someone in the bathroom with you?"

Cyndi looked into his pleading eyes. He looked so concerned. She wanted to tell him everything.

"It wasn't you. It's just...I...."

There was a part of the story last year that she had nearly forgotten. At the time, it had seemed so insignificant next to all the violence and death she had witnessed. Back then, she had just wanted to forget it, as if it had all been just some nightmare. That little part of the story had begun to weigh heavily on her over time, but it had never nagged at her as much as it did right now.

Remember you promised.

Cyndi's mind began to rewind back to last summer.

*   *   *

The house seemed so unreal as they pulled up into the driveway. Cyndi looked up and saw her window upstairs. It felt good to see something so familiar despite the fact that her life had completely changed in the past week. She knew her room wouldn't have been touched, it would still be exactly as she left it over a week ago, but after everything she had been through, she almost expected everything in there to be drastically different.

Her father opened the car door and held out a hand to help her stand up.

"Dad, I can walk fine," she said solemnly.

He only stared at the bruises on her neck for a second, he seemed to be having trouble comprehending them. Then he nodded apologetically and went to get her suitcase out of the back of the station wagon.

The bruises on her neck had taken on a rotten yellow color and were fading quickly. The cuts on her legs had scabbed up nicely. There was still a large bandage on her left side. Cyndi was sore, but she didn't want to be treated so delicately, she wasn't a baby. What she wanted most was to be left alone, crank up some records, and mentally escape for a while.

Her bedroom hadn't changed a bit, just as she had expected, but it still seemed odd and out of place. Her dad brought the suitcase and her backpack up to her room.

"Well, here ya go," he shrugged. Both of her parents stood in the bedroom doorway as she walked around, running her fingers lightly over everything as if to confirm its existence. She looked back over her shoulder and saw them staring at her with wide eyes.

"What?" she asked.

"Nothing," her dad said with a guilty smile.

"Why do you guys act like you're afraid of me?"

"Honey, we're not afraid of you, it's just..." her mother trailed off and turned to her father.

"If you need anything, we'll be right downstairs, okay?" Dad picked up the slack.

"Thanks." Her dad put his arm around her mom's shoulders and led her away.

As soon as they were out of sight, Cyndi sat down on her bed gingerly. It seemed so much softer than she had remembered it. She supposed that after spending one night in a raft, and the next up in a tree, anything would feel too soft.

Cyndi sat in silence for the next two hours and let her body and mind settle.

Before she realized how much time had passed, she heard the doorbell ring downstairs. She glanced at the clock. *Who could be here at 2:30 on a weekday?*

She got up and walked over to look out her window. Down at the end of the lawn, parked on the street, was a shiny black stretch limousine in front of her house.

Before Cyndi had time to ask herself what a stretch limo was doing at her house, the doorbell rang again. Cyndi ran over to her bedroom door, opened it just a crack, and listened. Her room was at the end of the hallway and she wouldn't be able to see who was at the door unless she crept over to the top of the stairs.

Downstairs, Cyndi's father gave his wife a

20

perplexed look. "Who the hell could that be?"

"I don't know," her mother whispered back.

They answered the door and from upstairs Cyndi heard the deep, cheery voice of a middle aged man.

"Mr. and Mrs. Stevens?"

"Yes."

"My name is Kurt Carver, I'm the C.E.O. of Bright Smiles Corporation. My family owns Camp Kikawa. I was hoping I could talk with you and your daughter. Is this a good time?"

"Uh...well..." Her parents sounded utterly flabbergasted. "Sure, come in."

"Thank you."

There was a brief shuffling of footsteps and Cyndi quickly laid back down on her bed, trying to act casual.

Downstairs, Cyndi's mother whispered to her father. "I'll go get her."

"Uh, why don't we go into the living room, Mr. Carver?" her father asked.

"Please, call me Kurt."

"Okay, Kurt. And why don't you call me, Bill?"

Cyndi listened to this muffled exchange and then heard her mother's soft footsteps coming up the stairs. There was a light knock on the door and her mother opened it. She looked very intimidated, almost starstruck. Cyndi imagined she would have a similar look on her own face if she were to ever meet The Go-Go's face to face.

"Cyndi, honey? There's a man downstairs who wants to see you."

"Who is it?" Cyndi asked.

"It's the owner of the summer camp. Do you feel up for this?"

Cyndi shrugged, "I guess."

Together they walked downstairs, her mother close behind her. They went into the living room and Cyndi saw the back of a large man's head as he sat in her father's easy chair. The chair was turned in the opposite direction so she couldn't see his face yet. Her father saw them coming and stood up. The man briefly looked over his shoulder, saw them walking in, and also stood politely.

"Uh, Cyndi, honey, this is Mr. Carver, the owner of Camp Kikawa. This is my daughter, Cyndi," her dad made the introductions.

As Mr. Carver turned around, Cyndi caught her first glimpse of his face, and her mouth dropped open. He grinned at her with the same smile and the same huge perfect teeth as the killer's white mask. Of course the mask had been a cartoonish exaggeration, but the resemblance was uncanny. His face resembled the mask as closely as President Reagan's face resembled one of those rubber masks they made of him that you could get at the costume stores around Halloween.

"Hello, Cyndi. It's a great pleasure to meet you." He held out his hand. Cyndi had to force herself to politely shake it and close her shocked mouth.

"Nice to meet you," she replied very quietly.

Mr. Carver was a huge, solidly built man. Cyndi guessed he was maybe six foot four. He spoke with an air of authority, and had an impeccable sense of style. He wore a very expensive looking pinstripe suit and a large gold watch. There were several huge rings on his fingers. His hair was dark black and perfectly slicked back, hanging down almost to his shoulders. Cyndi couldn't help but stare at him as her mother offered him a drink, which he politely declined.

They all sat down on the couch with Cyndi protectively placed in between her mother and father.

"First off, I'd just like to thank you for taking

22

the time to sit down with me. I only wish I could've met you under, uh, brighter circumstances. My father, Kent Carver, wanted to come as well, but he is eighty-two years old and I'm afraid his health has declined significantly over the last few years. But on behalf of my father, the Bright Smiles Corporation, Camp Kikawa, and myself, I just wanted to express how truly sorry we are for everything you went through. I can't imagine how awful it must have been and I'm deeply sorry."

He seemed sincerely apologetic and genuinely moved.

"Well, thank you," her father muttered.

"Yes, thank you," her mother agreed. "This means a lot, you coming here. Doesn't it, Cyndi?"

Cyndi could not pull her eyes away from the man's face, his lips had pulled back in that eerie grin again. Her mother jabbed her elbow into Cyndi's side and she remembered her manners.

"Uh, yeah. Thanks," she mumbled.

"You're very welcome. There's also another reason I came here today. The inattentiveness of the staff at Camp Kikawa was unacceptable, and I wanted to personally assure you that there have been major changes in personnel since the tragedy." Cyndi imagined this huge, intimidating man yelling at Head Counselor Sheehan, and maybe even that bitchy bunk leader Morgan, then firing the both of them. "We have also been working very closely with the police in their investigation of...what happened."

"Well thank you, that's good to know," her father replied.

"We would also like to make it up to you, Cyndi. We'd like to offer you a full ride scholarship to the college of your choice once you graduate high school in a few years."

Her mother and father's eyes widened and their

mouths opened in excited surprise. Mr. Carver's grin widened as well. Cyndi's father patted her on the back, and her mother smiled down at her, squeezing her hand.

"That's very generous of you, Mr. Carver, I mean Kurt."

"We don't know what to say."

Cyndi looked down at the floor, trying to process all of this information.

"Don't mention it at all. We're more than happy to do it. Although..."

The smiles fell off her parents faces instantly. There was always a catch.

"We were hoping that in exchange for full college tuition, your family could do us a tiny favor. If word of this unforeseen tragedy got out to the public, it could cripple my family's company. In fact, it could damage the company so severely that your scholarship may not even be there waiting for you when you reach graduation. So you see, what's best for the company is best for you."

The parents exchanged worried looks, their daughter's entire college tuition was at stake.

"Well...that shouldn't be a problem. Should it, honey?" her father asked her mother.

"No. Not a problem at all," she replied. Neither one of them even gave Cyndi a questioning glance before smiling back at the generous Kurt Carver.

"Excellent. I just knew we would see things eye to eye," Mr. Carver beamed. He reached into his jacket and pulled out a neatly folded piece of paper. "This is a confidentiality agreement. It's a very basic form that states that you will not discuss, either verbally or in writing, anything that happened after you left Camp Kikawa, and in exchange the Carver estate will provide you with a full ride scholarship to the college of your choice. It's that simple."

He unfolded the contract and handed it to Cyndi's father across the coffee table. Her dad squinted down at the contract, trying to skim through it as fast as he could. Cyndi took a look at it. It was only one page, but the words seemed too small and deceptive. Cyndi looked back at Mr. Carver as he pulled a fancy pen out of the front pocket of his jacket. They locked eyes and he grinned again.

A deal with the devil, she thought.

"Isn't this the kind of thing you'd usually have a lawyer bring over?" her dad asked warily.

"I understand your concern, Mr. Stevens, and believe me, under any other circumstances, absolutely. But these are extreme circumstances, and I thought it would be more personal if I handled this myself. Think how insensitive it would be for me to show up at your house with lawyers, especially after your daughter has just returned from experiencing such a horrific event."

Her father shrugged. "That makes sense. And I appreciate your thoughtfulness."

"Of course." Mr. Carver handed her father the pen and he scratched down his signature. He handed it to her mother.

"Are you sure about this, dear?" her mother asked hesitantly.

"It's fine, honey. It's all right there in plain English."

"I completely understand your concern, Terri, but there's nothing to worry about. Take all the time that you need to read through it. I know a rare opportunity like this must seem too good to be true, but we only want what's best for Cyndi."

"Well...okay, I guess." Her mother scratched her signature in at the bottom and handed the contract and the pen to Cyndi. She stared down at the contract and the pen in her hand.

This isn't right, her thoughts raced. *He can't just come in here and hush us up like this. Not without giving me some kind of explanation as to just what the hell happened.*

"Honey, it's okay. Go ahead," her mother whispered.

Cyndi put the pen down on the table and looked up at Mr. Carver. "Before I sign, there are some things I need to know."

"Cyndi, please," her father pleaded. She ignored him.

The grin remained on Mr. Carver's face, but there was an icy coldness lurking just under the surface of that grin.

"It's all right, Bill. I'd be more than happy to tell you anything I can," he said calmly.

"What the hell *was* that place?" Cyndi asked point blank.

"Cyndi!" her mother said, shocked at her daughter's frank language.

"No, no. Please. It's perfectly all right. She can ask anything she'd like," Carver held up his hand defensively to Cyndi's mother, then turned to Cyndi. "You and your friends had stumbled onto some private property owned by my family. It's a secluded spot deep in the woods about twelve miles southwest of the highway. Very few people know about this, but we have been designing and testing amusement park rides there."

"Rides?" her father asked curiously.

"Yes. I'm afraid I can't reveal too many details about them, as we like to keep our designs very private to protect our investments. I can tell you we're planning on selling these rides to several water-based amusement parks around the country in exchange for free advertising. The rides are mostly for publicity for the company, but we were also planning on keeping the prototypes in working order as sort of a private getaway for our family and friends."

"Wow. So that's how the other half lives," said her mother admiringly.

Carver shrugged. "I know it all seems a bit extravagant. My father, Kent Carver, spent some time in Vaudeville before he got into the dental industry and started Bright Smiles. Walt Disney is his idol. And I can assure you, my father is still very, uh...theatrical." He chuckled.

"The guy who was after us, who was he?" Cyndi asked without hesitation.

He seemed to suppress his grin. "At this point, we still don't know. Like I said, we are working with the police and a private investigator to discover anything we can about him. We think he was most likely a member of the construction crew. He may have just...snapped. The police have narrowed his identity down to half a dozen potential suspects based on the bodies that have not been found and positively identified yet, but, unfortunately, we will probably never be able to find *all* of the bodies."

"Jesus," Cyndi's dad muttered. Her mother looked pale and cupped a hand over her mouth.

"And the mask?" Cyndi asked.

Carver grinned. "I noticed you staring at me earlier. My face looks familiar?" Cyndi nodded gravely. Carver only laughed. "Kaptain Smiley was the first advertising campaign that my father introduced for Bright Smiles way back in 1947. It was discontinued in 1964. The face was a caricature based off of his own face. He was, well, actually *still* is, known for his winning smile. I'm told I am the spitting image of him, although I don't see it." He waved a demonstrative open hand underneath his chin, and grinned. Cyndi's parents laughed, but she did not. He looked eerily too much like the mask. "To answer your question, we have absolutely no idea where he got that old mask, or why he wore it."

Cyndi sat in silence trying to wrap her mind around all of these new revelations. All of the mysteries of the past week of her life seemed to be explained. It seemed too easy, too convenient, but what other explanations could there be?

"Is that everything you wanted to know?"

"I...guess so," she shrugged, trying to think of any other questions.

"Before I forget, there's one more thing I have for you." Next to the easy chair, Mr. Carver picked up a small gift-wrapped box with a purple bow and handed it to Cyndi. She opened the box, and inside, sitting on a piece of cotton padding, was a brand new Walkman tape player with a new pair of orange headphones. Its silver sides seemed to sparkle. "We found your cassette player broken and I thought I would replace it for you."

"Aww, that was so sweet of you, Kurt," Cyndi's mom beamed at him.

"It's my pleasure."

Cyndi stared distrustfully at the Walkman, then looked up at Mr. Carver. His smile seemed genuine. That ice behind the grin seemed to have melted.

"Thank you. Thank you very much," Cyndi said, giving him her own smile.

"Now if I can just get that last signature from you, I'll get out of your hair and we can put this whole mess behind us."

"Go ahead, Cyndi," her dad pushed.

Cyndi picked up the pen, took a deep breath, and signed her name in her loopy neat handwriting.

"You made the right decision," Mr. Carver said as Cyndi handed him the agreement and the pen. He glanced at the three signatures, folded the paper, and made it disappear back into his suit jacket. "Well, I'd like to thank you for letting me into your home. If you have any more questions, or if there's anything you need at all, here's my card. Call anytime, tell my assistant who you are, and if I'm not available, I'll get back to you as soon as I can."

They all stood up and walked Mr. Carver to the door. He shook their hands and told them how very nice it was to meet them. Then he walked down the front walkway where his driver stood stoically near the back door of the limousine. Cyndi couldn't help but feel that everything had all been explained too easily, like there were more layers of the story yet to be uncovered. She looked down at her brand new Walkman and an image came to her. It was the image of Stacy's body lying dead and motionless after Cyndi had pulled her out of the slow current of the Lazy River. She remembered how she had placed Stacy's limp delicate hand over the jagged wound in Stacy's stomach. Wasn't this exactly what Carver was doing? Conveniently covering up a bloody mess?

"Mr. Carver," Cyndi called out. He stopped and turned back. Her parents looked down at her alarmed. "What happened to his body?" Her parents glanced at each other nervously.

He paused, looking down at the concrete and gathered his words. "All you need to know is that you can put it behind you now."

"I'd sleep better knowing what happened to his body."

He nodded to himself, as if he'd expected that she would ask this particular question.

"I haven't the faintest idea what happened to it."

Carver gave her one last grin, then turned and stepped into his limousine. The driver shut the door behind him and he disappeared behind the dark tinted windows. Cyndi watched as the limousine drove away.

Later in her room, she pulled out Zack's gray T-shirt with the monster truck and the cut-off sleeves, and

Stacy's pink shirt, the ones she had taken from the picnic area before escaping the water park. She laid them out on her bed and looked at them for a while, trying to remember her friends. The new Walkman lay on her bed next to it. Mr. Carver's words came back to her: *All you need to know is that you can put it behind you now.*

Cyndi neatly folded the shirts and put them on top of the new Walkman. Then she placed the whole bundle back into the bottom drawer of the dresser she kept in her closet. And for the next two months, that was where they stayed.

*   *   *

Cyndi had come home one day in late August, about two months later, full of a nervous tension that she hadn't felt in weeks. She and her mother had been out running errands when she saw the sign advertising *Thrill River* currently under construction less than five miles from her house. They had even used the same grinning Kaptain Smiley character on the sign.

"That son of a bitch," she said out loud, slamming her bedroom door behind her. Carver had known all along that they were testing rides for this new water park. He had known that any bad publicity would slow him down. *So here you go Cyndi, too bad you survived. Here's some hush money and a contract to sign.* She felt completely used. He could have at least had the decency to take all of that Kaptain Smiley crap out of the advertising.

Cyndi dug through the piles of junk and papers on her desk. Carver's business card had to be somewhere around here. She was going to call and give him an earful. After searching for ten minutes, tossing everything off the desk and onto the floor, she found it. One of the corners had folded and some makeup powder had smeared on it.

Breathing heavily, she picked up the phone and dialed the number with shaking fingers. As she waited for him to pick up, everything suddenly became real and she was hit with a wave of doubt. All of her nerve seemed to be draining out of her. *Maybe this isn't such a good idea.*

There was a click and a cheery, professional-sounding woman picked up. "Bright Smiles Incorporated, how may I direct your call?"

Cyndi sat silently for a moment, then slammed the phone back down into its cradle so hard it dinged once.

What difference does it make? It's over now isn't it? Besides, it's not like he's going to say, 'Oh you're right. Gee, I didn't even think about that. Sorry Cyndi. I'll take down the smiley faces right away.'

She picked up the phone again and began dialing Johnny, her new boyfriend's, number. She had to vent about this-- She stopped herself four numbers in.

You can't. If you tell him about it and they find out, all that hush money goes down the drain. You can't let them get away with this AND cut off the scholarship.

Reluctantly, she put the phone down again. She walked over to her closet and yanked open the drawer. She dug through her clothes and pulled out Stacy and Zack's T-shirts. With careful, delicate hands, she unfolded them and neatly laid them out side by side on her bed.

"God, I wish you guys were here," she said aloud. She spoke softly to the T-shirts, venting her feelings to them, as if Zack and Stacy were both sitting right there patiently listening and commiserating. Twenty minutes later she had no words left, but felt better. As she folded up the shirts and put them back in the drawer, her hand brushed against the unused

31

Walkman and she pulled it out. She could use some nice, loud, angry rock and roll right now. Maybe some Joan Jett, or better yet, Motorhead. She hesitated, not wanting to use the hateful bribe gift. Then she gave in, and dug through her tapes for some of the angry ones. She finally settled on her Suicidal Tendencies tape and popped it into the Walkman.

"This doesn't change anything," she told Carver through the Walkman. She put the fresh new headphones on over her ears, pressed play, and sat down at her windowsill.

*   *   *

Everything came flooding back as she sat in Johnny's car under the streetlight. There had been a few other times throughout the past year when she wanted to tell him what happened last summer, but she had never felt the need to talk about it as urgently as she did now. The words were on the tip of her tongue, fighting and clawing against her closed lips.

"I...I..." she continued to stammer. That confidentiality agreement stood in the way, nagging at her. Johnny didn't push her, he never did, but his silent anticipation didn't make matters any easier.

Cyndi remembered that the killer was still out there somewhere. He might have followed them through the darkness. Surely if he knew where the school was, he knew where she lived. She scanned the dark front yards for even the faintest glimmer of that white grinning mask.

Johnny sighed, defeated. He knew she had been so close to telling him her secret. It had been there since the beginning of their relationship. Cyndi would mention something about one of her friends, then clam up immediately. When they had watched the big world premiere of Michael Jackson's "Thriller" music video on MTV back in December, Cyndi had looked pale and sick and couldn't finish the video.

He knew that she had gone to a summer camp last summer and had gotten sent home early for some reason. He imagined that her friends there had done something really bad, like hurt someone, or gotten seriously injured themselves. Maybe one of them had even gotten killed, he doubted it, but the thought had crossed his mind a few times. Cyndi must have gotten in trouble by association. That was about all Johnny knew, and he didn't dwell on it. Dwelling on it would make him want to push her to talk about it, and he never wanted to do that. God knew how much he hated when he didn't feel like talking about something and his mother would nag at him relentlessly. *What's bothering you? Tell me, Johnny. I'm your mother, you can talk to me about anything. Are you sure you don't want to talk about it? Are you really sure? If you talk about it you'll probably feel better. Why don't you want to talk about it?* It was if she thought she was a psychiatrist or something, and it drove him nuts. So he gave Cyndi her space.

"Look, Cyndi. I don't care if you don't want to talk about what happened. It's fine, really. But we're gonna have to figure out something to tell your parents if you ever want to be able to see me again. They're paranoid enough about me," he explained.

"I'll just tell them I got really sick to my stomach," she said.

"Sounds okay." He shrugged and put the car in gear again. He drove her the rest of the way back to her house.

They pulled up less than five minutes later and Johnny shut off the car.

"Well, it was fun while it lasted I guess," he

sighed.

"I'm sorry I ruined tonight," Cyndi said quietly. Johnny looked over and saw that she was on the verge of tears.

"Hey, hey. Come on. You didn't ruin tonight." He reached over and wiped the tears that were gathering on each eyelid away with his finger. His fingertips were smeared black with mascara. He leaned closer and hugged her, rubbing her back with his hand.

"We didn't even get to have our first dance together," she said with her head on his shoulder.

Johnny pulled away from their hug and looked into her eyes. "There'll be other dances. I'm not going anywhere." He gave her that crooked smile of his. Without thinking, she leaned in and kissed him hard on the mouth. Johnny was so understanding, nothing ever seemed to bother him, and he always knew what to say to make her feel better. She was falling for him hard.

It was a long kiss. When they broke apart, they could only stare at each other in silence, feeling the electricity between them. At that moment, they both desperately wanted to just take one another up to their room and stay together all night. They wanted to lose themselves in that electric heat and fall asleep in each other's arms. It was a nice dream, but one they both knew was impossible, at least for a few years.

Finally Johnny broke the silence. "Come on. I'd better take you in before your mom and dad see us out here."

Cyndi nodded in agreement.

He walked her to the door and they shared another brief kiss. Then they went in, and both had to fend off intense questioning and suspicious looks from her parents.

*   *   *

Cyndi stayed up almost all night sitting at her window in the darkness, watching for the killer. She replayed the events of tonight over and over in her mind. It didn't seem like it had really even happened, it was like some kind of vivid nightmare. She picked the scenario apart, asking herself questions. *If that really was him, then where is he now? How did he get out of the pipe last summer? Why has it taken him this long to find me if he's really still alive?*

She waited, listening for odd sounds in the house: the tinkle of broken glass, the thump of a door, the creak of footsteps coming up the stairs, or the rattle of someone trying to open her locked bedroom door. She heard nothing but the crickets outside until she fell into a deep, dreamless sleep at the windowsill around 3:30 in the morning.

Several hours later, she awoke with a jolt of panic, but sighed with relief when she saw the sunlight. She had made it through last night. But what about tonight? Or the next night? She would have to stay alert.

Cyndi sat down at her vanity and began brushing out the knots in her hair. In the corner of the mirror she saw Kurt Carver's business card. She put the brush down and picked the card up.

Call him. Tell him what happened.

But what good would it do? He wasn't a police officer, he probably wasn't even in this state, and he was trying to keep the whole thing quiet. Besides, if nothing had happened all night, maybe that psychopath hadn't really been at the dance at all. Maybe, it had only been her mind playing tricks on her. If he had really found her, wouldn't he have followed her home last night and started their chase again?

If anything else happens, I'll have to tell

someone. Either I'll have to talk to mom and dad, or the police, or I'll have to call Carver. If just one more thing happens, I'll call...

She set the card back down and continued brushing her hair.

*   *   *

Two hours later, Bill Stevens, Cyndi's dad, walked out to the garage and got into his station wagon. He was on his way to the hardware store to pick up a plug for the downstairs toilet, it had been leaking constantly for the last two weeks. It was Sunday and he wanted to spend the day in his easy chair, but he knew if he put this trip off any longer, the damn water bill would be through the roof.

He backed the station wagon carefully out of the garage and down the driveway. He was trying to predict how much the water bill might amount to this month when something caught his eye. The gate on the side of the house leading into the backyard stood wide open.

"Oh, damn," he muttered. "Must've left it open yesterday."

Bill put the car in park, pulled off his seat belt, and got out. He walked casually over to the gate and closed it. The latch locked the gate into place and it rattled briefly before settling.

"Coulda' sworn I closed it."

On the ground beneath the gate were thin muddy tracks on the octagonal bricks leading into the backyard. Bill didn't notice these tracks though, his mind was elsewhere.

Chapter Three:

Job Search

Nothing much happened over the next week. Cyndi gradually settled back into her regular sleep schedule. The more time passed with nothing eventful happening, the more she felt like seeing the masked maniac at the dance had just been a hallucination and nothing more. In the daylight she could forget about it, but at night the arguing voices in her head would speak up.

There was just a fight at the dance, that's all. You thought you saw that mask, but it was probably just your imagination.

How do you explain what happened in the bathroom then? Who walked in, clicked off the lights, and started kicking in stall doors?

That could have been anyone.

The sound of that breathing was pretty damn unmistakable. You should know.

He's dead. He drowned and got washed away in that pipe last year.

Is he?

She would hear a sudden creak from downstairs, and imagine someone creeping around down there, making their way slowly up the stairs toward her bedroom. Coming for her. With a knife.

Nothing would happen though. She would lie awake for another hour and fall asleep. She woke up just fine every morning with the rising sun chasing away the shadows. *Is he?* In the morning light, those two little words seemed ridiculous.

The coming end of the school year also raised Cyndi's spirits. Middle school had begun, flown by, and ended in a blink. She was more than ready to bury her middle school memories away in the past alongside the memories of last summer. She had gained a new small circle of friends and a boyfriend, but all of them were already in high school (unless you counted Christie, Johnny's little sister, who was only in seventh grade). In middle school, she was still just a quiet, friendless, lonely girl. Once she was officially in high school, she could become the girl she wanted to be.

Every morning seemed to get progressively warmer and more exciting as she neared the approaching summer break. The birds were getting louder, and the golden shine that the sun cast on everything seemed to get brighter.

On a particularly gorgeous Thursday morning, almost a full week since the dance, Cyndi came downstairs humming "Yes Or No" by The Go-Go's. It was currently in her rotation as one of her new favorites. She sat down at the breakfast table and her parents greeted her. Her dad put down the paper he was reading and they both scooted their chairs closer together. Cyndi watched as they glanced at each other, preparing themselves.

"Oh God, I know that look," she said.

"Cyndi, honey, we need to have a little talk," her

dad said, ignoring her comment. "Your mother and I think it would be really good for you if you looked for a summer job."

"A job?" Cyndi asked with an expression of horror.

"It would help give you a taste of responsibility," her mom chimed in.

"Not to mention all the extra money you'd have. You could buy all kinds of records or clothes or whatever."

"I'm not even in high school yet. How am I supposed to get a job?" Cyndi argued. Her father picked up the newspaper he had been reading, and flipped through it until he reached the classified section. He pulled it out and tossed it across the table.

"I seem to remember two weeks ago you came home fifteen minutes late and your exact words were, 'Chill out, Dad, I'm practically in high school already.'"

Cyndi couldn't take it. She dropped her face down onto the table dramatically, the silverware rattled as her skull thunked down.

"What about Johnny? He's gotta gas up that car of his somehow." Her mother hesitated slightly before the word *car*. She worried for her daughter's life every single time she got into that rusty, old accident-waiting-to-happen.

"He's training to be a lifeguard at the Countryside Pool," Cyndi replied without lifting her head.

"Well, see? He'll be working too. I was thinking you should try to work at that record store at the mall. You'd be perfect for that." Cyndi was irritated to find that her mother's idea actually sounded pretty cool, so she made no response. "And while you're there, you can check out some of the other stores you like too."

Cyndi lifted her head an inch off the table and

banged it down lightly a few times. Her father rolled his eyes and sighed in exasperation.

"Oh, Cyndi, for goodness sakes. It's not gonna kill you," her mother added. Cyndi finally lifted her head, a sly, accusatory expression was on her face.

"Isn't that what you said about going to camp last summer? Because I seem to remember that's almost exactly what happened."

Both of her parents mouths dropped open in shock and horror.

"Cyndi! For goodness sakes!" That was her mother's trademark saying.

"We all agreed we weren't going to talk about that anymore," her father said, trying to sound calm and reasonable.

"That doesn't change the fact that it happened, Dad."

"This is a completely different situation. You are going to at least *look* for a job, is that clear?"

Cyndi glared at her parents for a second, they didn't flinch. "Crystal. I'm not hungry anymore."

She got up and left the table while her father grabbed the newspaper again and pretended to get back to the article he'd been reading before the discussion. He felt his wife staring at him, wanting him to say something.

"Teenagers," he grunted. It was all he could think of to say.

*   *   *

Cyndi was dropped off at the Westview Mall the next day after school by her mother. She wore a black blouse that her mother had insisted she wear in order to look more "presentable." She brought along the Walkman with one of her dozens of mix-tapes, and left

40

her headphones on during the entire car ride over. She draped the left shoulder of her blouse off to one side, and her mother put it back into place as she pulled up to one of the mall's dark-brown brick-lined entrances.

"Mom," Cyndi grumbled. Her mother ignored her and pulled off one of her orange earphones.

"Make sure you put these things away in your purse before you walk in anywhere," she said loudly.

"Okay, okay," Cyndi wriggled her way out of her mother's grip and got out of the car. She wished Cyndi luck and watched her walk into the mall. *Oh Lord, she doesn't stand a chance with that attitude,* she thought. *She'll just have to learn things the hard way.*

Ironically, the song that came on as Cyndi walked through the glass front doors into the mall was "Money Changes Everything" by Cyndi Lauper. She couldn't help but wonder why certain songs always seemed to play whenever the lyrics were oddly appropriate to her own personal situation. Was it just coincidence, or was it the universe's way of trying to give her some kind of message?

There were dozens of middle school and high school kids hanging around in little groups throughout the mall. Cyndi recognized a lot of them from the hallways of her own school. She always loved the fresh new clothes and recycled air smell that seemed to permeate every crevice of the mall. She also loved the raised medians that divided the center of the mall and the bizarre jungle of real and fake plants that filled them. Holding her hand out, she let it brush against the plants, feeling their smooth, waxy textures as she walked.

Cyndi reached a green-carpeted gap between two sections of median, and crossed over to the other side, the record store was only a few doors down from here. She glanced over at a tiny pond and fountain at the end of the median. A group of high school sophomores were clustered around a wooden bench in front the pond. One of the kids, a guy in a leather jacket with curly black hair, leaned back, reached into the fountain and splashed a brunette girl in a tiny pink denim jacket who was talking a mile a minute. The girl gave an exaggerated gasp of surprise and immediately went after him. For a second, Cyndi was reminded of Zack and Stacy. Hadn't Zack and Stacy done that exact thing last summer at the--

Nope, now is definitely not the time to be thinking of that, she stopped her own train of thoughts.

The record store was now in sight, with its pink neon stripes and the bouncy illuminated words *Sam Goody* near the ceiling. Cyndi could already hear synthy New Wave music blasting from inside and she recognized the song as soon as she took off her headphones. It was "The Metro" by Berlin, another song that she had on one of her mix-tapes back at home.

Cyndi took her headphones off and put them into her purse as she walked in. The guy behind the counter was busy ringing up some teenage girl, so she decided to browse around and see if there were any new albums that she just had to get. After the girl went away, Cyndi walked up to the counter.

The guy at the counter greeted her with his usual blank stare. He looked like a brain-dead version of Billy Idol with his bleached spiky hair. He had rung her up dozens of times but never seemed to recognize her.

"Uh, hi," Cyndi said, trying to speak loudly over the music. "I was just wondering if you guys were looking for any help over the summer."

The dude stared at her awkwardly for a moment as if he were trying to comprehend what she said. She was about to open her mouth to say something when he finally spoke up.

"You sixteen?" he asked in his monotone voice.

"Umm no, I'm fourteen...and a half." She

immediately regretted adding that last bit, it made her sound like a dumb little kid.

"Sorry, kid. Gotta be at least sixteen to work here."

"Oh, okay. Thanks anyway." He nodded to her and watched her as she walked out. She put her headphones back on to drown out the noisy store. She somehow got the feeling that the jerk with the spiky hair had been lying to her. *Whatever. I didn't want to spend all summer working with that moron anyway.*

Now where? She had been really counting on the record store being her first and last stop on this job hunt. Now she would have to walk through the mall alone and look for *Help Wanted* signs hanging in store windows.

Over the next hour, she found two clothing stores with *Help Wanted* or *Now Hiring* signs. She was again told by both that she would have to be at least sixteen years old. She stopped at the Orange Julius near the middle of the mall and thought, *Hey, I'd probably get free Orange Julius all the time if I worked here.*

At the counter, she asked if they were hiring for summer help. A perky girl with pigtails sticking out from her Orange Julius cap said that they were and she handed Cyndi an application and a pen. Cyndi sat down at one of the booths and filled out the application. *At least, now I'll have something to tell my parents to get them off my back.*

After finishing and handing in the application at Orange Julius, she passed the center of the mall where four huge colored balloons rose up to the ceiling and drifted back down again. They sat on a low island in front of a series of water fountains bubbling thin streams four feet into the air. In front of this huge decorative centerpiece were four wide, carpeted steps where parents sat watching their young children run around

43

energetically in front of the balloons. She remembered a time, not so long ago, when she herself ran around down there with her own parents sitting up on the higher green-carpeted steps. The memory made her feel a little sad, especially now that she was having to do something as boring and mundane and adult as looking for a job.

Cyndi went to the far end of the mall towards the pet store. She admired the fuzzy little puppies and kittens that were rolling around and playing in straw bedding behind the windows. *This might not be a bad place to work either,* she thought. She had always loved animals, but had never been able to have any pets growing up because her mother was allergic and didn't want to have any "filthy animals" in the house. She went in and asked the guy behind the counter if they were hiring for the summer. He shook his head and politely told her they had just filled a position. She thanked him and left.

Feeling dejected, Cyndi stood outside the pet store. She had reached the end of the mall and had seen no other stores with *Help Wanted* signs. It was time to go find a payphone and call her mother to come pick her up. She walked toward the nearest side entrance and exit doors to the mall, knowing there would be payphones there. Taking a left in front of the movie theater, she went down the corridor toward the group of four payphones near the exit doors.

Looking to her left, Cyndi saw the Red Baron Arcade with its dark, noisy interior filled with flashing video games and pinball machines. The arcade had always struck her as sort of an oddly dark and sinister place, considering that it was made for kids. It seemed like the only lights that were ever on in the place were the glowing video-game screens and pinball machines. The constant blaring electronic 8-bit sounds of phasers, explosions, gunshots, and monsters roaring made it sound like some futuristic war zone. It was never very crowded with kids either. There never seemed to be more than a few kids in there, playing at a machine or two. It was as if most kids had somehow learned to stay away from the arcade.

She was about to turn to the payphones when her eyes locked onto the grinning white mask.

There he was again, standing back in the shadows. He stood in a dark corner behind the Skee-Ball machines, deep within the bowels of the arcade. The spinning red light on the top of the farthest Skee-Ball machine lit up one side of his mask intermittently, while a cold blue neon light lit up the other side. She had almost missed him in the middle of all the visual chaos, but that awful, unmistakable grin couldn't escape her sharp eyes.

Cyndi felt the blood drain from her face and she slowly began to step backwards. This small corridor of the mall was completely deserted. He had caught her alone. He cocked his head in the strange slow way she had seen him do last year, as if wondering whether or not to give chase in this public place in the middle of the day.

She kept her eyes locked on his mask, knowing that he was slippery. If you took your eyes off him for one second, he would disappear into the shadows, and then she would *really* be in trouble. *Is he real or am I just imagining this whole thing?* she wondered. She took another step backward, hoping to coax him out of that corner.

"Cyndi! Hey!" a girl's voice broke in, startling Cyndi out of her thoughts. She looked over and saw Christie, Johnny's little sister, and two of her friends waving and walking towards her. She forced a smile at them, then quickly turned back to the corner of the arcade. No one stood there in the darkness behind the Skee-Ball machines.

45

Christie and her friends approached. Cyndi recognized Christie's friends from school. They were identical twins in Christie's grade, one looked dark and punky, the other looked bright and preppy.

"Hey, Johnny's here," Christie said. "He's looking for you."

Cyndi's eyes darted back and forth over the dark corners of the arcade but she saw no sign of the masked man. Christie had noticed her staring into the back of the arcade as she walked up and had looked back there herself. "What are you looking at?"

Was he still there? Cyndi imagined him stepping back into the darkness, staring back at her and Christie from the safety of the shadows.

"What?" Cyndi asked distractedly.

Come on, she thought. *There isn't anyone there. You're probably jumping at shadows, just like at the dance. And after everything that happened last summer, who could blame you? Even if there had been some creep standing back there in the first place, he's probably had his fun and is long gone now.*

"I said, what are you looking at?" Christie repeated.

"Oh, uh, i-it's nothing. Forget it." Cyndi smiled at Christie and watched the younger girl's face light up.

Christie was thirteen, only a year younger than Cyndi. She had light brown hair that she had recently bleached blonde with *Sun-In*, and crimped in the same style as Cyndi's hair. Today she wore thin suspenders over a loose light-pink button-up shirt. She had rolled her sleeves halfway up her arms, and her pant legs halfway up her shins. Ever since Johnny had first brought his new girlfriend home and introduced her to his family, Christie had idolized Cyndi. She had been twelve when she first met Cyndi and was just starting to take her first steps into the teenage phase of her life. She had begun searching for her own sense of style and identity. Then along came Cyndi with her off-the-shoulder T-shirts, dozens of bracelets, bows in her crimped blonde hair, and her dark eye makeup. Something in Christie had clicked, this was what she was looking for. In her eyes, Cyndi was cool and mature, the ultimate template for teenage style.

Soon after their first meeting, Christie stopped to talk to Cyndi in the halls of their middle school whenever she saw her. Cyndi noticed as Christie's new outfits and dark eye makeup began to look remarkably similar to her own. Every time she went to Johnny's house, Christie managed to show up and hang around until Johnny chased her away or yelled for their mom to come drag her out.

"God, she's so annoying," Johnny had once told Cyndi.

"Oh, leave her alone. It's fine if she wants to hang out," Cyndi had replied. In Christie, she saw herself tagging along with Stacy at Camp Kikawa last summer. She figured that this was what it must have felt like to be Stacy back then. The warm memories of Stacy made her feel good and she liked Christie even more.

"Johnny's here," Christie repeated. "I think he's at the food court with Eddie."

"Oh yeah?" Cyndi asked. "Well let's go meet up with them."

She and the three younger girls ventured back into the main part of the mall. Looking back over her shoulder at the arcade, she saw the entrance standing empty as it always did. Maybe she had just imagined it. She continued forward, staring back at the arcade, and bumped right into another girl.

Startled, she spun around to see a fourteen-year-old girl with pink barrettes in her thick dark brown hair. Cyndi's heart dropped. It was Jennifer, her ex-best

47

friend, and three of her groupies, their arms loaded with shopping bags.

"Why don't you watch where you're going, loser," Jennifer said icily. The other girls in Jennifer's group giggled at her comment, and scowled at Cyndi as they walked past. Cyndi's only reply was an angry glare. Jennifer and her friends had been particularly hostile and nasty toward Cyndi throughout this entire year at school for no apparent reason.

Cyndi could hear the other girls snickering and talking about her in low voices as they walked away.

"Oh my God, what a geek!"

"Look what she's wearing!"

"Why is she with those two little kids?"

"It's because she's too much of a freak to make friends her own age," Jennifer piped in. Some of the other girls laughed and looked back at Cyndi. Christie's friends looked around at the other stores embarrassed and began to distance themselves from Christie and Cyndi. Christie angrily glared at the group of snotty girls and tried to think of something to yell back at them. She hadn't played the teenage game long enough to realize that anything she said, unless it was the best comeback in the world, would only make them look worse. Cyndi noticed Christie's clenched jaw and fists.

"Forget them. They think they're hot shit," Cyndi said dismissively. She silently prayed that Christie and her friends wouldn't say anything stupid and just keep their mouths shut. Cyndi gave her a reassuring smile that she couldn't help but return. "Come on, let's get to the food court."

As they walked away, Christie noticed Cyndi looking back at the arcade again. There was nothing to see. When Cyndi turned back around smiling, Christie forgot all about the man she thought she had seen Cyndi staring at in the dark corner of the arcade.

*   *   *

Eddie sat alone at a table near the middle of the food court. He was tipping his chair back precariously against a big potted plant and reading a Thor comic book. It had Thor on the cover fighting some huge villain with a half-black, half-white face. He wore an old blue T-shirt with a cracked and fading Superman S symbol on the chest, and had his ragged red Converse All-Star tennis shoes propped up on the table. His curly auburn hair looked wilder than ever.

Eddie was even more crazy about comic books than Cyndi was about music. He had a huge collection of superhero comics dating all the way back to his prized 1940's Batman issues. He hoped to be a comic book writer, or maybe even an illustrator, for Marvel Comics or DC Comics one day and work on the big superhero titles. He had a thin, skeletal build and an awkward, geeky face that one would expect from a comic book nerd, but he was friendly and his sense of humor made most other kids accept, rather than ostracize him.

"Hey, Eddie!" Cyndi said as she, Christie, and Christie's friend walked up to his table.

"What's happenin'?" Eddie replied without looking up from his comic.

"Have you seen Johnny?"

"He's grabbing a couple slices of pizza. Sit down, I'll be right with ya.'"

Cyndi looked up and smiled at Johnny as he crept up behind Eddie. He held a finger to his mouth to keep the girls quiet. Christie couldn't help but start to giggle. Johnny put two huge New York style slices of pizza and a couple of Pepsi's on the table behind Eddie. All at once he gave a panicked scream, grabbed Eddie's tipped back chair, and gave it a quick jerk.

"Gaahhwhat the hell?!" Eddie shouted. His whole body tensed up for a second. The girls immediately burst out laughing.

"Don't tip back in that chair, young man! You'll break your darn fool neck!" Johnny scolded in an elderly woman's voice while pointing a crooked finger at him. It was an inside joke between the two of them about their French teacher. Eddie examined the cover of his comic book, which he had crinkled slightly in his panic.

"Aww, dude! You made me crinkle it," he complained. He held the comic in front of Johnny, who examined the tiny crease as he picked up the drinks and the slices of pizza from the other table.

"Oh, it's not that bad," Johnny shrugged, sipping his Pepsi and walking toward Cyndi.

"Uh-uh. Get back here," Eddie said holding up his fist.

Johnny gave a resigned sigh, set down the food, and leaned toward Eddie, his upper arm pointing at him. Eddie reared back his thin arm, punched him with a bony fist, and they both roared with laughter like Neanderthals. This had been their ritual since the fourth grade when they first met.

"You guys are stupid," Christie laughed. "Are all high school boys as stupid as they are?" she asked Cyndi. To Christie's pleasant surprise, this made Cyndi laugh even harder.

"Get lost," Johnny waved Christie away dismissively.

"She can stay," Cyndi said as Johnny leaned down and kissed her. Christie put her finger in her mouth and made gagging sounds.

"It's bad enough that I've got Captain Comic-Geek over here," Johnny pointed at Eddie.

"I heard that," Eddie chimed in with a mouthful of pizza, he had returned to his Thor comic book, finishing up the last page. "Besides, everyone knows I'm the cool one here."

"Uh-huh," Johnny said sarcastically. "Well, I'm not having my dorky little sister hanging around too. Buzz off."

"Fine. I don't wanna hang around with you butt ugly jerks anyway," Christie said. "See ya, Cyndi."

"See ya later, Christie," Cyndi said with a smile. Christie's friend gave Cyndi a wave, and she returned it before Christie wandered back into the mall to find her friends again.

"Don't encourage her," Johnny said gravely.

"Oh, she's fine. I like her."

"How can you like her? She follows you around and copies everything you do, like she's your little shadow or something."

"Hey, the girl's got good taste."

Johnny rolled his eyes and changed the subject. "How was the job hunt? Love the outfit by the way. You look like you mean business." He said that last sentence in an ultra-white, straight-arrow voice, enunciating every syllable with anal retentive clarity.

"Shut up!" she said, shoving him. "My mom made me wear this."

"Yeah, I can see that. It's quite different from your usual attire."

"You love my usual attire."

"Yeah, you're like my sexy MTV video chick. But hey, you look good in this too, really. I mean it."

"Yeah?"

"Yeah." He leaned in and kissed her again.

"Oh, here we go," Eddie groaned. Apparently, he had finished his comic book.

"Anyway, how'd it go?" Johnny said. He

51

always tried to keep the lovey-dovey stuff with Cyndi to a minimum whenever Eddie was around. Eddie never had much luck with girls, and Johnny didn't want Eddie to feel like he was rubbing anything in his face.

"Ugh, don't remind me," Cyndi said. "You practically can't get a job anywhere unless you're sixteen."

"What about the record store?"

"Same thing. Plus that wannabe Billy Idol dude in there's a real jerk."

"Yeah, I know exactly who you're talking about. I never liked that guy either," Eddie added. "He always looks like this." Eddie did a dead-pan, slack-jawed expression while drool dripped out of his mouth and they all cracked up.

After their laughter died down, Johnny said, "Well, why don't I talk to Mr. Matthews? He's gonna be my supervisor at the pool. I think the age limit for lifeguards is sixteen too, but I bet I could get you a job at the snack bar."

"I don't know," Cyndi said. The idea of being stuck in that hot, cramped snack bar at Countryside Pool all summer sounded less than appealing.

"Oh, come on. It'd be great. We'd get to see each other everyday. Plus you'd have a ride there and back. And--" His voice dropped lower and he leaned in close. "After hours swimming." He raised his eyebrows and winked at her lecherously. He looked so goofy that she couldn't help but laugh. "Seriously, it'd get your parents off your back too."

"That *is* true." Suddenly the snack bar at the pool wasn't sounding so bad after all.

"You mean you actually want to spend your entire summer with this creep?" Eddie asked.

Cyndi shrugged, imagining getting to see Johnny's tanned shirtless body everyday.

Eddie threw up his hands in the air. "Your loss."

"I'll call Mr. Matthews tomorrow."

Cyndi took a sip of Johnny's Pepsi, and saw Jennifer and her group walking into the food court. They sat down at a clean table about thirty feet away. Jennifer noticed Cyndi also and their eyes met. Cyndi quickly looked away.

"Oh, God. Just what I need. It's Jennifer," she said, trying to look as if she hadn't even noticed her.

Johnny looked over and saw the bratty looking brunette glaring at his girlfriend.

"So what?" Johnny asked.

"She bumped into me while I was walking over here with Christie and her friend. She's always such a bitch to me."

Eddie had noticed Jennifer also. "I don't know, I think she's pretty hot. You think I should go ask her out? We could go on double dates." Cyndi gave him a horrified look.

Suddenly Johnny grabbed Cyndi's shoulder. "Kiss me," he whispered.

"What?"

"Just do it. It'll make her really mad, trust me."

Cyndi leaned toward him and they shared a long passionate kiss. Eddie opened the Thor comic book again and stared at Jennifer over the top edge of it. The other girls at Jennifer's table were all chattering and giggling, but Jennifer sat there squinting at them hatefully.

"It's working," Eddie mumbled.

Before they broke away from each other. Jennifer violently turned her head back to her friends and joined in their laughter. They heard her overcompensating cackle, and broke away smiling.

"Got her," Johnny said smiling that crooked

smile of his.

Cyndi glanced over at Jennifer. She saw quite clearly how the tables had turned, now Jennifer was trying hard to ignore *them*. "How did you know that would work?"

Johnny only dusted off his hands and placed them behind his head.

Cyndi surprised herself by thinking, *Hey, this job hunting trip to the mall actually turned out pretty good after all.*

Chapter Four:

Good News and Bad News

A scratching sound awoke Cyndi. She opened her eyes and looked around her dark bedroom. It wasn't coming from the window. The door maybe? No, the angle was all wrong. The light scratching continued off to her right. It was coming from the other side of the folding closet doors.

Cyndi slowly pulled the covers back and stepped out of bed. She supposed a mouse had gotten into her closet somehow. She walked over to the closet doors only half awake. As she stood in front of the doors, the scratching suddenly stopped and there was a faint rustling sound made by clothes she had up on hangers.

"What the--?" she mumbled. No mouse could reach her clothes, they all hung at least two feet off the floor. She put her hand down on the knob and began to pull just as her tired, sluggish mind gained control of itself.

Wait! Don't! she thought frantically. But it was too late, she had already pulled the closet doors open.

A gaseous, putrid smell wafted out from inside the darkness. It was a smell she remembered well, it had been the smell of the pool at the end of the Dead Man's Drop ride back at the water park. She stepped back, gagging and choking from the stench of rotting bodies. Underneath the oppressive, rotting smell there was a sharp bleachy tang of chlorine.

Then she saw it and her heart stopped cold. A dead person was standing back in her closet. She could see a pair of bluish black decomposing legs standing back in the shadows. Above the coat-hangers, there was the outline of a head covered with stringy ropes of wet hair.

The hanging outfits suddenly split down the middle and were flung to the sides with a harsh whisk sound.

Stacy stood back in the shadows. Her skin was a fishy, whitish-blue, covered with a slimy sheen from the chlorinated water of the Lazy River where she had died. The bottoms of her hands and feet had turned black where her blood had pooled and coagulated. Her eyes were gone, leaving only dark, sunken pits. Her mouth hung open and was coated with a black viscous liquid that dribbled out over her purplish lips and down her chin. The ripped gaping gash in her stomach was still there and more of the black liquid poured out of it.

Stacy uttered a low creaky scream, choked with water and full of rage. She lunged toward Cyndi with outstretched arms and her fingers hooked into claws against her throat--

Cyndi woke up at once, a guttural, panicky scream tearing out of her throat. In her sleep, she had felt herself pull her own head up off the pillow. Gasping for breath, she felt the bed and looked around wildly, trying to regain her bearings. She knew it had been a nightmare as she was having it, but it felt so real. She leaned over to her night table and flicked on the lamp as fast as she could. Every time she had one of these nightmares, and she'd had a lot of them over the past year, it felt as if something was still in the room with her until she turned on the lamp beside her bed and the light chased it away.

In the warm glow of the light, her room looked ordinary and safe. She turned quickly, facing the closet doors. They were firmly closed, just as she had left them before falling asleep. She stared at them distrustfully, wondering if anything might be hiding in there.

Open it. Make sure there's nothing in there. Make sure this is reality, where dead people are just dead, and they don't come back, she thought. It was stupid and completely irrational, but she knew the frightened part of her mind would not let her rest until she saw the inside of that closet.

Cyndi stood up on the bed, staring down the closet doors, daring them to make a move. They remained perfectly still. She stepped down off the bed, took a few shaky steps until she was an arm's length away from the doors.

Just do it, open it. You're being stupid. There's not going to be anything in there.

All at once, she yanked open the closet doors and flinched, expecting the nightmare to repeat itself, expecting to see a dead Stacy come shrieking out of the darkness. Inside, the clothes hung neatly on their hangers above the dresser just as they always did. There wasn't even a trace of that disgusting Dead Man's Drop smell. Nothing out of the ordinary in here.

Told you.

She remembered that Stacy's T-shirt was in the bottom drawer of her dresser folded neatly on top of Zack's T-shirt. The thought of the shirt brought up the image of that dead ghost Stacy from her dream again and she quickly suppressed it.

"Just another stupid dream. That's all," she mumbled to herself. She closed the doors firmly and got back in bed, knowing that she'd have to listen to some music before she would be able to get back to sleep. She looked at her mix tapes, doing a mental inventory of what she had recorded, but she couldn't decide what to listen to. Despite her vast library of records and tapes, she didn't seem to be in the mood for anything.

The radio it is then. Cyndi clicked on the radio dial on the corner of her Walkman. It was already tuned to her favorite pop station, and a familiar song came blasting into her headphones, "Girls Just Want To Have Fun." She immediately clicked it off. She had nothing personal against that song, but it had been one of the ones that psychopath had played in the water park. She figured that it had probably been playing while either Stacy or Zack had died, and it made her feel kind of sick and sad to hear it. These days it seemed like they played it every two hours on the radio.

She had also heard it last year when she and her mother had been driving and she had seen that sign for the new Thrill River water park. That was one place she would not go near this summer. Countryside pool would be the closest she got to any kind of water park thank you very much, at least, *if* she got the job.

That reminded her, she had to try to get some sleep because her job interview with Mr. Matthews, the guy in charge of the pool, was coming up in a few hours. Johnny had set the whole thing up and was planning on driving her down to the pool at ten. She turned onto her side, her most comfortable sleeping position, and stared at the closet door in uncomfortable nervous silence. She would have to wait for a few minutes until that song was over before she would turn the radio back on. Even with the radio, she had a feeling it was going to be a long night.

*   *   *

A few days earlier, not long after Cyndi's fruitless job search at the Westview Mall, Johnny had called with the great news that his boss, Mr. Matthews, wanted her to come down for an interview that upcoming Saturday. Cyndi's parents drilled her all week with potential job interview questions, and her mother insisted that she wear another nice outfit. She tried to avoid them as much as possible.

Saturday morning, just hours after her nightmare of Stacy, Johnny picked her up and drove her to the pool in his Bel Air. Once they were out of earshot of her parents, he screamed, "Ow! Lookin' sharp!"

Cyndi punched him in the arm playfully and he flinched, causing the car to swerve. Johnny grinned at her and rubbed his arm where she had punched him. "You know, you hit really hard for a girl. Harder than Eddie, but I guess that's not sayin' much."

She held up her fists like a boxer and began punching the dented dashboard in front of her. It was what Zack had been doing the first time she met him on the bus last year and it had always stuck with her as one of her clearest memories of him.

"You know you'll just be selling candy and sodas and chips, right? I mean, it's not like your going in for an interview at Goldman Sachs or anything."

"Believe me, I told my parents the exact same thing," Cyndi said. "You know how they are."

"Ah, they're not so bad. I've seen worse." She shrugged in agreement.

Cyndi had gone swimming at the Countryside pool with Jennifer a few times as a kid. That had been back when she and Jennifer had still been friends. She

59

hoped that if she got the job at the snack bar, she wouldn't have to run into Jennifer and her group very often.

The pool was in the middle of a public park surrounded by a tall chain-link fence. It was nothing special, just a small rectangle. There was a curved kiddie water slide at the shallow end, and a diving board at the deep end. Tall cottonwood trees stood near the fence and provided half of the grassy seating area around the pool and snack bar with constant shade. Looking at them, Cyndi thought that they would definitely come in handy on those sweltering hundred degree days in July. The pool had been built sometime in the fifties. Originally, the snack bar and changing rooms had simply been a small cinder block building near the shallow end of the pool. In the late seventies they had added on an air conditioned entrance building and connected it to the old cinder block snack bar and changing rooms. To enter the pool, you had to go through the new entrance building, buy your ticket from the front desk, then walk through the damp changing rooms in the old part of the building to get to the pool. Because of the twenty year age gap between the two connecting buildings, their styles clashed. The old building looked tacky and worn, while the new building looked fresh and modern.

Johnny parked in the small paved parking lot in front of the entrance. As they walked up to the building, Cyndi heard the voices of men working somewhere behind the chain-link fence at the pool. Johnny opened the tinted glass door to the entrance building, and a rush of fresh, air conditioned, chlorine-scented air blew out at her.

"He's gotta be around here somewhere," Johnny said, looking around the deserted building for Mr. Matthews. Cyndi followed him behind the front desk and he opened an unlocked door along the back wall.

Looking over Johnny's shoulder, Cyndi got her first good look at the tiny snack bar. It was maybe half the size of her bedroom. There was a big, glass fronted refrigerator right next to the door they were looking through, fully stocked with all kinds of soda and ice cream bars. Directly in front of them, along the opposite wall, was a fading red counter-top and a huge open window that looked out at the drained, empty pool. Below the counter were shelves stuffed with boxes of candy bars and small bags of chips. A couple of hard bar stools that Cyndi and another employee would be sitting on sat neatly in front of the counter.

Johnny and Cyndi leaned against the door frame and looked around. The sounds of loud, clattering equipment and men's voices drifted up more clearly now, coming from down inside the empty pool. Johnny recognized Mr. Matthews voice as one of them.

"Ah, there he is," Johnny said and immediately went back into the main entrance room. Cyndi quickly followed him past the counter and into the men's changing room. As they walked past the rows of showers and lockers, Johnny turned around and jumped as if frightened.

"What are you doing in here? This is the *guy's* locker room!" he cried in mock horror.

Cyndi shook her head at him and laughed as they continued out into the pool courtyard.

"Ay, Mr. Matthews!" Johnny called out as he walked up to the edge of the pool. Cyndi saw two guys in rubber boots down in the pool near the deep end. They were knelt down, working with some kind of large pump and a thick canvas hose that ran up over the pool's edge and drained in the grass. A puddle of dark water filled with last autumn's decaying leaves sat stagnant in the deep end, and they were trying to clean some of that debris out of the pump. Mr. Matthews looked up, saw

Johnny, and waved at him briefly.

"Hang on, I'll be right there," Matthews shouted over the noise of the pump. Cyndi had expected him to be fit and tanned, instead she found he was short and stocky with an unshaven, gruff look about him. After a minute, he reached up and began climbing the ladder out of the deep end of the pool. Johnny introduced them as he approached.

"Cyndi, nice't'meetcha," he said, giving her a firm hand-shake with his strong, calloused grip. "So this dipshit actually tricked you into dating him, huh?" Johnny burst out laughing. Cyndi was taken aback, she definitely did not expect him to use bad language.

"Yeah, I guess he did," she replied laughing.

Matthews laughed. "Well, I'm sorry for you. Why don't you guys come on back?"

Johnny and Cyndi followed Matthews back into the snack bar area where he motioned for them to take a seat on the bar stools near the counter. He left them briefly to rummage through the drawers under the front counter in the main entrance, then finally returned with a job application and a pen. He handed them to Cyndi to fill out on the faded red snack counter-top while he and Johnny made small talk. She finished it up, handed it back, and he looked it over briefly.

"First job, huh?" he asked.

"Yes, sir. I hope so," she said loudly, remembering her parents insistence that she speak loudly and clearly. Johnny smirked at her, he had a running joke about what he called her "grownup voice." Cyndi glanced over and stuck her tongue out at him while Matthews was still looking over her application. Matthews reached the bottom of the application and nodded to himself.

"Okay, well uh, I'm not sure how much Johnny told you about the job," he began. He spoke in an indifferent, no-nonsense tone, rattling off facts about the job. Cyndi had a hard time trying to figure out whether he liked her or not. "It's part-time, between twenty-five and thirty-five hours a week. Umm, pay is three-fifty an hour. Paychecks come out every other Friday. We have Countryside T-shirts that you have to wear. It's a pretty easy job. We'll train you up on everything during orientation. Uh, any questions?"

"No, none that I can think of," Cyndi shrugged.

"All right, well I'm glad you're both here because I've got good news and bad news. Good news is the job's yours if you want it. The bad news is that you're probably not gonna be working with this guy."

"Me? What?" Johnny asked confusedly as Matthews pointed at him.

"Yeah, the word just came down this morning from Mr. Harrison, he's the executive director of the Parks department. They need lifeguards over at that new water park they're putting in. That, uh, Thrill River or whatever the hell they're callin' it. So they're transferring you over there."

Cyndi felt her heart drop at the mention of the water park, a chill wormed its way up her back. The thought of Johnny among all those creepy grinning faces all summer....

"Isn't that a whatchamacallit? A *corporate* water park? What does it have to do with the city?" Johnny asked.

"Yeah it's technically corporately owned, but it's on public land. They worked out some kind of discount deal for the residents if they used some city employees to help build it and fill the lifeguard staff positions for the rides over the first few years, I guess. I don't know, all that shit's above my pay grade. Hey, look on the bright side though, you get a big raise. They're paying five an hour over there."

Johnny's eyes lit up at the mention of five dollars an hour. He had never made that much money from any job before, and it was a lot more than he had originally expected to make over the summer. At the Countryside Pool they only paid the lifeguards four dollars and twenty-five cents per hour. He smiled at Cyndi, but the smile left his face when he saw the tense expression on hers. He knew she had been counting on getting to spend the summer with him, and here he was, cheerfully getting ready to up and leave for an extra measly seventy-five cents an hour.

"Well, that's really generous. But if it's all the same, I was kinda hoping I could stay here for the summer," Johnny said as politely as possible.

"I'm sorry, man, but it's not my decision to make. Trust me, if it was up to me, I'd have you here in a second."

Johnny was torn. He didn't want to leave Cyndi alone at the pool, but he had to admit that the extra money sounded good. Matthews turned back to Cyndi.

"So do you still want the job?" he asked. She hesitated. The job was the last thing on her mind now. She was imagining Johnny among all those grinning white faces, and picturing his body joining the rest of the bodies floating in the putrid water at the bottom of the Dead Man's Drop.

She forced herself out of her dark thoughts and smiled at him. "Uh, yeah. Sure." He returned her smile and held out his hand.

"Then welcome to Countryside." She reached out and shook his hand.

*   *   *

Johnny drove Cyndi home in tense, awkward silence. He knew she was mad by the way she stared out the window, avoiding eye contact with him since the moment they got into the car. He had to say something, had to break the silence.

"Look, I'm sorry, Cyndi," he blurted out. "Believe me, I would much rather spend the summer at the pool with you. I really would. But five dollars an hour? I mean, come on, you wouldn't be able to pass that up either."

Cyndi looked over at him reproachfully and her only response was an irritated sigh.

"It's not like I had a choice or anything. You heard him, *he* didn't even have a say in it. It's not like I wanted to just ditch you or--"

"That's not what I'm upset about," she interrupted.

"Okay, well, what are you upset about then?"

"I'm not even upset. I'm... I just..." Johnny kept silent while she struggled with her words. Early on in their relationship, he had figured out that this was the only way to get her to communicate with him. Not even her own parents had quite figured it out yet. "It's just...I don't want you over there. It's dangerous."

Careful, Cyndi, careful. You're telling him way too much, she thought.

"Dangerous?" he laughed. "What are you talking about?"

"Never mind," she said quickly. *Why couldn't you just keep your mouth shut?*

"Cyndi, I'm sure those rides are perfectly safe."

Yeah, that's what Brad thought. He got on one of those rides and we never saw him again. "And you know I'm a great swimmer. That's why I'm a lifeguard, remember?"

"Look, let's just forget it, okay?"

They pulled up in front of Cyndi's house and she quickly unbuckled her seat belt. "I better get going."

65

"Don't you still want to hang out today? I mean, we've still got the whole rest of the day."

"No, I really didn't sleep very well last night. I think I'm gonna go lay down." At least she wasn't lying to him. "Thanks for getting me the job." She leaned over and kissed him briefly, then got out of the car.

"You're welcome," he replied. He waited until she got inside before pulling away. "What the hell was that about?" he asked himself.

Upstairs in her room, Cyndi went to the window and watched him drive away from her house. She desperately wanted to tell him about last summer. She wanted to tell him everything, and then urge him to quit his job, because she had a bad feeling deep down about this new water park.

She looked back at her closet door, remembering the nightmare about Stacy. *Maybe I'm not quite all there anymore. Maybe my mind was messed up from all those bad things that happened last summer. But maybe I'm right to be scared. Just maybe....*

"If anything weird starts to happen there, I'll tell him. I'll have to tell him for his own safety. And I'll have to call that creep, Mr. Carver. But until then, I'll just keep my mouth shut," she swore to herself. Saying it out loud made it a promise, a plan that she would stick with. She still couldn't shake off the image of Johnny surrounded by those white grinning faces, or of him getting on a ride and never being seen again.

Please, God. Please don't let anything happen to him, she thought as another chill wriggled down her back.

Countryside T-shirt. She felt like ripping it off.

"Oh, I get it. Since they don't make little kid's sizes, you had to just settle for the smallest one they had, right?"

"What do you want?" Cyndi asked dully.

"Well, that's not a very nice way to talk to customers, is it, girls?" Jennifer taunted. The other girls quickly agreed with her. Below the counter Cyndi's fists clenched.

"Can I help you?" Cyndi said through gritted teeth.

"That's better. Get me a Pepsi."

Cyndi turned around, opened the glass refrigerator door, and pulled out a can of Pepsi. She turned back to the counter and Jennifer spoke up again.

"No, not that one. The one next to it."

Cyndi turned back and exchanged one can of Pepsi for another.

"No, the other one."

Cyndi exchanged cans again. She brought this can to the counter.

"Fifty cen--"

"Mmm, no. I changed my mind. I'll have Dr. Pepper instead."

Cyndi sighed again, glaring at the girls as they all laughed like loons. Jennifer kept a smug smirk on her face through all of it. Cyndi put her hand on a can of Dr. Pepper, knowing exactly what was coming next.

"No, the other one."

"Hey, come on. Quit holding up the line, will ya?" said a man with a toddler in his arms. None of them had noticed that he had walked up to the counter almost immediately after they did.

"Oops, I forgot my money. Sorry," Jennifer said quickly and in a mocking innocent tone. She rushed away from the counter and her flock trailed behind her, laughing hysterically. The man stepped up to the counter as Cyndi put the can of soda away.

"Sorry about that," Cyndi muttered.

"Ah, don't worry about it. Stupid kids," he said. "I'll take a juice box and a bag of Doritos."

Cyndi smiled appreciatively at him for putting a premature stop to her torture and turned to get his order.

*   *   *

A few hours later Johnny parked his Bel Air in the Countryside Pool parking lot. He and Brady were starving after a long day of swim drills at the hands of their hard-ass boss Mr. Sheehan. They had both been craving pizza all day, so they stopped at a Little Caesars in the corner of a strip mall a mile away from Thrill River and each bought a pizza. As they walked out with their pizzas, Johnny explained that he was going to meet his girlfriend working at the Countryside Pool after work. Brady had suggested that they bring the pizzas there, he claimed that there were always a ton of babes at the pool on opening day.

They walked out into the pool courtyard still in their red swim trunks. Both of them wore tight muscle shirts with Johnny in white and Brady in black. Johnny side-stepped over to the snack counter. There was no line at the moment.

"Hi, Girlfriend," he joked loudly as if that was the only name he knew her by. Cyndi had been spacing out, listening to some radio commercial, and was so surprised to see him that she jumped.

"Oh my God," she laughed. "Hi, Boyfriend." She laughed at his geeky entrance, and leaned forward to kiss him.

"Hungry?" he asked, lifting the lid of his pizza box and waving a demonstrative hand in front of the pizza. It smelled like heaven.

"Yeah, a little," she said, feeling her mouth to water at the smell.

"Take a piece. By the way, this is Brady. He used to work here. Now he works with me at the water park. Brady, this is my one true love, Cyndi."

Cyndi already knew Brady and suppressed a distasteful sneer at seeing him again. She'd had encounters with Brady Johnston years ago. He was Jennifer's older cousin, and the few times she had seen him at Jennifer's house were enough to make her think that he was a total scumbag. She remembered a few years back when a sixteen-year-old Brady had tried to get Jennifer and Cyndi to get high with him. At the time, both girls had been only eleven years old. Jennifer had taken one hit of the joint Brady handed her, and started coughing violently. Cyndi refused the joint, and had to endure their condescending remarks until her parents came to pick her up.

"Hey, nice to meet you," Brady muttered. He thought she looked familiar, but couldn't remember where he had seen her before. She also looked way too young for him, so he skipped his usual charm and flirtatious remarks. As they walked in, the pretty brunette lifeguard overlooking the pool had caught Brady's eye and still had most of his attention.

"Nice to meet you too," she said warily. He didn't seem to remember her, so she decided to pretend that she didn't remember him either.

"Hey, hold this for a second, will ya?" Brady shoved his box of pizza in Johnny's arms and walked off to go talk with the new lifeguard girl, intent on getting her phone number. Johnny watched him go and smirked. He recognized the lifeguard girl from the halls of DeAngelo High, but couldn't remember her name.

"Working his magic already," Johnny laughed.

81

He turned back to Cyndi and saw the distasteful expression on her face. "Oh, don't mind him. He's convinced that all the hotties are here on opening day. Anyway, how's it been so far? Any problem customers?" Johnny opened his pizza box and handed Cyndi a slice.

Brady brushed his hair back as he walked over to the lifeguard girl. He was debating on one of two possible pick-up lines to use when all of a sudden, someone shrilly screamed his name.

"BRADY!" Jennifer called out. She ran up to him and threw her arms around his shoulders in a big hug. Brady's heart sank as he saw his chances with the lifeguard fly away.

"Hey, little cousin," he said in a voice loud enough to be heard by the lifeguard girl.

"When did you get back in town? I feel like I haven't seen you in forever. How was college? I missed you!" Jennifer rattled off excited question after excited question without taking a breath. Brady noticed the lifeguard girl glance over and smile.

Oh, okay. So she digs the whole older cousin thing. Maybe there's some hope after all, Brady thought. He bragged to his friends about his ability to read women like a book, and in truth he actually was pretty good at it.

"Hey, slow down. I'll tell you all about college, but first I gotta get some food. Me and my buddy over there picked up some pizzas. You want a slice?"

"Ohhh! You answered my prayers. I'm starving!"

"Hey, Johnny! Come on, dude!" he called.

Jennifer looked over and saw Johnny standing at the snack counter talking with Cyndi. She recognized him instantly as the cute guy she had seen Cyndi with in the food court of the Westview Mall a couple weeks ago.

"In a minute, man," Johnny replied, he turned back to Cyndi. "Do you have a break coming up?"

82

"You're too late, I had my last one before Jackie left a half hour ago. Now it's just me until close."

"Come on, man! Pizzas are getting cold!" Brady called.

"Well, come sit with us if you can, okay? I gotta go." Johnny leaned in and gave her a quick kiss before rushing off to join Brady and Jennifer. Cyndi watched him go, and a jealous, disappointed feeling settled over her like a sheet. Here she was, watching her boyfriend go off with some of the worst people she knew, and she couldn't do a thing about it. *Could this day get any worse?*

The three of them walked over to the shady corner where Jennifer and her friends had been all day. Her group was down to three now, Lisa had gone home at five.

"Hey, pretty girls," Brady said, turning on that old Brady charm. "Anyone hungry? You look like a bunch of skinny supermodels over here, you know that?" The girls all screamed giggly laughter. Brady sat down with his cousin, and Johnny sat down on the empty chair Lisa had been on earlier.

"Hey Johnny, this is my little cousin Jennifer and her friends," Brady introduced them. Johnny set his pizza box down and he recognized the girl with the pink ball shaped barrettes in her thick, dark, waist-length hair. She was that girl from the mall a few weeks ago, the one who had been glaring at Cyndi. Like Cyndi, he decided to play it cool and pretend that he didn't remember her.

"Nice to meet you," he said smiling.

Jennifer also pretended that she didn't recognize him from the mall. She glanced down at his toned arms and tanned chest. *How the hell did that goofy little geek, Cyndi, get a cute guy like this?* she thought.

"Nice to meet you too," she said. She turned back to Brady. "So are you home for summer break,

83

Brady?"

"Oh yeah. Home for the summer. Me and Johnny here are working over at that new water park."

The girls were all impressed. "Ooh, I can't wait to go over there!"

"Yeah, you're gonna love it. Trust me."

Brady told them all about the new water park as he and Johnny wolfed down their pizzas, but Jennifer was only half listening. The wheels were turning in her head, plans were being made. That little brat Cyndi's boyfriend was cute, no doubt about that, but Cyndi wasn't here, was she? She was stuck behind that snack counter in that ugly, sweaty T-shirt. She wondered how hard would it be to take this cute guy for herself, sticking it to Cyndi in the process. Jennifer smiled at Johnny again, seductively biting one corner of her lower lip. He looked up at her as he pulled out another slice of pizza, returned her smile, and quickly looked away.

Perfect, Jennifer thought. There was something in the way he looked at her and the way he turned his eyes away that told her all she needed to know. Like her cousin, she had a talent for reading the opposite sex.

The snack counter traffic had died down as the evening wore on, and Cyndi watched the back corner like a hawk. She helplessly witnessed Jennifer's eyes constantly crawling all over her boyfriend. About a half hour after they finished their pizzas, Johnny, Brady, and the three girls began jumping into the deep end of the pool. The girls screamed and laughed, then joined in as Johnny and Brady splashed each other playfully. Eventually, Brady swam over and struck up a flirtatious conversation with the lifeguard girl, leaving Johnny alone with Jennifer and her friends.

All Cyndi could do was sit back miserably as they laughed and splashed in the water.

Chapter Seven:

After Hours

The sun reluctantly set, bringing a bittersweet end to that gorgeous first day of summer break. Most people had cleared out of the pool by twilight. Johnny and the others left together about an hour before closing time. Cyndi had been helping a customer and didn't get to say goodbye. As Brady and the girls dragged him off, Johnny managed to give her a wave behind the customer's back. She gave him a small smile and returned his wave, hoping to God that he wasn't driving those girls home.

Finally, the lifeguard girl that Brady had been talking to most of the evening had to tell everyone left that the pool was closing and they would have to go home. They groaned, but reluctantly obeyed.

Jackie had worked the early shift and took off a few hours ago, now Cyndi was all by herself. She pulled down the rolling metal snack counter shutter and locked it up with the padlock, just as Mr. Matthews had instructed. She went back to the closing duty checklist that hung on a clipboard underneath the counter, and wrote her initials next to the *Close/Lock Window* column under today's date. Next, she remembered she had to count the cash in the register, and type it into the clunky, old adding machine. One of her favorite songs, "The Waiting" by Tom Petty and the Heartbreakers, played softly in the background, but she kept the volume on the stereo down low so she could concentrate. The snack bar seemed unnaturally quiet and still after the noisy chaos of opening day.

Cyndi was down to the nickels when there was a startlingly loud thud followed by a scratching sound on the metal counter shutters. She jumped in surprise, her hand jerked and a few nickels dropped to the dirty floor. Her heart immediately began hammering and her shoulders tensed. She waited for a second in silence, wondering if she would hear a voice. Maybe it was that lifeguard girl wanting to get in. Maybe she was being chased again by a huge crazy man in a white smiling mask.

Stop it! Stop it! Stop it! Do NOT start thinking about that now. Not after dark.

The pounding started up again and she involuntary stepped away from the window, getting ready to run.

Get a hold of yourself and ask who it is for God's sake.

"Wh-who is it?" she asked in a trembling voice.

"Can I get a 3 Musketeers bar?" someone said in a gravelly, growling, yet still recognizable voice. Cyndi sighed and let her tense shoulders relax.

"Johnny? Is that you?" she asked in a much louder, more confident voice. She immediately felt stupid about overreacting.

"Yeah it's me, come on out," Johnny laughed in his normal voice.

"Hang on. Let me go turn in the cash drawer at

86

the front," she said.

Cyndi quickly finished counting the change, rushed into the front entrance room, and put the drawer in the thick safe below the counter. She made her way back through the women's locker room and came out into the pool courtyard.

The sound of crickets filled the cool night air. The lights were still on in the pool, sending out blue, bouncing, lightning lines of reflection to everything above the calm surface of the water. Johnny sat near the shallow end, quietly looking out at the water. He had lazily kicked his sandals off on the concrete, and sat with his legs down in the water. He turned back and smiled at Cyndi when he heard her footsteps echoing through the concrete locker room. She was irritated and a little distrustful of him after he had spent the evening with that bitch Jennifer, but his smile was already starting to melt that cold irritation away.

You and that damn crooked smile, she thought.

"What are you doing here? The pool's closed," Cyndi asked.

"When you've got connections like I do, you get to enjoy the perks of the pool. Like swimming after hours," Johnny said in a cocky voice.

"Oh really?" she asked with her arms crossed, pretending to be stern.

"Well, actually Mr. Matthews let me in. He's inside somewhere, I think. Come sit with me."

She took off her white Keds and socks, sat down on the edge of the pool, and dipped her legs in next to his. The water felt great on her aching feet, and it was surprisingly warm. He leaned over to kiss her, expecting her to lean in and meet him halfway. She held back, forcing him to lean all the way over. He felt the cold irritation behind her kiss and pulled away.

"How was your first day?" he asked. He

ignored the unresponsive kiss and kept the smile on his face, but he had a bad feeling that he was going to have to do some serious relationship damage control.

"Could've been better," she replied.

"You don't like the job?"

"The job is fine. It was some of the people that were the problem."

"Yeah, well.... There's good days and bad days. It'll get better, trust me."

Johnny held out his arm to wrap around her shoulders, hoping he could break the ice between them and have her snuggle up against him. She sat as still as a stone.

"What's the matter?" he finally asked.

"Nothing," she shrugged. Johnny frowned, knowing that was a bullshit answer.

"Come on, out with it. What's with you?"

"I think you know," she said. He rolled his eyes and sighed.

"Uh-oh. Jealous girlfriend, watch out," he joked. He laughed at his own joke, but shut up when he saw that Cyndi wasn't laughing at all. "Look, I'm sorry, okay? I thought it was just gonna be me and Brady hanging out. I didn't know What's-Her-Face was gonna be here. I didn't even know that her and Brady were related."

"Uh-huh. Did you give them a ride home?" Cyndi asked, her eyebrows raised.

Uh-oh, he thought. *If you tell the truth, she'll be pissed. If you lie, she'll see right through it.*

"Yeah, so." Johnny had nothing to hide and he wasn't about to start lying to his girlfriend.

Cyndi sighed in exasperation and looked away from him.

"What? It's not like I was alone with a bunch of girls. Brady was there, I dropped him off last. Ask him if you don't believe me."

"Oh yeah, Brady.   Real great guy," she said sarcastically.

"What?   Brady's cool.   We work together." Cyndi's only reply was a sarcastic look. "Okay, maybe he's not the greatest guy in the world," Johnny conceded. "He's harmless though, really.   And he's hilarious.   You should've seen what happened on Thursday.   They give us these radios on some of the rides.   They're kinda like bigger versions of Walkie Talkies, y'know?   So our boss is basically giving us this long lecture on how to use a Walkie Talkie and we're all falling asleep.   Brady went to school for electronics, so you know what he does?   He messes with the frequency or something on the top of the thing and suddenly he's got the police channel.   Then he switches it again and gets these Mexican guys who keep saying '*CopyCopy!*'   We were all cracking up.   Oh man, you should've seen the look Sheehan gave him.   It was so funny.   You wouldn't believe--"

Cyndi's head snapped toward him.   "Who?" she asked sharply.

"Mr. Sheehan.   He's our dick boss."   Cyndi's mouth dropped open.

Could it be the same Sheehan from Camp Kikawa from last year?

"What?   Do you know him or something?" he asked.

"Uh...no.   No.   I thought you said something else, that's all."

"Yeah, well you're lucky you got Mr. Matthews as a boss, because this Sheehan guy is a total asshole. He looks like he flunked out of gym-teacher college or something.   Takes his job way way *way* too seriously."

It sure sounds like him, she thought.   *What the hell is he doing here now?*   She halfheartedly listened as he continued his story about Brady Johnston and

Sheehan. She couldn't help but picture Brad and Zack fighting with Sheehan last summer. Everything Johnny said had a ring of familiarity to it that made Cyndi feel uneasy.

"You could tell Sheehan was so pissed. And they didn't come back from his office for twenty minutes. It was awesome." Johnny burst out laughing as he finished his story. He looked over and saw that Cyndi wasn't paying any attention to him at all. She stared out at the calm ripples along the surface of the pool. He decided to change the subject. "So what are you doing next Saturday?"

"Hmm? What?" she asked, coming back from some deep thoughts and memories.

"I said, what are you doing next Saturday?"

"Oh, uh, I got the lucky shift, next Saturday off."

"Great! Because it's opening day at Thrill River and they're letting all of the employees invite two people to come to the park for free. Then after work, we're having a big party for all of us lifeguards and our guests. You wanna come?"

Cyndi felt her blood run cold. The thought of going into that water park and reliving the nightmares from last summer made her want to scream.

"I was gonna give my two passes to you and Eddie if you guys wanna go," he continued.

"Uh... I-I-I don't know..." she stammered.

"It'll be really fun," he said enticingly. "You should see that place, it's really incredible. They've got this... well, I don't want to spoil it. You'll just have to see it for yourself. It blew me away when I first went in."

"I don't think I can go."

"Why not? It's not like the rides are *that* scary. Trust me."

Oh, you have no idea how scary the rides can

be, she thought, trying to force back the image of the bodies floating at the end of the Dead Man's Drop.

"I just can't."

"Oh come on, Cyndi. What's the problem? I mean, ever since I got that job you've been acting all weird."

"No I haven't."

Now it was Johnny's turn to give Cyndi the same sarcastic look.

"I'm not acting weird," she reiterated more firmly.

"Okay, fine. I'll give my pass to Christie then. The little brat's been begging me for it anyway."

They sat in silence for a while. Johnny thought over something he had suspected for a long time. He always avoided the subject because he knew Cyndi didn't like to talk about it, but this conversation had been bad from the start. What more could it hurt?

"Can I ask you something?"

"What?"

"What happened to you last summer?"

The question hit Cyndi like a truck. Johnny didn't push the question and he didn't elaborate. He sat in silence, waiting patiently for her answer.

Screw it, just tell him, she thought. *This has gone on long enough. Don't you see what it's doing to your relationship? Just tell him already.*

Cyndi took a deep breath. "It's a long story."

"We've got all the time in the--"

"Time to go, lovebirds!" shouted a voice from behind them. They looked over their shoulders and saw Mr. Matthews standing in the locker room doorway. "We're locking everything up. Come on."

"Spoke too soon," Johnny said to Cyndi with an edge of irritation in his voice.

They stood up and picked up their shoes, their

legs dripping water onto the concrete. Cyndi's feet were too wet to put her shoes on, so she held them in one hand as they walked out to Johnny's old Bel Air in the parking lot.

"So, go on with your story."

"Not tonight," Cyndi said. The Countryside parking lot seemed to be full of shadows. She definitely did not want to tell him the story of last summer in this dark parking lot. "I've gotta get home. I'm late as it is. My parents are gonna kill me."

"Okay, but promise me you'll tell me sometime."

"I promise."

"I'll be waiting."

Don't make promises you can't keep. That old saying rose in her mind suddenly. Johnny gave her another crooked smile as they sat down into his old car. She loved that smile of his, it made her feel like everything was going to be all right. *Maybe it won't be so hard keeping that promise after all.*

He fired up the engine and began driving her home.

"You really should come next weekend, though," Johnny said after a few minutes. "It's gonna be great. We get discounts on food there too. They've got these great burgers called Big Kahuna Burgers. Me and Brady were talking about getting you guys lunch or something."

"Who's Brady bringing?" she asked.

"I don't know. I guess he'll probably give one of them to that Jennifer girl you don't like."

Cyndi remembered the greedy way Jennifer had been staring at Johnny today. She remembered the way Jennifer flirted with him, laughing too loudly at his jokes, touching his arm. If Jennifer were to act like that right in front of her, what would Jennifer do when she wasn't around? Cyndi knew if she wanted to keep her boyfriend, things were going to have to change. She would have to tell him what happened last year, and she would have to keep a watchful eye on him whenever Jennifer was around.

They pulled up to Cyndi's house and shared a long kiss. It felt like it had been forever since they last kissed. Staring into Johnny's eyes, she made her decision.

"You know what? I think I will go next Saturday."

It was a decision she would live to regret.

Chapter Eight:

Opening Day at Thrill River

The radio blared to life with a harsh burst of static. Cyndi jumped. Her parents would kill her for having her stereo so loud this early in the morning. She rushed over to the stereo just as a familiar song began to play. It was "Girls Just Want To Have Fun" again, and Cyndi felt her stomach drop. She quickly spun the volume knob to the left but it didn't make any difference. Now the pitch of the song was wavering.

"What the hell's wrong with this thing?" she asked aloud, thumping her fist on its side. The stereo must have been broken. *Oh great, what next?*

A car horn honked outside, Johnny's horn. He was early. She rushed over to the window and saw his old Seafoam Green Bel Air pull up to her front yard.

Shit, I'm late. Cyndi rushed over to the closet to grab her swimsuit. She flung the folding doors open and bent down to look through one of the lower dresser drawers. Inside, Zack and Stacy's T-shirts were unfolded and spread over her clothes. *This isn't where I left these shirts. This is the wrong drawer. What's going--*

A gray, putrid hand clamped down over her wrist. Suddenly, the smell of rotting corpses was all around her. Zack slid out between two of her hanging dresses from the dark depths of the closet, his slimy skin leaving a nasty residue on her clothes. His face was crushed and misshapen, one cheekbone way too high, the other a dark scabby pit. Only splintery fragments of his teeth remained, they were covered with specks of black mold. Dark blood oozed out over his drooping lower lip. There were moist splits across his milky, dead gray eyes, making them look like rotting grapes.

"CYNDEEEEE!" his low voice gurgled as more black blood dripped out of his mouth. His grip on her wrist tightened, she felt her bones grind. She began to scream in short bursts.

Zack's other arm shot out and grabbed her free hand just before she could turn to pull herself away from him. He held her arms crisscrossed in front of her chest in a tight death-grip. He walked forward out of the closet, lifting her helplessly off the floor. Waves of his horrible stench drifted into her nose and mouth as he came closer to her.

He spun her around to face her bedroom window. Now it was wide open, and the lipped edges of a water slide ran over the edge. A red current of blood rushed down the slide to some dark pool below. She kicked her feet desperately as Zack dragged her toward the slide. He was too strong, she could barely move, barely even breathe.

Zack shoved her toward the slide in the open window and she could see Johnny's Bel Air idling at the curb again. The driver had gotten out of the car and come halfway up the yard, but it wasn't Johnny. The killer stood there in his grinning mask and black, dripping jumpsuit. In one hand he held that rusty sharpened stake. His other arm was raised in the air, and he slowly beckoned with a fish-white hand, inviting her to ride the bloody slide down to him.

Cyndi jumped out of bed screaming. It had all been just another nightmare, but this was one of the worst ones yet, maybe even the worst she'd had in her entire life. She spun around, glancing around the room wildly, trying to get her bearings and stifle her short screams. She was safe in her own room, all alone. Both the closet door and the window were safely shut. The stereo was turned off.

She sunk to her knees on the floor near her bed, put her head down, and burst into tears. How could she go to the water park after that? In just a few hours, Johnny's mother would be picking her up and dropping her off at the front gates of Thrill River. The thought of actually setting foot in another water park terrified her.

Thankfully, her job had distracted her all week, and she had kept her conversations with Johnny to a minimum. Now the week was over and she felt totally unprepared. She imagined this must be how it would feel if she had a big final exam that she hadn't studied for at all.

The night before, while Cyndi picked at her dinner, her parents had asked if she had any plans for the weekend.

"Johnny's getting us into the water park for free for opening day tomorrow," she mumbled without even a hint of excitement.

Her mother dropped her fork onto her plate. Both of her parents looked at each other with alarm, then turned back to her.

"You're actually...*going* there?" her father asked, breaking the silence.

Cyndi nodded.

"Honey, are you sure that's a good idea?" her mother asked cautiously.

"Mom, Dad, please. I really don't want to talk about it. Please."

"Okay," her father said solemnly. Her parents exchanged another worried glance. Much to Cyndi's surprise, they didn't bring it up again.

Behind closed doors that night, her mother and father had argued in whispers.

"I just don't get why she would even want to go in the first place," her mother said.

"Isn't it obvious? She's doing it for that boy," her father said.

"We can't let her go through with it."

"What are you gonna do? Ground her? It's not like she's doing anything wrong."

"Well, we can't just sit here and do nothing."

"She's not a little girl anymore, Terri."

"But she's already been through so much. I don't want this to...damage her even more."

"She's a survivor, honey. She's strong. We had no idea just how strong she really was until after she came back last summer. She survived all that. She'll survive this too."

"It's just so hard to see her like this." Her mother began to feel the sting of tears in her own eyes, and her husband held her in his arms.

"I know, I know. She'll be okay. We just have to give her some space and let her deal with this in her own way."

Now Cyndi sat sobbing with her head down on the bed to muffle the sound, but her cries hadn't gone unheard. Cyndi's mother had been startled awake by the sounds of her daughter's screams down the hall. Her husband slept like a rock and simply rolled over. She quickly threw on a robe and slowly opened her bedroom door. On tiptoes, she crept down the hallway, approaching Cyndi's door as quietly as she could. She softly pressed her ear to the door and heard the muffled sound of her daughter crying into her bed.

She raised a hand to knock, but hesitated. Part of her wanted nothing more than to rush in, wrap her arms around her daughter, and make everything all better.

She's a survivor. Her husband's words echoed through her mind again, and she knew he was right.

With a great effort, she held herself back. She listened for a few minutes as Cyndi's sobs began to taper off, then crept back down the hall to her own room.

*　　　*　　　*

Mr. Matthews didn't notice that anything was wrong at the Countryside Pool until he felt the broken glass crunching underneath his feet. He was in the middle of a sip of hot coffee from his old blue thermos and almost burned his tongue when he heard it and stopped walking. He looked down beneath his heavy work boots. For a second he thought it was gravel, then his mind put the pieces together. The front door hung open and there was a gaping, jagged hole in the glass.

"Oh, shit. What the hell?" he whispered in disbelief. The hand holding his thermos had lowered in his state of shock and now hot coffee was spilling onto the concrete. "Shit." He set the thermos down on the concrete, cautiously walked up to the door, and peered inside.

Even though the inside of the main entrance building was dark, he could see it was in shambles. There was a lot more broken glass on the floor directly in front of the door. Papers were scattered everywhere and the supplies from the front desk had been thrown around the room wildly.

Matthews almost stepped in, but stopped

himself at the last minute. *What if the burglar is still inside? What if he was some druggy, all hopped up on God knows what? He could be dangerous and unpredictable.* He stepped back, trying to control his frantic thoughts.

Finally, he came to a decision. He ran back to his truck, reached into the truck bed, and pulled a battered old toolbox forward. He opened it up and rummaged through, glancing back at the building every few seconds. He finally dug out the heavy, rusted pipe wrench he used for the pool plumbing and irrigation lines. If there were any twitchy, drug-addled psychopaths still in that building trying to get the drop on him, they had a big surprise coming.

Walking as quietly as he could, Matthews went back up to the front door. The main lobby looked clear. He pushed the door open a few inches farther and slid inside, being careful to step around the broken glass. He took a deep breath as silently as he could, then crept toward the front desk. On tiptoes, he peered over the edge and saw no one crouching below. He allowed himself to sigh a little and walked around the corner of the desk, eager to get a look at the safe on the lowest shelf.

Coming around the corner of the desk, he saw the metal front of the safe still intact. Thankfully, it was still here and still locked. It had been moved slightly, as if someone had tried to open it and gave up.

"Thank God," he muttered under his breath.

Matthews looked up and saw that the door to the snack bar was also ajar. Peering through the open crack between the door and the jamb, he saw no one inside. He braced himself and pushed the door open with the heavy pipe wrench, it thunked against the metal.

The snack bar area was a total disaster. Melted ice cream covered the floor and there were filthy footprints everywhere. Matthews saw this and decided not to set foot in the snack bar until after the police got here. Sticky soda was sprayed all over the walls. The room had a stale sour smell from the spoiled food. He glanced up at the shelf where the stereo sat. It was gone, along with the speakers that young Cyndi Stevens girl had brought from home. All of her tapes were gone as well.

"Well, so much for her sound system," he frowned. That girl had been so excited about it, and now she was shit outta luck. He'd have to break the news to her tomorrow when she came back to work, or maybe he'd call her later after the police got here.

He pushed the door open a bit farther and saw what the burglar had left on the rolling metal shutters of the snack counter. It looked like the guy who broke in had taken one of the bottles of ketchup for the microwavable hot dogs and painted a huge grinning Smiley-Face on the metal. It wasn't just a simple one either, it had grotesque detail like a caricature with huge over-sized teeth. It gave him the creeps all over again.

"Goddamned kids," he said shrugging off the chill that was attempting to worm its way down his back. "Thanks for that. It's a real work of art."

At least they hadn't gotten any of the money, and at least *he* had found this mess first and not one of the kids. Matthews sighed and walked back to the front desk.

"Oh God, I really don't need this shit today," he growled. He picked up the phone off the floor behind the desk. It was making that harsh, pulsing off-the-hook noise. He set the phone back down on the cradle, then lifted it again to call the police. He turned and looked back into the snack bar at that Smiley-Face again as he waited for the police to pick up. From out here, it almost looked like it had been drawn in blood.

                    *   *   *

    The doorbell rang just after 9:15 that morning. Cyndi looked out the window and saw Johnny's mother's station wagon parked out front, right where Johnny usually parked his old Bel Air. Johnny worked out a deal with his mother, giving Christie his second free ticket in exchange for his mother picking up Cyndi and Eddie and driving them all to Thrill River. He had gotten an extra discounted ticket for Eddie.

    Underneath Cyndi's tiny pink shorts and loose white T-shirt that cut off just below her rib cage, Cyndi was already in her new swimsuit. It was a two piece with a wild black and hot pink tiger-stripe pattern. The old white one from last year had been permanently stained in the Dead Man's Drop and in the tunnel, and it had been thrown out the day she came home.

    Cyndi turned off her stereo, picked up her small backpack, and walked out of the room.

    A light green and blue beach towel hung across the banister at the bottom of the stairs, and she flung it over her shoulder.

    "Mom, I'm taking off," Cyndi called out. Her mother came into the room drying her hands on a dish towel.

    "So soon?" her mother asked.

    "Well, they open the gates at 9:45, and Johnny said we should probably get there early to get a place in line."

    "Okay, be careful," her mother sighed. She held out her arms and Cyndi walked over to hug her. She thought her daughter looked too pale, and the circles under her eyes were too dark, but she held her tongue.

    Cyndi opened the door and Eddie stood there in an unbuttoned yellow and black plaid shirt with his

                              101

aviator sunglasses on. His swim trunks were also as yellow as a school bus. He flipped the shades up onto his forehead.

"Hi, my name is Edward and I'll be your substitute boyfriend for the day," he said in a joking suave voice. Cyndi laughed out loud and gave him a playful shove. Eddie's goofy presence always eased her tense nerves. Eddie waved at Cyndi's mother and she returned it politely. "Hi, Mrs. Stevens. You all set, Cyndi?"

Cyndi glanced back at her mother and could practically see the worry buried under her pleasant expression. Cyndi gave her the most reassuring smile she could muster.

"See ya," she said and walked out the door.

Her mother stood there staring after her. Cyndi had left so abruptly, she couldn't just let her go without saying something. She rushed to the door and flung it open. Behind her the phone began to ring. She glanced distractedly at it, but decided to ignore it. Cyndi was already halfway down the front walk.

"Cyndi, wait!" she called out.

Cyndi turned back, the smile she put on for Eddie and the others quickly faded and her real expression came forward. Her mother noticed how wide Cyndi's eyes were, how tight her fists were clenched. She looked so young and afraid.

"What?" Cyndi asked, her voice low, barely a whisper.

"If anything happens, *anything*, you call me and I'll come get you. You understand me?"

Cyndi glanced at Eddie and saw the perplexed look on his face. She had to think of something quick to say or Eddie would start asking questions.

Oh God, me and my big mouth, her mother thought as she noticed the weird, questioning look on

102

Eddie's face. For a brief moment, she had a terrible vision of her daughter's college tuition and that confidentiality agreement swirling down a toilet bowl.

"What could happen?" Cyndi asked with a fake shrug and a matching fake smile.

Her mother returned the fake smile. She knew Cyndi had gotten the message. *She's a survivor. She's strong.* How right her husband had been.

Cyndi turned away and she and Eddie walked down to the station wagon. As Cyndi and Eddie got into the car, her mother waved at Johnny's mother, a woman she had only met once briefly. The station wagon pulled away, and they were on their way to Thrill River.

She watched the car drive off, then rushed back into the house to answer the phone. The ringing had already stopped by the time she made it into the kitchen and picked it up. She heard only the dial tone and set the phone back on its wall-mounted cradle. *Oh well, I'm sure if it was important they'll call back.*

If she hadn't chased Cyndi out the door, she might have answered the call and heard a very disturbing message from Cyndi's boss Mr. Matthews. She might even have had time to stop Cyndi before Mrs. Vesna's station wagon pulled away from their house. Matthews himself may have even called back later to tell Cyndi that her tapes and speakers had been stolen. Unfortunately for Cyndi, her mother forgot about the call, and Matthews got distracted by other things.

*   *   *

To Johnny's surprise, Brady actually showed up on time for work. Usually, he was around five minutes late, and if Mr. Sheehan was around, he would start asking Johnny questions about Brady's whereabouts. Johnny would simply shrug and say, "he'll probably be

103

here any minute," and he always was.

Today, Brady pulled into the employee parking lot on the northwest side of the front gates, right behind Johnny.

"What are *you* doing here so early?" Johnny asked amiably.

"Don't remind me," Brady grumbled, looking miserable and slightly disheveled. As they walked in together, Johnny noticed the thick aroma of beer-sweat underneath the layer of Brady's sunscreen.

They stood in a small semicircle with a dozen other lifeguards outside the control room, just like they had on that first orientation day. Sheehan faced them all, reciting their scheduled stations one by one for the day.

"Let's see...Vesna," Sheehan flipped through the papers on his clipboard. "Okay, you'll be on first shift at Lazy River Cliff. Once you get your relief you'll head up to The Falls up on the tower, lunch at two, then the rest of the day you'll be on two stations at Hurricane Bay."

Johnny nodded solemnly. He wished he had known his schedule ahead of time so he could tell Cyndi, Eddie, and Christie where to look for him.

Sheehan turned to Brady, found his schedule, and read it to him. Brady nodded, keeping his bloodshot eyes on the floor, and gave him a sarcastic salute. Sheehan gave him a wary, irritated look. Johnny expected Sheehan to make a comment about how obviously hungover Brady looked and smelled.

Sheehan squinted at him. "I better not catch you away from your stations, Johnston. There's gonna be hundreds of people here today. This is for real. No horsing around, got it?"

"Sir, yes sir. Safety is my top priority, sir," Brady said enthusiastically. It was a phrase Sheehan had hammered over and over throughout the past two weeks of training. Behind Sheehan's back, two kids covered their snickering smiles with their hands. Sheehan gave him an annoyed look, Johnny noticed the muscles in his jaw clench. He squinted at Brady one last time, then moved on to the last two people on his list. He looked over the faces in the group, checking for them.

"Has anyone seen Greg Cosetto or Shelly Wilkins?" he asked.

All the other lifeguards looked around for them as if to confirm that they weren't there. Greg and Shelly were assigned in their group, and rumor had it that they were in the middle of a hot and heavy relationship. Johnny knew them in passing from school and didn't doubt the rumor's validity. He had noticed the way they were always looking at each other, and the way Shelly laughed at everything Greg said, usually touching his arm lightly. He thought it was strange for them to both be gone on opening day of the park. Turning to Brady, he tried to give him a questioning look, but Brady only stared blankly at the ground with heavy-lidded eyes, too hungover to care.

"Anyone have any idea where they are?" Sheehan's question was met only with blank stares and shrugs. He gave a grunt that sounded sarcastically perplexed, as if he expected no better from the two of them, then scratched their names off his clipboard. "Okay, that'll be all. Call me on the radio if any of you have any questions."

Sheehan hurried off to his next group, checking the time on his wrist watch. The group dispersed. A few of them muttered questions to each other about their missing coworkers. Johnny had more important things on his mind than two no-shows. He could feel the nervous excitement in the air like electricity before a lightning strike. He felt something else too, something sour just below the surface, like something bad was going to happen.

*   *   *

"Hello. Wake up, Cyndi," Eddie said. He whistled at her and snapped his fingers in front of her face. She had been staring out the station wagon's window at the rolling hills and empty fields. Somewhere down below the crest of the hill running alongside the road was a line of tall cottonwood trees, probably lining some stream that she couldn't see from here. They had also passed a group of rundown apartment buildings and a rough old residential neighborhood a mile ago. She wasn't really looking at much of that though, she was thinking about her nightmares, and trying to brace herself for her first glance at the park. She wondered how closely it would resemble the park from last year.

Now Eddie finally caught her attention and she turned to him. "What?" she asked.

"I said, what was up with your mom back there?"

Cyndi looked forward and saw Christie also looking back from the front seat. She had a look of admiration on her face, and she seemed to be soaking in every move Cyndi made. Cyndi noticed that sometime in the past few days, Christie had refreshed the blonde in her light brown hair again with Sun-In to look more like Cyndi, although her roots were still darker than the rest of her hair.

"Oh, uh, you know, that's just my paranoid mom," Cyndi quickly covered.

"Hey, say no more. I know all about that," Eddie agreed.

"Moms are supposed to worry, that's our job," Johnny's mother, Laurie Vesna, said from the front seat. She was a tall woman in her mid forties. She had Johnny's sandy blonde hair and grayish blue eyes, but

106

looked exactly like Christie. Cyndi really loved Johnny and Christie's parents. Her own parents were kind of bookish and reserved, but Johnny's parents were the complete opposite. They were two of the friendliest, most talkative people she had ever met. They were always going out and doing fun things, unlike her own parents who stayed home most of the time. Sure Cyndi loved her own parents, but she wondered just how much more fun life would be if they acted more like the Vesnas.

"You don't have to worry about me, Mom," Eddie said, he had known her for years and jokingly referred to her as his second mom. "If any perverts try to touch me, I'll scream my head off."

"Good," she returned his sarcasm with more sarcasm, then turned to Christie. "And you, young lady, stay with Cyndi and Eddie. Even if you see some of your friends, I don't want you wandering off with them. You need to stick together."

"Mom, I'm not a baby. I'll be fine," Christie protested. She turned back to Cyndi. "We'll stick together, right Cyndi?"

"Yeah. Stick together," Cyndi said.

Right as the words came out of her mouth, a memory flashed through Cyndi's mind that made her heart skip. *We gotta stick together, y'know?* Stacy had said that, and Cyndi had given her the exact same response. Now the roles were reversed, Cyndi was the older girl and Christie was the younger one. Cyndi felt a sudden chill, as if Stacy's ghost had reached out and touched her heart. She turned away from Christie and looked out the window, trying to suppress a shudder.

Now that she thought of it, making that promise to each other was probably the clearest memory she had of Stacy, but they had broken that promise. They hadn't stuck together in the end, things might have ended differently if they had. Now, a full year later, the words still came back to haunt her.

Well, I'm not Stacy, she thought. *I won't leave her side for anything. Stacy might not have left my side either if she'd known what lay ahead.*

And just what does lay ahead?

"There it is!" Christie shouted from the front seat. Cyndi looked up at once. To the right, Cyndi saw the black wrought iron gates and the concrete steps leading up to the park. A small crowd gathered around those gates with towels slung over their shoulders, coolers at their feet, and beach bags in their hands. Back behind the bars were the blue painted ticket booths. Hung in the center of each booth, between the top of the ticket window and the peak of the roof, was the grinning cartoon face that had haunted her dreams all these long months. It looked exactly as it had on the metal doors leading out of the Gold Mine Tunnel, the doors that had locked them in. Now here the face was again and again, plastered high in the air, inviting everyone in.

Eddie grabbed Cyndi's shoulder. "Check it out!" he said excitedly.

Cyndi gave a nervous little laugh and tried her best to smile. Eddie was too overcome with excitement to notice the hard goosebumps that had broken out all over her arms and legs.

The station wagon pulled into the already crowded parking lot, passing families with kids bouncing around excitedly. Laurie stopped the car at the drop off lane in front of the concrete steps where everyone was gathering.

"Okay, you kids have fun. Christie, remember: *Sunscreen,*" Laurie put extra emphasis on the word.

"I know, Mom," Christie said with irritation, unbuckling her seat belt.

"Put it on again at lunchtime. And don't go

running off."

"I *know, Mom*," Christie whined, getting out of the car.

"Keep an eye on her, okay?" Laurie told Cyndi and Eddie.

"*Mom, God!*" Christie shut the car door hard.

"Christie!" she scolded, frowning with disapproval.

"We'll keep her out of trouble, Mom. Don't worry," Eddie said.

Cyndi stepped out of the car and felt a wave of fresh heat baking off the pavement. It was going to be hot today without a doubt. As she walked around the back of the car, her gaze fixed on the white smiley-face looming down from the nearest ticket booth. Its black eyes seemed to be ignoring the rest of the crowd, staring straight down at her.

Welcome to my NEW house, Cyndi. Don't you love it? Couldn't you just DIE for it?

Eddie and Christie walked up and took their place in the growing crowd in front of the gates. The coconut and medicinal aromas from a wide variety of sunscreens filled the air.

"You got the tickets, kiddo?" Eddie asked Christie.

"Umm, I think Cyndi has them. And don't call me kiddo," she replied. Eddie crossed his eyes briefly at Christie. They both looked back and saw Cyndi standing in the gutter, staring wide-eyed at the face painted on the ticket booth.

"Paging Dr. Cyndi Stevens," Eddie said in a monotone voice, cupping his hand around his mouth. Cyndi jumped and looked down at Eddie. "You mind giving us the tickets before you get run over by the next car that comes by?" Cyndi hadn't even realized that she hadn't fully stepped out of the street.

"Oh, yeah, sorry," Cyndi said. She joined Eddie and Christie, then dug through her pack for the tickets that Johnny had dropped off two nights before.

The low murmur of the people in the crowd suddenly rose to a cheer as Cyndi found the tickets. She handed them to Eddie and looked up. A teenager with bushy brown hair and a patchy, peach-fuzz mustache walked up from the other side of the wrought iron gate with a set of keys. He wore a white Thrill River T-shirt and red lifeguard swim trunks. The crowd cheered him on. A few people even blew loud whistles between their fingers as he bent down in front of a small electrical box to the right of the gate. He opened the box and stuck a key into an unseen lock. There was a loud metal clunk and an electric whirring sound as the gate automatically slid open to the right along its track. People at the front of the crowd started milling in as soon as there was enough room to cram themselves through.

"Hey, perfect timing. Right on!" Eddie yelled in his surfer dude voice.

As the crowd moved forward, Cyndi's heart began to pound like a drum. They followed the herd of water park patrons up the steps to the main open area in front of the ticket booths. They looked so slow and naive to Cyndi. She imagined herself crying out at them, warning them to leave or they would be next, just like the guy at the end of that old movie *Invasion of the Body Snatchers*. That would make her look crazy though, and she wasn't crazy (she hoped). The crowd thinned out as two thirds of the people quickly formed lines in front of the four ticket booths. Cyndi, and anyone else with free passes, bypassed the booths and went up the slope toward the main entrance.

Just past the ticket booths the concrete path leading toward the main entrance forked around a big decorative flowerbed. There was another set of concrete steps to the left and a smooth ramp to the right, both led up the hill to the turnstiles at the main entrance. The raised flowerbed in between the two paths was bursting with color, and was surrounded by round, softball-sized chunks of white river rock. Cyndi stopped dead in her tracks as soon as she saw what stood in the middle of the flowerbed. It was a life-sized bronze statue of the grinning Kaptain Smiley character holding hands with two bronze laughing children. The two kids were in the air, caught in the middle of jumping or skipping.

Cyndi's mouth dropped open, it was as if the killer were standing right in front of her again. To her, the two bronze children almost looked like they were screaming instead of laughing, being dragged down to some dark, bloody pool to be drowned.

Oh God, I can't do this. I just can't. I just--

"Come on, Cyndi," Eddie urged. "We gotta get up there so we can get a good place in line for the rides."

Eddie and Christie had somehow gotten past her again and were halfway up the ramp to the right of the statue.

"Sorry," Cyndi laughed, putting on the brightest smile she could manage. She rushed forward, glancing back at the statue the whole time. She half expected the ugly thing to turn its head and watch her as she ran past.

Eddie walked hurriedly up the ramp, Cyndi and Christie almost had to jog to keep up with him.

"Slow down, Eddie," Christie whined. "We've got all day."

"Move it, girls," Eddie called back without slowing a bit. "Pump those short-ass pygmy legs."

"Hey!" Cyndi and Christie both yelled defensively at the same time. Both girls were the same height, only five feet tall, although Cyndi had a feeling that Christie would probably grow at least a few more inches and end up taller than her.

The three of them made their way up the ramp and got in the lines forming at the turnstiles. The chattering crowd around them was pretty loud, so they waited in silence, rather than shout to hear each other talk.

Cyndi looked up at the building off to the right of the line. She instantly recognized the familiar design of the wooden stairs leading up to the blue metal door. It looked exactly the same as the Control Room building at the other park. She remembered sprinting up those stairs in the dark, running from the killer. Then had come the sting of rusty metal stake as it jabbed forward, slicing open her left side. She lifted up the left side of her short T-shirt, and looked briefly at the white, puckered scar on the side of her stomach. It was the length of a pencil, but slightly wider. She could almost feel a phantom pain underneath the scar, and she resisted the urge to touch it.

Christie glanced back at Cyndi, saw her looking down at her stomach, then noticed the scar.

"Where'd you get that?" Christie asked.

Cyndi immediately dropped her shirt guiltily.

"I, uh, got it at summer camp," she said thinking quickly. "This guy was chasing me and I fell."

"Ouch."

Cyndi couldn't help but notice how easy it was to lie when there was an element of truth behind it.

"That's nothing, check this out," Eddie pointed out a large white scar that ran from halfway down his forearm to his elbow, a scar on his right knee, and his right foot. "Got all three of those all at once."

"Yikes, what happened?" Cyndi asked, happy to shift the topic away from her.

"Well, let's just say I'll never wear sandals while riding a bike with no hands ever again."

Both girls laughed. "You *would* do that," Cyndi said.

"Yeah, your boyfriend was there when it happened. That asshole had the nerve to laugh his head off at me. At least, until he saw how fucked up I was."

Just past the control room building were the main entrance turnstiles. There were six kids in white Thrill River T-shirts collecting the tickets and ripping the ticket stubs, keeping the flow of traffic into the park moving. Cyndi thought she even recognized one of them, a pimply-faced kid from school. The line finally inched its way to the front. Eddie and Christie went through the turnstiles first. As Cyndi waited behind them, she contemplated just turning and running.

Last chance. It isn't too late to just get the hell out of here and never look back.

She looked forward at the eager smiles on Eddie and Christie's faces. Christie looked so young and vulnerable. Cyndi's promise to Mrs. Vesna came back, *make sure you two stick together.* Stacy had run off, leaving Cyndi on her own. Cyndi wouldn't make the same mistake.

With a forced smile on her face, she handed her ticket to the kid with the pimples, and stepped into the park.

*   *   *

"All right, let's check this place out," Eddie said excitedly. The three of them followed the crowd up one last short set of concrete steps just behind the ticket turnstiles, and Cyndi immediately saw another familiar sight. Shiny metal lockers lined the edge of another long building on her left. Near the end of the building was an opening that went all the way through to the other side. Unlike at the other park, a sign with the words RESTROOMS clearly marked this building. Cyndi guessed that if she were to walk in there, she would already know the exact layout.

"Well, there's the lighthouse," Eddie said, pointing fifty yards ahead. A thirty foot high lighthouse stood at the top of the hill, towering over the rest of the park. This park, like the one last year, was built on a high hill. The restrooms building and the lighthouse seemed to be at opposite ends of the top of this hill. Cyndi figured that the rides must be on the other side of the hill. At the base of the lighthouse was some kind of gift shop. "Johnny said to just walk past the lighthouse, and get a spot down the hill, whatever that means," Eddie said. "He was all mysterious about it. Said he didn't want to ruin the surprise."

"I know. He wouldn't tell us anything about the park either," Christie agreed.

Cyndi half listened as they chattered about the excited, secretive attitude Johnny had adopted whenever he talked about the park. She stared back at the bathroom building, lost in her memories. There had been wild woods in front of the bathrooms at the old park. Here, there were picnic tables and chairs placed neatly in between the bathrooms and the Lighthouse. There was also a big snack bar advertising various foods: pizza, burgers, churros, ice cream. The mouth watering scent of frying food drifted out from the snack bar.

"Oh my God," Eddie exclaimed. "Get a load of *that!*" Christie and several other people in the crowd around them gasped as they reached the crest of the hill beside the lighthouse. Cyndi looked forward and gasped aloud herself at the sight before her eyes.

At the bottom of the steep hill, sprawled out before the crowd, was a huge wave pool. It stood in the center of the park and was the size of a couple of football fields. It was shaped like an arrow, but with a round, blunted end. It was narrow and rectangular at the deep end, but halfway down the length it fanned out into the shallow end. Crystal blue water rippled calmly across its empty surface, the lifeguards hadn't let anyone in the water yet. A green AstroTurf beach with neat stacks of brand new reclining lawn chairs surrounded the wave pool. A building made to look like a row of little beach-front huts housed another snack bar on the left side of the AstroTurf beach.

"Fuckin' A," Eddie said quietly, his eyes sparkled with excitement. "Man, Johnny wasn't kidding, this place is amazing!"

At the back of the wave pool stood a twenty foot high painted wall. Jagged letters spelled out the words *Hurricane Bay* along the top of the wall. Underneath the letters, a huge grinning caricature of Kaptain Smiley from the waist up was painted in the center of the wall. He stood among raging, swirling storm clouds with his arms stretched out almost as wide as the wave pool itself.

Near the back of the wave pool on the left side, a plastic Great White Shark hung upside down over the water from a wooden gallows. It looked like a grotesque trophy.

A loud, electronic bell chimed loudly off to their left. Cyndi jumped and let out a short, startled scream. There was a familiar white speaker mounted up on one of the eaves of the lighthouse gift shop. A man's cool, deep voice boomed loudly from this speaker and all the others throughout the entire park. It wasn't the first time Cyndi had heard this voice.

"Hello, everyone. This is Kurt Carver, President and CEO of Bright Smiles Incorporated. All of us here at Bright Smiles want to thank you for coming today, and welcome you to the park. We're so glad you could make it to our Grand Opening here at Thrill River. Have a thrrrrilling day!"

The welcome message ended with a harsh

crackle of static. A chill ran down Cyndi's spine as she stared up at the speaker.

Down below at the bottom of the hill, a loud buzzer sounded from somewhere around *Hurricane Bay.* All eyes turned toward the wave pool as a thunderous roar came from the deep end. A huge, churning wave that began at the back wall of the pool surged forward, bubbling and foaming. The wave had to be at least four feet higher than the surface of the calm water, and it gathered speed as it rushed toward the shallow end. The tidal wave spread out and lost some of its height as it rushed toward the shallow end, but it still didn't seem to lose any of its fury.

A cheer rose from the crowd on the hill watching the wave and the people began to walk quickly down the hill toward the huge, frothing wave pool.

"Come on, Cyndi!" Christie and Eddie both said. Each of them grabbed one of her hands, and tugged her forward with the rest of the crowd. She stared at the painting of Kaptain Smiley standing with his arms spread out in front of those dark, brooding storm clouds, as if he were commanding them to rain death and destruction. Cyndi felt so alone, realizing that she was the only person in the whole crowd of smiling, sunscreened people who had any idea just how prophetic that painting actually was.

Chapter Nine:

The Wave Pool

"Okay, what do you guys wanna ride first?" Eddie asked eagerly, slapping his hands together. The three of them, along with the rest of the crowd, had walked down a winding concrete path that led to the AstroTurf beach in front of *Hurricane Bay*. Neat stacks of reclining lawn chairs stood at ten foot intervals along the water's edge. They grabbed three chairs, found an empty spot, and set their towels down. Now that they had their base camp set up, Eddie and Christie were chomping at the bit to go explore the rest of the park.

"I don't know," Christie answered, pulling off her own T-shirt and shorts. She wore a light-blue one-piece swimsuit with a wild, brightly-colored flower pattern. "Maybe we should go check out what they have."

"I say we wait for the next wave," Eddie said.

"Maybe we should go find Johnny," Cyndi suggested.

"He said not to worry about trying to find him," Eddie explained. "The plan was that he and Brady would keep an eye out for us and meet us up by that lighthouse at two o'clock when they get their lunch break."

"We should get on some of the rides before the lines get too long," Christie suggested.

"I like the way you think, little sister. We gotta beat those lines." Eddie held out his hand for Christie to slap him five, then expertly snatched it away from her. "Oh, too slow."

Suddenly, the loud buzzer went off again, signaling the approach of another monster wave. The crowd around the wave pool roared its approval.

"Oh, shit!" Eddie said. He yanked his yellow plaid shirt off in one quick movement and tossed it back at the girls. He kicked off his sandals and sprinted into the water toward the thunderous wave that loomed ahead. His feet splashed and made dunking sounds in the water as he ran. The water level rose rapidly above his knees as the wave rushed toward him. With his fists raised in the air, he screamed out and dove into the foaming massive wave.

No one else had set foot in the wave pool yet. A team of a half dozen lifeguards stood in a tight circle, getting their orders for the day from their boss. One of them finally heard Eddie's triumphant scream and noticed that he was in the pool. Their shrill whistles immediately rang out, but Eddie was already underwater and couldn't hear them.

From the white-washed concrete shoreline, Cyndi and Christie saw the lifeguards rush into the water, blowing furiously on their shrill, metal whistles. Eddie's head and one raised fist popped out of the water as the huge white wave washed over him.

"Hey! Get out! You're not supposed to be in there yet!" a few of them shouted at Eddie.

"Eddie!" Christie called out with her hands

cupped over her mouth. All of their shouts were lost over the roar of the powerful wave.

The wave dissipated as the pool widened and fanned out towards the shallow end. The bubbling surface calmed and Eddie splashed up again. He turned back to scream for the girls to come in, but he quickly went silent as he noticed the lifeguards whistling and shouting at him.

"Get out! *Get OUT!*"

"Huh?" Eddie asked, utterly confused.

The leader of the team of lifeguards, the guy who had been giving out the group's orders, stood on the shoreline bellowing at Eddie.

"We don't have the lifeguards stationed yet! Get out NOW!"

Cyndi looked over at the large guy screaming at Eddie and her mouth went dry. The sound of the man's booming voice had first caught her attention. He stood with an air of authority. He had long, dark-brown hair, curly and neatly feathered. He wore a tight white Thrill River T-shirt, high red shorts, and a whistle around his neck. Cyndi would have recognized that no-nonsense expression anywhere. It was her old head counselor Sheehan from Camp Kikawa.

So it really was the same Sheehan after all, Cyndi thought, remembering her conversation with Johnny the previous week. *What the hell is he doing here?*

"Oh, sorry," Eddie shrugged, laughing. He sheepishly trudged out of the water toward the shore. All the lifeguards glared at him as he walked back to the chairs.

Sheehan looked over to make a mental note of the group of kids the little troublemaker was returning to. He always kept mental notes on troublesome kids, remembering them for future reference. Troublemakers

119

had burned him too many times in the past. He looked briefly at Christie, then locked eyes with Cyndi. She saw the flicker of recognition in his eyes and knew he remembered her.

Why would he forget? You cost him his job remember?

Neither one of them greeted each other. They simply stared at each other with quiet caution.

The other lifeguards began to take notice, and Sheehan intentionally looked away, ignoring Cyndi. She saw the curious expressions on some of their faces as they turned to look at her, and she hastily turned away herself, staring at the ground. She felt the curious eyes of the lifeguards still watching her as Eddie walked up, his yellow trunks dripping.

"Jeez, touchy aren't they?" he commented.

"You idiot! You're gonna get us in trouble," Christie scolded with her hands on her hips.

"Ah, forget it. I thought it was supposed to be open. It was an honest mistake," he shrugged, dismissing the lifeguards with a wave of his hand. "This place is so big, I bet we won't even see them again today. Hey, it was still worth it. *I* was the first person to ever get in that wave pool. How do ya like that?"

"Eddie! Gosh!" Christie acted so exasperated with him, it made her sound so young to Cyndi.

"Oh, come on, little sister. Give me a hug!" Eddie, still soaking wet, rushed forward and wrapped his skinny, slippery arms around Christie. He lifted her off the ground in a bear hug.

"Eww! No! You're all wet!" she screamed in protest.

Cyndi couldn't help but laugh and shake her head.

"You too, Cyndi!" Eddie called out, putting Christie down. "I'm your substitute boyfriend for the day, remember?"

"Ohh, no!" Cyndi immediately tensed her shoulders and ducked back from Eddie's reaching arms. He chased her around the chairs briefly. "Christie, help!" she yelled laughing.

Christie obediently snapped into action, climbing up on her lawn chair and jumping on Eddie's back. Eddie begrudgingly calmed down and took a moment to catch his breath. Cyndi looked off to the left to get another look at Sheehan. The little group of lifeguards had dispersed and were heading toward the high ledges overlooking the deep end of the wave pool. Sheehan was nowhere in sight.

People were now beginning to slowly wade into the water.

"Oh sure, *now* they let people in," Eddie complained. "We've gotta catch the next wave, you guys." He and Christie stood up and headed toward the wave pool.

"Actually, I think I'll wait for you guys," Cyndi said hesitantly.

They both turned back. "What's the matter? Can't you swim?" Eddie asked.

"Yeah, I can swim, it's just...My stomach isn't feeling too good right now." Cyndi clutched her stomach, hoping they'd buy that excuse.

"Ooh, not good." Eddie grimaced sym- pathetically.

"Are you gonna be okay?" Christie asked.

"I'll be fine. I think I'll just sit here for a while and get some sun."

"Okay well, we'll come check on you after the next wave hits," Eddie said in an unusually serious voice. He had a sensitive stomach himself and didn't mess around when it came to digestive issues. He pointed off somewhere to the left of the AstroTurf beach. "I think I saw a sign for some bathrooms over there if... y'know."

"I'll be all right. Go have fun."

Cyndi watched as they dashed off into the water. Christie's body immediately tensed at the cold temperature, and Eddie threatened to pick her up and toss her all the way in. *Maybe I should go out there with them and just try to forget about all of that stuff from last summer,* she thought. Being here felt so strange though. She knew there were major differences between this park and the one out in the woods, but some of the similarities were uncanny. The bathrooms and control room buildings were exactly the same. Then, minutes ago, as they walked down the winding path to the wave pool, she had looked up and seen two of the Ragin' River slides. They looked exactly as they had out in the woods. Also, those the smiley faces were everywhere again: on the buildings, the maps, the signs for the rides, the trashcans. There was Sheehan too.

There were a lot of people around though, and music. It played from those mounted speakers just loud enough to be pleasant but not overbearing. Music almost always had a way of putting her mind at ease. She decided to wait for a little while and try to relax. Maybe when she got too hot she would go join her friends.

*   *   *

"What's up with Cyndi lately?" Christie asked. They had waded far out into the wave pool just past the high ledges where the lifeguards stood looking down with aviator sunglasses and hawk-like solemn expressions.

"Her stomach's upset," Eddie explained.

"No, it's more than that. She seems...freaked out or something. I'm kinda worried about her."

"You sound like your brother," he laughed.

122

"You both worry way too much about that girl."

"I'm serious, Eddie."

"She's fine," he said dismissively. "Look, I'll tell you the same thing I told Johnny: She'll come around."

The buzzer blared out again. It was much louder down here in the wave pool. Eddie's fist shot up out of the water with a splash. A cheer erupted from everyone in the wave pool, it sounded like the crowd at a DeAngelo High School football game after a touchdown. A roaring rumble thundered from the back wall beneath that larger-than-life Smiley character. The water rose at the deep end, bubbling and roiling.

"Here we go!" Eddie shouted at Christie. They waited in excited anticipation, watching the huge wave rush at them. The water level rose up to their chins and they had to kick off from the bottom of the pool to keep from going under. The wave was only ten feet away, rolling toward them with incredible force. They both took deep breaths, bracing themselves for impact.

Just before the wave hit, Eddie kicked and paddled furiously, trying to shoot up as high as he could. He wanted to ride the top edge of the wave. He turned his head to the right at the last moment to keep the water from rushing up his nose, and he caught a brief glimpse of something that looked like a pyramid beyond the wave pool. Then he was engulfed.

The wall of water smashed into them, shoving them backwards and whipping their arms and legs around wildly. They completely lost control of their bodies in the wave's fury. The wave shoved them back a full fifteen feet, then let them go. As the water began to calm, a cloud of tiny air bubbles swelled around them, tickling their skin as they swam upwards. They burst up to the surface, gasping for air.

"FUCK YEAH!" Eddie cried out. Christie

123

came up laughing and coughing. They watched as the little kids who stayed near the shallows ran in terror from the diminishing wave. It had lost a lot of its force by the time it reached the shallow end of the pool, but it still washed over the little kids mercilessly.

*   *   *

Back at the chairs, the sun already felt like it was baking Cyndi's skin. She still didn't fully trust the rides here, but the cool, crystal clear water of the wave pool was looking more enticing all the time. It wasn't even eleven o'clock yet, but she could already feel a sunburn coming on. She decided to put on more sunscreen.

Rummaging through the essentials she had brought in her small, neon-green backpack, she found her tube of Banana Boat sunscreen. It already felt warm despite being in the backpack. She sat on the edge of her pool chair, squeezing out a small glob of sunscreen. Then she set the tube down on the AstroTurf and began lathering up her arms.

A fit of familiar, giggling laughter cut into Cyndi's ear from off to her right. Instinctively, she turned her head, but regretted it as soon as she did. As usual, it was Jennifer's group of giggling, irritating hyenas, all in their skimpy swimsuits and stylish sunglasses, walking in her direction across the AstroTurf beach. She wondered why they always had to giggle like that whenever they were near her. *What is so goddamn funny?*

She only gave them a brief glance, trying her best to ignore them, but something felt wrong. She looked back and realized that Jennifer, their fearless leader, was nowhere in sight.

Jennifer suddenly ran past Cyndi and stomped

down on the tube of sunscreen. A huge white glob of sunscreen squirted out onto the AstroTurf.

"Oops!" she taunted.

"Hey!" Cyndi yelled at Jennifer with more anger in her voice than she intended.

"Sorry," Jennifer called back over her shoulder, and her group of friends erupted in hysterical laughter. They all ran off, glancing back at Cyndi and congratulating Jennifer. Cyndi clenched her fists and began to grind her teeth.

"Fuckin' bitch!" she growled under her breath. She stared down at the pathetic glob of wasted sunscreen, and it only made her angrier.

All of a sudden, the heat was too much. The sun was too bright in her eyes, her skin felt too hot, and her blood was boiling. She had to cool down. Afraid or not, she had to go cool off in that water or she thought she might just explode.

Cyndi stood up, leaving the sunscreen where it was, and stormed off into the wave pool. Her feet sent up little splashes as she walked in. The water was blessedly cool as it washed over her feet and calves. She dodged the little kids and families that floated around in the shallows, hurrying out to the deep end as fast as she could.

Once the water level reached her thighs, it began to slow her down. She went out a little farther, then dove in. The cool water relieved her hot, reddening skin and she instantly felt a little better. Her skin felt slippery from the fresh sunscreen she had put on her arms. She swam forward a few feet under the surface, her legs kicking hard. She didn't want to bump into anyone so she let her eyes open underwater. Other than a few blurry bodies off to the left, she was in the clear.

She kicked forward once again. Her blonde hair trailed out delicately behind her, the cold water washing away the heat the sun had baked into it. She came up for air a few times as she swam out, quickly took a huge gasping breath, then dove back under immediately. Under the surface, she swam hard, letting out all of her aggression towards Jennifer and her stupid friends.

After a few more minutes of hard swimming, Cyndi finally felt like she had gone far enough. She came up for air and looked around, blinking away the chlorine that stung her eyes. She hadn't realized how far out into the deep end she'd gone until now. The bottom of the wave pool was at least four feet below the tips of her toes, and the nearest swimming person was at least fifty feet farther back. She was all alone way out here. The deep end of the wave pool was eerily calm and quiet. Back here the noise of the crowd seemed insignificant and far away.

Cyndi spun around and looked up at the towering painted Kaptain Smiley holding his arms wide. Whatever heat the sun baked into her was now fully gone, lost in the chills that seemed to emanate from that garish, grinning face. She felt goosebumps rise on the skin of her arms and legs as she tread water and kicked.

Above her head, a thick red safety rope had been strung across the wave pool. The safety rope was strung about five yards in front of that plastic shark that dangled over the left edge of the pool by its tail. She stared up at the rope and realized that she was unintentionally moving towards it. The wave pool was sucking her in, pulling her toward whatever machinery controlled the waves. She looked up at the back wall and the grin on Kaptain Smiley's face almost seemed to have widened slightly.

She turned to swim away, her heartbeat jumping up to a frantic pace. Remembering the swim classes she took at the rec center as a little kid, she laid face-down flat against the surface, and paddled as if she were swimming laps for the 1984 Summer Olympics. The faster she swam, the harder the water seemed to tug at her.

She held her breath for as long as she could and paddled hard, but exhaustion in her arms and legs, and the need for air, finally overcame her. She came up gasping for air and spun to face the back wall again, the water still seemed to be relentlessly pulling her back to the deep end.

If it starts pulling me too hard I'll scream. I'll scream for help. There's people here now. I'm not alone. I'm not alone.

But you are alone. Way out here in the deep end it's just you and me.

A cold, pruny hand grabbed her shoulder. Cyndi jumped and whirled, spraying the owner of the hand with a fan of water.

"Cyndi, I thought that was you," Eddie said smiling. "Why didn't you come find us?"

Wet locks of Eddie's curly auburn hair were pushed back from his forehead haphazardly. Cyndi saw Christie farther back, standing in water up to her chin and waving. Cyndi waved back, she had never felt more glad to see familiar faces.

"I looked for you, but I guess I lost you in the crowd."

"Yeah, I guess so. I didn't even see you swim past us. Isn't this place incredible?"

Before she could answer, the alarm buzzer went off again. Eddie screamed in joy, throwing his fists out of the water. The screams of the people in the wave pool erupted behind Cyndi. The sound of all those screams made her skin crawl.

The rumbling wave burst up from the back wall and rolled toward them. Eddie was bouncing, trying to make the wave shoot him up as high as he could go.

Cyndi, on the other hand, decided to go under it. She had no desire to be pummeled by that chaotic mass of water. She took a deep breath, paddled up with her hands, and let her body sink to the bottom of the pool.

Cyndi touched the bottom with her feet and crouched. She had made it back to the six foot depth during her frantic swim away from the deep end. She opened her eyes again to watch the wave approaching overhead. Something else caught her eye, something near the bottom of the pool. Everything was blurry underwater, but she could make out a black shape coming with the wave, coming straight toward her. She squinted trying to make sense of the image. As it came closer, its movements became more recognizable. It was a man dressed in all black, and he was swimming toward her.

She screamed underwater, bubbles came out of her mouth and brushed past her face on the way to the surface. She kicked off the bottom of the pool, launching herself upward, and came up the middle of the foaming chaos of the wave.

It knocked her backward, sending her in a flailing underwater somersault. She had no control over her body for a few terrifying seconds. Then the wave passed and she found herself floating at a strange diagonal angle. Her head finally figured out what was up and down, and she went for the surface. She burst into the sunlight with a great gasp, and saw she was facing the shallow end. Whirling around, she tried to locate the man that had been swimming toward her.

There was no one under the surface. She ducked under the surface again looking left and right. The man was gone.

Was it my imagination again?

"Ohh yeah!" Eddie shouted from behind her. She turned to look at him, forcing a half smile on her face. "Intense, huh?"

"Yeah, intense," she agreed. *That's one way you can put it.*

Cyndi looked over her shoulder, searching for any sign of the swimming man in black. Two sets of smooth white stairs ascended out of the wave pool on both sides, but no one was walking on either of them. *If there really had been someone down in the water, wouldn't you see him by now? That's a long time to be underwater, even for him.* There had been so many other times in the past few weeks that she thought she had seen the masked man: at the dance, at the mall in the arcade, in her nightmares. Maybe there had never been anyone there at all.

Cyndi smiled as Christie rejoined them, but inside she wondered yet again if she might be losing her mind.

Chapter Ten:

The Rocky River and The Falls

"Come on, you guys. Let's go check out these rides," Christie suggested. They were sitting at the chairs in front of the wave pool and catching their breath. Eddie and Christie had been discussing their experiences with the huge waves. Cyndi nodded agreeably whenever they turned and asked, *'Right?'* Now they stood up to go see what the rest of the park had to offer.

"Okay, let's go check out that pyramid thing over there," Eddie said. "I saw it from the wave pool and I gotta go check it out." Eddie had a deep love for Ancient Egypt. He had told Johnny and Cyndi that someday he planned to get a tattoo of Egyptian hieroglyphics around his arm.

The three of them walked along the right side of the wave pool toward the pyramid. On impulse, Cyndi turned and looked back at their towels on the lawn chairs, hoping no one would touch them while they were gone. Suddenly, she had a strong sensation of déjà vu. Every time they had left their belongings last year at the other park, she had looked back just like she was doing now. There had been picnic tables on a wooden deck area that was built right up to the edge of the river. The wave pool had taken the place of the picnic area at this new park, but it still felt all too familiar. Would they come back to find their towels shredded and thrown around, with those horrible smiley face drawings all over them this time too?

Don't be ridiculous, she scolded herself. *There are at least a hundred people sitting around here, nothing's going to happen.*

It was only a short walk to the entrance of the pyramid ride. They walked up to the fake wooden sign with a cartoon picture of Kaptain Smiley wearing an Egyptian headdress and standing in that classic bent-arm Egyptian pose. The ride was called *Pharaoh River,* and tacked underneath the writing was a yellow sticker that said *OPENING AUGUST 3!* A waist-high metal crowd control barrier blocked the concrete path leading to the line switchbacks for the ride.

"August? Aww, man!" Eddie said glumly. He looked up at the huge pyramid shape that stood farther up the hill behind a grove of thick bushes and pine trees. To Cyndi, the pyramid looked dark and brooding sitting back in the shadows of the trees like that. "Why couldn't they have just had it ready when the park opened?"

"I know," Christie agreed.

"Oh well. Come on, you guys. Lots more to see," Cyndi said, grabbing Eddie's arm and pulling him back away from the metal barrier. She hoped she didn't sound too eager about not having to ride the Pharaoh River.

They wandered back up the hill, away from Hurricane Bay. There was a set of simple open white slides along the left side of the concrete path that didn't look too threatening. Riders got on at the top of the hill on an elevated wooden platform, and slid down with their arms and legs crossed, spraying water off each side of the slide. Eddie and Christie were pleasantly surprised when Cyndi volunteered to try them, but their surprise turned to disappointment when they reached the top of the hill and saw the size of the line. It stretched far back along the grass behind the wooden platform, and had no shade from the blazing sun. Everyone in line looked bored and hot.

"You guys wanna wait?" Cyndi asked without enthusiasm.

Christie shrugged.

Eddie looked back, judging whether the ride was worth it or not. "Mmm, nah. Maybe later. Let's see what else they got."

They moved on, wandering along the path at the top of the hill back toward the entrance of the park. *This is where the Dead Man's Drop would have been,* she thought. *Thank God they didn't include that awful ride.*

Past the lighthouse gift shop and the picnic tables, that déjà vu feeling came back. Cyndi looked to her right and saw that they were walking past the slow meandering start of the Duelin' Rivers. The plants and trees around it were slightly different, but the ride itself looked exactly the same. She remembered climbing under that rock overhang, and crouching behind the bubbling fountain. She could almost feel the rough texture of the rock that had dug into her hands and feet. Eddie and Christie marveled at the shady start to the Duelin' Rides.

There were two boys in one large green tube, playfully splashing two girls in the tube behind them. The girls screamed and laughed, holding their hands up defensively. For a second, Cyndi saw herself with Stacy, Brad, and Zack in those tubes, and a wave of sadness washed over her. She had only known them for about a week, but sometimes she missed them terribly. She often thought how strange it was that a person could get attached to a group of friends in such a short time. Every now and then something would remind her of them, and an empty, lonely feeling would clamp down on her heart. Most of the time when this feeling came over her, she was at home and could pull Zack and Stacy's T-shirts out and look at them. Those shirts were all she had left of them, souvenirs of her long lost friends.

"Ooh we'll have to check that one out," Eddie said. Christie nodded in agreement. Cyndi gave them a brief smile.

At least that was one of the safe rides. Unless they changed it.... She hoped she wouldn't have to find out.

Cyndi's feeling of déjà vu faded as they passed the Duelin' Rivers entrance and crested a small hill. They looked down at an area that was completely new and unfamiliar to Cyndi. Four rides that she didn't recognize were clustered together in a flat area off to the left of the main entrance. Cyndi guessed that if the Lazy River had been recreated like the Ragin' and Duelin' Rivers, then this area would be directly uphill from it.

Off to their left, winding down along the slope of the small hill that they now stood on, was an open ride called The Rocky River. It looked like a cross between the Duelin' Rivers and the Lazy River. Riders on single person blue tubes sped down the twisting river. The ride seemed to speed up on shallow quick stretches, then slow down in deep water around a few wide curves and whirlpools. Cyndi saw several of the riders holding hands, creating a chain from tube to tube.

That doesn't look too threatening, Cyndi thought.

Another ride called The Screamin' Demon stood on the highest part of the little hill. It started under a covered wooden gazebo structure with a short line of people out the back. A lifeguard stood at a sloping wooden platform, assisting the riders as they put bright red, heavy plastic sleds with little wheels onto a set of metal tracks. As Cyndi and the others watched, two riders, a father and a young son, climbed on board the sled and gripped onto little handles on the sides.

"You guys ready?" the lifeguard asked. The father and son both agreed enthusiastically, then counted to three. At three, the lifeguard pulled a metal lever and the sled rocketed down a steep wooden ramp lined with diagonal safety barriers covered with green AstroTurf. At the bottom of the steep ramp, the tracks ran out and the sled shot into a long pool, skipping along the surface of the water. It finally slowed and sunk near the shallow end. Both father and son let out adrenaline-filled cries of joy as they reached the end of the ride.

"Whoa," Eddie whispered, completely entranced as he watched the Screamin' Demon in action. He had never seen or heard of anything like it before in his life. "Oh, we're gettin' on that!"

"Uh-uh," both Cyndi and Christie said at the same time, shaking their heads. Christie knew she wasn't brave enough for a ride as scary as that, and Cyndi, still battling her own memories, didn't know if she could trust any of the rides here yet.

The centerpiece of this entire area was a large playground structure called Smiley's Beach, with tiny water slides, chaotic jets, and waterfalls placed randomly everywhere. Soaking wet little kids ran around this area with limitless energy. It was like any playground, freeing kids up from the tight, oppressive parental shadow they had to live under almost all the time. It wasn't for grownups, it was for kids, period. Another small AstroTurf beach filled with pool chairs, like the one surrounding Hurricane Bay, sat in front of the play area.

"There you go, little sister," Eddie said, putting a patronizing arm around Christie's shoulder. "We'll drop you off there so you can play with all the other little kids while me and Cyndi go ride the big people rides. That sound fun?"

Christie turned and bit playfully at the hand Eddie held against her shoulder. Eddie laughed and jumped back, not expecting it.

At the opposite end of this cluster of rides, there was a three story wooden structure that looked kind of like a guard tower or a lookout tower with a large tree-house at the top. Three enclosed tunnel slides hung from the top of the tower and ended in a triangular blue pool below. The two slides on the left and right looped around in wide circles before letting the riders spray out into the pool, but the middle slide seemed to drop straight down. This ride was called The Falls.

The girls had less than thirty seconds to admire all of this before Eddie took them both by the hands and began dragging them down the hill toward the rides. They had three awesome looking rides to choose from, and Eddie intended to ride all of them.

*   *   *

While Cyndi, Eddie, and Christie were looking out at the cluster of rides, Brady sat shirtless at the top of The Falls looking down into the end pool. It was the tallest ride in the park, built up on thick stilts thirty feet high in the air. Wooden steps wound their way up to the top, a little wooden shack where the three Falls slides began. The walls inside were decorated with nautical, pirate objects. On one of the side walls hung a pirate flag. Mounted securely on the opposite wall were two extremely old metal swords crossed in an X.

The three enclosed slides were the Seafoam-

Greenish color of garden hoses. Water burbled from jutting jets at the smooth start of each and rushed down into the darkness. The wall above the slides was open, so that riders could look down at the end pool and the entire upper area of the park. Brady's job was to sit on a little wooden perch above the slide on the left and watch another lifeguard standing below at the end pool. Once the riders were completely out of the pool, the lifeguard below would signal to Brady with a thumbs-up, and he would let three more riders slide down screaming. The job also required him to direct the riders to cross their arms and legs before going down the slide, but he really only gave them a lazy grunt and a wave of his hand.

There was a high shelf above the three slides and the open wall where the riders looked down. It was decorated with the skull of an alligator and a few old shark jaws. Brady had a put a little portable Sony radio up there, tuned it to his favorite rock station, and cranked the volume up loud. Sheehan didn't approve of this station, or the volume level, but Sheehan wasn't around so Brady did what he wanted. The wild drum beat at the beginning of "Hot For Teacher" by Van Halen began to pound out of the radio. It was one of Brady's absolute favorite songs and he shouted a triumphant, "YES!" and pumped his fist.

Brady glanced back at the line and saw a gorgeous brunette girl in a purple bikini waiting for the left slide. He couldn't help but stare at her thick dark hair and deep cleavage behind his Ray-Ban Wayfarer shades. She was a perfect ten. She had come up with her dweeby little brother and let him ride down first. Brady tried to start up a conversation with her after the brother went down, but she had only given him brief responses, keeping her eyes mostly on her little brother as he splashed into the end pool below. Then it was her turn to ride, and she slid down underneath Brady.

A few seconds later, she splashed out into the end-pool. Brady watched as she sunk underneath the water, got her bearings, then bounced back up. Her thick, voluminous hair had been dry at the start of the ride, but now it was perfectly slicked back and hung down to the middle of her back. She turned around laughing, and Brady noticed the exposed tan-line on her chest. Both of her ample breasts had popped out of her purple bikini top and were glistening freely in the sunlight. She hadn't noticed it yet, and Brady's mouth dropped open as the topless babe waded toward the edge of the sparkling pool, looking like a goddess. He lowered his Ray-Bans down the bridge of his nose and stared at her over the top rim of the sunglasses.

"Holy shit!" Brady said to himself in complete awe at the sight in the pool.

Behind him, a mother standing in line with her small son frowned in total disapproval and put her hands over his ears. She didn't approve of the loud rock and roll song with its crazy guitars and foul lyrics, and she certainly didn't approve of the vulgar young lifeguard attending this ride.

"Excuse me," said a polite voice behind the mother. Johnny, also shirtless, smiled at her gratefully as she stepped to the left. She looked away from him without returning the smile.

It was time for Johnny's shift on The Falls. He had gotten his relief from the Lazy River cliff early and called Brady on the radio to see if he wanted a drink or anything. Brady hadn't answered, so Johnny brought a spare radio with him, figuring that the battery might be dead. Now Johnny heard the deafening, distorted Van Halen song blaring out of the portable radio up on the high shelf. He saw the two-way radio sitting next to the portable Sony. Brady was looking down at the pool intently. No wonder he hadn't heard Johnny calling him

137

on the two-way.

"Hey, Brady!" he called, but Brady still couldn't hear him over the splash of the slides and the blare of the music. Johnny reached up, pulled the portable radio down off the shelf, and quickly turned down the volume. Brady noticed the lack of sound and guiltily turned around.

"You know Sheehan's gonna have a cow if he catches you like this, dude," Johnny said.

"Yeah yeah. You see that girl down there?" Brady asked, pointing down at the goddess. Johnny leaned forward and caught a glimpse of her just as she sheepishly pulled her bikini top up over her breasts again. "Mm! Damn! You think she'd come party with us tonight?"

"I don't know, man. Maybe. Well, hey, I'm taking over for ya. You better get down to the wave pool and relieve Misty."

"Oh, perfect! Maybe I can catch up with that chick!" Brady jumped off the platform, nearly colliding with the disapproving mother, and dashed past the line of people.

"Go get her number, dude," Johnny called out in his surfer voice. Then he suddenly remembered the extra two-way radio he had brought up. "Wait! Bring this extra radio back down!" Brady was already halfway down the stairs though, and out of earshot. Johnny rolled his eyes and stuck the extra radio up on the high shelf near the ceiling.

Glancing down, he saw the empty end pool and the lifeguard impatiently waving at him, signaling for the next riders to come down. He waved back and let the next group of riders go. As he propped himself up on the wooden perch, he noticed the mother glaring at him. He tried to give her another polite smile, but she turned away, looking absently at the other people in line.

Jeez, Lady.   What crawled up your ass and died? he thought.   It occurred to him that it was a very Brady-like thought to have.   He shrugged off the lady's glare and looked back down at the end pool.   He listened to the music on the portable radio and wondered if he would see any other girls pop out of their tops over the next couple of hours.

*   *   *

Within ten minutes Cyndi, Christie, and Eddie were standing in a short line waiting for the Rocky River's clear blue single tubes.   Standing in front of them was Brady's goddess, the brunette in the purple bikini, and her little brother.   When they had gotten in line, Cyndi had seen one of those familiar, fakey, rustic-looking signs with a painted cartoon drawing of the Smiley-Face guy.   In this cartoon he was at the front of a river raft paddling his way down a whitewater river lined with jagged rocks.   Behind him in the raft were three happy, laughing caricatures of kids.

Apparently they still haven't given up that whole river theme, Cyndi thought.   Another wave of déjà vu washed over her again, but she couldn't understand why. Of course, there had been signs like this at the other park, but there had been no Rocky River ride.   She turned away from the sign, determined not to look at it.   She knew she would have to get on something eventually, otherwise, she might as well go home.   *How weird would that seem to everyone?   Just keep it together, you're doing fine.*

A few metal switchback railings went back and forth underneath a high wooden deck that was reserved as a break area for the lifeguards.   Underneath the deck, where they now stood waiting, another one of those heavy rope and fishnet railings blocked off the edge of a

139

deep drainage pool down below. The water from both the kid's play area and the Falls end pool overflowed into this low pool, and it was closed off to the public. The rippling surface of the drain pool was about six feet beneath their feet, and it was littered with leaves, twigs, and trash. To Cyndi, the deep, dirty water seemed somehow sinister.

A hollow roar of falling water echoed from somewhere beneath her feet. Cyndi leaned forward over the rope and looked below. Another one of those metal grates, like the one she had seen last year at the Lazy River, was mounted beneath her feet. *He* had been standing in the shadows behind that Lazy River grate last year, watching them. Could someone be standing down there now, looking up, crouching in the water like a crocodile? From her upside-down angle it was impossible to tell. Cyndi backed away from the rope, trying to ignore a growing feeling that she was being watched from somewhere down below.

"Wake up, Cyndirella," Eddie said from ten feet farther up. She gave him an embarrassed smile and glanced back apologetically at the impatient people waiting behind her in line.

"Shut up, Eddie Munster," Cyndi retorted, walking forward.

"Why do you guys call each other those names?" Christie asked.

"What? You didn't you know that Cyndi was short for Cyndirella?" Eddie asked.

"Really?" Christie gazed at her with intrigued eyes.

"Ignore him. It's not short for Cyndirella," Cyndi corrected.

"It's true," he defended.

"Yeah. Shut up, Eddie," Christie immediately jumped to Cyndi's defense.

The PA system suddenly erupted with static. Cyndi whirled and looked at the closest speaker mounted high in a cluster of fake plastic palm trees near the big water playground. "Footloose" by Kenny Loggins had been playing before, and it continued to play, but another song had somehow broken through and loudly played over it, creating a chaotic mess of music. Cyndi recognized the new song at once, she had it on one of her records at home, as well as one of those mix tapes that was now at the Countryside pool. It was "Hello Again," by The Cars.

Eddie, Christie, and dozens of other people turned around to look at the speakers, the sudden cacophony catching their attention. They murmured confusedly to each other over the crazy sound of two conflicting songs.

"Uh-oh, technical difficulties," Eddie laughed. Cyndi barely heard him, staring intently at the speakers. The two songs played on for another forty-five seconds.

"Is someone gonna fix that? It's hurting my ears," Christie grimaced. As if someone had heard Christie's complaint, both songs abruptly shut off, leaving the park sounding too quiet. Eddie looked around at them with a strange smile on his face.

After a brief moment of silence, "Footloose" started up again at the beginning of the song. There was no harsh crackle, just the smooth sound of the song at a tolerable volume level.

Eddie laughed again. "Someone just got--" he ran a thumb across his throat and made a choked sound.

Cyndi gaped at him. "What?" she asked.

"You know, someone just got fired for that one."

"Oh, yeah. Right," she sighed. For a second, she thought he had somehow known about the strange music and the corresponding deaths at the park last year. His words had an ironic double meaning of which he was totally unaware.

The line moved forward again, and before Cyndi moved with it, she made a conscious effort to take her hands off the thick rope that blocked off the drainage pool. She had been gripping it so tight that her knuckles had gone white.

Technical difficulties, that's right. That's all it was. It's the first day, something's bound to go wrong, she thought. Deep down though, she wondered....

Once they reached the end of the line, they stood in ankle deep water between the end pool of the Rocky River and a small picket fence draped with more decorative fishnet. The water flowed over their feet from the playground through the Rocky River end pool, went under the picket fence, and splashed down into the low, dark, drain pool below. They waited patiently as riders awkwardly got off their clear blue tubes at the end of the ride and handed them off to the people in line.

As soon as all three of them got their hands on fresh wet tubes, they made their way up a winding concrete path towards the start of the ride. Eddie dribbled his tube up the hill like a basketball.

"He shoots," he began. Then he lifted his tube off the ground and dropped it over Christie's head. "He scores!"

"Eddie! Knock it off!" Christie cried. She dropped her own tube and struggled to fling his off of her shoulders. Eddie erupted in wild cheering as if he had just won a championship basketball game. Cyndi couldn't help but laugh, she was grateful that Eddie was here today to distract her from her memories. He was a spaz, but at least he always found a way to make her laugh.

"Okay," he apologized. "I'm sorry, little sister. I'll tell you what, why don't I carry your tube the rest of the way for you?"

"You better!" Christie said. Eddie picked up both tubes off the ground and held one in each arm.

"You gonna carry mine up too?" Cyndi asked. "After all, you are my substitute boyfriend."

Eddie couldn't stop himself from laughing at that, he could think of no snappy comment.

"All right," he conceded, lowering his head. Cyndi lifted her tube and hung it around his neck like a huge round necklace. He turned and continued back up the hill with both girls laughing and following him up.

The path wound around to the top of the hill again and they stopped to wait in a short line just in front of the small entrance pool. Eddie turned around and lowered his head again. Cyndi thanked him and took her tube back. He pointed at her with his thumb and index finger, and made a double click sound in his throat.

They dropped their tubes down into the entrance pool and got on next to a huge bubbling fountain just like the one under the rock overhang at the start of the Duelin' Rivers. It felt strange to be on a tube again. Cyndi hadn't even gone swimming after coming home last summer. She had enjoyed being home, safe, and dry. Now, here she was at a water park again. The sensation of the bobbing tube and refreshing cool water on her legs and back actually did feel good, physically at least.

A teenage lifeguard with a shock of feathered brown hair and a peach-fuzz mustache stood in the waist deep water, ushering each tube underneath a waterfall that splattered down on each rider from a high rock arch overhead. The lifeguard lightly pushed Eddie under the waterfall, then Christie who gave out a tiny scream and cringed as she went under the water. Cyndi came last, bracing herself for the cold rush of the waterfall. Without a word or a glance, he gave her tube a push, and Cyndi was instantly soaked. The waterfall completely shut out the rest of the world for a few seconds. She emerged into the sunlight again, wiping water away from her eyes. Her tube slid down a slight slope and bumped its way into a crowd of a dozen other tubes that had gotten caught in a circling whirlpool surrounded by pine trees.

"Cyndi, grab my hand!" Christie shouted, smiling. Cyndi reached for her outstretched hand, but the water made their grips too slippery. In Christie's other hand, she hung onto Eddie's right foot. "Come on, reach!"

A beefy, hairy guy in his own blue tube circled around, unintentionally bulling his way in between Cyndi and Christie. They pulled their hands back. The whirl-pool's current pulled Eddie and Christie farther away from Cyndi. People in tubes kept coming out from behind that waterfall, sliding down the slope, and joining the other tubes caught in the spinning current. Cyndi had to crane her neck and peer past them to catch a glimpse of Christie and Eddie. She told herself not to panic, they would join up again once they escaped the whirlpool.

They were on opposite sides now. Christie and Eddie had come full circle and were near the waterfall and the first short slope again, while Cyndi had her back to an open channel of water that slowly drifted toward one of those familiar drop off points. Up ahead, she could see the water swirling around the smooth concrete sides of the ride and speeding away down a fast slope.

The whirlpool was filled to capacity. A fat lady, who yelled 'Yahoo' as if she were a cowboy, came out from behind the waterfall and bumped into the crowd. Christie and Eddie laughed at the lady's goofy exclamation. On the opposite side of the whirlpool, the force of the fat lady's entrance traveled through all the other tubes and pushed Cyndi out into the open water. Her heart raced as she drifted away from the whirlpool. She hadn't thought she was going to face this ride alone, and now fear settled deep into her stomach.

Cyndi looked back, desperately hoping that Christie and Eddie would come around again, floating right behind her, but they were lost in the crowd. Her tube tipped forward, and she looked down at the fast stretch of river ahead just as the current caught hold. No turning back now, she would have to ride this thing down to the end, with or without her friends.

She slid down a long stretch that was lined with thick, jagged gray rocks. Tall pine trees stood behind the rocks on grassy peninsulas between the Rocky River's wild twists and turns. The breeze blew back her wet locks of blonde hair and chilled her skin.

Near the end of the long slope, the ramp of that sled ride, the Screamin' Demon, crossed overhead, held up by thick concrete pillars. She looked up at the wooden bottom and angled AstroTurf sides of the ramp as she passed underneath it. Another one of those sleds rocketed by overhead. She heard the ramp's wooden boards shake, and the delighted screams from the people on board the sled.

The Rocky River curved wildly just past the high ramp, spinning her around a full one-hundred-eighty degrees. More thick pine trees and jagged rocks surrounded the ride. Some of those pine branches reached out close enough to touch. That déjà vu feeling came back at the sight of the rocks and trees. She had never been on this ride before, but she felt as if she knew every twist and turn.

Her tube carried her down another steep slope, slowed briefly in deeper water, then sped up again. She hit a bumpy stretch that jostled her, making her feel as if she were a live bobble-head doll. Another wild turn was coming on too fast. She leaned far away from the huge gray boulder that loomed ahead, but the current was too fast. Her elbow bumped against it and she cried out as a shockwave of pain flared up her arm and--

The memory flashed into her mind, Brad cracking his arm on the rock in the wild river just before they had entered the park. It suddenly made sense to her now. They had designed this ride to be just like the real river that was outside the other park. She hadn't ever been on this ride, but she had been down the real river on which it was based. Her elbow throbbed, and she thought that maybe they had been a little too faithful in their designs.

She went down another familiar steep twist and splashed into deeper water. The front of her tube went under the surface for a second, just like the raft had done in the real river. There was another close call with one of those thick, gray rocks, she had to lean so far away from it that she almost fell out of her tube.

Finally, she rounded another curve and went down a steep stretch into the end pool. She could imagine the mine tunnel looming ahead, but of course there was no mine tunnel here, this was a different park. There was only open air and a lifeguard standing by at the end of the ride to help people get up out of their tubes and back on their feet again.

Clear water splashed up in small waves as her tube hit the deep water of the end pool. She sighed with relief. There were dozens of people around again, she wasn't on the secluded ride anymore where anything could happen. This ride had been relatively safe, but she still didn't know if she should trust any of the other rides though.

Cyndi got up off her tube easily and handed it to the next person in line, a little girl with dark pig tails. She wanted to pull the tube back and tell her *this ride is too scary for you, why don't you go play in the nice little play area over there?* She handed it over anyway, with a smile on her face and a sick feeling in her stomach.

146

I hope you don't hit your elbow or fall off, little girl, she thought.

Cyndi stepped out of the water and waited for her friends on the AstroTurf beach. Her mind played over the similarities between the real river from last year and this re-created, all-too-real river. She couldn't help but wonder why they would base a ride off of that dangerous river.

After a few uncomfortable minutes of dripping dry over old memories, she glanced over at the Rocky River's cartoon sign at the front of the line. She had forced herself to turn away from it earlier, not wanting to look at that grinning face. Now, taking a longer look at it, her skin broke out in thick goosebumps. The three cartoon kids riding on the raft behind Kaptain Smiley looked eerily familiar. They could almost be caricatures of three people she used to know. The girl had blonde hair in a side ponytail, one boy had blonde feathered hair, and the other boy had slightly curly, greasy black hair. Stacy, Brad, and Zack.

A wet clammy hand dropped on her shoulder. "Hey, have you been waiting long?"

Cyndi let out a scream and Eddie stepped back, holding his wet hands up defensively.

"God, Eddie. You scared the shit outta me!" she sighed.

"Jeez, sorry," he laughed. "You're pretty jumpy, you know that?" Cyndi only shrugged in response. "Christie will be down soon, we got separated. Did you like the ride?"

"Uh, yeah. It was okay. You?"

"Yeah, it was really cool going under that sled ride. But they gotta do something about some of those turns. I hit my elbow twice on those rocks. It fuckin' hurt." He clutched his tender elbow.

"Yeah, me too. They gotta fix that," Cyndi

147

agreed. They looked over at the ride just in time to see Christie come down the final slope and splash into the water at the end. She got off her tube and approached them.

"I told you to wait for me, Eddie," she complained.

"I tried to wait for you, but there were other people behind me. I'm not gonna hold up the ride for you."

As they argued Cyndi looked back at the sign. Maybe those caricature kids didn't resemble Stacy, Brad, and Zack *that* closely. They could easily be three random kids. Maybe she was just so freaked out being here that her mind was making all sorts of connections that were really only coincidence. Maybe....

*   *   *

Johnny could've seen Cyndi, Christie, and Eddie riding down the Rocky River from his high vantage point on The Falls, but he had been distracted.

Somehow the weather today was turning out to be even more gorgeous than it had been last weekend. There wasn't a cloud in the sky, and all the water down below sparkled in the sunlight. It seemed like everyone at the park was smiling and having fun, and it put Johnny in a good mood.

The little silver portable radio was blaring out some old Beach Boys song. *Cyndi would know the title, what album it came from, and what year it came out*, Johnny thought. To him, it was just part of the sunny, summer soundtrack along with the screaming kids and rushing water. Shrill giggling cut into his summer soundtrack, and he turned to see a couple of familiar faces in line for the ride. It was that Jennifer girl, Brady's cousin, looking right at him. She smiled and

148

waved at him, and he returned the wave. Two other girls stood behind her, giggling hysterically. He also recognized the other two girls from when they had all met last week at the Countryside Pool.

"Shut up, you guys," Jennifer scolded in a whisper over her shoulder.

Johnny looked down, saw the thumbs-up signal from below. He turned to the three twelve year old boys waiting eagerly on each of the slides and said, "Okay, cross your arms and legs. You guys can go." They went down the slides screaming.

The girls stepped forward. Jennifer went up to the slide on the left with her arms crossed. He tried to avoid looking at her ample cleavage and the bottom of her red and black swimsuit that went past her hips in a sexy, stylish V-shape. She was only fourteen, but seemed to have already grown into the curves of her adult body.

"Hi, Johnny," she said.

"Hey, uh, Jennifer, right?" he asked casually. He knew damn well what her name was.

She nodded. "So I've got a question for you. How come the water is so cold here?"

"Well, it's not bad if you're in the sun. I'm baking up here."

Jennifer reached out and put her hand on his arm, her fingers really were cold and felt good on his red, sunburned skin.

"Ooh, you're right. You *are* hot," she said, letting her cool, soft fingers linger on his arm. Johnny was at a loss for words as she stared up at him with her dark brown eyes and lightly bit the corner of her lower lip. Her thick, dark hair hung over her right shoulder in wet strands. The other girls erupted into a fit of more giggles.

Suddenly, a shrill whistle sounded from down

below.   Johnny tore himself away from Jennifer's seductive stare. The lifeguard down below at the end pool gave him an irritated thumbs-up.

"Uh...you girls can go," he said in an awkward rush. Then he remembered what he was supposed to tell all the riders. "Oh, and cross your arms and legs."

"See ya later, Johnny," Jennifer said and threw herself down the slide with a wild scream of excitement. The girl on the farthest slide, the one who seemed to always be chewing on Bubblicious gum, popped a huge softball-sized bubble.

"She thinks you're hot!" she blurted out, then flung herself down the slide. Johnny caught the double meaning of her words, shook his head, and laughed. It felt damn good to be told that someone thought you were "hot," no matter who it was.

"Hey, right on, dude!" said a geeky twelve-year-old kid with braces who stepped up to the middle slide. He had been watching the whole exchange. Johnny laughed at him and looked down at the pool. The girls were climbing out of the water and screaming about how cold they were. Jennifer looked up and waved to him one last time as she climbed out of the pool. He returned her wave politely again, and all three girls ran off laughing. The lifeguard below gave him the thumbs-up signal.

"You guys can go," he said absently, still watching as the girls ran out of sight. He turned back to his job just at the last second. The geeky twelve-year-old kid was inches away from sliding face first down the middle slide, the one that went almost straight down. "Whoa, wait! Stop!" The kid clung to the sides of the slide, his hands made little rubbery slipping noises against the smooth sides. "You can't go down that way."

"Why not?" the kid asked.

"Because you'll break your neck. You gotta go

down feet first, dude. And cross your arms and legs."

"Okay," the kid said begrudgingly. Johnny sighed with relief as he watched the kid disappear down the slide. *That was too close,* he thought. If that kid had gone down head first and gotten hurt, Johnny would've been in serious trouble. That girl's sexy stare with her dark eyes had somehow temporarily melted away his common sense. He had to admit to himself, that Jennifer girl had a great body. He thought of her long hair and those curvy--

Easy, you've got a girlfriend, remember? Plus, even if you were single, Brady would probably kick the shit outta you if you got mixed up with his cousin, he thought. Somehow he couldn't seem to get Jennifer out of his head. He looked down and saw that goosebumps had raised on his warm arm from where her cool hand had touched him.

*   *   *

Eddie practically dragged Cyndi and Christie up the slope toward The Falls.

"Eddie, I don't think I can do this one," Cyndi protested. Her eyes darted back and forth from the high enclosed slides. From here, she saw that as they circled around near the bottom, they ran underground before emptying into the end pool. She dreaded what may or may not be hiding for her in those dark, humid slides.

"Oh, come on, Cyndi," Eddie insisted. "It's just a ride. You're a big girl, you can handle it. Look, even Christie's getting on."

Christie only gave Cyndi a nervous shrug. She didn't exactly want to get on the ride either, but she wanted to look brave and mature in front of Cyndi. Now, the uneasy look on Cyndi's face made her think twice about the ride.

151

"Why don't you guys go without me?" Cyndi suggested.

"But there's three slides and three of us. It'll be perfect. Look, I'll even take the really steep one in the middle, okay? I'm sure it's perfectly safe. They wouldn't let people on if it wasn't safe."

Our throbbing elbows from the last "safe" ride might disagree with you on that, she thought.

Eddie had known Johnny since the second grade. He had known for years that Johnny, for the most part, was a good, well behaved guy. He also knew that sometimes if you wanted to have a *really* good time, you had to leave your best behavior at home. After years of observation, he had learned that Johnny could really loosen up and have a great time, but first he needed a little push. With a little cajoling, Johnny usually gave in, and they would go off on some wild adventure. Today, he had discovered that Christie was the same way, and why not? They were brother and sister. He mistakenly assumed that Cyndi was also like them, and he persisted in trying to push her to have a little fun too.

They reached the wooden steps that circled around the thick wooden support beams up to the top of the ride. Cyndi looked up at another one of those fake wooden signs at the base of the stairs. It showed the Smiley-Faced character grinning and diving off of a raging cartoon waterfall. Cyndi ignored the sign, but as she took her first tentative steps up the wooden stairs, she couldn't get the image of the cartoon Stacy, Brad, and Zack out of her head.

Last year at the Ragin' Rivers, Stacy had told Zack, *'don't get on that ride.'* She had saved his life, at least temporarily, and she had been right. Stacy's words echoed through Cyndi's mind, and she stopped on the fourth step. Eddie was already at the top of the first flight of steps, looking down at her over his shoulder.

152

I can't do this. I can't get on this ride. This park is just as bad as the other one. It's hiding some dark secrets, I can feel it.

There's something very wrong in this place, Stacy had said. *Can't you feel it?*

"I'm sorry, you guys. I-I- just can't," she stammered. Her mind raced, trying to think of an excuse but none came. "I'll wait for you at the bottom."

Eddie felt torn. Looking down at Cyndi, he could see genuine fear in her face and he regretted pushing her so hard.

"It's fine," he said, dropping his usual jokey tone. "No problem. We'll just see you at the bottom, 'kay?" Cyndi gave him a nervous smile and walked off the stairs.

"Actually, I'm going to wait with her," Christie said. She followed Cyndi back down to the bottom. Eddie gave a resigned sigh and hurried after them. He hoped no one, especially no one from school, was watching him do the dreaded "Walk of Shame" off the ride.

"Okay, we'll go ride something else," he said solemnly.

"Eddie, really. It's all right if you want to ride it. We'll wait," Cyndi said.

"Well, I'd look pretty stupid coming down all by myself." In truth, he felt too self-conscious and embarrassed to stand in a line and ride something by himself. High school had a way of making a person more self-conscious than they wanted to admit. Sometimes it seemed to him that strength in numbers was the only antidote for being an awkward teenager.

"To be honest, you look pretty stupid most of the time," Christie said. Both Cyndi and Eddie turned to her in stark surprise.

"Okay, I walked right into that one," he

153

admitted, and they cracked up laughing.

They had taken only a few steps away from the ride when Jennifer and her gaggle of giggling friends came around the corner. They had joined up with two other girls who had just come off the Rocky River not long after Cyndi, Christie, and Eddie.

"Well, well, well. Look who it is," Jennifer taunted. Her voice raised an octave in a patronizing, baby-talk voice. "Aww, are the little babies too scared to get on the big girl ride?"

"Aww, poor baby," another one of them called and popped another of those loud bubbles with her gum.

The laughing girls all egged Jennifer on. Christie put her hands on her hips and her face flushed with anger. Eddie gave them a frown that was half anger, half pity. Insults from young girls didn't anger him as much as insults from people his own age, but it was still pretty annoying and embarrassing.

"What the fuck is your problem?" Eddie asked.

"You! You're my problem," Jennifer challenged without missing a beat. She had a rare talent for getting in the last word and catching her enemies off guard. To her, Eddie was just another geek, someone to look down on and step over. Her true enemy was Cyndi.

All five of the girls stepped in closer to Cyndi and stared her down. It was five against one, or two if you counted Christie who was younger and smaller than any of Jennifer's friends. Cyndi and Christie stood their ground, fists clenched, waiting, dreading the inevitable first punch.

Eddie saw where this was going. In his mind, he saw himself being escorted out of the park by a burly security guard with a bruised and battered Cyndi and Christie at his side. He had no intention of leaving the park early over something as stupid and petty as this. He finally stepped in between the standoff, grabbing Cyndi and Christie by the shoulders. He led them around the group of girls.

"Yeah, okay. Thank you, middle school girls. This was real fun, but we're gonna get going now," he said sarcastically.

"That's right. Run away, you babies," Jennifer called after them. "Run back to the little kiddie rides!"

Cyndi glanced back at them with fire in her eyes. If looks could kill, she would have struck them all dead that second. Eddie rushed Cyndi and Christie away, and the laughter and cat-calls followed them until they were out of sight.

Chapter Eleven:

Stronger Than Déjà Vu

They walked away from the Rocky River/Falls area, heading back downhill toward the wave pool. In their walk around the park, they had circled around the Duelin' and Ragin' Rivers, and would soon end up near the Lazy River cliff. Tall blue spruce trees surrounded the steep and secluded path they were on. Not many people were around and it was very quiet.

"You should've let me fight her," Cyndi said through clenched teeth. Both she and Christie were still furious.

"Yeah, Eddie," Christie agreed. "If I see them again, I'll--"

"Nah, it's not worth it," Eddie dismissed. "They're just a bunch of goofy middle school brats."

"Did you even hear what they said to us?" Christie asked.

"Big deal. They're all just jealous of you, Cyndi."

"Why the hell would they be jealous of me?" Cyndi asked.

"Because you're hot," Eddie blurted out. Cyndi and Christie gaped at Eddie, making him realize the implications of what he had just said. It was a thought that had danced around in his mind, but never fully occurred to him until now. "Well, I mean, hotter than them. I mean, not that you're not...good looking, or whatever...because you are. But...you know what I mean."

Cyndi and Christie exchanged gossipy looks and Eddie felt compelled to continue stumbling around for the right words.

"I mean, *I* don't have a thing for you. You're my best friend's girlfriend, you know. I'm just saying...if you weren't...well...I mean, you know."

"Yeah, I get what you're saying, Eddie," Cyndi stopped him with a forgiving smile. "Thanks."

"Well, yeah. You know. Forget those skanky bitches!" He reverted back to his usual joking to clear the air, and the girls cracked up laughing. Inside, Eddie felt thoroughly embarrassed, like he had just revealed some deep scandalous secret. Silently, he prayed that they wouldn't bring it up to Johnny, he had no idea how he would explain that one. He planned on spending the rest of the day pretending that their last bit of conversation had never happened, stricken from the records. He tried to act casual, but was unusually quiet the rest of the way down the hill.

As Cyndi's anger wore off, that déjà vu feeling settled back in. She began to recognize more of those familiar re-created landmarks from the old park as they walked down the hill. The first one she noticed was the lifeguard's cliff overlooking the Lazy River off to her left. Then she recognized the last stretch of one of the Duelin' Rivers off to the right. Mentally, she braced herself for what she might see at the bottom of the hill.

Cyndi came around the corner at the bottom of

the hill and there they were, side by side, just as she remembered them: the end pools for the Duelin' Rivers, and the Ragin' Rivers. They looked exactly the same as the originals, she supposed the Ragin' Rivers (which were made of thick plastic mounted on wide concrete pillars) might even be the exact slides transplanted here. They even had the same wooden faux-rustic signs labeling them with the same names and cartoony pictures. The only major differences were the long lines of anxious people standing in the metal switchback railings that had been built in front of the end pools. Still, the feeling of déjà vu had never been stronger in her life.

Cyndi remembered a trip to Disneyland she and her family had taken when she was only seven years old. Being there and walking through familiar movie landmarks like Cinderella's castle had felt unreal. In the movies, all those settings and places seemed impossibly far away and unattainable, yet at Disneyland, there they stood in real life for everyone to see. This part of the park felt a lot like that, except it wasn't a re-creation of a movie, it was a re-creation of her own horrific past.

"Ooh, we better get on this one before the line gets any longer," Christie said impatiently, tugging them toward the Ragin' Rivers.

Oh God, not the Ragin' Rivers. Christie, no, Cyndi thought.

Eddie and Christie picked up the pace. He glanced back and saw Cyndi lagging behind them, staring warily at the slides.

"Hurry up, Cyndi. The *line,*" Eddie whined. Cyndi smiled apologetically and hurried forward.

There were two lines split evenly between the four slides. Christie and Eddie decided to get in line for the two slides on the right first because it was closer and seemed slightly shorter. They entered the metal line corral that reminded Cyndi so much of a mouse maze. Eddie, who seemed to have the patience of a four-year-old, walked his body forward with his hands on the waist high bars, letting his feet dangle a foot off the ground. He spun around to Cyndi and Christie, speaking to them in a deep manly voice.

"Hey, girls. I, uh, went through puberty overnight, now I'm eight feet tall. What do ya think?"

"Yeah, remind me what fourth grade was like again," Cyndi joked.

Still holding himself up with his hands, he inched toward her, looking down menacingly. "Hey, whoa. I can see the top of your head. Oh, wait." He lowered himself back down to his normal height, but bent his knees so his feet still hung off the ground. "You're so short. I can always see the top of your head. I guess it's not that big of a deal. Oh! *Burn!*"

Christie and Cyndi couldn't help but laugh. Cyndi gave him a playful shove just as he was inching backwards on his hands, and he bumped hard into the hairy back of a beefy guy who was standing in front of them in line. The man turned around with a threatening glare on his face.

"Watch it, kid," he snarled, his red face turning even redder.

"Sorry, sorry. It was an accident. I'm sorry," Eddie blurted out, holding his hands up defensively. The beefy guy seemed to growl as he turned back around. Eddie turned back to the girls clenching his jaw in a tight, nervous expression. They stood in silence through the rest of the wait.

Once they reached the front of the line, the beefy guy and his beefy family headed up the hill toward the start of the ride. With him gone, Eddie and the girls relaxed a little. They waited for the riders to come flying off the slide in their tubes, splashing into the rippling slow water in the end pool. Cyndi kept a close eye on the second slide from the right, the slide where Brad had disappeared. She kept expecting to see an empty tube slide down without a rider, but time after time each tube was occupied with happy, laughing people. They splashed down into the pool and got off the tubes in the waist-deep water. With smiles on their faces, they waded over to the side and handed their tubes up to the next person in line.

Eddie and Christie finally got their tubes, then waited for Cyndi. The same fat lady that had yelled 'yahoo' on the Rocky River ride, came down cackling in a strange hyena laugh. She careened down the slide on the far right and flipped over backwards as soon as her tube hit the water. Everyone in line laughed. She slowly got to her feet, then lazily shoved her upside-down tube to the side of the pool where Cyndi stood waiting.

Cyndi bent down and picked the slippery tube up out of the water. She flipped it over to grab one of the handles. It was a bright green color, just like the tubes on this ride from the other park, except for one major difference: now that smiley-face logo was painted in the center between the two handles. She would have to ride down with that ugly grinning face staring up at her between her legs.

"Don't worry," Eddie said. "There's enough chlorine in that water to clean off all of that lady's sweat." Cyndi looked up at him, confused for a moment, then she understood what he was trying to tell her. He must have assumed that she was looking disgustedly at the tube, as if it were covered in the fat lady's greasy sweat.

"Oh, I know. It's fine," she said smiling. She noticed Eddie and Christie were beginning to give her a lot of strange, questioning looks. They were probably wondering why she was acting so distracted and edgy.

160

She decided that she'd have to do a better job of hamming it up for them. She added an enthusiastic, "Let's go," then lead the way up the hill.

The hill toward the Ragin' and Duelin' Rivers looked almost exactly as she remembered it: a short, wide set of wooden steps, then a curving concrete path with a grassy slope on the right, and wildflowers on the left. There were fewer trees, and those that were here were mostly young saplings, freshly planted and tied with stakes on either side to keep them straight as they grew.

As they reached the familiar fork in the path, Cyndi turned right toward the Ragin' Rivers without any hesitation. She noticed only after it was too late.

Oh well, too late to pretend you don't know where you're going now.

A short way past the fork they joined the end of the line on the wooden bridge over one of the Duelin' Rivers and waited. Eddie leaned his tube against the railing and looked down just as one of the Duelin' River tubes came around the corner loaded with three screaming fourteen-year-old boys whooping and cheering. Eddie and Christie watched with delighted eyes as they went under the bridge, then ran to the other side with them. Christie's eyes lit up as she recognized the boys.

"Hey, TJ!" Christie shouted. One of the boys with wild spiky black hair looked up just as they were about to turn the corner.

"HEY, CHRISTIE!" the boy, TJ, shouted back. He waved and the other boys looked up just as they rounded another wild corner and disappeared from sight. Cyndi thought she remembered having the TJ boy in one of her classes last year.

"He's Nina and Dawn's older brother," Christie explained, her face growing red.

"Oooh, is he your boyfriend?" Eddie asked, nudging Christie with his elbow.

"No!" she said just a little too defensively to be fully convincing. Cyndi and Eddie gave each other doubtful looks. Christie groaned and turned away from them, feeling her cheeks and the tips of her ears growing hot.

"Oh, man," Eddie said enviously. "I don't know where that ride starts, but we're riding it next."

"The line for it is right next to the line for this ride," Cyndi spoke up.

"How do you know?" Eddie asked.

Shit, me and my big mouth again. Get it together, Cyndi.

"I saw the big green tubes that they were on while we were waiting in line for this ride." For all the times her brain fell asleep at the wheel, sometimes it seemed to work lightning fast.

Eddie shrugged. "Guess I wasn't paying attention. I was too wrapped up in this place. Isn't it awesome?"

"You can say that again," Christie said, and they slapped a high five. Eddie held out his hand for a low five fake-out, but Christie had already turned to Cyndi.

"Yeah, totally," Cyndi agreed and smiled at her.

As they approached the slides on the other side of the bridge, the line split in two. Eddie was next in line for the slide on the left, the one Zack had taken. Cyndi and Christie waited for the one on the right, Brad's slide. Cyndi had begun to get a bad feeling about riding this slide, and desperately tried to think of excuses to get Christie to bail out.

"Are you sure you want to ride this, Christie?" she asked.

"Sure I do. It looks fun."

"You sure it won't be too scary for you or

162

anything?"

"Yeah, you might as well go ahead and chicken out now. I'll beat you to the bottom," Eddie taunted.

"No way, Jose! You're going down!" Christie snapped back in a competitive growl.

Eddie's words had the exact opposite effect on Christie that Cyndi had hoped for. There was no stopping her now, Cyndi would have to cross her fingers and hope for the best. The promise she made to Mrs. Vesna came back in her mind, *Stick together.*

A pretty, dark-haired, teenaged lifeguard with silver sunglasses stood in her red swimsuit uniform between the two slides. "You guys can go," she mumbled. Eddie and Christie stepped forward into the slow moving water, dropped their tubes, and quickly got on. They paddled toward the fast part of the slide as quick as they could. Cyndi restrained the urge to reach out and pull Christie back.

"Am I beating him?" Christie asked Cyndi as she tipped toward the fast part. Eddie was already on his way down the other slide.

"Better hurry," Cyndi said with a fake smile. Her heart pounded, she couldn't help but wonder if this was the last time she would ever see Christie alive.

The current caught hold of Christie's tube and she slid forward. She went fast down the first slope and looked back up at Cyndi just as she rounded the first corner. She caught only the briefest glimpse of the worried, terrified look on Cyndi's face before sliding out of sight.

Cyndi stood alone, facing the twin brother of the slide where Brad had met his end. She remembered something else Stacy had said last year as they stood in front of this ride, *How do we know the rides are even safe?* Now her turn to ride the dreaded Ragin' River slide had finally come. She would finally find out what

Brad had seen in the last moments of his life, just before the ride claimed its first victim.

"You can go," the lifeguard girl muttered to Cyndi.

Cyndi stepped forward, her legs shaking. She dropped the tube in the water, and couldn't bring herself to go any farther. The tube began to drift forward with the current, she would have to hurry to catch up to it.

"You need help?" the lifeguard asked.

Cyndi stared at her for a moment, then that lightning quick brain snapped into action again. "I think I'm gonna be sick." She stepped back from the edge of the slide and walked quickly past the line with her head down. She felt completely humiliated, felt all the eyes of the people standing in line staring at her as she took what Eddie liked to call "the Walk of Shame." They were all watching her, assuming she was chickening out on the ride. They were right, but her reasons for chickening out were much deeper, and much darker than they knew.

*   *   *

Eddie stood at the bottom with his back to the ride looking back and forth anxiously. His pale skin and curly auburn hair, freshly soaked, had that glossy look. Cyndi approached him and he let out a sigh of relief.

"Cyndi, there you are! Where were you?" he asked. "I've been looking all over for you guys."

"Where's Christie?" she asked, glancing around.

"I don't know, I thought she was with you," Eddie said in exasperation.

"What?" Cyndi grabbed his arms. Her eyes were blazing and her blood suddenly ran cold.

"I waited for you guys, but I didn't see either of you."

"You must've seen her get off the ride. She was

right behind you."

"I fell off my tube right at the end. I didn't see her at all."

"Shit!" Cyndi whispered. She whirled, looking back at the Ragin' River slides. Another happy kid came down Christie's slide. She looked left and right, scanning the crowds of people for Christie's bleached hair or her light-blue, flowery swimsuit. Christie was nowhere to be seen.

"Christie! Christie!" Cyndi shouted. Eddie noticed how pale her face had gotten, and how frantic her wide eyes looked.

"Relax, Cyndi," he said. "She's gotta be around here somewhere."

Cyndi ignored him and continued to call out Christie's name. Some of the people in line were beginning to stare at them. Eddie saw several concerned looks from people. He grabbed Cyndi's shoulders, pulling her close.

"Whoa, Cyndi. Hold it. Stay calm. We'll--"

She smacked his arms away. Her mind was racing. She was in full survival mode now. "Just shut up and listen to me! Stay down here and look for her. Don't walk away from the crowds. You hear me?"

"What?" he tried to ask, but she was gone in a flash.

Cyndi cut in between slow moving herds of families. She looked around desperately for any sign of Christie, and continued to call out her name. She worked past the crowds and went back up the path, following the wandering Ragin' River slide that Christie had ridden.

This is how it starts. This is how it was last time. We let our guard down, then he took us one by one. And I just let it happen again.

Cyndi ran up the wooden steps two at a time, tracing the path of the Ragin' River slide with her eyes.

The slide wound around the heavily wooded hillside, curving crazily between thick bushes and trees. There were no people walking around in the dense, woodsy area between the slides. She took a deep breath, then ventured into the bushes with a sick feeling of dread deep in her stomach, knowing that she would find something horrible.

*   *   *

Brady met Johnny near the Big Kahuna Grill by the bathrooms building and the Duelin' Rivers entrance. The girl who had come to relieve him off The Falls had shown up early. Now he could see from the huge clock near the lighthouse gift shop that he still had ten minutes before Cyndi, Eddie, and Christie were supposed to show up. He exchanged a high five with Brady and sniffed the air, salivating at the smoky scent of burgers and french fries cooking in oil.

"I'll tell you what, I'm glad we got the late lunch. There's no way I could've eaten anything earlier," Brady said. "But now I'm fuckin' starving!"

"Yeah, you can say that again," Johnny said, his own stomach had been rumbling constantly for the past hour. "I was half tempted to grab one of those kids on The Falls, give 'em a five, and say, 'hey, kid, go grab me a burger.'"

"Shit, if you're gonna throw your money away that easy, you might as well give me some."

Johnny grinned. "Your hangover all gone?"

Brady held out his arms and gave him a huge game-show host grin. "Natch, baby. Natch. All sobered up and ready to rock."

Johnny laughed and shook his head. "I don't know how you do it, man."

"What do you think you do every day in

166

college? Go to class and study? Fuck no!"

"Didn't you flunk out of college?" Johnny asked petulantly. Brady cackled a goofy, sarcastic laugh, then punched him on the arm. Johnny only continued to laugh.

"No, I didn't flunk out, asshole," Brady muttered, then began to laugh himself. "Where's your chick?"

"I don't know, I haven't seen them all day. They'll probably be here soon. I told them to meet us here at two."

Brady looked around secretively, then lowered his voice. Leaning in toward Johnny, he conspiratorially spoke out of the corner of his mouth. "Well, then let's go smoke up real quick before they get here. I got the good shit."

"Nah, that's cool, man. I don't do that stuff." Johnny didn't want to admit to Brady that he had never smoked even so much as a cigarette in his life.

"No, you're gonna smoke up with me, man," Brady countered, completely ignoring his refusal. "You gotta get warmed up for the party tonight. I got a surprise for us."

Johnny was about to protest when he felt a cool, soft arm slip around his waist. Jennifer slid in between the two of them and wrapped her arms around both their waists.

"Hey, boys," she said. She did that little seductive lip bite again as she smiled at Johnny.

"Hey, little cuz," Brady said. "You're just in time. We're gonna go smoke up before lunch."

"You guys are gonna get high?" she gasped excitedly. "I wanna come too!"

Brady clapped a hand over her mouth and glanced around nervously. "Keep it down, what are you: stupid? You wanna get caught?"

"Oh, sorry," she whispered, then made a lip-zipping gesture.

Brady looked around once more, then motioned for them to follow him with his hand.

"All right, let's go."

"Hey, I think I'm gonna stay here and wait for--" Johnny tried desperately to make up an excuse, but Jennifer suddenly grabbed his right arm with both hands, slung it over her shoulder, and dragged him off after Brady. As she dragged Johnny off toward the wooded areas between the rides, he became aware that his hand was dangling dangerously close to the swell of her considerable cleavage, and he found himself at a complete loss for words.

Brady led them around the Duelin' Rivers' entrance and into the woods between the slides. In the shade, he tilted his Ray-Ban's up on top of his head. They went over a winding treacherous path past pine trees and thick undergrowth, and ended up in a secluded, grassy clearing near the middle of one of the Duelin' Rivers. On one edge of the clearing was a rocky outcrop that bridged over the Duelin' River slide. Johnny had ridden both Duelin' Rivers, and figured it had to be one of those tight three hundred and sixty degree tunnels. On the other side of the clearing, a small stream surrounded by cattails flowed by. Tall pine trees shaded the clearing, blocking out almost all of the heat and glare of the sun. It was remarkably quiet compared to the rest of the park.

Brady went over to the rocky outcrop and opened up a small metal door set back deep in the rock. Johnny figured it must be a plumbing access to the jets of water that fueled the ride, or maybe one of the surprise waterfalls. He opened up the metal door and reached deep inside. Up on a metal edge above the little doorframe, he found what he had hidden a few days earlier.

"Ta da," Brady said, pulling out a small baggy filled with a few dozen white, rolled joints and a metal lighter. Jennifer grinned at him and clapped her hands as if he had just performed some magic trick.

"You're crazy, dude," Johnny said with wide eyes. "If Sheehan finds that, you're a dead man."

"He won't find it," Brady said dismissively as he stuck one of the joints between his lips. He kept his lips tight as he continued to speak, and the joint bounced up and down with his words. "That guy's got his head up his ass. And even if he does find it, so what? They can't prove it's mine."

Brady lit it up, took a deep drag, held it, then coughed out a skunky smelling cloud of smoke.

"Oh yeah," he coughed lightly, then passed it to Jennifer. Johnny looked around warily as she delicately picked up the joint. As secluded as this spot seemed, he felt sure that someone, maybe even Sheehan himself, would come around the corner. If that happened, he was quite sure he could kiss this job goodbye.

Jennifer began to cough immediately after taking her own drag off the joint.

"H-h-holy sh-sh-it," she said between coughs, passing the joint to Johnny.

Johnny shook his head and held up his hands defensively.

"You gotta take a puff, dude," Brady said. "It won't make you sick or anything. Trust me."

"I've been doing it since I was eleven," Jennifer giggled.

Johnny glanced around again. The coast was still clear. He looked down at the smoldering joint, Jennifer practically held it right under his nose.

Just one. That's all. It'll get them off your back.

Johnny gave them an exasperated sigh, then took the joint from her hand.

"Just one," he said. He brought it up to his lips and inhaled lightly. The smoke burned his throat and lungs instantly and he began to cough worse than Jennifer had.

"Oh shit, there he goes," Brady said, and Jennifer erupted in laughter. Johnny passed the joint back to Brady. As his coughing died down, he noticed that a swimmy light-headed feeling in his head refused to go away. He was reminded of when he and Christie used to spin around in circles in the living room on rainy days when they were kids.

Well, scratch that off the list of things I've never done, he thought.

"This *is* good stuff, Brady," Jennifer said as she took another small puff. "Where'd you get it?"

"I got my resources," he said, leaning back in the grass and looking up at the sky. Jennifer held the joint out to Johnny again. He held a refusing hand up to cut himself off.

"Come on." Jennifer leaned toward him, resting her hand on his thigh. She gave him a smile that he couldn't refuse.

What the hell? You're already feeling it, might as well take another hit.

Johnny took the joint from her and had another puff. He handed it back to Brady who was staring blankly up at the few wispy clouds in the sky.

"I thought you were only gonna hit it once," Brady said.

"Yeah, well... Once, twice. What's the difference?" Johnny replied, and Brady began to laugh.

"That's my man. Just wait 'til tonight. I've got something real good for you guys then."

"Oooh, what is it?" Jennifer asked, almost pouncing on Brady.

"It's a secret."

170

"Tell me what it is."

"Nope, you'll have to just find out later."

Jennifer pouted on the grass, crossing her arms over her chest. Johnny found himself staring at her again and tore his eyes away.

Brady took a final drag, then crushed the joint out on the bottom of his flip flop. "All right, that should hold me over for a while. Now I *really* want those fuckin' burgers." Johnny and Jennifer both agreed with him. "You guys stay here. I'll go get the food."

"I'll go with you," Johnny said eagerly, remembering that he had to go meet Cyndi, Eddie, and his little sister. He stood up too fast and he felt a thick rush to his head. He stumbled and caught his balance awkwardly before he fell down. Brady and Jennifer laughed and shook their heads.

"No, you better stay here, dude," Brady chuckled. He grabbed Johnny's arm and helped him sit back down on the grass.

"But what about Eddie and Cyndi and Christie," he asked thickly.

"I'll wait for 'em and bring 'em here with the food."

"But...But..."

"You really should stay here, man. If that dickhead Sheehan sees you stumbling around out there, you'll be in deep shit."

"You're right, man. You're right. I know you're right." Johnny knew he was repeating himself, but couldn't help it.

"Be right back, you guys," Brady said. He pulled his Ray-Ban's back down over his eyes and took off into the woods again. Johnny listened to the sound of Brady's feet crunching over bushes and beds of pine needles. The sound was so mesmerizing and clear, as if he could hear each individual leaf, each individual pine needle--

"So it's just you and me, huh?" Jennifer said. Johnny turned and there she was, sitting right beside him. Their shoulders were almost close enough to touch.

"Yeah, just you and me," he said. "What happened to your friends?"

"They're with Lisa's mom down by the wave pool having peanut butter and jelly sandwiches. Yeccchh!"

"I hate packed peanut butter and jelly. The bread gets all soggy."

"Me too. Besides, I wanted to have lunch up here with you guys. You're *way* more fun than them."

"Oh yeah?"

"Yeah." She got up on her knees and faced him directly. Her dark brown eyes seemed to look deep into his. In Johnny's inebriated state, the dark-brown color of her irises looked so rich, like the color of delicious tap root-beer. Her face and body seemed to fill the world.

"You like to have fun, don't you, Johnny?"

"Yeah, of course." His voice was down to a quiet mumble as he stared at her. She seemed to be getting closer and closer to him, inching her way forward.

"You need someone who knows how to have fun, don't you? Someone more fun than who you have now."

"What are you talking about?" he asked softly.

"I think you know," she said. Her face was now inches away from his. Her hands had somehow come down to rest on his thighs, they kept creeping higher and higher. She pushed herself forward, leaning on top of him and their lips connected in a kiss. It was slow and soft at first, then she became more insistent. Her mouth opened and suddenly her tongue was in his mouth, all wet, soft, and urgent. It was nothing like any kiss he ever had with Cyndi--

Oh shit. Cyndi, he thought dimly. *I'm gonna get it for this one.*

Jennifer lifted her leg up and brought it down on the other side of his waist, straddling him as she continued to kiss and press herself against his body. Johnny found it impossible to stop.

*   *   *

A hush fell over Cyndi as she passed into the brambly, wooded area between the slides. It wasn't quite the complete silence she remembered from the woods last year, but it felt eerily similar. Like everything else here, it felt like an imitation of that original park. The sounds of screaming kids, laughter, and even the music faded deep into the background, like the sound of a radio coming from a house three doors down.

Cyndi rushed forward in a panic, trying to stave off the horrible images of Christie being dragged through here by a white-masked killer. She tried treading lightly to soften the sound of her footsteps crunching through the undergrowth. With shoulders tensed, she looked around warily. Even in daylight, she couldn't be sure that no one was sneaking up on her. She felt like a trespasser, and felt like she was being watched.

In the lengthening afternoon shadows, Cyndi followed the winding Ragin' River slide. It stood on concrete pillars ten feet off the ground in some places. She stopped and listened to the swish of a tube sliding down. Following the tube's progress with her eyes, it went around another curve, then passed behind a tall stand of pine trees that blocked out the swishing sound.

They have no idea that I'm down here watching them, she thought. *Anyone could be down here and no one would know.* The thought did nothing to ease her

173

mind. She imagined the killer sitting below the ride, watching as random people went by, cocking his head as he listened to their excited cries. She wondered if the killer had climbed up one of those pillars, reached out with clutching fingers, and yanked Christie off the ride as she came around one of those curves. Could that have been what happened to Brad too?

"Just keep moving. I gotta find Christie," she whispered aloud to herself. She called out Christie's name and listened for a moment, hoping desperately for any kind of response.

Was that a noise behind her, a branch snapping maybe? Cyndi glanced over her shoulder, still running forward, and almost ran right off the concrete edge onto one of the Duelin' River slides. She faced forward at the last second and skidded to a stop over dry pine needles. A choked cry escaped her throat. The tips of her flip flops hung over the high concrete lip of the slide. A small drift of dirt and pine needles rained down four feet to the bottom of the slide below, and were washed away by the fast moving current. From farther up the slide, she heard the whish of an approaching tube and the excited laughter of riders. She stepped away from the edge, not wanting to be seen.

Looking up, she saw that the Ragin' River slide rounded around another curve high above her head. Somehow she would have to cross this Duelin' River to get to the other side. Trying to drop down onto the smooth surface of the Duelin' River was a bad idea, she'd go tumbling and scraping her skin on the concrete all the way to the bottom.

The tops of the Duelin' River rider's heads suddenly came into view. She ducked down and watched them like a tiger. The riders disappeared as they shot into one of those rocky circular tunnels, she remembered the layout of the ride well. *That's it*, she realized. *That's how I'll get across.* She would have to double back a little bit, then she could cross over the rocky top of the tunnel and continue to follow the Ragin' River slide.

Doubling back made her impatient. Time could be running out for Christie. If Cyndi didn't find her soon it may be too late. She ran to the rocky tunnel and began climbing. Her flip flops felt too slippery, but she pressed on, finding precarious footholds. She made it to the top of the tunnel and looked down at the ride. Three laughing kids riding in another tube came around the nearest high curve and slid towards the tunnel. One of them looked up and noticed Cyndi standing up there. He called out, "Hey!" and pointed in her direction. The other two kids looked up to see what he was pointing at, but Cyndi was already scrambling down the other side.

She jumped the last two feet down onto the ground. The Ragin' River slide swung away to the right and she started off toward it again, but then she heard a noise to her left. It came from around the other side of the rocky Duelin' River tunnel. Cyndi stopped in her tracks and listened. There it was again, the sound of a girl's muffled murmur.

"Christie," she said aloud. Equal amounts of relief and dread ran through her nerves as she rushed towards the girl. She desperately hoped she would find Christie still alive.

Cyndi came around the corner and was immediately confused. There were two people lying on the ground, but they weren't Christie and some masked killer. It was two teenagers, a boy and a girl, and they were making out. She instinctively turned away, embarrassed at her own intrusion. Then she recognized them. It was--

"Johnny?" she cried out in horror.

Johnny whirled, his lips glistening with

Jennifer's saliva. He jumped in surprise, and his eyes instantly went wide with fear and guilt. All the color drained out of his face as he scrambled to his feet, shoving Jennifer away.

"Cyndi? I-I-I-- Uh..." Johnny stammered. He walked toward her with his hands up.

Cyndi was dumbstruck, she couldn't believe this was happening. She had expected to find the butchered body of one of her friends, but at the moment, this felt just as bad. She couldn't find any words.

Jennifer stood up and brushed herself off. Her own lips were also wet with Johnny's saliva. She looked directly at Cyndi and smiled smugly. *Got your boyfriend, bitch. I won, and you lost. What are you gonna do about it?* Jennifer thought. She covered her glistening mouth with her hands as she started to laugh.

"Cyndi, please. I-I-- Listen, I..." Johnny continued. Cyndi wasn't even looking at him, she was staring hard at the crafty, triumphant smile on Jennifer's face. Each little laugh stung. Cyndi's jaw clenched and her fists balled up. Her muscles tensed up so hard she began to shake.

"Oops," Jennifer mocked, just like she had when she had flattened Cyndi's tube of sunscreen. That one word was the straw that broke the camel's back.

Cyndi rushed toward Jennifer. Johnny reached out for her shoulders, but she roughly slapped his arms away. Jennifer barely had time to react. Before she could brace herself, Cyndi was right in front of her. Cyndi's arms flashed forward and she gave Jennifer a hard shove backward. Jennifer fell back into the pine needles, landing on her butt. She slid back in the dry dirt. Her elbows painfully scraped against the ground, and she looked up at Cyndi in surprised shock. She honestly had no idea that Cyndi would've ever had the guts to lay a hand on her. Cyndi had always been such a gutless wimp before, what was she now?

Cyndi didn't slow down after the hard shove. She advanced forward and crouched down on top of Jennifer. Less than thirty seconds ago, Jennifer had been on top of Johnny in the same position, only this wasn't sexual, it was savage. Cyndi roughly grabbed the center of the swimsuit top between Jennifer's breasts and pulled her forward.

"Don't fuck with me!" Cyndi shouted in a hoarse growl. She pulled back her clenched left fist and slammed it down with all of her strength. The first punch mashed in Jennifer's lips, and without hesitation, she reared back and punched her again between her cheekbone and her nose. Cyndi screamed out cries of rage and effort with each punch. She reared back for another punch, but someone caught her fist.

"Jesus Christ, Cyndi! What the hell are you doing?" Johnny screamed, holding onto her forearm tightly. She looked back up at him with feral rage, her jaw clenched and her lips pulled back in a snarl. Johnny didn't look guilty now, he looked afraid, afraid of *her.*

Cyndi panted, each breath was almost a growl. She looked up at Johnny, wanting to hate him and somehow wanting to apologize to him at the same time.

There was movement behind Johnny and she lowered her gaze. Eddie, Christie, and another boy stood there, their mouths hung open in shock. Cyndi recognized the boy, he was the friend Christie had seen riding down the Duelin' River slide while they had waited in line for the Ragin' Rivers. Brady also stood there behind Johnny, his arms full with boxes of food and tall cups of soda. His sunglasses were up on his head again, and his bloodshot eyes were wide and full of disbelief. Out of all four of them, Cyndi looked longest at Christie, who stood there alive and well.

"Christie. You're okay," she said softly.

Jennifer had begun to cry and clutch her bleeding mouth and nose, she crab-walked backwards. Cyndi felt Jennifer's top tug backward in her clenched right fist and she let go, barely giving her a second glance. Sniffling, Jennifer turned around and crawled away from her.

"I-I'm fine," Christie explained. "I just went over to talk with TJ for a minute." She pointed at the boy with the spiky black hair beside her who nodded in agreement.

They all stood there gaping at Cyndi, not knowing what to say. Jennifer whimpered and clutched her red beaten face. Her mashed lips had split and one of her nostrils was oozing blood. Seeing Jennifer like this should have given Cyndi a sense of savage satisfaction, but she only felt guilt and pity.

Brady set the food down on the ground and rushed over to help his cousin.

"What the fuck is your problem, bitch?" he mumbled as he passed Cyndi.

Cyndi stood up and looked down at her punching fist, her knuckles were beginning to ache and were lightly smeared with Jennifer's blood. Johnny reached out and touched her arm.

"Look, Cyndi. I can explain," he began. It was too late for that though. Cyndi yanked her arm away from him and ran.

Chapter Twelve:

Can't Talk About It

Johnny stood on the ledge above Hurricane Bay watching the crowd of swimmers as they braced themselves for the last wave of the day. The crowd had thinned, and the average age of the people swimming in the wave pool became noticeably younger as the day wound down. The kids and teenagers still splashed and screamed, but fatigue had set in, and the energy level in the wave pool had died down. He hadn't even had to jump in and pull out any drowning kids in the last two hours. He had changed into a white sleeveless T-shirt to protect his skin from getting even more sunburned.

From the loud speakers came an announcement, "Attention, guests. The time is now 5:55 PM. Thrill River will be closing in five minutes."

Thank God, Johnny thought. He had stood on different points of this ledge all afternoon, and the time seemed to drag on forever. This afternoon had felt longer than the longest school day as he stood alone with his thoughts and came down from the pot he had smoked with Brady and Jennifer. He replayed the day's events over in his head again. The look of betrayal and horror on Cyndi's face was crystal clear in his memory, and it gnawed on his conscience all afternoon.

You fucked up big this time. What were you thinking? he scolded himself internally. *How am I ever gonna convince her to talk to me again? How can I ever convince her to let me explain, or give me a second chance?*

That awful, heartbroken look on Cyndi's face had burned into his brain. Then, before he could even blink, she had pushed down Jennifer and started pounding her face in. He was still completely stunned about that. Could that really have been Cyndi actually beating the shit out of someone else?

When Cyndi ran off he had tried to rush after her, but he tripped in the underbrush. His head had still been swimming uncontrollably. Christie and Eddie could only stare at him in disbelief. He did not look like the old Johnny, the nice guy they had known and grown up with. The old Johnny had been a loyal friend who could let loose, but usually stayed on the side of caution. The new Johnny in front of them was high on drugs and disoriented, the new Johnny had kissed a girl who wasn't his girlfriend.

Brady had partied enough to build up a major tolerance to pot. He was still high, but he settled back into a mature, adult persona easily. He gently helped Jennifer to her feet as she fought off the last of her tears.

"I gotta get her over to the infirmary," he said without the slightest hint of his usual attitude. "Save me some of that food," he added over his shoulder as an afterthought. He pushed some of the low tree limbs out of their way, and they quickly disappeared from sight.

"I'm gonna go back and find my friends again. See ya later, Christie," the spiky haired boy, TJ, said and he also ran off.

Then it was just the three of them left; Eddie, Christie, and a bewildered Johnny sitting on the ground looking stunned and guilty.

"What the hell was that all about?" Eddie asked. Johnny sighed, put his head in his hands, then reluctantly told them everything.

Christie only stuck around for another half hour after the showdown. She felt like she was partly to blame for the fight between Cyndi and Jennifer. They had left the shady clearing and brought the food to one of the picnic tables near the Big Kahuna Grill. Eddie explained how Cyndi went into some kind of frenzy and ran off looking for Christie after they rode the Ragin' Rivers. No more than two minutes later, Eddie had spotted Christie off by the entrance of the Lazy River talking with her friend TJ.

Then they turned their questions on Johnny.

"What were you doing with that chick, man?" Eddie asked. Johnny heard a touch of disgust in Eddie's voice that he didn't care for at all.

"Hey, *she* was the one who kissed *me,* okay?" he shot back defensively.

"Yeah, but why were you even with her in the first place?" Christie asked.

"She's...she's..." *What? She's hot? She's cool? She's all over me with her huge--* "She's Brady's cousin. They're friends of mine." His brain was sluggish, it felt the same as when his old Bel Air backfired and sputtered if he gave it too much gas at a green light.

Eddie and Christie exchanged a look of shame, as if he had just explained that he had befriended Nazis.

"What? I'm allowed to be friends with whoever I want." Although, he didn't much feel like hanging out with Jennifer anymore. She had gotten him into enough trouble today.

"And you guys were getting high?" Eddie

181

asked.

"Yeah, so?"

"Oh, Johnny," Christie said, shaking her head. In that instant, she sounded exactly like their mother, a master in the fine art of guilt trips. "How could you do that to Cyndi?"

"I didn't do anything. I told you *she* kissed *me*."

Christie and Eddie simply looked down at their food in silence.

"Hey, what is this anyway? A fuckin' interrogation?"

They said nothing. Now he realized he sounded like Brady, minus the cool, likeable sense of humor. He sounded like a petulant, young kid trying to copy some asshole older brother that he idolized. He sounded pitiful and embarrassing to his own ears.

The rest of the lunch was spent mostly in awkward silence. At the end of lunch, Christie announced that she felt like going home. She stood up to go find a payphone and call their mom to come pick her up.

"If you tell Mom about any of this, I'll kill you," Johnny threatened.

"Shut up, Johnny. You're being a jerk," she shot back.

"I mean it. You better not tell Mom, or I'll tell her who broke the vacuum." A few months back, while their parents had been out looking at carpet samples, Christie had used the vacuum to clean up a fresh puddle of her cat, Bear's, puke. Johnny had caught her in the act and told her to stop, but she had stubbornly refused. Two weeks later, the vacuum died and a putrid, burnt smell came from the vacuum bag. When their mother questioned them about it, Johnny kept his mouth shut. Later, he had whispered, '*You owe me, big time,*' in the privacy of Christie's room. He had dragged out this

182

secret at every opportunity since then, and she was getting tired of it.

"Fine! I don't care," she shouted and stormed off.

Eddie had also been about to leave when Brady finally came back from the infirmary. He told them that Jennifer had been patched up and then immediately changed the subject. To both Johnny and Eddie's relief, he drove the conversation, telling them funny stories from college. He had gotten them both genuinely laughing, and for a while Johnny let himself forget all about Cyndi and Jennifer and the whole mess.

As soon as he went back to work, standing up on that ledge over the wave pool, the unpleasant thoughts came right back. Three guilt-ridden hours later, he was still here. He envied all the kids down in the wave pool who were having such a sunny, carefree day.

Over the loudspeakers, some song by The Human League ended and a rare slow song began to play. Johnny recognized it immediately, having heard it with Cyndi dozens of times. It was one of her favorites: "Mercenary" from her favorite band The Go-Go's. As he listened to the song, he couldn't help but look up at the gorgeous setting sun off in the distance. Thoughts and images of Cyndi filled his mind. How could things with her have been so perfect, then gone bad so fast? Could this really be the end of all that? Would this song (and every other song) be ruined forever for him, tainted by memories of a relationship that he had washed away just as easily as that huge, destructive wave?

I've gotta call her as soon as I'm done here. I've gotta at least try to talk to her. It can't be over just like that. There's still so much unresolved.

Cyndi still hadn't told him about last summer yet. She had been so close the other night at the pool. Not finding out would be like reading a book with the last few pages torn out. He felt more and more that it somehow had something to do with this place. Maybe she'd had a bad experience at a water park last year, maybe it was even another Thrill River. There weren't any other Thrill Rivers though. Throughout their week of training, Sheehan had repeated certain sayings over and over. *'We want to show our guests something brand new, something they've never seen before. Make their very first Thrill River experience a great one.'* He had said that maybe fifteen times over the last week, and each time Johnny had struggled not to roll his eyes.

You're living in a dream world if you think she'll trust you enough to tell you now.

Doesn't matter. I still have to try.

The song ended and the clock bell chimed over the loudspeakers. He and the other lifeguards up on the ledge stuck their whistles in their mouths and blew hard. Then, just as they'd rehearsed, Johnny and the lifeguard across the way jumped in and began herding the guests out of the wave pool. After the last few stragglers trudged out of the wave pool, Johnny looked up and was startled to see Eddie standing on the shore in front of him.

"Hey, man. What are you still doin' here? I thought you would've gone home by now," Johnny said happily.

"Nah," Eddie shrugged. "It's too hot today to be cooped up at my house. Besides, I wanted to stick around for the after party."

"I don't know if I'm gonna stick around for the party anymore. I was just thinkin' I'd rather go home."

"Come on, man," Eddie protested. "I waited around all afternoon for ya.' You're gonna let me down, just like that? You can't let that chick stuff get you down. Just have a good time. You and me, man. Just like the old days."

"Well..." Johnny said. Eddie had a point, he would feel even worse leaving now since Eddie had waited all afternoon for him.

"Forget those girls. Just find some hot lifeguard girl."

"It's not over with me and Cyndi. At least I don't know for sure."

"Okay, then find *me* a hot lifeguard girl."

Johnny laughed. "Okay. You talked me into it."

"All *right!* I knew you'd come around." They slapped each other a high five. Eddie went back to his chair and put his yellow and black plaid shirt on, but left it mostly unbuttoned. He stuffed his towel into his backpack, and they both headed back up to the picnic area at the top of the hill.

Sheehan and some of the other lifeguards were already there setting up a small space for the party. They helped lay out two-liter bottles of Pepsi, plastic cups, and napkins. A lifeguard named Adam McAvery had brought a bulky boom box and set it down on the table as well.

By the time Johnny and Eddie reached them, the party was about to start. They walked over to ask what they could do to help set up, but Brady got to them first. Now that work was over, he had put on a black tank top. He slyly squeezed in between them, wrapping his arms over their shoulders.

"All right, come with me guys," Brady said in a conspiratorial low voice and clenched jaw. "I gotta go grab a couple of cases from my connection at this liquor store. I'm gonna sneak 'em in and bring 'em to the spot. I need a couple of lookouts."

"I don't know, man. I don't think it's a good idea," Johnny said hesitantly.

"I thought you said you liked beer, dude. You turnin' down free beer?" He sounded and smelled like he had already had a few drinks. He shook Johnny's shoulder chummily, then turned to Eddie. "Lookit this guy. You believe this guy?" Eddie shrugged and Brady turned back to Johnny. "You can't turn down free beer. The fuck's wrong with you, dude?"

"I really gotta go make a call, man," Johnny pleaded.

"To who? That little blondie chick? She'll wait for you, man." He grabbed Johnny's cheeks and looked at Eddie. "See this face? Would you wait for this face?"

Eddie laughed and shrugged.. "Uh...ye--uh...why not?"

"See? Now come on, while Sheehan's still distracted."

"No, really. I--"

"I'll go," Eddie suddenly spoke up. "You go, Johnny. Make your call. Put your mind at ease. Then come back and have some beers with us, man." Eddie, always good at reading people, saw that there was no arguing with Brady, and offered him a compromise to free Johnny up. Johnny couldn't help but admire how smooth he always was at that.

"My man," Brady said, shaking Eddie's shoulder. Brady looked over his shoulder at Sheehan, then quickly moved away from the crowd.

"You gonna be all right with him?" Johnny whispered to Eddie.

"I can handle him," Eddie whispered back dismissively. "Just promise you'll introduce me to some of these lifeguard girls." He glanced around at a few of the ones he had spotted already. Johnny knew they were all out of Eddie's league, but he agreed anyway.

"I promise," he said sincerely.

It was a promise he never got to keep.

*   *   *

186

Twelve people stood in line waiting to use the payphone.

"Oh you gotta be kidding me," Johnny said as he came around the corner and caught his first glimpse of the line. The payphone stood around the corner from the picnic area where they were setting up for the party. It was on the far opposite side of the bathrooms and lockers building. The line stretched out down the concrete steps to the entry turnstiles where the last few slow-moving families and groups of kids were shuffling out.

"Thanks. Hope you had a thrilling day. Thank you. Have a good night. Thanks," the boy and girl stationed at the turnstiles said to the guests on their way out.

A fourteen-year-old girl stood at the payphone arguing with her mother on the other end of the line. "But Mom, all the other girls are gonna be at Becky's house...Mom, you never let me do anything...Come on, please...." The other kids behind her in line craned their necks and listened to her conversation. It didn't look like it would end soon. Several of the kids near the back of the line threw up their hands and rolled their eyes impatiently.

Well, there's another payphone over by The Falls, Johnny thought. *There will probably be less people there.*

Johnny turned to make his way back toward The Falls ride, and there stood Jennifer. She was still in her red and black swimsuit, but now she also wore a huge gray T-shirt that draped off one shoulder. She had brushed her hair and put on fresh black eyeliner, but her injuries still stood out on her face. Her lip was swollen and dark, and there were dried flakes of blood around her nostrils. She gave him a condescending, sullen smile.

"Where's your girlfriend? Did she run home crying to her mommy?" Jennifer asked sarcastically.

Johnny decided it would be best to just ignore her. He rolled his eyes and walked around her. "You tell Cyndi that this isn't over. This isn't over by a *long* shot."

Johnny stopped walking and looked back over his shoulder at her.

"You really want to keep pushing her? Because I seem to remember that last time you pushed her too far, she kicked your ass pretty bad." The smile on Jennifer's face immediately turned into a scowl. Johnny mimicked the condescending smile that she had just given him a second ago, then turned and walked back toward The Falls area.

Jennifer watched him and began to grind her teeth. All afternoon she had been repeating the same phrase to herself and her friends: *I'm gonna get that bitch. I'm gonna get that fuckin' bitch.* Now she added more to the end: *I'm gonna get that bitch and her stupid boyfriend too.*

A wicked idea suddenly popped into her mind. She didn't have to wait, she could start the punishment she planned for Cyndi and Johnny right now. She glanced casually in all directions, making sure there was no one around who she recognized. Other than the few strangers leaving the park who didn't give her a second glance, she was alone. Jennifer smiled as she made her way out to the parking lot.

*   *   *

Cyndi's mother paced back and forth through her living room, trying to figure out what to say to her daughter. Halfway through this uncomfortable, nerve-wracking day of waiting, she had gotten Cyndi's brief call and went running for her. The whole ride over to the park she kept repeating the same thought in her mind: *I knew something would happen. I just knew it.* Ten minutes later, she pulled the station wagon up in front of the curb. Cyndi sat there with her towel and neon green backpack, she had run back to the chairs and grabbed them before calling her mother. She got in the car and the furious barrage of questions that she had expected started up.

"What happened? What's the matter? Are you all right?"

"Mom, I don't want to talk--," Cyndi said through clenched teeth.

"I don't want to hear that, Cyndi. Now tell me what's going on."

"Mom, can we please just get out of here?"

"Just talk to me, Cyndi. I'm your mother. I'm on your side--"

"Mom, please!" Cyndi shouted. Her mother felt like she had been slapped just by the sheer volume of Cyndi's voice. She saw the rage burning in her daughter's eyes. She had never witnessed such raw anger from her daughter before. It was far more terrifying than the prospect of her daughter growing up, or going out with boys, or driving. Cyndi's hard stare remained locked on her mother's eyes until she shifted the station wagon into drive. When the car was finally in motion, Cyndi sighed, lowered her head, and rubbed her eyes. Without a word, her mother sped away from Thrill River.

In ten minutes, they were back at home. Cyndi rushed upstairs to her room, slamming the door behind her. Her mother paced downstairs, imagining a thousand different possibilities that may have caused Cyndi to react as she did. None of them seemed very plausible. She had given Cyndi her space all afternoon, even though she was burning with curiosity. Just what the hell had happened at that water park?

I'm her mother and I have a right to know what's going on, she thought, knowing full well that it would be a battle trying to drag a single sentence out of Cyndi. She and her husband seemed to be the two people in the whole world that Cyndi wanted to talk to least. It was irritating. What had they ever done to her to make her so uncommunicative? They had never beat her, or mistreated her in any way. They had always gotten her just about everything she wanted.

"Just be firm with her. That's all," her husband said from his easy chair. Since last year he seemed to have given up on trying to reach Cyndi. Maybe he was right.

She turned to go upstairs and try to talk to Cyndi again, bracing herself for a screaming match, when the phone rang. She gave an exasperated sigh and went to the kitchen to answer it.

"Hello?" she answered, a little more sharply than she had intended.

"Uh, hi, Mrs. Stevens. It's Johnny. Is Cyndi there?" He sounded a little nervous talking to her.

"Johnny, what the hell happened over there?"

"Uh...Well, I'm sure Cyndi told you everything, but look if I can just explain to her..."

Now she was more confused than ever. Johnny sounded guilty and apologetic.

"She wouldn't say a *word* to me, you know how she is. Now tell me what's going on. Is Cyndi in some kind of trouble?"

"She got in a fight."

"A *fight?!* A fight with *who*?" This was getting even more confusing. Cyndi doesn't fight. Her daughter was timid and delicate, not some rough, antagonistic--

"It was Jennifer Johnston. She, uh...well, Jennifer tried to kiss me." He blurted out the last of it in an embarrassed rush.

Her eyes went wide. Suddenly, she felt almost as uncomfortable as he sounded. She felt as if this were something private that she had no business knowing. Yet the gossipy details were also undeniably fascinating. Wasn't Jennifer one of Cyndi's oldest friends? The two of them had practically grown up together. Was Johnny lying, or not telling her the whole truth? She initially imagined that Cyndi had had some sort of nervous breakdown brought on by memories of the terrors she had survived last year. These new details were nothing like what she had originally expected.

"Look, if I could just talk to her, or maybe..." he paused, formulating an idea. "Could you do me a favor?"

"What kind of favor?" she asked suspiciously.

"Can you tell me what happened to Cyndi last summer?"

"I don't know. How much has she told you already?"

"Nothing."

"*Nothing*? She really hasn't told you *anything* about it?" She and her husband had discussed the possibility of Cyndi breaking the confidentiality agreement and telling Johnny. They both agreed that she would confide at least some of it to him. After all the time they spent on the phone together, how could the subject have been avoided? On the other hand, it was *Cyndi* they were talking about.

"No. If I knew what happened, maybe I could help. Maybe I could...I don't know, understand her better."

She sighed. "Well, Johnny. I'm not sure it's my place to tell you. And I wasn't even there, she's never told me all the details."

"But she probably told you enough of it to make sense."

She laughed. "You think she talks to *me?* I can barely get a few sentences out of her on a good day."

"If you want her to talk to you, just don't try so hard."

"Don't try so hard? What do you mean?"

"Well, don't come at her with all these questions. Just kinda act like you don't care if she tells you one way or the other. If it's something she really needs to talk about, she'll talk. Trust me."

"How do you know that'll work?"

"I don't know. That's how my dad gets me to talk about stuff."

"Believe me, Johnny, I've tried everything to get her to open up to me."

"Well, I don't--"

The operator spoke up suddenly. "Your time is up, sir. Please deposit ten cents."

"Ah, I gotta go. Can you just tell her something for me?"

"Sure."

"Tell her that I'm sorry. And tell her if she hates me and doesn't want to see me again, I'll understand. But if she wants to talk, I'll still be here for her. I'll still be waiting. Can you please tell her that?"

"I'll tell her."

"I'll be at the park for another few hours then I'll--"

The phone clicked, breaking the connection. He had run out of time.

She felt sorry for the boy. He sounded so sincere, and he truly seemed to care about her daughter.

I'll still be here for her. I'll still be waiting.

What exactly did *that* mean? It sounded romantic though, and she felt a touch of nostalgia for the hectic swells and waves of young love. How long had it been since she felt any of that old, exciting drama? It all had a kind of soap opera quality that tugged at her heart.

Act like you don't care if she tells you one way

or the other. If it's something she really needs to talk about, she'll talk. She had tried that tactic a few times, but her impatience always seemed to get the better of her. Had she really ever stuck to that strategy, followed through with it until she got results? Besides, who was Johnny to give her parenting advice? What did a sixteen-year-old boy know about being a parent? Still, maybe it was worth a try.

*   *   *

Cyndi pretended not to hear the knock at her bedroom door. Over the last few years she had gotten pretty talented at being able to hear the extraneous noises beyond her Walkman headphones. With that talent came another ability: the ability to make people believe that she hadn't heard them over her mix tapes. Unfortunately, it had been a long time since she had been able to use that to fool her mother.

The door opened with a soft snick, and her mother poked her head in. She held a tray with a sandwich and some potato chips. Cyndi lay on her stomach on her bed, facing the wall. She tossed her pink and black tiger stripe swimsuit on the floor, and had put on a fresh white off-the-shoulder T-shirt and a tiny pair of pink acid-washed shorts. Her mother wasn't surprised to see those orange foam-covered headphones were over her ears. For a moment, she watched Cyndi, trying to gauge her mood and figure out the best way to proceed. Cyndi had a boy's T-shirt and a girl's T-shirt laid out on her pillow in front of her, and she stared at them with her chin resting on her arms.

Her mother stepped in quietly and sat down on Cyndi's bed. She lightly scratched Cyndi's heel over her green sock to get her attention. Cyndi didn't make the slightest reaction.

"Cyndi, honey?" she asked. "I made you a turkey sandwich."

"Not hungry," Cyndi muttered without moving a muscle.

"Okay," she shrugged. "I'll leave it in case you get hungry." She set the tray down at the foot of Cyndi's bed and got back up. She walked slowly to the door, intentionally not giving Cyndi the slightest glance back. *Keep it together. Don't give in. Just leave her alone. Leave her alone.* She opened the door and walked out, closing the door softly behind her. Just as the latch touched the door frame, Cyndi's voice called out.

"Mom?" It was soft, as if she wouldn't mind not being heard, but loud enough to warrant attention.

She poked her head back into Cyndi's room. "What?"

Cyndi turned around, sat up, and looked up at her. Her face had a washed out, weary quality that made her look prematurely old. Her mother didn't care for that look at all.

"Am I crazy?" Cyndi asked.

She shrugged. "Do *you* think you're crazy?"

Cyndi seemed to honestly consider the question. "Sometimes. After today everyone probably thinks I'm crazy." Her mother said nothing, didn't even move, and sure enough Cyndi continued. "I don't know what came over me, I just... I keep seeing these things. Sometimes they're just little...coincidences, and I can tell myself that I'm just being paranoid. But sometimes it feels like everything that happened last year is starting again. It feels like everything that was dead and buried is all coming back up."

Her mother was so engrossed in listening to her daughter speak that she forgot her strategy and dared to ask a question. "What happened today?"

Cyndi shook her head. "Everything was going

fine, well, fine enough I guess. It was just kind of weird at first. It felt like, I don't know, if Disneyland built a ride out of my life or something. But it was more than that. We were in this little group, just like before. It was like Eddie was Zack, I was Stacy, and Christie was me. It was like we were actors doing one of those re-enactments on TV. Then they wanted to go on those damn Ragin' Rivers. Christie got on that slide, the same one Brad went on before he disappeared, and I just panicked. Because that's how it started last time, that's when things turned bad." She looked down at Zack and Stacy's T-shirts in front of her, remembering her friends.

"Then what?" her mother asked impatiently.

"That's just *it!* *Nothing* happened. Christie was fine. There's nothing there but people and rides. But before I found her, I found Jennifer and Johnny. She was...all over him. I didn't even stop to think about it, I just knocked her down and started punching her, right in the face. And you know what? I felt exactly the same as I did last year, when I...killed that guy. It was like I could've killed her too. And everyone knew it. They just stared at me like they were afraid of me." Tears welled up in Cyndi's eyes and her voice became frantic. "But they don't get it. They weren't there. None of them saw what *I* saw. They didn't do what *I* had to do." She noticed the T-shirts she had balled up into her tight fists and let them go. "I just want to be normal."

Now it was her mother's turn to cry. She turned away from her daughter, her face scrunched up with thick emotion, and the tears spilled out uncontrollably. Cyndi was shocked out of her own thoughts, suddenly concerned. She had rarely ever seen either of her parents cry.

"Mom? What's the matter?"

Her mother sniffled and shook her head, trying to compose herself enough to speak.

"That's all I've ever wanted for you," she choked. "I wanted you to be able to live a normal life. This is supposed to be the time in your life that you should be having fun with your friends. And now I've made it worse for you."

"What are you talking about?"

"It was that fucking summer camp. We should never have sent you. I don't know what I was thinking."

Cyndi stared down at Zack and Stacy's shirts in her hands, remembering the good times with them, and the good times that had come afterward with her new friends. She imagined how empty her hands would be without them now, and how empty her life would be.

"But I wouldn't be who I am if you hadn't sent me there."

"I know, but..." her mother trailed off into more sobs. Cyndi hated to see her like that.

"Aww, Mom. Come here." Cyndi stood up and her mother practically fell into her open arms. They hugged for a long time, both of them with tears streaming down their eyes. They finally pulled away and wiped their eyes, laughing a little with mild embarrassment.

"You know what your father says about you?"

"What?"

"He says you're a survivor. He says you can get through anything. We're both so proud of you." Cyndi rolled her eyes. "I mean it. You're so strong. You've faced down terrible things. Things that I can't even imagine. And after all that, I don't think you're crazy at all."

Cyndi smiled at her mother, a rare sight from a sulky teenager. "Thanks."

"I love you, Cyndi."

"I love you too, Mom."

Her mom sighed and got up. "You know, this is

the longest conversation we've had since...I can't even remember."

"Yeah, I know."

"Johnny called and taught me how to get you to talk. He's pretty smart."

"He called?" Cyndi asked curiously.

"About a half hour ago, he wanted to talk to you. He told me to tell you he's sorry. And that he's still waiting, whatever that means."

Cyndi remembered that night at the pool last week. "I know what it means."

"You really didn't tell him anything?"

"You said I couldn't because of that stupid contract thing."

"Yes, but I didn't think you'd actually stick to that. I thought you would've told him the whole story in secret by now."

"Well, you know me. I can't keep my mouth shut," she said sarcastically.

"Maybe that's the problem. Maybe that's what's making you feel crazy. You know I'm always here for you, but you need someone your own age to talk to. You should tell him what happened." Cyndi was shocked at the sudden change in attitude from her mother. She had just suggested that she do exactly what had been on her mind for the last year.

"Maybe," Cyndi said, thinking of Johnny. Her trust in him had been shaken, but she hadn't exactly been Girlfriend Of The Year either. The past had driven a wedge between them, and it had gotten deeper and deeper. Maybe it was time to pull it out. "But what about the contract?"

"I don't care about that stupid contract. I care about you."

"Maybe you're right. I'm gonna call him."

Cyndi walked over and picked up the phone.

"Wait. He's not home yet. Right before the phone cut off, he said he'd be at the park for an hour or two." Cyndi felt a sting of disappointment. She wanted to blurt out the whole story right here and now.

"Oh yeah. I forgot about the party."

"Well, just give him an hour or two, then call."

"Yeah, okay."

"Well, I'll leave you alone. You can come downstairs if you want."

"Maybe in a little bit."

Cyndi's mother walked out of her daughter's room feeling an uplifting sense of accomplishment. She had finally reached her, finally broken through.

Cyndi sat on her bed with some of the weight lifted off her chest. She wasn't crazy. She was a survivor. She could get through anything. Suddenly, she had an idea.

"Mom?" she called, just before her mother closed the door again. "Can you do me a favor?"

"Sure, anything."

"Can you take me back to the water park?"

Chapter Thirteen:

This Party is Dead

Only twenty-five of the forty-five lifeguards bothered to stick around after work, and now almost half of them were gone. Red plastic cups and paper plates littered the cluster of picnic tables, practically no one had bothered to clean up after themselves before ditching this sorry excuse for a party. Even their jerk boss, Mr. Sheehan, had ducked out early. Most of the lifeguards would have agreed that he had been strangely absent all day.

"This party is dead. Where the hell is everyone?" Shaina asked, looking around at the few scattered groups of people eating slices of pizza and making small talk. She was a recent graduate of DeAngelo High with a sunny smile and wild, teased brunette hair that exploded out from under her pink headband.

"They're probably off with Brady Johnston. He said he was gonna sneak in some beer," said Lori, another recent DeAngelo graduate.

"Oh right, he told me about that earlier." Brady

had come up to her earlier while she was working the Duelin' Rivers end-pool station, and conspiratorially told her about his plan to spice up the after-work party. "You wanna go try to find him? I bet you five bucks that's where everyone is."

"No, I've had enough of this place for one day," Lori said. "Ronnie Everly's having a real party while his folks are out of town at their vacation house. I was thinking about stopping by. Why don't you come with me?"

Shaina gave Lori a half-grimace and a shrug. She had no desire to attend another spoiled-drunk-rich-kid party hosted by a stuck-up asshole like Ronnie Everly. "I think I might just head home."

"All right, well, I'm gonna take off too. I'll see you tomorrow, 'kay?"

"Yeah, see ya."

Lori said her goodbyes to a few other people and headed for the parking lot. Shaina glanced around at the eleven other people left and saw no one that she knew well enough to approach and strike up a conversation. She wasn't unusually shy, but she wasn't exactly a social butterfly either. Looking past the entrance of the Duelin Rivers into the woods between the slides, she suddenly thought about Brady again. Most of the lifeguard staff at Thrill River had been secretively talking all day about Brady Johnston's plan to have a little side party. She knew Johnny Vesna and at least two other acquaintances from school would probably be down there. Also, it was too early to go home, the sun wasn't even down yet. She took one last look back at the two tight-knit little groups of strangers lost in their own conversations, and that settled it for her. She would go find Brady Johnston and the others, maybe she'd even have a beer or two before heading home. As with the others who had already ventured back into the depths of the park in hopes of enjoying part of a rumored beer stockpile, no one took much notice as Shaina slipped away from the party.

The sun was setting quickly, and the wild, woodsy areas between the slides were prematurely dark and filled with shadows. Shaina walked slowly over the rough terrain, her feet crunching on the pine needles. The sounds of Madonna's "Lucky Star" coming from the boom box and laughter from the party had become muffled and distant almost immediately. The woods seemed to have closed in around her, and she could barely hear the party at all. It was the first quiet moment she'd had since she arrived here early this morning. She was unaccustomed to the silence, it gave her an odd, unwelcome feeling, like she had walked into a stranger's house.

This place really is kind of creepy at night, Shaina thought. She shrugged away her nervousness, assuring herself that she would be with the others out here soon.

A black form moved between the shadowy trees up ahead. Shaina figured it was one of her fellow lifeguards wearing a black sweatshirt or something. They were all probably trying to stay quiet so that Mr. Sheehan wouldn't catch them and fire them all. She walked a little farther, then ducked underneath the low limbs of a big old pine tree because it was the most direct route. When she stood up straight, she saw Brady wearing his black shirt and crouching down with his back to her and his head lowered. She saw a few pairs of white legs lying down in the underbrush past Brady.

"Hey, got any more of those beers for me?" she asked in a hushed voice. As the words fell out of her mouth, she noticed those splayed legs looked too motionless, as if they were asleep. The pale shins and calves were also covered in muddy water or something,

201

but it was really getting to be too dark to tell.

The figure whirled at the sound of her voice and stood up to his full height. Shaina gasped and her scream caught in her throat as she realized that the huge, hulking man standing before her was definitely not Brady Johnston. She had an instant to recognize the ghastly grin on his white mask before his arms raised, and he brought something incredibly heavy and sharp down on her skull.

*   *   *

Eddie was getting irritated. Brady was taking forever to get the beer, Johnny was taking forever to make his phone call, and it was starting to get dark. Down at the Ragin' Rivers' end pool, the flow of water coming down the slides had been turned off for the night, and the slides sat silently drying in the lingering heat from the day. Eddie stood across the sidewalk in front of a white painted gate marked *Employees Only.* The gate stood slightly open, exposing a small stack of deflated tubes, a tube patching work station, and a compressed air tank for re-inflating them. Beyond this little inflation station was a dirt access road for the maintenance and construction crew trucks.

Before he left, Brady had explained his plan to drive over to the liquor store and secure two cases of Miller Lite from his "connection." He would drive back to the park, through the back gate, and up the dirt road to the inflation station to unload the beer. Then he, Eddie, and Johnny would carry it up to his little hideout spot in the woods near the Duelin' River slide. A few other trustworthy people would meet them there, and they would have a *real* party, not some "G-rated, baby bullshit," as Brady put it.

In the meantime, Eddie was Brady's lookout.

Brady had pointed out their boss, Mr. Sheehan, up at the picnic area. Eddie recognized him as the buff-looking, older lifeguard that had yelled at him for being the first one in the wave pool this morning. If Sheehan came down this way, Eddie would go out on the dirt road and wave his arms as soon as Brady turned in. Brady would then drive away, and they would wait for Sheehan to leave.

Now, after what felt like an hour (although he figured it was probably less), neither Brady or Johnny had come back, and Eddie was getting impatient.

"Come on, man," Eddie said out loud. "What's the hold up?" He had spent too much of today by himself, and he was eager to get back in the company of friends. As an only child, he was used to loneliness. He didn't like it, but he was used to it. Too often he found that when he was by himself, his mind got him in trouble. Today had been no exception.

Around four o'clock that afternoon, he had been enjoying floating in the slow current of the Lazy River. With one arm draped over his eyes to shield him from the hot sun, his thoughts had turned back to Cyndi. He felt a slight stirring of something, some feelings for her, and tried to suppress it. *Give me a break. She's your best friend's girl, come on.* But was she? Maybe not anymore. He didn't know.

Eddie and Cyndi had always gotten along pretty well. She had gotten used to his relentless sense of humor very quickly, and she didn't seem all snooty and stuck up like some of the girls that Johnny had briefly dated in the past. Today had been the first time he and Cyndi had ever spent time together without Johnny, and now, for some reason he couldn't understand, she seemed much more attractive than she ever had before. He tried to articulate the feeling, but the only word he could come up with was *close.* They seemed somehow *closer* now

203

than they had ever been.

Then there was the big blow up and Cyndi just ran away. She didn't even bother to tell them goodbye, just grabbed her backpack and towel and took off. Eddie wasn't about to lecture Johnny on the subtleties of relationships, God knew he had no experience or authority in *that* area. Though, regardless of his inexperience, he wondered just what the hell Johnny had been thinking.

If I had a girl as hot as Cyndi, you'd never catch me acting like that, he thought. *Who does Johnny think he is, Mr. Amateur Party Animal? Cyndi is way hotter than that Jennifer chick. If Cyndi was my girl....*

Eddie's overactive imagination created images of Johnny and Cyndi breaking it off officially. Then he saw himself calling her and talking for hours. He would make her laugh, and maybe she would start wondering about him the same way he was wondering about her now.

Later, sitting by the wave pool, he had pulled his sketch pad out of his backpack. Without thinking, he began to draw. Occasionally, he just unplugged his mind from reality and let the pencil do all the work. From time to time, he glanced up at the orange sky and the setting sun, unaware that he and Johnny were both watching it and thinking about the same girl. He drew twelve sketches in quick succession, all in the same action-pose, heavily-shaded, comic book style. All twelve of his stylized drawings featured a girl with blonde crimped hair that was unmistakably Cyndi. He started with a drawing of her face and shoulders. Then he did an action shot of Cyndi holding Jennifer's swimsuit with one hand, her other fist cocked back. This was followed by Cyndi standing in front of a giant broken heart shape, its broken edges crumbling like old rock. The theme of the drawings changed then and became darker and more sinister. He drew a picture over Cyndi's shoulder looking out at the wave pool and the Smiley mural at the back. Cyndi and some of the rides they had observed today covered the next few drawings. He did a full page of Cyndi with that nervous look on her face that he'd caught several times, and above her like a bunch of floating ghosts were dozens of those weird Smiley-Faces that were all over the park.

When his hand started to cramp up, he put the pencil down and looked over his work. They were great drawings and Eddie really wanted to keep them, but he felt guilt begin to gnaw at his conscience. What would Johnny think if he came across these? He closed the book and made a mental note to hide this sketchbook away where Johnny would never ever find it, maybe under his mattress back home.

Now standing here with his backpack slung over his shoulder, he almost pulled out those drawings and looked at them, but stopped himself at the last minute. He didn't want Johnny or Brady to come back and see them. He thought about the payphone sitting off near the snack bar next to the wave pool. Cyndi was only seven digits away, and he had some spare change in his backpack right now. Maybe he could call and just check up on her.

No, no, no. Just give it time. He decided to let Johnny and Cyndi's relationship end if it was going to end. Then maybe....

"Come on, come on, come on," he sighed. Even now, standing in front of the silent dry Ragin' Rivers, he couldn't stop his brain from returning to that *maybe*. He didn't want to wreck his friendship over this, that would be as stupid and self-destructive as getting high and kissing another girl. What he needed more than anything was some company and a distraction. Something to distract him from that bright blonde hair that swept down

205

to one side, and those full pouty lips, and--

There was a dull, mechanical *clunk* from somewhere under the concrete beneath his feet. Eddie looked down, the images in his mind evaporating. He felt vibration under the soles of his flip-flops, and he heard a low, bubbling gurgle. In the growing darkness, it almost sounded like low laughter.

Water began trickling somewhere above ground. Eddie looked up and saw dirty brown water flowing down the Ragin' River slides, then it began to rush down in a torrent. Just for a moment, Eddie thought it was diluted with dark clots of blood, and his mouth dropped open in horror and disgust. Then the water cleared and flowed down the slides normally, swirling and foaming in the end pool just as it had earlier. The scent of bleachy chlorine lightly drifted through the air. Eddie allowed himself to sigh a little. *Get real, man. It wasn't blood. Quit acting so nervous.*

Still, there was the question of why the slides had been turned back on in the first place. Eddie glanced around, scanning the area for that guy Sheehan or anyone else, maybe some maintenance guys were coming to work on the ride. No one was anywhere near this area, he was alone. But he didn't *feel* alone. He felt like someone was out there in the woods watching him. He felt like he was being set up for some humiliating practical joke.

Eddie turned around and poked his head out through the painted white gate. The dirt maintenance road was still empty. He listened for voices, still expecting to hear the sound of maintenance guys, or maybe some of the lifeguards coming down one of the paths toward the Ragin' Rivers. He realized the rush of the water splashing into the end pool would make it impossible to hear anyone coming until it was already too late. Taking a few soft steps forward, he watched for any movement on the path or in the dark woods between the white, smooth slides. He saw nothing but shadows.

The sun was almost below the tops of the higher trees on the west side of the park now. *Sun's going down. Better get home before all the vampires and ghosts come out.* He shook his head, ridding himself of the thought of ghosts. If there was one thing under the whole umbrella of horror fiction that never failed to get under Eddie's skin, it was ghosts.

Just quit it. There's no such thing as fucking ghosts, and there's no one out here except you. Brady will be back soon, and these stupid slides will turn back off. It's probably just a glitch or something. Don't be so jumpy, for Christ's s--

From off to Eddie's left, the wave pool buzzer went off, cutting jaggedly through the air. Eddie jerkily snapped his head toward the sound. The AstroTurf beach and the wave pool were up past a short set of concrete steps from the lower Ragin' and Duelin' Rivers area, just out of Eddie's sight. He couldn't see it, but he heard the tidal wave's thunderous rush toward the shore. Without the sounds of happy laughter and cries of joy from dozens of people, the wave sounded like the rush of grim death.

Eddie looked over his shoulder and saw that the Duelin' Rivers were up and running again as well. The wave pool buzzer went off again, and Eddie faced forward to hear another wave crashing toward the shore. It was as if all the rides were turning on by themselves.

"What the fuck?" he whispered. He slowly walked to the concrete steps and went up toward the wave pool, fully expecting to see someone, anyone, standing around up there. At the top step, he looked out on the clean, deserted AstroTurf beach. Tall stacks of reclining pool chairs were clustered symmetrically along the back edge of the beach. The stacks were neatly arranged in rows and columns like classroom desks. The waves tumbled to the shore, but there was no one here to enjoy them.

Maybe the vampires are coming out for opening night, and maybe the ghosts are already here. Yes, hundreds of ghosts could be all around me right this very second.

"Knock it off," he scolded himself. It was the disjointed mixture of rides and fun, mixed with the deserted, empty silence that was getting to him.

Feedback ripped into the silence as if on cue, and Eddie screamed. The nearest speaker was mounted up on a corner of one of the snack bar buildings along the left side of the AstroTurf beach. Music began blaring out of the speaker, ringing in his ears. It was a strange song that he had once liked so much that he bought the 45, "Der Kommissar" by After The Fire. Ordinarily, he would have shouted a triumphant *YES* at the start of this song, but now it sounded slightly warped and off pitch. The sheer volume of the song was piercing. The music made his stomach flip as if the whole park had turned into one giant, sickening ride, and he was riding it alone.

Eddie walked away from the speaker, toward the wave pool. He stopped on the AstroTurf beach directly in between the speaker that had startled him and another speaker mounted on a pole along the back edge of the fake beach. The sound blared out from speakers all over the park, echoing like at a big stadium concert. Over the constant driving beat, tinny synths, and hectic rap verses, Eddie heard the harsh bray of the wave pool buzzer go off a third time. At the back of the huge wave pool, the Kaptain Smiley figure painted on the mural seemed regal, basking in the glory of the waves. Its black eyes looked hungry though, and they seemed to be staring right at him across the pool.

What the fuck is going on? he thought.

A black streak dashed between the tall stacks of pool chairs to Eddie's right. He whirled to the right, seeing only a long, empty aisle between the stacks of chairs. Someone was back there hiding somewhere. Eddie could almost feel their presence.

Suddenly he thought he understood everything. This was all a big joke. Johnny and Brady had set this whole thing up to mess with him. Johnny knew he liked this song, and Brady, well...Eddie just didn't trust Brady. Just another joke on losery old Eddie. His animosity toward Johnny rose all over again.

"Hey, I saw you guys back there!" he shouted, cupping his hands over his mouth. He wondered if they could even hear it over the blare of the music. "Okay, you got me. You can come on out and turn that fuckin' music off now! It's giving me a migraine!"

No response from behind the stacks of chairs. Eddie started toward them.

"Okay, I'm coming over so you can jump out and scare me! Let's get this over with!"

The stacks of chairs had been arranged in a big grid: four rows spaced evenly down six columns. Each stack was at least six feet tall, about four inches taller than he was. It reminded him of the corn maze he and Johnny had gone to last fall. Eddie went down one of the aisles formed by the chairs, and the blasting music was blocked out a little, his ears rung. He waited in between the first two stacks, bracing himself, then jumped into the open aisle again. No one there, in all four directions. Beyond the waves crashing up against the shoreline, that mural still seemed to be looking at him.

Nope, not that aisle, the painted Kaptain Smiley seemed to speak in his mind. *Keep going. Maybe the surprise will be down aisle number two.*

Eddie silently tried to take a slow deep breath even though there was no way anyone would hear it over that pounding music. He hated when people jumped out at him, and promised himself that Johnny was gonna get it for this. He took two great big steps forward, then jumped forward and whirled in all directions. Again, nothing. He sighed and clenched his jaw in exasperation.

Just walk casually, he decided. *They're gonna jump out at you either way.*

With tense shoulders he slowly walked forward, peering around the corners of the stacks. Each chair fit perfectly on top of the one below, it was impossible to see through them. He was pretty sure the movement he had seen in his peripheral vision had been down the third or fourth aisle, but before long, he passed both aisles with no end to his suspense.

They're moving around me. Probably behind me. Now that he thought of it, he actually *did* feel like someone was behind him.

The second chorus of the song blared out, and in his mind he registered the lyrics. They weren't just random, it was as if they were warning him. Eddie turned his head to look over his right shoulder, and as he did something cold and hard flew into his mouth. It was a metal baling hook, its jagged edge ripped into his left cheek, its hard tip poking the back of his throat. He gagged, tasting his own blood and rusty metal, then let out a choked cry. He dropped his backpack to the ground. His hands flew up to his mouth to pull out the object, but his head was instantly yanked hard to the left.

In a blur of motion, another hook whistled in front of Eddie's face. It tore down into his throat. He didn't even have time to feel the pain, he only felt an unnatural chunk of metal sticking out of the soft flesh of his throat. In a panic, his fingers wildly scrabbled over the metal hooks, trying to pull them out.

He doubled over, choking and coughing out clots of blood that dribbled and splattered on the green

AstroTurf. The blood turned dark brown as it soaked in.

The two hooks suddenly yanked in opposite directions with brutal force. The man wielding the hooks had pulled his hands apart savagely, ripping the hooked ends out of Eddie's cheek and throat. Eddie felt his skin stretch and tear, and he screamed a bloody, bubbly gurgle. His legs gave out, and the force of the yanking hooks spun him around backwards.

Eddie landed flat on his back and what little wind he had left was knocked out of him. He clutched at the shredded holes in his mouth and throat as he stared up at his murderer for the first and only time. The white mask on the man's face was like something out of a nightmare. It was an awful 3D real-life image of all those weird smiley-faces around this place. His bulky frame, clad in a tattered black jumpsuit towered over Eddie. In his white-knuckled heavily scarred hands, he held up two baling hooks. Each hook was slick with blood, and Eddie dimly felt the droplets falling off and landing on his legs. Eddie's vision began to go gray as a huge dark puddle of his own blood spread on the AstroTurf underneath him.

In one quick movement, the man in the mask whipped the baling hooks up into the air and brought them down on the metal edge of the nearest stack of pool chairs. Eddie realized what the killer meant to do at the last second and tried to cry out *NO,* but his vocal chords had been ripped out, and he only managed a bubbly wheeze.

The killer yanked the hooks sideways, putting his whole body weight into it, and the five hundred pound stack of lawn chairs toppled down on Eddie's head and chest. Tumbling metal and plastic chair webbing blotted out the last few shreds of daylight that Eddie ever saw.

*   *   *

Heads turned and faces cringed as the feedback and music began to blast out eardrums. The nine kids left at the picnic table party ceased all of their conversations and looked around anxiously at each other, searching for some kind of explanation. No one had any answers. A few of them waited to see if it was just some sound system glitch like the one that had happened earlier today. A few minutes into the song, a beefy kid with wavy feathered hair spoke up.

"Is this shit gonna go on all night?" he shouted with a hand cupped over his mouth. A few kids shrugged in response. "Let's get outta here, you guys." The others nodded in agreement and quickly walked out after him. They left Adam McAvery's boom box playing on the table. Adam had told another girl to keep an eye on it for him. He had said something about going to find that Brady Johnston guy who was apparently sneaking in some beer.

The nine remaining kids got in their cars and drove away, disappointed that the party had been such a dismal failure. Their disappointment turned to shock and relief the next day when they heard about what happened that night at Thrill River.

Chapter Fourteen:

The Last Ones Left in the Park

By the time Brady got back to Thrill River, the music had stopped and the park was utterly silent. He shifted his dark red Datsun into park outside a little maintenance tool shed next to the inflation station and looked for Eddie. On the floor of the passenger seat, underneath an old sweatshirt he kept for emergencies, beer bottles clinked softly. He had scored two cases of Miller from a friend named Jimmy Donahan who worked at his uncle's liquor store. Jimmy had to take care of a long stream of customers before he could sneak the beer out the back door to Brady's car. Brady had handed him the money and sarcastically thanked Jimmy for taking his sweet time, and Jimmy told him to get bent. They laughed and Brady hurried back to the park.

He got out of the car and saw no sign of Johnny or his goofy friend Eddie.

"Hey, Johnny. Eddie. You guys still out here?" he said in a low but audible voice. No response.

Uh-oh. That's not a good sign, he thought. An image of Sheehan standing behind Johnny and Eddie flashed through his mind, and he suppressed an urge to simply get back in his car and drive away.

Brady closed his car door softly, trying not to attract any attention in case Sheehan was around. As he walked around the front of his car, he briefly glanced at the tool shed. One of the wooden double doors hung askew and tools were scattered all over the floor, but he didn't take much notice of that. He went up the short set of wooden steps onto the tube deck and peeked out through the fence opening. The Ragin' River and Duelin' River rides had been turned back on for some reason. There was no sign of Sheehan, which was good, but there was no sign of Eddie or Johnny either.

I don't believe it. Those assholes bailed on me. Brady sighed in exasperation. Here he was going out of his way to teach those high school kids how to *really* party and have fun, and they couldn't even keep a lookout for thirty lousy minutes. He figured they must have gotten scared when someone turned the rides back on. They must have run away, afraid to get caught. What a couple of wimps. Well, his little cousin Jennifer and some of the other kids he'd invited to his "opening day party" were probably already at the spot waiting for him. He couldn't keep the beer sitting in his car.

Brady took one last look to make sure Sheehan wasn't lurking around the corner, waiting to pop out and bust him with the beer. His eyes lingered on the running rides again. Why the hell were they on again? He tried to think up a logical explanation but none came to mind.

"Whatever," he muttered as he walked back to the car.

Carefully, he stacked one case on top of the other, trying to keep the clinking noises to a minimum. He set them on the hood while he closed the passenger door softly, like he had with the driver's side door. Brady had to turn his back to the gate at the inflation station, and back into the park holding the two full cases of beer in front of him.

"Hey!" someone said, clapping him on the back. Brady jumped and spun around, the beer cases in his arms teetered precariously. Johnny stood in front of him smiling.

"Jesus Christ!" he said in hushed shout. "You scared the livin' shit outta me, man!"

"Sorry, dude," Johnny said, matching his low tone of voice. Brady looked around nervously. "Where's Eddie?"

"No idea. Here, take one of these and follow me. Keep quiet 'til we're off the path." Johnny lifted a case off the top of the stack in Brady's arms, and they set off.

They followed the path between the Duelin' and Ragin' Rivers in silence, keeping an eye out for Sheehan the whole time. Once they were over the short set of wooden steps near the bottom of the hill, they veered off to the right and went into the underbrush. Johnny wondered if they were taking the same path Cyndi had taken earlier when she dashed off to look for his sister.

"Okay, I think we're good now," Brady said, still keeping his voice low. "What happened to your goofy friend?"

"I thought he was with you," Johnny explained.

"I told him to wait at that gate for us."

"That's weird." Johnny looked around the woods, wondering if that loud music had anything to do with Eddie's absence. "What the hell is going on around here?"

"What do you mean?" Brady asked.

"After you left, I went to call Cyndi at the payphone over by the Falls. Then I was heading back up that path between the rides to get some pizza for us before it was all gone, and all of a sudden the music

215

system starts up, like, way too loud. I mean, it was blast-out-your-eardrums loud."

"What the fuck?"

"Yeah, that's what I said. It played one song, then just stopped. I don't know, it was really weird. So I came down here looking for Eddie and he was gone. I went around to see if he was over by the Lazy River, but he wasn't there either. I came back and that's when I ran into you."

Brady grunted noncommittally. He didn't really care where Eddie was one way or the other.

"I'm his ride home, so he'll probably turn up," Johnny continued, still looking around for Eddie. He was more worried about him than he let on.

"Yeah well, you better keep an eye on that guy, dude," Brady suggested. "He totally wants your chick."

"What? What are you talkin' about, man?" Johnny laughed at the absurdity of the thought. "No he doesn't." Brady gave him a skeptical raise of one eyebrow. "Trust me, man. He doesn't like her."

"I don't know. I saw them waiting in line for the Ragin' Rivers before lunch. He was totally checkin' her out."

"You're crazy man. He doesn't like her, trust me." Johnny remembered his conversation with Eddie earlier at lunch, he had seemed a little overly defensive about Cyndi. He couldn't help but wonder....

Brady shrugged. "If I were you I'd let him have her, unless she's great in the sack or something. Is she a freak?"

"I don't, uh..." Johnny almost said, *I don't kiss and tell*, but stopped himself. That would've sounded lame. "Well, we haven't done a whole lot yet, but..."

"Aww, you're still a virgin aren't you? You're killin' me, man." Brady laughed condescendingly.

"Get bent," Johnny shoved him. Brady didn't

press Johnny anymore on the subject. He only laughed a little longer, then dismissed the conversation altogether, much to Johnny's relief. Brady had planted the seed of something in Johnny's mind though, and he wondered again where Eddie was now. He looked around at the trees in the growing darkness, half searching for Eddie, half taking in the shadowy scenery. "This place kinda gives me the creeps at night."

"Yeah," Brady said solemnly. "Either that or you're just a fuckin' pussy!"

"Eat shit and die," Johnny laughed.

They reached the rocky tunnel where they could cross over to the other side of the Duelin' River. Brady climbed up the jagged rocky side first, Johnny handed him up the beer, then climbed up himself. Brady stopped and looked around, seeing only trees and shadows. No one was waiting for them at their spot.

"Where is everybody? Are we the last ones here?" Johnny asked warily, joining him at the top.

"I don't think so. You hear Adam McAvery's stereo up there? No way he'd leave without that."

Johnny listened and he could faintly hear the boom box up at the picnic area through the trees.

"Yeah, I hear it," Johnny replied. "Maybe Sheehan found a bunch of people waiting down here and sent them back up the hill."

Brady squinted suspiciously into the woods. Something just didn't feel right, and both of them felt it. Brady would never admit that he felt a nervous fluttering in his stomach, but Johnny was right, this place was creepy at night. He needed to get one, two, or maybe six beers in him to ease his nerves.

"Come on, let's get this party started before he comes back. I've got a surprise for you, dude."

They climbed down into the clearing and Brady opened up his secret storage cabinet in the rock.

"What surprise?" Johnny asked. Brady reached his arm way back into the far corner of the plumbing access where he'd hidden the joints this morning. He pulled out another crumpled plastic baggie with a bulging twisted corner stuffed with white powder. He held the baggie out in front of Johnny with an expression of lecherous pride.

"I'll let all those other assholes have a couple of beers, but I saved the real party for you and me, man. And, my cousin too, wherever the fuck *she* is."

Johnny stared down at the ugly little baggie and felt his blood run cold. Smoking a joint was one thing but this....

"Is that what I think it is?"

"Well, it's not fuckin' powdered sugar," Brady laughed, pulling a small mirror and a razor blade out of a protective blue rubber sleeve.

"Is it...coke?"

Brady laughed the same way he'd laugh if one of the kids in line for The Falls asked him if the ride was scary.

"Uh yeah, it's coke," he rolled his eyes at Johnny. "I know you're Mr. Straight-Arrow, so let me show you how it's done."

Brady set the mirror flat on the ground, untwisted the corner of the baggie, and poured a little of the white powder out onto the shiny surface. With the razor blade he pulled a fine line across the surface and tapped off the excess. Johnny watched with trepidation as Brady lowered his head to the mirror, plugged one nostril with his finger, then snorted the entire line in one smooth motion. He threw his head back suddenly and held his breath with his eyes closed. Then he began to snort and cough a little, rubbing his nose anxiously.

"Hell yeah," he said. "Now you."

Excuses raced through Johnny's mind. He had

218

to talk his way out of this somehow. Brady could be pretty persuasive, but this had already gone too far earlier. He decided to play it straight with Brady. If he didn't draw the line somewhere, Brady would drag him down whatever mad, destructive path he was taking through his life.

"No, I don't do that shit, man," he hoped the profanity would offer him a little bit of redemption. Brady saw right through it.

"Aww come on, man. Do you have any idea how much it costs to score a gram of this shit? I got this for you, dude, to teach you how to really party. So here." He stood up and practically shoved the baggie and the mirror into Johnny's hands. Johnny stepped backwards, he didn't even want to touch the stuff. He wished desperately that Eddie were here. Eddie always knew how to talk his way out of, or into, anything.

"No, man. I'm not... I can't... Just, no."

"Look, I'll even set it up for you so you won't fuck it up." Brady poured out a little more of the white powder and drew out another thin line across the mirror. He completely ignored Johnny's protests.

"I can't get too messed up. I gotta drive home. Plus, we have to be back here early tomorrow too, y'know?"

"Here, it's not gonna kill you." Brady practically shoved the mirror up under Johnny's nose, forcing him to step back even farther. Johnny had backed up almost all the way out of the small clearing now.

"Listen, man. I'm sorry, but I'm not doin' that shit. Period," he finally forced himself to speak in a clear firm voice.

Brady's face darkened. He slowly shook his head in bitter disappointment. "You're a fuckin' pussy, you know that? Here I am trying to add a little fun in your life, and you're too goody goody."

"Yeah, I know. I'm sorry, man. Let's just have a couple beers and--"

"No, just get the fuck outta here. You too good for my coke? Too good for my beers? Fuck you. You're out."

Johnny looked at Brady with wide-eyed shock. How had this guy, who Johnny considered a good friend, turned so ugly and mean so fast? Maybe it was just the drugs that were making him crazy. Maybe he could talk Brady back down and leave on better terms.

"Hey, calm down, man. I'm not too good for you, it's just--"

"You're out," Brady repeated with an aggressive edge that Johnny didn't like at all. Johnny noticed that his eyes looked bloodshot, all of his movements were becoming too quick and jerky. He was starting to look like a mad rabid dog, ready to attack at the slightest provocation. Johnny began to back away slowly. He wanted to talk Brady down, make him see reason.

"Seriously, man. I'm s--"

Without even the slightest hesitation, Brady bent down, scooped up a thick river rock the size of a large egg, and threw it at Johnny as hard as he could. Johnny instinctively stepped to the right and held up his hands to deflect it away. It whistled in, chipping his left elbow, and hitting his funny-bone. His left arm immediately went numb and tingly from the elbow down.

"Hey! Are you fuckin' crazy, man?" Johnny asked. He was outraged and more than a little frightened.

"YOU'RE OUT! YOU'RE OUT!" Brady screamed. To Johnny, he looked and sounded as if he had completely lost his mind. He bent down again, but this time he could only find tiny pebbles. He chucked them at Johnny, but in his fury, his aim was off and the pebbles bounced off into the woods.

Just get the hell away from him before something else happens. Haven't you had enough of this trouble for one day? Without a word, Johnny turned and walked back up the hill.

While Brady looked for a bigger rock to throw, he remembered the coke again. He bent down and snorted up the second line of coke. Johnny was through the trees when he heard Brady call out one last thing to him.

"If you tell anybody about my stash I'll fuckin' kill you!"

Hadn't Johnny said the exact same thing to his little sister earlier today? The weight of that hit him hard. *Did I really almost become that?* All at once he realized how much time he had been wasting with Brady over the past two weeks, and how much he had been neglecting his true friends. The problem with Cyndi hadn't been Cyndi, it had been him. He wanted desperately to grab Eddie, get the hell out of this park, and put an end to this long crazy day.

*   *   *

Johnny was so deep in his own thoughts that he hadn't noticed how quiet the party had gotten until he was crossing the bridge over the Duelin' Rivers. He looked up and was startled to see only remnants of the party scattered over the deserted picnic tables. He stopped in his tracks and looked around, half expecting the other lifeguards to pop out of some hiding places and give him a good scare. No one did.

Johnny slowly walked toward the picnic tables, searching for anyone. The boom box on the back table near the snack bar was still on, blaring Lionel Richie's "All Night Long." It was an upbeat party song, but without anyone to listen or enjoy it, it seemed inappropriate. It hollowly reverberated off the picnic tables and Lighthouse gift shop walls.

"Hello? Where the hell is everybody?" he asked aloud. It was somehow more comforting to hear his own voice out loud. The setting sun still gave a little comfort, but the daylight was fading fast. It made Johnny want to just get in his car and put the pedal to the metal. Maybe, like Brady said, he was a "pussy," but this place was just too creepy. Was Eddie even still here?

"Eddie!" he called out, cupping his hands over his mouth. He didn't really expect a response. He just felt like Eddie was gone. Just to be safe, he figured he should call Eddie's house and make sure he had actually gotten a ride home with someone else. After all the stupid things Johnny had done today, he did not want to add *Leaving His Best Friend Behind* to the list.

Johnny left the abandoned picnic area and walked past the showers to the payphone where the line had been earlier. Now the payphone sat just as silent and lonely as the picnic tables were. He scrounged in his pockets for change, then remembered he'd spent the last of it on the phone call to Cyndi's house.

"Shit," he said. He sighed, ran his hands through his sandy blonde hair, and slapped them down on his thighs. He would have to go out to his Bel Air in the parking lot and see if he could find some more change in the glove box, or maybe under the floor mats.

He went down the concrete steps and hopped over the entry turnstiles, making his way toward the parking lot. As he passed the Guest Services building, he glanced up at the wooden staircase leading up the concrete sides of the building to the control room. He had never been up there, but he had seen Sheehan come out from that metal door at the start of almost every training day. Sheehan had always been careful to lock the door behind him and give the metal handle a quick tug for safety. The blue metal door stood open now and warm light from inside spilled out down the wooden steps.

Yet another weird piece to add to this weird day. Johnny almost shrugged it off and continued to his car, but he stopped himself at the last second. *Wait, there's probably a phone up there.* He considered it, then shrugged. Maybe this was where Sheehan had been hiding all day. In fact, he may have an explanation for why the party seemed to be over so early.

Johnny turned and began up the stairs. The wood was new, but it was already creaking and squeaking under the weight of his feet. He listened for voices or any noise from inside the control room, but heard none. It almost looked as if someone had left this room in a hurry, especially considering the obsessive way Sheehan locked and double-checked it everyday.

He slowed his approach as he reached the top of the stairs, and peered into the room from the wooden landing. It was another one of those identical layouts from the other park that meant nothing to Johnny, but Cyndi would have recognized right away. Thin dark red carpet on the floors and halfway up the walls, tinted windows in the far left corner, electric switching boxes along the right wall, and soundboards and control panels on long tables to the left.

Johnny knocked softly in case there was anyone in this strange room.

"Hello?" No answer. The room, like everywhere else in the park, seemed to be devoid of human life. He pushed the door open a foot farther and glanced around the room. Just to the left of the door there was a table with a pile of at least thirty cassette tapes scattered haphazardly all over it, and on the wall behind it was a phone. Johnny walked over to the phone, lifted it off the cradle, and glanced down at the tapes on the table. He had dialed the first two numbers to Eddie's house when one of the tapes near the edge of the table caught his eye.

The label along the top of the cassette read *Go-Go's MIX*. He recognized Cyndi's small looping handwriting from a mile away. He had flipped through Cyndi's tapes dozens of times when she couldn't decide what she wanted to listen to. Running his hands over more of the tapes he recognized more of her labels. *Jun RADIO MIX, CARS MIX, BEAUTY AND THE BEAT, PUNK MIX*. He quickly realized that these were all Cyndi's tapes.

Johnny's mind was suddenly filled with questions. *Why the hell are these here? Is Cyndi here right now? Did she bring all these to the park today?* Though the most unsettling question that came to his mind was: *Did something bad happen to her, something to do with this place?*

The wooden landing outside the door gave off a slight squeak behind Johnny. He dropped the tape and began to turn. Before he saw who had snuck up behind him, something heavy and hard slammed down on the back of his head. Johnny's world went black.

*   *   *

Little did Johnny know that he wouldn't have been able to leave the park anyway, all four tires on his Chevy Bel Air were completely flat. Right after their last exchange near the payphone, Jennifer had casually wandered out into the parking lot and found Johnny's beat up old car. A few people were still filtering out of the park, most of them were kids climbing into their parents cars idling in the pick-up lane at the front steps. No one seemed to be paying any attention to her.

Jennifer glanced at them as she walked right up to the car and intentionally dropped her purse, spilling some of her belongings out onto the simmering pavement.

"Shit," she said realistically for anyone that may have happened to be looking in her direction. She hoped if anyone did look her way, they would only see a nondescript girl stooping to pick up her purse and would mind their own business.

A rusty red Volkswagen slug-bug was parked two spaces down, blocking her from sight of the front entrance. She ducked down low and gathered a few of her belongings that had scattered onto the hot pavement, but the object she really wanted had been in her hand the whole time: a thick metal nail file sharpened to a point. The parking lot was quiet, it was time.

Eat this, Johnny. She stabbed the sharp point of the nail file into the side of the left front tire as hard as she could. A jolt of panic shot through her as the nail file initially stuck tight in the rubber. With both hands she tugged the file free, and a satisfying hiss of air leaked out after it. Jennifer grinned.

She crawled alongside the car to the back left tire and stabbed that one too with that devilish grin on her face. The old clunker had begun to visibly lean to the left. One look at that drunken lean and Jennifer had to put her hands up to her mouth to stifle a fresh round of giggles.

As she crawled behind the trunk to the other side of the car, she felt a sudden nervous shiver lightly caress her upper back and shoulders. It felt like someone was watching her. She guiltily glanced around. This side of the parking lot and the road in front of the park were completely empty. Directly in front of the car was a grassy hill that led up to the wrought iron fence that surrounded the park. Beyond the fence were thick blue spruce pine trees. She felt she was being watched from somewhere deep within those shadowy limbs. Narrowing her eyes, she tried to catch some movement, or even the faint silhouette of a person. After a full sixty seconds, she decided there was nothing to see.

Relax. Everyone left in the park is either down at Brady's spot getting some beers or up at that stupid party. Just get this done.

Jennifer finished the job, but didn't take as much pleasure in it as she had with the first two tires. That eerie feeling was too distracting. When it was done, she stood up, dusted off her hands and knees, brushed her long dark hair back, and walked back into the park. She glanced back over her shoulder at the old clunker and saw the lopsided tires resting flat on the pavement. The car was now noticeably lower to the ground, looking crippled and pathetic. She gave off a tittering, high strung laugh and started up the steps.

That's just the beginning for you two, she thought. *Lots more where that came from.* Now she felt satisfied enough to let thoughts of Cyndi and Johnny go for the day. She knew Johnny would probably be with Brady down by his spot drinking some beers, and she would have to play it cool with him. She didn't want to give off any suspicious vibes.

With the nervous excitement of pulling off a costly and nasty prank, plus the drop in temperature from the approaching dusk, she felt goosebumps rise all over her arms, thighs, and back.

"Brrr," she said aloud, rubbing her arms with her hands. Her skin had a dried out, flaky feeling. *Yecchh, I gotta get in the shower and get out of this itchy swimsuit.* She remembered there were showers here in the locker rooms by the front entrance. Maybe she could jump in, clean herself off, and change clothes before heading down to meet up with Brady. It would certainly make the rest of the night more comfortable.

As she passed the ticket booths, all closed and locked down for the night, she glanced back at those tall pine trees behind the fence again. They were far off on her right side now as she made her way back toward the entrance turnstiles. She glanced over, wondering if this new angle would allow her to see if there had been a person over by those trees watching her. This angle was even worse though. With the setting sun behind the trees, all she could make out were black silhouettes.

Her foot came down precariously on uneven ground and she quickly faced forward. She gasped as she looked right into the face of a tall man in a grinning mask and sea captain's uniform. It was that stupid bronze statue out in front of the park, Kaptain Smiley holding hands with the two laughing kids. She had been so focused on trying to spot a person by those tall pine trees that she had stepped into the bed of river rock and flowers, and almost walked right into the statue.

"God! Fuckin' thing." There were a lot of things that Jennifer hated, but somewhere up on her top ten all-time hate list was being startled. On impulse, she cocked back a foot to kick the statue right in its bronze shin, then thought better of it. She definitely did not want to add a broken foot to today's list of injuries. With an icy smile, she leaned close to it and in a low voice dripping with venom she said, "Fuck you, Smiley-Face."

Just as she finished that last word, "Der Kommissar" erupted from the speaker mounted on the backside of one of the ticket booths behind her. She screamed and jerkily spun around. The music was loud enough to make her ears ring, and she glared at the speaker. "Fucking piece of shit sound system."

Enough was enough. She'd had more than enough of the lonely jitters for one night. The grinning statue stood there passively as if mocking her. She gave it a final squinty glare, then jogged to the showers.

Before Jennifer turned and walked into the ladies' room, she saw the lifeguards clustered around the picnic tables. None of them noticed her. Over the harsh blare of the music on the speakers, Jennifer didn't hear the beefy kid with the wavy hair say, "Let's get outta here, you guys."

Jennifer went around the curved brick wall into the ladies' room and the music became a bassy, muffled echo behind the tiles at a blessedly lower volume. The lights were still on and she had the whole bathroom to herself. She went to the second shower stall on her left, set her purse down, and turned on the warm water. It came out in a high pressured jet that roared in the quiet bathroom and drowned out that music even more. She pulled off her gray off-the-shoulder T-shirt and pulled her pink ball barrettes out of her hair. In the mirror on the opposite wall, she caught another glimpse of the bruises on her face. She sneered at the sight of her injuries, but smiled when she remembered the four flat tires on Johnny's old car.

Have fun with that tonight, Johnny, she thought as she kicked off her flip-flops and pulled the shower curtain closed behind her. Under the warm water, she peeled off her wet, red and black bikini, and hung it over the left side of the shower stall.

If not for the loud music outside, one of the lifeguards may have heard the running shower, and stopped to make sure Jennifer had a ride home. If not for the roar of the shower, Jennifer might have heard them leaving, asked where they were going, and asked for a ride home herself. Noise canceled out noise though, and Jennifer became one of the last few people left in the park.

A minute after she started her shower, Jennifer noticed that it had seemed to quiet down outside the ladies' room. She slicked back her dark hair behind her ears with her fingertips, and listened. There was only the roar of the shower now. Someone had finally fixed that broken sound system, and turned off that awful, ear-splitting music.

"About time," Jennifer muttered and forgot all about the music.

Jennifer liked to take long showers. Her dad was always getting on her case about the water bill. He and her mother were cold, uptight people who were almost never around. They lived in the rich houses up on Hart Street, and spent almost all of their time at work, some social event, or at Indian Hill Golf Course. There they put on fake smiles and charmed their friends and coworkers. At home, they were free to be themselves: unpleasant, hostile, and bitter. After a week long business trip, Jennifer's father usually greeted her with, *"Look at this phone bill,"* or, *"Look at this water bill. You think we're made of money, Jennifer?"* Anytime he brought it up, she wanted desperately to shoot back her own questions about the bills. What about *his* golf club bill? Or *her mother's* designer dress bill? Or *both of their* liquor store bills? She didn't contribute when it came to the bills though, and comments like that would have only brought her a quick backhand to the face. So she kept her mouth shut, hating them in silence.

This wasn't home though. Here she could stand under the hot water and wash this long, hot day away as long as she wanted. With her eyes shut, she let everything go; her parents, that little bitch Cyndi and her stupid boyfriend Johnny, those lifeguards that kept yelling at her and her friends, and her friend Lisa's bitchy mom who had flat-out refused to let Lisa keep her company and stay late for the party. She let the water wash over her face, inhaled the fresh steam floating up from her wet body, and exhaled out all of her bad feelings.

One feeling refused to evaporate with the rising steam though: that ugly, violating feeling that she was being watched. She had forgotten about that feeling as she thought over the day in her mind, shampooing her long mane of dark brown hair, but now it crept back under her skin. She couldn't tell why that feeling wouldn't go away, she was alone in here.

Are you? Are you really alone?

That was enough to make her wipe the shampoo off her face and open her eyes. It felt like there was someone in here with her. She hadn't heard any squeaky shoes on the tile, or seen any shadows along the back wall, but she felt someone's presence just the same. Also, she'd had her eyes closed and her ears plugged up with running water as she washed out her hair.

"Hello?" she called out, her voice reverberating loudly on the tiles. The echoes of her own voice faded and the silence seemed to be waiting, holding its breath, not moving a muscle. "Stupid," she whispered to herself. Of course she wasn't alone. There were people right outside. She could still even hear their boom box playing some synthy new wave hit.

Despite her own reassurances, the goosebumps that had disappeared under the hot shower stream returned on her arms. She let out an irritated sigh and rubbed her arms with her hands. Leaning forward, she put her head directly under the water again. The pressure tickled her scalp, and the warm water ran down into her ears. She opened her eyes again, and behind the blurry stream of water, a shadow had fallen over the pink tiled back wall. It was as if someone was standing right behind her, blocking the soft light bulbs that were mounted above the mirrors on the other side of the room.

Jennifer spun, her bare feet squeaking on the shower floor. She wiped the water out of her eyes, clearing her blurred vision. There was no shadow behind the translucent pink shower curtain. If someone really was in here, they were doing a damn good job of pretending they weren't. An idea occurred to her that maybe it was someone pulling a prank. Maybe one of those lifeguards, maybe Brady, or Johnny, or even that goofy, moronic friend of theirs. *That would be fitting wouldn't it? You ruin Johnny's relationship and slash his tires, so he peeks on you naked in the shower. Tit for tat, literally. That would be just wonderful.*

Just peek out there and see. She slowly reached for the edge of the shower curtain. Now she held her own breath, meaning to catch the prankster off guard. She hoped to catch them red-handed. If it was Johnny or one of his pervert friends, she would scream *Rape* at the top of her lungs. Then they'd see who was laughing.

Her fingertips stopped an inch away from the curtain and she braced herself, mentally counting down: *1, 2, 3!*

Jennifer ripped the curtain back, the metal loops rasping harshly along the shower rod above. She made sure to pull the plastic curtain back behind her body, covering herself up so she wouldn't expose anything to those pervs. Her eyes darted back and forth, but there was no one to see. The bathroom was totally empty except for her. She even craned her neck and tilted her head to look under the toilet stalls, no one there either. It had all been her imagination, hallucinations of a guilty mind. It still might not be a bad idea to get her swimsuit back on though.

Just as she reached for her top, it slipped over the side into the other stall.

"Goddammit," she said. Well, at least now she knew there was no one in here, she could sneak over to the other stall and grab it quick. She peeked out from behind the shower curtain again, now noticing the cold air outside the stall, it made her want to shiver. She still had the bathroom to herself.

Holding her arms up to cover her breasts, she tiptoed out of her stall, shivering and dripping all over the place. She flung open the shower curtain.

A huge, hulking man stood slightly bent forward in the shower stall. The killer lunged forward, hard white hands groping for her throat. Jennifer let out a piercing and echoing shriek. She fell back a step and slipped on the smooth tiles. Her bare butt hit the floor hard.

For a second, she thought the bronze statue in the front of the park had come to life and followed her into the showers. He had the same white grinning mask on his face, but this mask wasn't perky and fresh like the one on the statue outside. It was drawn and fading, giving it a sick, sad look.

The man lumbered out of the shower stall toward her, and she scrambled back away from him, her naked flesh squeaking against the floor. In her panic, she had let him herd her back into her original shower stall.

"HELP ME!!! OH GOD, HELP!!!" she screamed. Someone would come running. They had to. No one came.

Panting behind that drooping smiley mask, he stepped into the shower stall with her, crowding her in, ignoring the running water drenching his black jumpsuit. His bulk filled the opening, there was nowhere to run. She screamed hoarsely and kicked out at him with her bare feet.

Hard bony fingers shot out, one hand catching part of the billowing shower curtain. They clamped around her throat, choking off her screams, reducing them to raspy gargles. Holding her by the throat, he lifted her up off the shower floor, pulling her face towards his own. Her legs kicked out desperately, sliding against the wet walls of the shower stall. She was close enough to smell his stinking, garbagey breath behind the mask. She tried to support herself and take some of the pressure off her throat by clutching his thick forearms. Water from the shower head ran into her face, blurring her vision and pouring into her mouth, nose, and ears.

Why won't they come? Someone... Anyone....

His fingers tightened around her throat and her head felt like it was going to burst. She could feel the blood pulsing in her eyes and brain. Now the water wasn't just blurring her senses, the world was going gray, starting to spin.

Someone... Anyone... Anyone at all... please....

*   *   *

The station wagon pulled up to the drop off lane in front of Thrill River for the second time that day. The front gates were still open, and there were close to twenty cars still in the parking lot. She looked up at the smiley-faces painted high on the ticket booths. In this darkening, dusky light, they looked much more like the horrors she remembered from last year.

They're just drawings that's all. I'm not crazy, she thought.

"I don't like this," her mother said from the driver's seat.

"Mom, please don't make it worse for me," Cyndi pleaded. "I have to do this. I have to talk to Johnny and get this off my chest. We've both waited long enough."

"Why don't I go in with you?"

"Mom!" The thought of showing up with her mom at a party, sent almost as much of a chill down her spine as those smiley-faces. "I'd die of embarrassment." Cyndi opened her car door and heard the faint sound of the boom box up the hill.

"Cyndi..." her mother couldn't think of anything else to say, she just had a bad feeling about this whole thing. She'd had a bad feeling about everything that happened so far today.

"Listen, can you hear that stereo? There's gonna be at least twenty other people here, maybe more. I have to go find Johnny." They had both glanced at his car in the parking lot when they pulled in, but neither of them noticed the flat tires.

"What if I wait for you?"

"Mom, please. You're being pushy."

"Okay, okay. But you call me if you can't find him."

"I will."

"And stay where everybody else is. Don't go wandering by yourself."

"I will." She had already pulled her seat belt off and was stepping out of the car.

"I love you, Cyndi."

"I love you too, mom. And thanks."

Her mother sighed in exasperation and threw up her hands. "You're welcome." She was coming to find out that there was just no reasoning with a teenager.

"See you soon." Cyndi shut the car door and walked up the steps into the park. Her mom watched until she was up the steps and out of sight, then pulled away reluctantly. She drove slowly, checking her rearview mirror often just in case Cyndi decided to come running back to the car to call the whole thing off. It was only wishful thinking. Her only consolation was that there were only a few more hours left to wait out this emotionally turbulent day, then Cyndi would come home and it would all be over.

Cyndi walked in between two of the ticket booths, and barely gave the bronze statue a glance. She kept reminding herself that it was only a stupid statue and the smiley faces were only stupid drawings. She walked quickly up the second set of steps, eager to join the crowd of lifeguards that she expected to see up at the party. The control room door was closed, she didn't even give it a glance.

The last sliver of sun was sinking below the horizon, and the eastern half of the sky was a moody, bruised purple. Cyndi noticed it, but didn't mind. She only planned on being here for a short while anyway. She would find Johnny and tell him they had to talk, tell him that she was going to tell him everything. Then they would get Eddie and Christie, and drive back to his house in his car. Once they were safely there, she would spill it.

As she walked toward the sound of the party, Cyndi felt like she was about to burst. The whole dark story was bubbling at the tip of her tongue, desperately ready to be brought out into the open again. She felt more free than she had in months, it brought a smile to her face. The smile faded as she reached the lockers outside the bathroom building. Something was wrong. She could hear the boom box playing some song, but nothing else. No laughter, no giddy flirtatious screams, no chatter, no other typical party sounds.

She slowed her pace as she approached the deserted picnic table area. Half-empty cups of soda sat randomly on the tables, a few had even turned over, spilling the sticky liquid onto the concrete. Napkins had fallen onto the ground and were fluttering away in the slight breeze.

"Johnny?" she called. "Brady? Anybody?"

Cyndi walked into the middle of the picnic area and stood there stunned like a lone survivor after the apocalypse. The combination of the twilight sky and the abandoned mess of the party somehow made her feel more sad and lonely than she had ever felt in her life. There had been people here before, now they were all gone and she had no idea where they went, or why.

She turned and looked at the boom box. It blasted out a song she knew from her own record collection: "All Through the Night" by Cyndi Lauper. *At least it's not "Girls Just Want To Have Fun,"* she thought. This song's eerie similarities to "Girls Just Want To Have Fun" worried her though. The volume on the boom box had been turned up loud, and the way it echoed through the rest of the park added to her feeling of desolation and abandonment. She walked over to the boom box, noticing that it looked almost new with hardly any scuffs or dents. *Who would just up and leave a boom box as nice as this?*

On impulse, she reached out and clicked off the stereo. The song cut off abruptly on the last loud swell of the synthesizer solo during the bridge of the song. It was one bizarre song, almost perfect for a bizarre setting like this. Now silence prevailed, except for the familiar sound of rushing water on the nearby Duelin' Rivers.

And you thought earlier today this place was a reminder of last year? That was nothing. There's the Duelin' Rivers start right over there. Why don't you go hide behind that waterfall? Remember that? Remember what happened after that? Remember how he had been waiting underwater and splashed up out of it?

All of a sudden Cyndi's paralysis broke. She sprinted for the front gate, jumping over the short sets of steps in great leaps. The thin soles of her flip flops provided little padding and her feet stung on impact. She glanced back to see if she was being chased, but there was no one. She sprinted past the payphone. No time to call anyone, she had to get out, just get the fuck out!

Cyndi ran past the ticket booths and out the front gate. She took the last steps two at a time, and

236

dashed out into the middle of the nearly empty parking lot. Breathing hard, and with her back still turned to the park, she slowed to a stop. She had made it out, gotten a safe distance away. There was no barbed wire, no electric fence. Just a deserted water park.

Am I crazy? No, no. I can't be. Maybe they just moved the party somewhere else. There's still a bunch of cars here. They have to be here somewhere, right?

An electric whirring and loud metal clunk started up behind her. It was the first noise she had heard from the park since the boom box. Cyndi turned around slowly. The masked man that she had seen so many times in her nightmares over the past year stood there in the center of the front entrance. The front gate slid closed in front of him as he slowly waved to her with his white, scarred left hand.

"No, no, I'm not seeing this. Nope. I'm not seeing this. I'm not," Cyndi mumbled as all the blood rushed out of her face. Her stomach lurched and her heart hammered crazily.

The faded grinning mask, the tattered black jumpsuit, the crooked, slump-shouldered way he stood, he was unmistakable. He continued to wave to her like an old friend. In front of the killer, the gate slid fully closed with a heavy, reverberating thunk. The shock wave of the gate closing briefly vibrated through the wrought iron fence. He had locked himself in.

He lowered the left hand and raised his right, pointing back over his shoulder towards the park.

First them...

Then his long fishy white finger swung around and pointed directly at her.

Then you.

Cyndi understood him perfectly well. Her mouth dropped open in terror and she almost sobbed.

"No," she whimpered. Then her breath grew deeper more rapid, she felt the scream rising in her throat. "NOOOOOOO!!!"

Cyndi ran back to the gate with her fists clenched furiously. She was in survivor mode again. It had been the same when she thought Christie had gone missing earlier. She had thought it was starting up again then, but she had been wrong. It had been waiting to start up again tonight, and she had to put a stop to it before it was too late for Johnny, or Christie, or anyone else.

In her half-crazed state, she ran toward the gate. She lost her footing and almost fell face-first on the pavement, but she caught herself and continued running. When she gained her balance and looked up again, the killer was gone.

She rushed back up the steps and slammed her fists on the gate. The gate clanked and the bars hummed with the impact of her fists. She tugged on two of the bars to pull it open again, but it only clattered against the heavy locking mechanism. He had locked her out before she could interfere.

Cyndi slammed her fists against the bars one last time and screamed. "JOHNNYYYYYYYY!" She had no idea where he was, or if he could even hear her at all. She hoped to God that she wasn't too late.

Chapter Fifteen:

Runnin' With the Devil

   Brady Johnston was completely out of his mind. He had only done coke once before, while waiting for a Van Halen concert to start. The first time he tried it, he loved the huge rush of energy it gave him. At the concert he had been drunk enough to really loosen up and have a great time, but the coke also made him alert and gave him enough energy so he could really appreciate the show. Toward the end of the concert, he had gone into a rage when some idiot tripped and fell into him during "Everybody Wants Some," one of his favorite songs. After a shouting match, Brady almost slammed his fist into the guy's irritating face, but the guy disappeared into the crowd.

   This time though, the rage had hit him instantly. Johnny's refusal to party struck a nerve somewhere in his brain, and he flew off the handle. It wasn't the first time he had been under the influence of something and gotten in a fight. His inebriated short temper was actually the real reason he had to come home from school and work at this water park with a bunch of high school kids. He had gotten in a fist fight with a kid at a dorm party back in April, and put him in the hospital. The school expelled Brady. He rarely talked about it with anyone, not because he was ashamed of it, but because he honestly couldn't even remember why he had done it, it was all a blur in his mind.

Johnny was smart to leave when he did, otherwise he may have ended up getting his face rearranged, just like the kid back at the dorm, or just like his little cousin Jennifer after she pissed off Johnny's little girlfriend earlier today. Brady knew Jennifer was all talk and childish pranks, but he was not.

After Johnny's departure, and Brady's second line of coke, he began to wonder why he should bother to share his beer with a bunch of assholes at all. If they were too good to come down the hill and party with him, screw 'em. He began to down his beers more quickly, so he wouldn't have to give so many away once someone came down the hill.

Brady lost track of time and lost track of beer. *Which beer was this? Seven or eight? Who knows? Who cares?* He still felt the rush from the coke, but it wasn't enough. He laid out another line on the mirror, and up it went. A fresh wave of energy rushed through his body and he yelled out, echoing into the night. Looking around the little clearing, Brady felt cramped. He had to get up and move, had to go somewhere or do something.

"I'm gettin' the fuck outta here," he murmured to himself. He jumped to his feet, wobbled a little bit, then stood steady. "Last call for alcohol!" he shouted with his hands over his mouth, giving the other lifeguards one last chance to finally come down the hill. No one came. "Fuck it."

Brady buried the unopened case of beer in a nest of pine needles under a nearby pine tree. With his foot, he pushed the other, mostly empty, case into his little cubby hole in the rock, grabbed one more for good measure, then kicked the door shut. He put the beer bottle in his mouth, planted his hands on top of the rocky overhang, and swung his legs up in one quick movement. He jumped back down off the other side just as quickly, landing in an agile, bent-kneed pose with his hands on the ground that reminded him of those old Spider-Man comics he used to read when he was a little kid. The coke made him feel like was a superhero right now, like he could do anything, lift any weight, kick anyone's ass.

It was full dark now, and the ground was treacherous, but it didn't slow Brady down. He trampled through the underbrush, making his way downhill and chugging his fresh beer in huge gulps. The beer had disappeared into him before he made it even halfway down the hill. He chucked the empty bottle off into the woods, and heard it shatter somewhere in the dark. He wished he had brought another one, or maybe two or three.

In the dark, Brady lost all sense of direction. He took a meandering path, stepping underneath Ragin' River slides and leaping over a Duelin' River every so often. Unfamiliar trees surrounded him, and thick, viney undergrowth seemed intent on tugging at his ankles and wrapping around his legs. He felt a tickly, squirming sensation on his shin, and looked down to see a big, brown wolf spider the size of a golf ball scrambling up over his left knee and onto his thigh. Attached to its belly was a huge, white egg sac that actually looked like a golf ball. With a disgusted cry, he slapped it away and began to shiver all over.

"Ugh! Fuck!" he shuddered. "I gotta get the fuck outta here."

A rip of feedback and a crunch of static responded to him. The sound came from somewhere off to his right and he turned that way. He listened as a swelling sound that reminded him of an oncoming train whistle blasted from the speakers all over the park. Then the sound faded off, and there was a low, pulsing bass note that began to repeat.

"Oh, fuck YEAH!" he shouted, his voice rising with excitement as it dawned on him. Whoever was running the sound system had happened to play his all time favorite song: "Runnin' With the Devil" by Van Halen. He ran toward the sound of the nearest speaker, eager to get out of this creepy crawly area.

In less than a minute, he ducked underneath another Ragin' River slide and emerged out of the woodsy area on a clear, grassy slope. At the bottom of the slope, a concrete sidewalk divided real grass from fake as the AstroTurf beach stretched out in front of him. Beyond that were the calm waters of Hurricane Bay, the wave pool, sparkling in the moonlight. Now he had his bearings again. He began bobbing his head to the driving beat, and played air guitar along with Eddie Van Halen. He noticed something was wrong with the recording though, it sounded like a warped record leaning slightly on and off pitch. At least the volume was cranked. When it came to "Runnin' With the Devil," Brady Johnston wouldn't have it any other way.

As Brady walked out toward the wave pool, he looked over at the tall stacks of pool chairs and a brilliant idea came to him. He decided to climb on top of the chairs as if they were a stage and rock out to an imaginary audience in the wave pool. Now he would really get to see what it was like on stage during one of those Van Halen concerts. Sure there weren't any real people here, but what the fuck? It was probably just the rush from the coke, but he felt like a rock star.

He ran over to the closest stack of chairs and began pulling himself up. The stack of chairs tottered, threatening to fall back on top of him. He hopped to the side and let them crash down onto the AstroTurf. If the light had been better, he might have seen the dark brownish-red pool of blood that he was standing in, it had soaked into the AstroTurf between the stacks of pool chairs.

Thin wisps of moonlight lit up enough for him to see between the rows of stacked pool chairs. Another one of the stacks had already fallen over too. Maybe some other clown had the same idea earlier. He tried to step up again onto a different stack, and the pool chairs tipped toward him.

"Motherfucker," he said, stepping down again. He suddenly lashed out, pushing against the stacks of pool chairs. He felt a childish sense of satisfaction as he watched them tumble like dominoes. The last stacks hit the ground and spilled out the top few chairs, they scattered onto the AstroTurf. He pushed the other few rows over and watched the huge dominoes fall. On a whim, he began to pick up some of the chairs and throw them around the beach. Some of their metal legs bent, and the plastic webbing broke as they hit the ground.

Eddie Van Halen's first guitar solo kicked in, and Brady stopped throwing chairs to listen to it. He looked back out at the wave pool in disappointment, his imaginary crowd was still waiting for him to take the stage. Then he understood, the stage wasn't here at all. This was the back of the stadium, the nosebleed seats. He had to go up to the front, past the premo seats in the deep end of the wave pool. There was a four foot ledge made of metal grates along the back mural of the wave pool that allowed the lifeguards to easily cross from one side to the other. Through the gaps in the grate, you could look down and see some of the pumping, churning machinery that created the waves. Since there was no guard rail, the ledge was off limits for the guests, but

Brady was no guest. He was a lifeguard, and right now he was the only one around. He might as well own this whole fucking area for all anyone knew. That back ledge was his stage, and the mural of that weird Kaptain Smiley character was his backdrop.

He ran to the back of the wave pool, cutting across the water in the shallow end, and singing along with David Lee Roth. He passed the lifeguard stations and looked down into the wave pool. Pale white moonlight glittered on the calm surface. Over the pounding music and the blood rushing in his temples, he could almost hear a crowd in the pool cheering him on. At the real Van Halen show, he had screamed his head off when the lights went low and they took the stage. The ghost crowd in the pool was going fucking nuts just like that, and it was all for him. Hot ghost girls were yanking their tops up, flashing their huge breasts at him. Other ghost girls were throwing their hotel room keys up at him. One of them was that hottie in the purple bikini from The Falls ride earlier. He pointed down at the ghost girls and they went even crazier.

Brady reached the back of the wave pool and stepped onto the ledge. Before he could look down at his admiring, imaginary ghost crowd, he stopped dead in startled surprise. A man in black stood on the middle of the ledge.

"Whoa, what the fuck?" Brady said.

Brady hadn't even noticed the guy at all until he had turned to face him. In the darkness the guy's black jumpsuit just blended in with the shadows and the mural. It was the stark contrast of his white face that caught Brady's attention. He was wearing some kind of rubber Halloween mask of the Kaptain Smiley guy that was on the mural and all over the park, only this mask looked like it had seen better days. It looked saggy and faded, making the eyes look almost sad, the grin drawn down almost to a grimace. Brady blinked his eyes, wondering if this guy was real or if he was just hallucinating him. It almost looked like he was seeing double between the guy's mask, and the huge identical face painted directly behind him.

"Who is that?" Brady asked loud enough to be heard over the blasting music. The guy only stood there staring at him. "What the fuck are you doing up here, man?" Again, no response.

The man stood slightly sideways to him, and Brady could see something metal in his other hand glinting in the moonlight. When the man turned a little, he saw it was one of those long poles the lifeguards used called a Life Hook. It was ten feet long and had a loop at one end that you could use to rope someone back to the side of the pool if they were drowning.

Brady was starting to get irritated with this guy. After everything he said, the guy just stood there staring at him like an idiot. He tried to think of who the guy might be. He was tall, maybe six four or six five, about the same height as Brady, and the guy was bulky too.

The masked man took a slow step toward Brady, then another. Brady took a step back.

"Whoa! Hey, asshole. You trying to freak me out or something?" Brady asked. "You don't wanna fuck with me right now, man. I'll beat the fuck outta you."

The guy only cocked his head and took another step forward.

Brady suddenly felt that rage building up inside him again like a fire. Was this masked moron seriously trying to play chicken with him up here? *Okay, he wants to play?*

Brady took his own step forward, the man didn't flinch.

A loud buzzer blared out behind Brady, it was even louder than the music. It was the buzzer to signal

245

the start of the waves. He was so startled that he broke his eyeline with the masked man. Then a rumbling vibration came from under the ledge, the wave machinery was cranking and revving up. Brady looked down to see white water rushing under the grates beneath his feet. Splashes of water at the back wall of the wave pool erupted upwards.

Brady looked back at the masked man just in time to see the metal pole swinging towards him. The hard plastic loop of the Life Hook slipped perfectly over his head. The killer yanked at the back end of the Life Hook and the loop tightened around his neck like a noose. Brady's hands flew up to his throat, trying to loosen the plastic loop as he began to choke.

Before he could even begin to yank the loop off of his neck, the masked man swung the pole to the left in a quick, strong pull. Brady felt himself lose his balance. He toppled off the ledge and splashed right down into the white hectic rush of the surging wave. The man held on with white-knuckled fury as the wave tried to wash Brady out towards the shore.

Brady felt his body flopping and tumbling helplessly in the water. The thick plastic loop dug deep into his neck in the tender spot just below his jawline. He choked and clawed at it with desperate fingers. In the rush of the wave, he had no control over his body. He could only kick feebly in the water. He felt the sting of water up his nose and in his eyes, but they were minor annoyances compared to the digging noose around his neck, cutting off all his air.

In his panic and drug-induced state, he used all his strength to free himself from the stranglehold of the Life Hook. The muscles in his arms and chest burned with effort. The loop loosened a little, and he managed to get his fingertips under it. He tried to gasp for breath, but only inhaled water. As he began to cough, the killer

246

yanked the noose tight again, reducing his coughing to harsh, gagging bark noises that ripped at his throat. His fingernails dug into the skin of his throat and only helped cut off more of his air and blood circulation.

The water pulled his body back toward the back wall again as the machinery sucked in water for another wave. As Brady tried to kick himself away from the wall, he realized that the killer had set the wave on a continuous cycle. He knew from his week of training that you didn't want to go anywhere near the back wall during a continuous cycle. The machinery acted like a set of lungs, pushing a wave out, then sucking water back in for another. There were safety grates at the bottom of the back wall where the waves came from, but the sheer force of the water could still hold you under until you drowned. The deep end of the wave pool was nothing to fuck around with. Brady kicked hard against the water's pull, knowing that if he didn't choke to death, the wave machinery might still suck him down toward those grates anyway.

Another wave surged forward, rolling and tugging at Brady. The killer refused to let go. He held the loop agonizingly tight around Brady's neck, pulling it in hard short bursts as if he were playing with him. Brady felt like his head was about to explode from the pressure. Blood vessels burst in his eyes, turning them a ghastly red as they flared with intense pain. The wave washed over him, and his face felt close to the surface. He tried to shriek for help, but all that came out was a gurgling, choked growl that bubbled under the water and was drowned out over the blare of the music.

He managed to free one hand and clawed at the metal pole itself, trying to pull it out of the killer's hands, but he had no leverage against the waves that were sucking him back toward the wall again. His fingernails scratched and slipped uselessly over the smooth metal.

247

His legs kicked and shook against the current, they began to convulse. He felt himself growing tired.

Oh God, no, no, no. I'm dying. Oh dear Jesus, I'm fuckin' dying! Gotta stay awake. Gotta--

It was a losing battle. The killer continued yanking in harsh tugs at the loop around his neck. He couldn't even breathe in great gulps of water with the noose cutting off his windpipe.

Stay awake, stay....

A fresh wave pushed forward and Brady let his arms drop into the current. Everything began to go gray. Some parts of his body had gone numb, and he couldn't even feel the water anymore. The last thing Brady Johnston heard was the faint bass thump of the end of "Runnin' With the Devil," his favorite song.

*   *   *

When the music started up, Cyndi almost turned and bolted from the park. She could have run down through the open field toward the slummy apartment buildings and into the rough older neighborhood, but it wouldn't have helped anything. What if the music was just a trick, a ruse to get her to run out in the open? That masked maniac was cunning, she couldn't trust him at all. That cryptic pointing gesture replayed over and over in her mind. *First them, then you. First them, then you.* He would come for her, oh yes, no doubt about that. If he had tracked her down this far away from Camp Kikawa, surely he could figure out where she lived. She had to deal with this now. It was either her or the killer, and she prayed that Johnny, Christie, and Eddie were still alive and safe somewhere in the park. If anyone knew what they were dealing with and could keep them safe, it was Cyndi, and finding them was her top priority.

Before the speakers began that eerie, deafening

song, Cyndi had gone to Johnny's car in the parking lot. She was far too young to drive, but this was an emergency. She'd thought that she could see if he had a spare key hidden somewhere. Johnny had never told her about any hidden spare keys, but that didn't mean there wasn't one there. Maybe she could drive to the nearest police station and tell them everything.

As she approached the car, she noticed the flattened bottom of the front left tire. She glanced at the back left tire, it had also been deflated and sat flat against the warm pavement.

"No. Oh God, no," she whispered, running around to the passenger side. Both tires on that side were flat too. "You son of a bitch!" She slammed her fist down on the hood in frustration. He had thought of everything. She desperately wished she knew how to hot-wire a car, everyone on TV seemed to be able to do it.

Just as Jennifer had done earlier, Cyndi turned around and looked up at the tall, shadowy blue spruce trees up on the grassy slope behind the wrought iron fence. Her friends were in there, and once again she had ignored Stacy's words: *We gotta stick together.* She had run home earlier today, and run out of the park a few minutes ago, but she wouldn't run home now. Plus there were payphones inside, and she would be able to call the police. Getting inside the park was the fastest way to get help.

First them, then you.
Better get going then.

Cyndi quickly walked west along the wrought iron fence searching for an opening. A lot of this side of the park seemed to still be under construction. Large construction equipment sat dead and silent, metal edges glinting in the moonlight. Cyndi stared at the concrete sides of a large in-ground slide whipping wildly down

249

the hill. She wondered what ride from the old park they might be recreating: the Dead Man's Drop maybe, or the Gold Mine Tunnel? The new slide didn't exactly resemble either of those rides as she remembered them.

The fence and the parking lot stretched back around the park. The hill that had seemed so steep near the wave pool and the Ragin' River slides began a slow gradual descent. Cyndi passed the farthest corner of the parking lot and continued alongside the fence. On her side of the fence, there was another large, open field that rolled downhill towards a small stream and a marshy area thick with cattails and tall cottonwood trees. Inside the park, she saw that fresh green sod had been laid in neat rows all the way up to the fence. It had barely begun to take seed before they opened the park.

At the bottom of the grassy hill inside the park, Cyndi caught sight of the new slide again. It led directly into a dark pyramid the size of a house, guarded by what looked like the rounded head and shoulders of a sphinx. For some reason, that pyramid filled her with a sense of dread. She slowed her pace and stared at the brooding Egyptian shapes for a moment, wondering what fresh terrors might be waiting for anyone stupid enough to go inside. Somehow this new ride seemed oddly familiar to her. Hadn't she seen something about it last year, a blueprint or something? She couldn't remember.

You're not here to sight-see, you've gotta get in there, she scolded herself. She forced herself to face forward and ignore the pyramid as she continued around the park.

Halfway down the hill, the wrought iron fence ended and a ten foot tall chain-link fence continued in its place. The chain-link fence was attached to the wrought iron with twisted metal loops, and the two fences overlapped for a few yards. Cyndi scanned the ground and found a thick twig resting in the tall weedy grass.

She picked it up and tossed it at the fence. It hit and fell to the ground harmlessly, with no hint of sparks or electricity. She reached a hand toward the fence slowly, half expecting to get a horrible electric shock. She tapped the fence with her fingertips, then immediately yanked them back. No shock, no jolt of pain, no seizure, no sparks.

With both hands she grasped the chain-link portion of the fence and tugged at it. It rattled but didn't budge more than an inch. So much for sneaking through. She looked up and saw ugly jagged loops of barbed wire around the top of the chain-link fence all the way down the hill. The wrought iron was too slippery to climb, and it had sharp points at the top of each bar. So much for climbing over. At ground level the chain-link had been buried in the dirt too deep for Cyndi to simply yank out the bottom and climb inside. So much for crawling under.

Of course not, did you really think it would be that simple? The only way in and out now is probably through another damned drainage pipe.

That was when the speakers roared to life with "Runnin' With the Devil." Cyndi let go of the fence and took two cautious steps back. She would've had the same reaction if she had been petting a big dog that suddenly turned to her and snarled.

"Shit," she whispered. Music meant trouble, trouble for Johnny or anyone else left in the park. "Johnny!" she cried out again, knowing that no one would hear her. From here, the music was a reverberating echo, but she knew that inside the park it would be ear-splitting.

Whatever you're gonna do, you better do it fast.

"Please God, don't let it be another pipe," she said out loud, shuddering at the memories and images that flew through her mind. She began to run.

As it turned out, Cyndi didn't have to face another pipe after all. She ran along the fence, scanning it for openings. Along the way, she listened carefully for the sound of screams over the blaring music, but heard none. At the bottom of the hill, the fence turned at the southwest corner of the park, and Cyndi began to follow the fence along the park's southern edge. Her shoes began to squelch and stick in the soggy ground, and she became surrounded by cattails and buzzing mosquitoes. Chirping crickets and a few croaks from a bullfrog somewhere in the marsh became loud enough to compete with the music. Without warning, her foot plunged down into ankle deep water. She had reached the stream on the far south side of the park. The chain-link fence crossed over the stream just ahead of Cyndi, and she could see its bottom edge hanging six inches above the lightly trickling water. If the stream had been at its regular levels, it may have been deep enough to cover the bottom of the fence, but the past week had been hot and dry so the water was low.

Cyndi noticed that the fence had a slightly bowed out look at the bottom, as if someone had grabbed it from the other side and tried to pull open a hole. Had the killer been messing with the fence? She didn't know. It looked like the best place to sneak into the park though.

She began pushing up the bottom edge of the fence, trying to force a wider opening between the stream and the chain-link. Bending down on her hands and knees she was able to lift the fence up another eight inches off the ground. She tried to ignore the mud that squished under her legs. *It's just mud, you've been in worse stuff than mud.* An image of one of the rotting faces from the Dead Man's Drop popped into her mind and she forced it away. With one arm holding up the fence, she slid underneath, her face only an inch above the mucky water. She was careful not to let her white shirt or pink shorts get stained. Her legs sloshed through the brackish water into the park, and she let go of the fence. It snapped back, pinching her fingers. She winced and pulled away from it.

Holding her aching pinched fingers, she stood up and looked back at the safe world outside the fence. Right then, the music came to an abrupt halt. Cyndi turned around and stared forward up a short slope into the dark silent water park. She was in, and she wouldn't see the outside world again until this was over. *That is, if I make it out of this alive.*

Chapter Sixteen:

The Screamin' Demon

      Cyndi steered clear of the wave pool. On the huge AstroTurf beach she would be completely exposed. She knew the staff party Johnny had wanted her to go to was long over now. Whether it had come to a quiet end or a horrible, destructive one she didn't know. Just past the fence, up a short slope and to the left, there was a huge covered wooden deck. Above the waist high railing, she could see crates and stacks of tubes in various sizes. It seemed to be some kind of spare tube storage building. Straight ahead, and farther up the slope, she could see the slanted blue tin roof of the building that stood at the deep end of the wave pool and housed the wave-making machinery. To the right of the wave pool was the long snack bar building. From the fake beach, the snack bar had looked like a perfect little set of huts you'd find on a real beach. At this angle, she could see that the building bent in the middle, kind of like a hockey stick. She assumed that the bent end of the building was the small set of bathrooms that was directly between the wave pool and the Ragin' Rivers slides. The back side of the snack bar building was ugly and unpainted. There had been no grass or flowers planted back here either, and her flip flops slapped on hard packed dirt and weeds. Only the employees were supposed to see what it was like on this side.

Cyndi crawled up the weedy slope, trying to remain inconspicuous. Before she made it halfway up the slope, she stubbed the toes of her left foot against something plastic lying in the weeds. She winced in pain and looked down to see the black curve of a telephone lying in the weeds. She picked up the phone and saw frayed wires dangling at the end of the flexible metal cord. Understanding dawned in her mind. It had been the payphone near the wave pool, ripped out by brute force and tossed away into the weeds.

"Figures," she whispered, dropping the phone back in the dirt at her feet. She had a feeling that all the rest of the phones all over the park were like this too. Now there was nothing to do but try to find Johnny and the others, then get the hell out of here.

Running in brief spurts and stopping behind whatever thick tree or bush she could find, she made it to the back side of the snack bar. With her back to the wall, she glanced left and right, then side-stepped slowly along the back side of the building. Every time she came to a back door leading inside the building, she braced herself and jumped past it, praying that the killer wouldn't jump out from behind one of those closed doors. She ducked and crawled beneath the few windows into the back kitchens. She planned to go all the way to the far edge of the buildings, dash past the Ragin' River's end pool, and sneak back into the woods as she had done earlier today. If Johnny and the others were still alive, they may still be at that little hidden spot of theirs between the rides.

The snack bar building ended and Cyndi crept up behind a wooden tool shed. She pressed her ear up against its white wooden wall, half expecting to hear cold, patient breathing muffled behind a rubber mask. She heard nothing but the sound of her own pounding heart. Creeping around the corner of the tool shed, she took extra care to make her footsteps as silent as possible.

A red Datsun sat parked at the end of a dirt road in front of the tool shed. Cyndi guessed that the road was reserved for staff and maintenance workers. From this side of the tool shed, she stared at the car, wondering who it belonged to. She wasn't very surprised to see that all four tires on this car were also flat. She leaned out farther around the front corner of the tool shed and tried to see inside the Datsun, looking for watchful black eyes or the white flash of a mask ducking behind the front bucket seats. The car seemed to be empty.

Finally she felt comfortable enough to step out from behind the tool shed. One of the shed's double doors stood open a few feet. It was almost pitch dark inside, but the moonlight illuminated enough to show her that it was a mess. Shovels and gardening equipment lay scattered, a burlap bag filled with grass seed had spilled out onto the ground. A rake hung halfway out of the open shed doors as if someone had knocked it down in a hurry and hadn't bothered to pick it up again.

Cyndi almost walked away from the shed, but stopped herself. *What are you doing? You have to grab something for protection. That masked psychopath already raided this thing, you should too if you want to stay alive.* She scanned the ground for something she could take with her.

A pipe wrench? *No, too heavy.* One of the garden trowels? *What are you gonna do, dig him to death?* A small sprinkler pipe saw? *Maybe.* Its dull edge didn't look very threatening though.

Cyndi finally decided on a small sod knife after

noticing its hooked three-inch blade glimmering in the moonlight near the open door. She picked it up and ran a finger along its edge. It was slightly dull from use, but the point on the end was still wickedly sharp. If she had to use it, the small knife would probably be able to do some damage against the soft vulnerable skin on the killer's white hands and neck. It was also small enough to fit most of the way into the pocket of her pink shorts in case she needed to use both hands. She wrapped her fingers tightly around the curvy wooden handle. Holding the blade sideways, she raked it sideways across an imaginary killer's throat, then gave the knife a satisfied nod.

Time to get going again. Cyndi saw the wooden inflation-station deck dead ahead, and looked past the stack of deflated tubes to the partially open gate. From here she could see that it led out to the walkway in front of Ragin' Rivers end pool. *Do I go the long way around or try this door?* She took a gamble, deciding that it would be best to get up the hill sooner rather than later, and walked silently up the wooden steps.

When Cyndi reached the top step, she peered out through the open gate and saw an eerily familiar sight, the Ragin' Rivers and Duelin' River's end pools sat deserted in the dark. Water ran down the slides and splashed into the end pools for no one. The coast was clear as far as she could tell, it was time. She silently took a deep breath and felt her hands and knees begin to tremble. She looked back over her shoulder, wishing desperately that she could just turn around and run all the way home. She knew she couldn't do that though. She'd gone too far to turn back now.

Before she could lose any more of her nerve, she sprinted through the gate. She felt a mad urge to shriek as she crossed the walkway and ran in between the two sets of slides. Panic and adrenaline shot through her nerves like electricity as she raced up the short wooden steps past the end pools and into the grass and the bushes that marked the edge of the woods. She whirled around raising the knife, fully prepared to slash out at anyone chasing her. She was alone.

Where the hell is he? she wondered. There was no sign of the killer or anyone else, and she had to have some cover. She stepped through the bushes for the second time that day.

As Cyndi followed the Ragin' River slide that swooped overhead atop its concrete beams, she thought about the question she had asked herself. *Where the hell is he?* He wouldn't just stalk her and follow her around, would he? Probably not. They had a history, and he most likely felt the need for vengeance. She was sure that if the killer was nearby, he would finish her off quickly and savagely. He wasn't though, and that could only mean one thing: there were other people still in the park. The killer was probably going after them right now. Maybe he was even saving Cyndi for last, savoring her terror. *First them, then you,* right?

Soon she was at the rock bridge that passed over the Duelin' River tunnel. She climbed over it, remembering the path she had taken earlier. She dropped down on the other side of the rocky bridge, and the smell of beer wafted into her nostrils. It definitely smelled like someone had been drinking over here, but there were no sounds of talking or laughter. *Oh God, that's not a good sign.*

Cautiously, she made her way around the rocky outcropping and gasped as she caught sight of what was in Brady's clearing. Three bodies now lay sprawled near the open doorway of a little maintenance access opening set in the rock. There were two boys and a girl, all wearing red lifeguard swimsuits. The girl's head was split open right down the middle, she stared up at the

258

night sky with flies buzzing in and out of her gaping mouth and eyes. Thankfully, the two boys were face down. A boy with a crew cut had dark yellow bruises on his neck, and another guy's head and shoulders were wet and drying slowly in the cool night air. The bodies looked as if they had been dragged here, and piled up for storage like they had been in the Dead Man's Drop. A dozen empty beer bottles were scattered around them, a few of them broken. The beer bottles seemed strangely out of place though. The only bright side to finding the three dead lifeguards was the fact that she didn't recognize any of them. Neither of the boys had Johnny's side-flipped sandy blonde hair, or Eddie's curly auburn hair.

Nausea gripped her stomach and she felt the sandwiches her mother made earlier wanting to come back up. She rushed to the far edge of the clearing, bent over, put her hands on her knees, and tried to fight off the urge to vomit.

That was when she heard the girl crying. Her head jerked up startled. Had that been real or had she imagined it? It came again, weak sobs coming from somewhere up the hill.

"Christie?" she asked out loud. The crying girl didn't respond. She sounded too far away to hear Cyndi's voice, but Cyndi didn't dare speak any louder and give away her position. Instead, she rushed out of the clearing past two tall evergreen trees, toward the voice. If Christie was still out here, she was still alive. Cyndi still had time to save her.

Her heart surged as she rushed through the trees. She wanted to sprint to the crying girl, and tell her that it would be all right. She tried to stay quiet, but her urgent need to reach the girl pressed her harder. As the sound of the weeping grew louder, Cyndi ran faster.

"Christie!" she cried out, unable to help herself.

She burst through the trees and looked around disoriented, not knowing exactly where she was in the park. There was a concrete path in front of her, leading up a steep slope to her left. Directly ahead stood tall plastic palm trees and the diagonally tilted green sides of some kind of slide. She suddenly realized she had walked down this concrete path earlier today with Eddie and Christie. It had led them down to the high grassy area with the Rocky River ride and those high slides called the Falls. The green ahead of her was the AstroTurf covered sides of that steep roller coaster ramp called the Screamin' Demon. Even Eddie had looked a little nervous about that one.

Where was the girl though? Cyndi couldn't see anyone in the darkness. Maybe they were up over the slope on her left at the picnic table area, the place where she had seen the abandoned remnants of the staff party. She turned to leave when she heard the crying again, clearer this time. Looking in that direction, Cyndi had to squint to make out the dark shape at the bottom of the Screamin' Demon ramp, it was barely moving. It was a girl's head.

"Help me!" the girl cried out between choking sobs. "Please! Anybody! Help!"

"Christie!" Cyndi shouted.

Cyndi ran over to the sobbing girl. She stopped near the green side of the ramp and her mouth dropped open as she realized that the girl, who's head seemed to be somehow attached to the slide, wasn't Christie at all, it was Jennifer.

Jennifer looked up at Cyndi and her eyes widened, she became frantic. "Cyndi! Oh my God! Thank God! Cyndi, please! Help me! For the love of God, help me!" Jennifer was somehow attached to the ramp, her head had been placed perfectly between the two metal coaster tracks. She faced forward up the ramp

260

and could only turn her head slightly in Cyndi's direction. Her long dark hair was a wet tangled rat's nest. From her neck down, she was completely underwater. Cyndi was dumbstruck, her jaw hung agape. She was completely at a loss for words as she tried to comprehend this bizarre sight.

"Cyndi!" Jennifer wailed, her voice cracking. Fresh tears ran down her face. "Please!"

That snapped Cyndi into action. She bent down at the edge of the pool and examined the situation. Through the rippling surface of the water Cyndi could see that Jennifer appeared to be naked and tied to a large wooden support beam underneath the slide ramp.

"He tied me up, Cyndi. I can barely fuckin' move! Oh God, it hurts!" Jennifer whimpered. Cyndi could see Jennifer's pale arms pulled tight against the thick beam.

"What do I do?" Cyndi asked. Her mind felt like a sluggish car's engine trying to turn, but failing to catch.

"Help untie me! Hurry before he comes back again!"

Cyndi climbed down into the water, ignoring its cold temperature and the fact that she was fully clothed. She ran her hands over the rope and Jennifer's limp, pruny fingers. Coarse rope, the same stuff used in all the nautical looking railings throughout the park, coiled around Jennifer's wrists which felt bloated and choked from the lack of circulation. Cyndi felt the thick knot below Jennifer's wrists. It was twisted in so many incomprehensible, overlapping loops. Another rope dug into the small of Jennifer's back several times, then came up over her shoulders and crossed her back in an X pattern. This second rope came together in an even bigger knot a foot below the first.

"Okay, okay. I got it," Cyndi whispered,

remembering the sod knife in her hand. She took a deep breath, trying to gain some sense of control over her panic. She plunged the little sod knife into the water and began sawing at the thick ropes. She felt the tough, soaked fibers slowly begin to rip apart.

"Thank God. Oh, thank God," Jennifer sobbed. "Cyndi, I'm so sorry. For everything. I swear I'll make it up to you. I'm so sorry. We can be friends again, I swear I'll be nice to you again." Cyndi was still struggling to wrap her mind around the whole situation. She hadn't really thought much about Jennifer since she decided to come back to the park. Now with Jennifer crying and completely at her mercy, she only felt embarrassed.

"Don't worry about it," Cyndi muttered, it was more of an automatic response than anything else. The last thing on her mind were her problems with Jennifer and her friends, which seemed so petty when compared with the danger they now faced.

"No, I mean it, Cyndi. Really. I'm sorry. I'll do anything you want. I'm so so sorry." As Jennifer cried, she pulled and struggled against the ropes. Cyndi felt the knife's edge slip against it a few times and she had to feel around with her fingers to find the cut that she had been working on.

"Just shut up and stop moving so much," Cyndi snapped. Jennifer's mouth clamped shut with an audible click.

The rope wasn't coming apart fast enough. Now Cyndi felt stupid for bringing this small knife instead of that little pipe saw from the equipment shed. She used all the force in her wrists but as the blade dulled, it became harder and harder to cut the rope. She had only made it a quarter of the way through, not nearly enough to free Jennifer.

"Shit, it's too thick," Cyndi growled through clenched teeth.

262

"Hurry!" Jennifer whined. Cyndi lifted the blade out of the water and ran her thumb along its edge. It felt dull and useless.

Suddenly there was a loud thud from up on the top end of the slide that vibrated all the way down the wooden ramp. Jennifer started to shriek in fresh terror. Cyndi's blood ran cold as she looked up and saw the killer in the little gazebo at the start of the ride, looking down at them with one heavy boot up on the top of the ramp.

"Get me out! Get me out! Cyndi! Please!" Jennifer screamed.

"Shit!" Cyndi whispered, her voice filled with panic. She slammed the blade back into the water and began to saw desperately at the rope. Jennifer struggled and yanked her body with all her force against the ropes, making it harder for Cyndi to cut it. "Stop moving, goddammit!" Jennifer ignored her and the ropes bounced up and down in Cyndi's hands. The small rippling waves around their heads became choppy with their frantic movement. One wave splashed up, dousing Cyndi's face.

There was another shuddering thud from up above. Cyndi glanced up and saw that the killer had grabbed one of those heavy red sleds from the neat stack at the top. The back wheels had thudded as he dropped them down on the track. As Cyndi watched, he dropped the front wheels down and the sled locked into place. Cyndi understood everything now, he meant to send the fifty pound sled down the track, crashing right into Jennifer's screaming head.

"No! Help me, Cyndi! Help! Help!" Jennifer shrieked and thrashed even more wildly now. Her brown eyes were huge with terror. She leaned back away from the tracks as much as the tight ropes would allow, but all she could do was expose more of her neck to the path of

263

the sled.

Cyndi felt overwhelmed with panic, she had no time to cut all the way through the rope. While she continued to saw at the rope, she glanced around, looking for someone else to help, or some alternative plan. There was no one, and nothing of use around. She looked up at the killer as he stepped off the track. He wrapped his long white fingers around the long metal sled release lever.

"No! Don't! Don't!" Cyndi screamed at the top of her lungs. It was the only thing she could think to yell. Under the water, she sawed furiously at the ropes with the sod knife.

Jennifer only shrieked over and over, pushing her body back with her feet up on the slippery wooden beam for leverage. Her arms and shoulders were white with strain, she would dislocate her shoulders before long.

The killer waited for a moment, savoring their screams. Then in one quick yank he pulled the release lever. The red sled began to roll forward down the track. It rumbled and shook the whole ramp as the girls screamed.

Cyndi watched in terror as the sled picked up speed, rocketing toward them. The last thing she could think of to do was hold her arms out and try to catch the sled before it struck Jennifer in the face and broke her neck.

As Jennifer watched her own death roll straight towards her, she felt a sharp stab of pain as something pulled loose in her shoulder blade.

The heavy sled flew towards them at thirty-five miles per hour. Cyndi reached towards it, bracing herself for the impact. *That thing's gonna break my arms,* she thought. At the last second, her instincts kicked in and she pulled her arms back.

264

"NO!" Cyndi shrieked.

The sled slammed into Jennifer's head. It caught her in the chin and her neck snapped back at a grisly unnatural angle. It made a loud crunch sound like wet celery. Her last scream was cut off immediately as the sled struck her jaw. Her front teeth clacked together, cutting half of her tongue off in one quick chop. Several of her other teeth shattered upon impact. Fragments of teeth and the bloody pink end of her tongue flew backwards into the water. The sled bumped over the bottom of Jennifer's chin, which now faced the sky, and actually launched four feet into the air.

Cyndi caught all of this in one nauseating glimpse just before she turned away in horror. She heard the sled splash back down, sending out a fan of water before it stopped and sunk to the bottom of the pool. She was unable to hold back her own agonized sob. She gagged in revulsion, trying to lean toward the pool's slippery concrete edge. The horrifying image of Jennifer's head snapping backwards had been burned deep into her brain.

A heavy clatter and thunk jerked Cyndi back to reality. She looked back over her shoulder, up the green-sided ramp at the top of the Screamin' Demon ride. The killer had tossed another heavy red sled onto the platform and straightened it onto the tracks with a heavy kick.

He turned away from Cyndi's line of sight for a second, then returned holding a blood splattered baling hook. With black eyes focused on Cyndi, he climbed on top of the sled. Cyndi realized with horror that he was coming for her. Defensively, she gripped her hand tight around-- Nothing.

"Shit," she cried, searching for her knife. She frantically felt around her shirt and pockets, then on the wooden ramp and the edge of the pool. In her panic before Jennifer's death, she had dropped the knife somewhere in the water. "No, no, *no, NO!* Where is it?" She ran her fingers around the wooden beam and the ropes she had been trying to cut through. A few times she touched Jennifer's rubbery, lifeless arms, they felt like dead eels.

Up above, the killer swung the baling hook at the metal lever and pulled it back again. He began rolling towards her.

"Come on, come on." With her feet, she felt around the bottom of the pool and suddenly her foot connected with a small solid cylinder. It was the knife's handle. "Yes!"

The killer's sled began to pick up speed as it rumbled down the ramp.

Cyndi wedged the knife's handle between her toes and lifted her leg up, trying to pick the knife up with her foot like a monkey. The handle slipped out from between her toes. She wedged it in her toes again, lifted her leg, and again it slipped out. She gave an impatient panicky scream as she looked up. The killer was rolling down towards her, gaining speed by the second. He raised his left arm across his chest, holding the baling hook out sideways with his white fingers curled around its thin metal handle. He meant to snag her with the wicked hook in the soft flesh of her neck, or underneath her jaw.

She tried to wedge the knife between her toes again, but it was too late. The killer was only ten feet away, racing towards her at suicide speed. He swung the baling hook at her head. She ducked down into the water at the last second, feeling the wind from the hook's sharp, bloody point as it sliced through the air mere inches above her head.

Underneath the surface, the cold water around her head seemed to give her a sense of extra clarity. As the killer's sled thumped over Jennifer's body again, she

266

felt the dead arms and legs jerk and convulse. There was a splash as the killer skidded forward.

Go! Go! Grab the knife and run!

Cyndi blew air out through her mouth and reached for the bottom. She wrapped her fingers around the knife and tugged. The curved blade was caught in some kind of drainage grate at the deepest point in the pool. She pressed one hand on the bottom of the grate to give herself extra leverage and felt several splintery shards of Jennifer's teeth on the grate's surface. She ignored her own revulsion and with a twist of her wrist, the knife came free.

She kicked off the bottom of the pool and gasped for breath as she burst into the open air. Behind the water running down her face, she saw the killer's grinning white mask sloshing towards her in the water. He waded through the waist-deep water, slashing ineffectually with the baling hook. Cyndi screamed and spun to the edge of the pool, glancing over her shoulder at the approaching maniac. He was too close, and gaining.

With the knife in her hand, she lifted herself up and out of the pool. In the process, she lost both her flip flops. Water cascaded down her body and splashed onto the concrete. She lifted her right leg out of the pool first and kicked herself forward, scraping her right shin on the rough concrete edge. The killer swung out just as she jumped away. The razor point of the hook came down inches behind the soft skin of her bare left foot, cutting into the concrete with a stony *chink* sound.

Cyndi tumbled to the grass next to the concrete path. Looking back, she saw the killer lifting himself out of the pool right behind her. She scrambled to her feet and sprinted back into the woods the way she came.

Zigzagging like a rabbit, she ran through the trees, ignoring the sharp stabs of pine needles and jagged rocks under her bare feet. The killer was almost a foot and a half taller than she was, and much faster. She glanced back every few seconds to see if he was within swinging range. She took a quick hairpin turn. He skidded to a stop in the underbrush, spraying up clouds of dust and pine needles, then tore after her again. With the baling hook, he hacked viciously at any low tree limbs that got in his way. She took two more sharp turns, and each time she heard the killer's raspy muffled breathing become more savage and murderous with frustration.

Her heart pounded painfully as she ran. Exhaustion was setting in too fast. Had she gotten this tired so fast last year? She made one last quick rabbit turn, almost a full U-turn this time, and headed back uphill. She curved around a huge pine tree and saw no sign of him. As she continued running she listened for him, but couldn't hear much over her own gasping breaths and thunderous heartbeat.

Oh shit, where did he disappear to? She allowed herself to slow down the tiniest bit and continued in her same direction. She looked around wildly, trying to get the drop on him before falling prey to one of his traps.

Cyndi came to a large bed of river rock at the edge of a familiar ride. It was the entrance pool to the Duelin' Rivers. She looked at the bubbling fountain under the rock overhang on her right and the stack of large green tubes across the water. It all gave her a weird feeling, like she had traveled back in time a full year. It was almost as if she had fallen asleep in the park, and everything that had happened over the last year had only been one long dream, and here she was again finally waking up.

No time for nostalgia now, unless you want to end up like Jennifer.

In her mind she saw Jennifer's head slam back violently and heard the wet crunch of her broken neck, it brought Cyndi back to reality. She shook away the feeling and spun around, putting the Duelin' Rivers start pool behind her. On her left she could see the gazebo at the top of the hill where you boarded the sleds to ride down the Screamin' Demon. On her right, wild trees and undergrowth tangled downhill in between the Ragin' and Duelin' River slides. The white mask was nowhere in sight. The crickets and the splash of the rides were the only noise.

"Fuck!" she whispered. He was out in those woods somewhere, hiding, catching his breath. She had to get back down the hill again. She had two choices: get the fuck out of here, or die. *But if my friends die.... No time to think about that now.*

If she wanted to get down to the bottom of the hill again, the fastest way was to ride one of the Duelin' Rivers down. The Ragin' Rivers were too far away, and she didn't trust them anyway, not after Brad. Her survival instinct kicked in, and she turned and ran toward the pool, jumping as far as she could across the slow-moving water. The last thing she wanted was to get caught wading across if the killer decided to come out of hiding. She made it three quarters of the way across before she splashed into the blessedly warm water. *I hope to God that he didn't hear that splash*, she thought. Her throat felt so dry from running that she was half tempted to bend down and take a few huge, chlorine-filled gulps.

She waded to the other side and climbed up the steps out of the pool. Water cascaded off her soaked pink shorts, and she had to pull up one of the shoulders on her sopping wet off-the-shoulder T-shirt. She tracked dripping wet footprints on the concrete as she walked over to the stack of tubes. After another long look and listen for the rushing footsteps of the killer, she safely tucked the knife in her back pocket, reached up, and yanked a tube off the stack by its black handlebar. She hurriedly bypassed the slow entrance pool part of the Duelin' Rivers, dragging the green tube all the way to the fast drop off point.

Once she finally reached the drop, she heaved the tube over the pool's edge right in front of the drop off. She hopped on and her forward momentum pushed it down into the fast current. The tube accelerated as it slid down the ride, its rubber sides whispering occasionally as it scraped against the concrete. The cool breeze chilled her wet hair and the wet T-shirt that clung to her body, and she began to shiver a little. She turned and looked back at the entrance of the ride, expecting to see that white face peering down at her, getting ready to jump on his own tube. He wasn't there.

Hadn't she tried to send a decoy tube down this ride last year? Maybe the killer would think that she had tried that again and would search behind the fountain for her. Or maybe that was just wishful thinking. When you were running for your life, sometimes wishful thinking was all you had to keep you going.

The tube slid up over the first high curve, carrying her out of sight from the entrance pool. She allowed herself a sigh of relief. She had made it this far at least. Suddenly, an awful image arose in her mind: the killer already down at the end pool waiting for her, one hand holding that bloody hook, the other waving to her as he had at the gates. The thought sent a fresh chill down her spine and she faced forward, silently praying that it wouldn't become a reality.

She came around another curve, heading towards that wooden bridge that led to two of the Ragin' Rivers starting points. Earlier that day she had been up on that bridge waiting in line for the Ragin' Rivers with

Christie and Eddie. A shiny glint high up above the wooden rails of the bridge caught her eye, a curved hook in the moonlight against a hulking black silhouette.

Cyndi shrieked as the killer jumped off the top rail of the bridge, his black form flying down through the air like a huge bat. She cringed and covered her head as he landed on top of her in the tube.

A hiss of air blasted in Cyndi's right ear as the sharp point of the hook punctured the green side of the tube only an inch from her head. His knees buckled as he landed unsteadily. She felt his entire weight crushing down on her. His animal panting and grunting seeped through the eye-holes in the mask, and his horrible breath washed sickeningly over her own face. He rocked back and forth, struggled to gain his balance as she screamed and beat at him frantically with hard fists.

The tube went up over another one of those wild curves and the whole world turned on its side. The killer rolled off of her and onto the side of the tube. It leaned alarmingly, threatening to tip over and spill them out into the raw current.

With her legs free, she began to wildly kick him in the belly and chest. He gave a hard grunt and slipped off the edge of the tube. He held onto the handle of the baling hook, and was dragged behind the tube on his stomach. White foaming water rushed up, spraying his mask.

In one powerful yank, he pulled himself forward onto the back edge of the tube again. With his free hand he caught Cyndi roughly by her blonde hair. She cried out in agony as she felt several wet chunks of hair rip free from their roots.

He twisted the baling hook, trying to free it from the rubbery side of the tube. She caught a glimpse of this as he pulled her head down at a painful sideways angle. Seeing the hook reminded her of the knife in her pocket. She pulled it out and wildly began slashing at his arms. His grip on her hair weakened, but he refused to completely let go. She forced herself to slow down and aim her next slash, then raked the sharp little blade across the white skin on the back of his hand. It tore open a deep, bloody gash.

He howled beneath the mask, let go of her hair, and held onto the baling hook's handle with a death grip. She reared back the knife again, and with a warrior's cry, she stabbed it deep into his shoulder.

At once, the killer let go of the hook and rolled limply into the rushing current. The wet handle of the sod knife slipped out of her wet grasp, the blade was still buried deep in his shoulder. Cyndi felt both panic at losing the knife, and a surge of triumph watching him roll slowly down the slide as her tube continued to speed forward.

Suddenly the tube leaned again and she almost fell over. She had been facing backwards throughout her struggle with the killer. Now she faced forward again and saw that she was going through one of those circular tunnels. In the tunnel, everything became pitch black for a second, then she rounded the corner and saw the dead boy hanging upside down from the overhang at the end of the tunnel.

Cyndi screamed again as the dead boy's limp hanging arms struck her in the face and shoulders, smearing her with blood. In the moonlight she could see the horrified expression etched into his face in death. His bulging eyes seemed to look at her. His throat was a raw, unraveled mess, with strings and ropes of gristle hanging down over his white chin.

She wiped the dead boy's blood out of her hair and eyes as the tube went down the final stretch. Red streaks stained her white shirt. She turned back, expecting to see the killer rolling down after her, but he was gone. As she approached the end pool, she looked back one more time, thinking he may have lost a lot of speed out of the tube. Still only rushing water followed her down.

Cyndi sighed uneasily. She had successfully fought him off, but he'd gotten away from her yet again. She had gained the advantage now, but she would have to hurry to keep it that way.

The tube hit the final reverse jets in the end pool, and it slowed to a stop. Cyndi jumped out of the tube, her legs splashing in the water. She twisted the metal baling hook out of its ragged puncture hole and it came free easily.

"Jesus," she said aloud. He had been only inches away from pulling it free and jamming it down into her leg, or arm, or something worse. With the baling hook in her hand, Cyndi ran back toward the south end of the park, hoping to sneak back under the fence and run for help. She took the most direct route, running toward the wave pool, Hurricane Bay, not knowing that fresh horrors awaited her there.

Chapter Seventeen:

Beach Party

What about my friends? The question kept nagging at Cyndi as she ran for the fence. What about Johnny, Christie, and Eddie? What about anyone else unlucky enough to be stuck in here tonight? What if they were all still here and alive? She couldn't just leave them like she left Stacy and Zack. She couldn't put herself through that again.

She remembered the brittle crunch sound of Jennifer's neck breaking, and a new dreadful thought occurred to her. *What if they're already dead? What if I'm the last one left...again?* The sheer loneliness that came with the thought chilled her heart. She shook her head, trying not to jump to conclusions.

Maybe there was still a chance. Maybe she had pissed him off enough that he would just keep coming for her, and she could lead him away from anyone else that was still in the park. All she wanted to do was get out, but in the darkness of Thrill River, the outside world seemed like it was a million miles away.

Cyndi's first impression as she ran up the

concrete steps and out onto the AstroTurf beach at Hurricane Bay was that it was full of scattered bones. White, twisted bones seemed to be scattered all over the beach, gleaming in the moonlight. That wasn't right though. She blinked and made sense of the image in front of her. They were too long to be bones, too shiny, and the angles were too perfect. Now she recognized the white shapes for what they really were: the pool chairs.

Dozens of chairs were strewn about at canted angles, some tilted on their sides, some upside down. They looked as if someone had taken them off their neat stacks and violently thrown them all across the beach. A lot of the chairs were now broken and bent, lying on top of each other and leaning drunkenly. The adjustable backs of some jutted into the air like dead arms.

Cyndi uttered a surprised gasp as she noticed that there were people sitting in some of the chairs. A dozen still, slumped people had been placed in them like moldering mannequins. Dead girls' legs spread in very un-ladylike fashions across them, and dead boys' heads hung back on lifeless necks. All of their faces were locked in tortured grimaces. Cyndi remembered how she and all of the other park patrons had sat on these chairs earlier in the sunlight, lounging in the heat and dripping dry from swimming in the wave pool. Now the dead people sat under the cold moonlight, and the only thing that dripped off their arms and legs was dark, clotting blood. Black puddles stained the bright green of the AstroTurf underneath the bodies.

Out on the silver surface of the water, around twenty more bodies bobbed up and down with the gentle rolling waves. She noticed that not all of them were kids. A few were grown men with scruffy beards and dark gray construction jumpsuits. The killer had taken some of the construction workers again. The whole scene looked like some kind of horrible graveyard beach party.

Cyndi clapped a hand over her mouth in horror. *My God, it's the Dead Man's Drop all over again, only this time it's bigger.* She hadn't even realized that her feet had carried her into the tangle of chairs toward the shore. *Better go, get the hell out of here. Find a phone, call the police. Unless you want to join the dead. Unless you want to be that psycho's grand finale, his final revenge for escaping last year.*

Cyndi turned to run, and stumbled into one of the chairs, jamming her shins on the metal. Her foot caught in its rubbery, plastic webbing, and she fell to her knees. The baling hook in her hand clattered to the green surface. Her hands came down in front of two dead feet, the blood pooling underneath the skin had turned the toes a bluish black color. This body was slumped down so low that she hadn't even noticed it rotting on the beach chair as she walked toward the wave pool. Now, from the ground, she looked up at it, her face only a few feet away from its head.

Eddie's wide, glazed eyes seemed to be staring directly into hers. His mouth hung open, covering only a small portion of the ragged remains of his throat. The color in his lips had faded to a pinkish-gray. Several dark purplish-yellow bruises covered a lot of his skin. Most of his bones looked fractured and misshapen beneath the graying skin.

"Eddie. Oh God, no," she whimpered, feeling fresh tears burn her eyes.

She slowly backed away from him, letting her tears fall freely, but being careful not to sob too loudly. She looked around at the other bodies in the chairs, then at those floating in the water. Was one of them Johnny, or Christie? A sick sinking feeling told her that they probably were somewhere out there. She would never have time to find them though, at least not if she wanted

276

to get out of here alive. Did she really want to find them anyway? Just seeing Eddie like that had been horrible enough.

They're all dead. All of them. I was too late. I never should've left them here.

Across the wave pool, the huge painted Kaptain Smiley on the mural held his arms out over the scene. This place, full of death, was his legacy. The mural had looked inappropriately dark during the day, but in the moonlight surrounded by bodies, it looked right at home. On the left side of the mural, she saw that the killer had even replaced the shark that hung by its back fin with the body of a teenage boy in red lifeguard trunks. The boy hung upside down from the gallows just like the shark. His pale arms and blonde hair swayed slightly in the breeze above the wave pool.

Suddenly there was a light splash from down in the water right near the shore line. Cyndi jumped. She looked down at a dead girl floating closest to the shore, the body was only fifteen feet away. Had it just moved? *No, no, no, don't be stupid. They're all dead. It was probably just the breeze.*

For only a brief second, she took her eyes off the floating body to pick up the baling hook again. She held it tight and began backing away, but bumped into another chair. A cold hand caressed her leg and she whirled, uttering a short scream. She had bumped into another of the corpses slumped in a chair. Its crushed, bloody ruin of a face gazed up at her with flat, miserable eyes. At the sight of that face, she felt another sick wave of nausea.

Time to go. No more of this. Just get out. Get out, that's all!

Cyndi turned her back on the bodies and walked away from the dead beach. She shuddered and brushed the wormy, slimy feeling off her leg where the dead boy's hand had touched her. Some of the weight lifted off her chest as she returned to the concrete path, away from the helter-skelter maze of tangled chairs and scattered bodies. Inside that stinking jumble of metal she had felt claustrophobic. Now that she was free, she began to run for the back fence, urged on by her own terror and revulsion. As she ran, she thought of Eddie again and wondered where Johnny and Christie's bodies might be. Would she have to spend the next year of her life having them visit her in her nightmares too, just like Zack and Stacy?

What if they're still alive?   What if they need me?

Why was that thought still nagging at her? Why did she feel so compelled to stay here?

On impulse, she turned and took one last look back at the wave pool again. She couldn't ignore the feeling that she was missing something. Something caught her eye off to her right and she slowed down. She had made it to the edge of the snack bars and the far back wall of the wave pool. From here she had a much better view of the dead boy hanging upside down from the shark gallows. His feet were tied together in loops of thick rope. His white, sleeveless T-shirt gathered and piled up under his chin in loose folds. She saw his feathered, sandy blonde hair hanging down and realized that she recognized him.

"Johnny," she gasped. Unable to stop herself, she ran to him across the grassy incline toward the high ledge and back wall of the wave pool. She went through a break in the fishnet fence that lined the edge of the wave pool, then out onto the grated ledge where Brady Johnston had taken his last steps less than an hour ago.

Cyndi stopped in front of Johnny and crouched down. His face looked red and flushed from the rush of blood, a thick vein popped out on his forehead. With one arm, she reached out and gently caressed the side of his head, wanting to pull him toward her for one last kiss. She felt clotted blood caked in his hair.

Johnny's eyes suddenly flew open and he gasped raggedly. Cyndi jumped back alarmed, not believing what she was seeing. Johnny looked around wildly, uttering confused grunts. Then his eyes met Cyndi's and some of his disorientation seemed to clear.

"Cyndi. Wh--" he wheezed. "What are you doing here?"

"Johnny." She put the hook down, grabbed his head with both hands, and kissed him firmly on the mouth. He winced briefly as her hands clamped down on the deep gash in the back of his head, but the pain quickly subsided and he gave in to her kiss. It was an awkward upside down kiss, but it was one of those unforgettable, magical kisses. She finally pulled away from him, then impulsively gave him another short kiss. He hissed in pain as her hands dug into his head wound again.

"Thank God. Thank God you're still alive."

"Hey, ah! Easy," he winced. "My head's fuckin' killing me."

His memories of the last few hours came flooding back: the deserted control room, the stack of Cyndi's tapes, then getting clobbered over the head. The rest of his memories were only fragmentary: being dragged by his feet over rough terrain, riding on a tube with water splashing up on his face, and a black, hulking figure wrapping loops of rope around his legs.

"Where's Christie? Did you see her?" Cyndi asked, interrupting his train of thought.

"Christie?" he asked, honestly confused.

"Is Christie still alive?"

"What are you talking about? Christie went home hours ago."

Cyndi let out a huge sigh of relief. "She did? Oh, thank God."

"Cyndi, you have to get out of here," he said hurriedly. "Get out and call the police."

"I'm not leaving without you," she insisted.

"No, Cyndi. Get outta here! Go!"

Her eyes followed the rope at his feet across the upside-down-L-shaped gallows over to the edge of the wave pool. The rope looped around a heavy metal cleat mounted near the base of the gallows.

"I'm gonna get you down, then we'll go."

Cyndi stood up and took a step backwards. Without her body blocking Johnny's vision, he saw the huge man in the tattered black jumpsuit standing behind her. He stared down at her hungrily from behind the eye holes in his white grinning mask. In his right hand he raised up a small knife, meaning to stab down at her.

"NO!" It was all Johnny had time to shout.

Cyndi spun around and the killer slashed out at her with the sod knife. She shrieked in surprise and terror as the knife swung towards her face. The deadly hooked blade caught her in her open mouth before she had time to even try to deflect it with her hands. It sliced smoothly through her right cheek and curved up in a vicious arc before tearing free from her skin. At first, she felt no pain, only a strange disconnected sensation that her mouth was open too wide. Then the taste of blood filled her mouth as it washed over her teeth and tongue.

The force of the slash spun her around in midair and she landed roughly onto the grated metal ledge. As she landed, the killer kicked out with one heavy boot. The steel toe caught her right under her rib cage, knocking the wind out of her and sending her rolling off the ledge. The baling hook rolled over the edge with her and splashed into the water. At the last second, she hooked her fingers into the grate holes and desperately

280

hung on. She gasped weakly for breath as warm blood streamed out of the gaping flaps of her sliced right cheek.

"FUCK! CYNDI!" Johnny screamed. He reached for her, but was strung up too high to help. From his upside down vantage, he saw her wide-eyed look of terror and agony as she clung to the grate.

Standing above them, the killer looked down from Cyndi to Johnny. The cheesy, faded white rubber mask shone brightly in the moonlight. Then he turned and walked off the ledge. Johnny watched him go in disbelief. Why hadn't he killed either of them?

Johnny turned back to Cyndi. *"Hang on! Just hang on, okay?"* He slowly began to rock his body back and forth, trying to get himself to swing toward the ledge.

The killer bent down at the base of the gallows and opened up a small electric control panel. He pushed a large red button labeled *GRATES.* There was a loud *thunk* from down in the water, and the back wall began to vibrate as unseen gears began to crank. Johnny looked down into the water and thought he saw movement on the wall deep down in the back corner. If he had been at the bottom of the pool he would have seen the four foot high safety grates that lined the bottom of the back wall descending into the floor, opening the wave pool up to the dark space behind the back wall where churning machinery pumped out the waves and sucked in more water.

The grates finally disappeared into the floor with another clunk and the grinding gears stopped vibrating. Turning back to the control panel, the killer pushed another red button labeled *CONT. CYCLE,* for a continuous cycle of waves. He had pushed this button before Brady had come up to the ledge earlier. Up above this button was a round timer dial currently set all the way to the right at *15 MIN.* He cranked the dial to the left, *0 MIN.*

The loud wave buzzer went off and Johnny's body jerked in surprise. Somewhere under the ledge there was a sudden electric whine and a bubbly roiling sound. He tilted his head back and saw the water below him begin to churn and flow from the wave pool jets. The swirling, foaming water beneath him made his stomach turn.

Suddenly he felt his body bounce as the rope around his legs and feet was given a strong tug. He let out a scream, briefly feeling like he was about to drop face first into the wave pool. Glancing over at the killer, Johnny saw that he held the rope that bound Johnny's feet in both hands. He gave the rope another hard tug and Johnny bounced again. The maniac was playing with him, enjoying watching him scream and squirm. The masked maniac looked like a giant, psychotic kid torturing a small animal. Even over the rush of the waves, Johnny heard eager panting breath behind the mask.

"NO, STOP! NO!" Johnny shouted. The killer ignored him.

He tried his best to ignore the bouncing rope, and went back to rocking his body back and forth again. The killer noticed Johnny's indifference and let go of the rope. He bent down and began unlooping the rope from around the metal cleat.

My God! That crazy fucker doesn't just want us to fall in the water, he wants us to get sucked into the wave machines, Johnny realized in terror. His only hope was to successfully swing himself forward and grab onto the grated holes of the ledge like Cyndi was doing. Putting all his effort into it, he picked up momentum with each swing. His fingertips brushed maddeningly against the metal ledge. He was still too high to grab onto it.

As Cyndi hung on for dear life, the gaping cut in her cheek began to burn with sharp pain. From where she hung over the wave pool, she had no leverage and wouldn't be able to pull herself up. If she could only get one foot up on the ledge again, she could climb up and help Johnny. She had regained a little of her breath now, and began to swing her legs left and right.

The killer made it down to the last few loops around the cleat. The twists of rope began to slide around its metal edges, and the killer grabbed the rope before it could slip out altogether.

Johnny cried out as the rope dropped, and pushed himself even harder to swing onto the ledge. The change in height allowed his fingertips to grip the edge better than ever for one maddening second, but they were slick with sweat. The metal slipped out of his grip as he swung backwards again. Johnny grunted with effort, trying to build up even more momentum.

Might have only one more shot at this.

The last loop slipped away from the cleat. The killer stood up, letting the rope drop another three feet. Johnny swung toward the ledge just as the killer loosened his grip. Before he dropped too low to reach the ledge, his fingers curled tightly around the grate holes.

Got it!

His legs dropped and he felt his body bend back in a painful U shape.

The killer cocked his head, watching Johnny curiously. The screams and the splash he had expected had not come. He leaned forward and saw the boy's fingertips clutching the grated ledge a few feet over from where the girl similarly held on. He unclasped his long white fingers in one quick movement, completely letting go of the rope. It slithered around the gallows like a snake and dropped into the roiling water below.

Johnny's legs dropped without the support of the rope, and his knees slammed against the back wall. He hung right-side up again. As the blood rushed out of his head and back into the rest of his body, and he had to struggle against intense feeling of light-headedness. He desperately clung to consciousness as his vision floated in and out between clouds of gray.

The killer watched with disappointment as Johnny hung on.

The other end of the rope still tied around Johnny's feet was sucked into the dark space at the back of the wave pool. It caught up in some grinding gears, and began to yank down at Johnny's legs. That brought the world back into focus again, and Johnny screamed as the ropes pulled hard around his ankles.

From the side of the gallows, the killer grabbed a decorative harpoon that sat next to where the fake shark had been. He ran a long finger over its sharp, rusty point, and headed out onto the ledge again.

Cyndi continued to swing her legs back and forth, the tips of her toes coming maddeningly close to the ledge.

Another wave surged forward, and Johnny felt the rope around his feet go slack again. Taking advantage of the break in pressure, he tried to pull himself up. He lashed forward with his left hand, grabbing the grate one foot farther onto the ledge.

Footsteps clomped toward him on the ledge and he turned just in time to see a sharp metal point drive down into his middle finger. He screamed as the killer slowly twisted the harpoon's point deeper into his finger, pressing in harder, drilling it down to the bone. His arm shook with pain as he tried to pull his finger out from under the sharp point.

The harpoon tip slipped off his finger and Johnny yanked his hand away. He felt his body drop back the extra foot he had gained, and his right hand began to ache in protest, it was the only thing holding him up now. The killer pointed the harpoon at Johnny's right hand and stabbed down. Johnny let go and launched his wounded hand back up on the ledge at the same time with a scream of effort. The bloody harpoon tip jammed down into the grate. Johnny's right hand grabbed hold of the ledge right next to his left. Taking careful aim, the killer stabbed down at his hands again.

Cyndi felt her toes cling to the ledge. She ground her teeth with effort as she put all of her weight on those toes. Once she was high enough, she grabbed onto the metal grate and heaved the rest of her body up. She looked over and saw the killer viciously stabbing down at Johnny's hands as he tried to pull them away. The killer had temporarily turned away from her, focusing all of his attention on the harpoon and Johnny's hands.

The wave machinery took hold of the rope again. Johnny felt his body being pulled down and was unable to let go of the ledge. This time when the killer stabbed down, Johnny couldn't pull his hands away. He yelped as the harpoon tip jammed down into the webbing between two of the fingers on his right hand. The killer raised the harpoon point again, aiming it over his knuckles. *This is it,* Johnny thought. *This is how I die.* He turned to get one last look at Cyndi, but saw she was gone.

Cyndi suddenly launched herself at the killer's leg and bit into his ankle as hard as she could. That red fury that had overtaken her during her fight with Jennifer was back. Even through the jumpsuit's pant leg she gnashed her jaw down hard enough to draw blood. He uttered a muffled, raspy cry behind the mask and dropped the harpoon. The sharp end stuck between the holes in the grate right in front of Johnny's fingers, and stood straight up.

The killer kicked back at Cyndi, but she had already let go and taken a step away from him. He fell to his knees at the edge of the ledge between Cyndi and Johnny. Then she launched herself as hard as she could at his back, shoving him over the edge.

He flipped over as he tumbled down into the water. With a last desperate effort, his arms shot out and grabbed the coils of rope around Johnny's ankles. His legs splashed into the frothing whirlpool and they were dragged into the strong, machine-made current.

Johnny cried out as the extra weight put even more unbearable strain on his fingers and arms. He felt his legs spinning in a circle as if he were attached to something caught in a fast powerful washing machine. The blood seeping out of his hands was making it hard for him to keep a grip on the metal grate. He felt the fingers of his left hand slip away, but two hands locked onto his wrist.

Crouching on the ledge, Cyndi held Johnny's wrist in a death grip. She pulled him up with all the strength she had. Through the bloody flaps of skin on her cheek, Johnny could see some of her teeth clenched together.

In the water, another wave washed forward and the killer's body was violently tossed around. The rope around Johnny's feet was beginning to slip off, and the killer would soon be at the mercy of the wave machinery. He let go with one hand and reached into his jumpsuit pocket, pulling out the sod knife. He furiously slashed long, deep, diagonal cuts across Johnny's calves and shins.

Johnny shrieked in pain with each cut. Cyndi looked past Johnny's face and saw the killer below, wildly slashing at his legs.

"WHATEVER YOU DO, DON'T LET GO!" she

screamed to Johnny. His only response was his continued yelps and shrieks.

Cyndi let go of Johnny's arm and reached for the harpoon. She tried to yank it up, but its barbed end was caught between two of the grate holes. Forcing herself to slow down, she carefully maneuvered the hook out from the grate just as the wave machinery began sucking the killer's legs into the dark space beneath the back wall. With a mad scream, she threw the harpoon down into the killer's chest like a javelin. He let go of Johnny's feet and the white water pulled him under.

Cyndi grabbed Johnny's hand and helped him slowly climb back up. He kicked the loosening loops of the rope off his feet and it got sucked down into the wave machines. Once his body was halfway up again, he swung his right foot up. Cyndi grabbed him by the waist, helping him haul his bloody legs up onto the ledge.

Johnny lay there panting and grunting as sheets of fresh stinging pain shot up from the gaping cuts in his calves. Beneath them, another wave roared as it went crashing out into the pool.

Cyndi looked over the ledge and down into the churning water below. The killer looked like a black rag doll with a white mask. In the darkness, she caught only glimpses of his mask and black clad arms flopping around helplessly in the water. He disappeared under a huge surge of white, bubbling foam, then was sucked back in again.

"The grates," Johnny shouted. "You have to close the grates!"

"Where?" Cyndi asked.

"The panel on the side there," he said, pointing to the gallows. "Push the button that says grates."

Cyndi ran off the ledge to the control panel. She quickly found the red *GRATES* button and pushed it in. She heard the same clunk and grinding gears as the grates began to raise up from the floor of the wave pool again. Cyndi looked down as the grates clunked into place, trying to see if the killer had escaped the wave machinery again, but another wave rushed forward through them and all she could see was white water.

She ran back onto the ledge to Johnny who was wincing and clutching his legs.

"Fuck! Ooh, that fuckin' hurts. Oh God!" he grunted through clenched teeth.

It was almost as if Johnny's pain reminded her body that it was also injured, and the sting from the cut in her cheek suddenly flared to life. She clapped her hand to it and bit back a scream.

"Where's a first aid kit?" she asked through clenched jaws.

"Should be one along the ledge just near the stairs there." He pointed toward the white concrete emergency steps leading out of the foaming wave pool.

"I'll get it," she said. "Wait here."

Cyndi stood up and ran off the ledge again. She looked out at the churning waves and saw the dark forms of bodies tumbling in the white water, being washed toward the shore. There were two bodies that weren't in that crowd though. She looked back at Johnny cringing and clutching at his legs. He was alive. Furthermore, Christie was home safe. They were both alive because of her.

"Thank God," she said aloud, and repeated it to herself over and over again. "Thank God, Thank God, Thank God."

Chapter Eighteen:

A Call For Help

They sat on the grass beside the wave pool. The waves had died down again, and the only noises were the crickets and the sounds of dying waves lapping against the walls of the wave pool. Under the moonlight, Cyndi wrapped as much gauze as she could around Johnny's bleeding calves. His left leg only had a few small cuts, but his right leg was a mess of deep meaty lacerations. While she wrapped gauze around his legs, he taped a bandage to the outside of her slashed cheek, and prepared another one to place inside her mouth. She had only been bleeding for ten minutes, but her white off-the-shoulder T-shirt was completely ruined.

"That's all of it," she said as she reached the end of the spool of gauze. She looked down at the blood seeping through the fresh bandages. "You're probably gonna need stitches." She spoke sparingly and kept her jaws firmly shut, it hurt too much to do more.

"Yeah, you too," he said. He handed her the bandage and she winced as she placed it between her teeth and sliced cheek. "Look, I want you to go to the payphone down there and call the pol--"

"Can't. He ripped the phones out."

"Well there's another payphone up by the--"

"*All* the phones," she interrupted. "And all of your tires."

"Wh-- My tires? What about my tires?"

"Flat. All four. I saw 'em. Gate's locked too. Only way out is under the fence." She pointed downhill, in the direction of the high fence where she had snuck in.

"How do you know that?" he asked.

"Long story," she mumbled. Her mouth was hurting bad now.

Recognition dawned on his face. "Oh my God. Last summer! Something like this happened to you last summer!" She nodded. "Jesus Christ! Why didn't you tell me? What happened?"

"It really hurts to talk right now," she said.

"Okay, okay," he relented. "Look, just leave me here and go find a phone. I'll be all r--"

"No!" she shouted. "I'm not leaving you."

"Cyndi, you have to. I can't fucking walk!" he shouted back.

"No. We stick together."

They sat in silence for a moment. Johnny tried to think of something, anything to get them out of this mess. Suddenly, he snapped his fingers.

"The radio!" Cyndi watched him, waiting for him to continue. "I accidentally left an extra radio up on The Falls earlier today. I brought one up there because Brady wasn't answering and I thought maybe his was dead, but he just had his little stereo turned up too loud. I stuck the extra one up high up on the shelf and never brought it back down. It might still be there."

"So? We're the last ones here, remember?"

"Yeah, but we might be able to change the frequency and get the police. Brady did it somehow while we were in training."

"Worth a try," Cyndi shrugged. "Can you make it up the hill?"

"I'll give it a shot."

She helped him get shakily to his feet, then slung his right arm over her shoulders and let him lean on her as they began to walk. Every movement sent sharp daggers of pain up all the way to his back. With every step he felt the sickening sensation of two sticky halves of his torn skin peel apart, then squish back together.

Cyndi kept her eyes on the ground, not liking the way the gauze wrapped around Johnny's leg seemed to be soaked with blood already. The bandage on her face was also already damp with her own blood.

One crisis at a time, she thought. *Just get out of here and get somewhere safe. Then worry about getting stitched up.*

Johnny surveyed the bodies at the beach. He had never seen a dead body until tonight. Now there were around thirty of them slumped in the pool chairs or floating in the shallow end of the wave pool. His face was white with shock (or maybe that just the blood draining out of his body through the gashes on his legs). He noticed that some of the bodies had been set in garish poses. One of them--

"Eddie?" he asked in a small voice, stopping to stare at the body. His eyes had locked on a dead boy in a pool chair with curly auburn hair and a yellow shirt. He looked like Eddie and was dressed like Eddie, but with his battered face and throat ripped out, how could one be sure? "No. N-no, it--it can't be. It's gotta be some other kid."

Johnny turned to look at Cyndi, but she only stared at the ground looking sick. That look on her face brought it home, the reality of Eddie's death came crashing down all at once for Johnny. His knees buckled and he legs felt weak. Cyndi struggled with his added weight.

"Oh God, no," he mumbled. "Oh, fuck. Oh--" He began to make involuntary gagging sounds.

"Don't!" Cyndi said forcefully. She grabbed his face and turned him away from the bodies. "Don't you throw up. Just keep walking. And don't look at them. You hear me? Don't look." He nodded weakly, still uttering a few short, shuddering breaths. His emotions for his lost friend were raging. He wanted to cry, but struggled to keep himself together and push forward.

By the time they reached the placid, flowing Lazy River, Johnny's sadness had turned into a seething, red rage, and he had found his words again.

"That crazy motherfucker," he growled. "He must have planned this all along. Must've been planning it right in front of our noses the whole time. That fuckin' psycho. That crazy fuck! Why? Why did he do it?"

"I wish I knew," Cyndi said with a shrug.

"You killed him," Johnny said. "You were amazing."

Cyndi smiled with the left side of her mouth. Inside though, she felt that old uneasy feeling of unfinished business again. She wanted to ask Johnny: *You sure he's dead?* She kept her mouth shut though, not wanting to tempt fate. Also, like she had told him before, it hurt too much to talk.

*   *   *

The walk up the hill felt endless at Cyndi and Johnny's slow, injured pace. Johnny winced with every grim step. *Gotta keep going. Gotta make it up the hill. Gotta get out of here.* He repeated those three sentences in his mind over and over, using them like a shield for the pain. Cyndi nervously kept an eye over her shoulder. They both felt like they had been limping along for hours by the time the towering Falls ride came into view.

"Almost there," Cyndi panted.

"You doing okay?" he asked.

"Fine. I'm more worried about you."

"Don't worry about me. I'm okay, really."

He didn't look okay though. His face had a whipped, tortured look that she didn't care for at all. His eyes were too wide and had dark circles underneath. His face was pale and his arm felt cool and waxy. A thought had begun to gnaw in the back of her mind, *What happens if we can't get the police? What happens if we have to stay here all night? Can we even make it 'til morning?*

Johnny stopped walking at the top of the hill. Cyndi saw he was looking down the length of the long Screamin' Demon pool. At the foot of the ramp, the crooked curve of a broken jaw and an open mouth pulled back in a grimace were the only things visible above the still surface of the water. Fanned out in front of the mouth was a cloud of dark hair floating in the water covering the rest of the face.

"What the hell is that?" Johnny asked in a small, terrified voice. From this distance he couldn't see it very clearly, though he knew it was probably awful.

"Jennifer," Cyndi answered in a cold flat voice.

Johnny let out a shocked breath and swallowed hard, but he said nothing else. He faced forward again, wishing he hadn't noticed the corpse.

They made their way across the wide AstroTurf seating area in front of the kiddie playground and the end pool of the Rocky River. Then they went up another small slope to the base of The Falls. Johnny stopped under the wooden archway at the foot of the stairs.

"Why don't you just run up and grab the radio?"

he suggested.

Cyndi honestly considered the question, then shook her head.

"I can't leave you."

"Cyndi, please," he pleaded, almost whined.

"What if he's still out there? What if he's been following us the whole time?"

"He's dead. No one could've survived that. And besides, how long have we been walking? An hour? Maybe an hour and a half? If he wanted us he would've gotten us by now."

"You don't know that. You weren't there last year. I'd think he was dead but he just kept coming back. I don't know how he survived everything, but he did."

Johnny stared at her, too tired to fight, and also too tired to keep going.

"Trust me, it'll be safer."

Johnny sighed, knowing that there was no arguing with her.

As they began the grueling climb up the three flights of wooden steps to the top, they both thought of their encounters with Jennifer earlier today. Johnny had been touched and seduced by her at the top of this ride, and Cyndi had almost started a fight with her at the bottom of it. Neither of them said anything about it to the other, but they both felt a strange guilt at the fact that Jennifer was now dead. Even though she had been nothing but trouble for both Cyndi and Johnny, the fact that she had suffered a brutal, painful murder was just plain awful.

The wooden steps creaked slightly as they went up. Even when they weren't moving the whole structure seemed to creak slightly whenever the wind blew. Johnny hadn't ever heard the creaks during the day, the noise of people and other lifeguards drowned it out, but now in the silence of the night he felt slightly unnerved at how creaky it was. He suddenly wondered just how safe this ride actually was.

"Wanna rest for a minute?" Cyndi asked when they reached the first landing. Johnny was panting and his skin looked pale and slick with cold sweat. He knew he probably didn't look very well, but he figured that if he sat down, he might not be able to get back up again. Also at this level, they stood directly underneath the wooden shack at the top. They were so close he could almost sense the radio.

"I'll rest at the top. Come on."

They made it up the last arduous flight of stairs, ascending along the right side of the wooden house at the top. As they turned the last corner, Cyndi looked out at the view. Behind the The Falls was the tall wrought iron perimeter fence, its sharp points were almost directly below them. Past the fence, the nearly empty parking lot stretched out, its fresh black asphalt shimmered a grayish-blue in the moonlight. Beyond the parking lot and a black silhouetted stretch of nearby trees, she could see streetlights, and on the horizon she could see the bright lights of the huge hospital building up on another hill five miles away. She stared longingly at all those lights before Johnny's cool arm gently pulled her forward into the wooden shack at the top of the ride.

"Made it," Johnny sighed and gracelessly sat down on the soft AstroTurf platform in front of the middle slide. Cyndi hadn't been up here before, and she looked around curiously at the pirate flag and the swords mounted on the wall, then turned to the three slides. The splash at the bottom of the slides echoed up hollowly in their ears. During the day, the inside of these slides were translucent, letting some greenish sunlight in. At night they were as black as a mine shaft.

Above the slides, they had a fantastic moonlit view of the cluster of rides in the upper area of the park.

Directly below was the triangular end pool of The Falls. Water from this end pool and the Rocky River's end pool cascaded into that deep drainage pool that had creeped Cyndi out while she stood in line for the Rocky River. Across the way, she saw the sweeping curves and slow pools of the Rocky River, and past that the chaotic jumble of the kiddie playground. Thankfully the playground stood in front of the Screamin' Demon, and tall pine trees and shadowy wooded areas also blocked the Ragin' and Duelin' Rivers from sight. Cyndi's heart lightened as she listened to the whirr of crickets and the soft trickle of flowing water all over this new part of the park. If not for her new set of terrible memories, this place, just like its predecessor from last year, just might have been beautiful.

"You see that shelf up there? I left the radio up there," Johnny explained. Cyndi looked up at a high shelf with the shark jaws and the alligator skull. From where she stood, she couldn't see the black, blocky shape of the radio, but she hoped it would be there. "Climb up on the platform and grab it."

She nodded at Johnny and carefully climbed up on the wooden platform where Brady and Johnny had sat earlier, using the top curve of the slide on the left as a step. Climbing up there, Cyndi became all too aware of the forty feet between her and the ground. She had to lean forward with her feet at the edge of the platform to reach the top shelf.

She pawed the flat surface of the shelf with her right hand. Two rows of sharp serrated shark's teeth scratched her palm. She reached around behind the shark's jaw and felt only flat, dusty wood.

Come on, where is it? Please don't tell me it's not here. Please don't tell me someone took it.

Johnny watched from the floor, silently sharing her thoughts.

Cyndi stretched herself out a few inches farther, taking more support away from her legs than she should have. Suddenly her bare feet slipped forward an inch and she screamed. Her scrabbling fingers gripped the edge of the shelf for support and it creaked under her weight.

"Whoa! You okay?" he asked.

"I-I'm fine. I'm okay," she stammered.

"Be careful," he said. Cyndi almost came back with a snappy comment, but kept silent. The cut in her cheek had opened again with her scream and she felt the sticky clots of blood peel apart. Now it was oozing fresh blood, and all she wanted to do was get down off this ride and go home.

After taking a deep breath to calm her nerves, she crouched down again and placed her feet more securely. She stretched forward again, farther than she dared to before and her fingers scraped against the back wall.

It's gone. All that effort for noth--

Then the small tip of the antenna, no bigger than a pencil eraser, tapped her pinky finger.

"Got it!" she cried through gritted teeth. She stretched her legs even more and gripped the tip of the antenna between two fingers. "Can you catch it? I'm afraid I'll drop it over the side if I try to carry it down."

"Yeah, I can catch."

With a quick jerk, she pulled the radio off the shelf. It bounced between the alligator skull and a shark jaw, and tumbled through the air. Johnny caught it a foot above the rushing water of the middle slide. Cyndi hopped down off the curve of the slide. With solid wood under her feet again, a giant weight lifted off her chest.

Johnny clicked the radio on and the rush of static was music to his ears. "Yes! It still works. Let's just hope the battery holds out." He cranked the volume so they could hear the radio over the rush of water from the slides.

Cyndi sat down next to Johnny as he fiddled with the small frequency knob next to the antenna. He thought back to that day in training when Brady had so easily picked up the police frequency and then that Mexican conversation. He tweaked the knob as delicately as he could and found only static. He wished Brady were here with them now, and realized that his body was probably back at the wave pool somewhere. The thought of all those bodies gave him chills.

A faint, staticky wave of voices was there and gone in an instant.

"There! What was that?" Cyndi asked excitedly.

Johnny only shook his head in frustration. He slowly twisted the knob, listening carefully for something, anything. At this point, he'd even be glad to find the Mexicans again. There was another short blur of a voice and they both inhaled sharply. He gave the knob an infinitesimal twist back but the voice was gone.

"Damn it," he grumbled.

Cyndi impatiently looked around the shack as she waited for him to find some kind of signal. She stared fixedly at those two swords on the wall for a moment, then across the room at the pirate flag.

Johnny tried a different approach, wildly spinning the dial to see if he heard even the briefest flash of anything. Static and silence were the only things he heard.

He growled in frustration. "Come on, come on!"

With a last hard twist there came a brief, garbled word.

"--iner," a woman with a flat, robotic voice said. Cyndi turned back to Johnny and the radio, her eyes wide with anticipation. Johnny twisted the knob as gently as he could and the signal became stronger. Only a faint hiss of static came through over the voice now. A deep man's voice answered the woman.

"That's a ten-four, dispatch."

"It's them!" Cyndi cried out.

Johnny clicked the talk button on the side of the radio and spoke loudly into the speaker.

"Hello? Police? Can anyone hear me?"

Silence from the other end.

"Hello? Anybody. Hello?"

They almost gave up when the man spoke up to them. "Dispatch, can you repeat that?"

"Yes! My name is Johnny Vesna. I'm at Thrill River water park. We need help! People are dead!"

The man now sounded irritated. "Kid, this is the Westview Suburban Hospital Security." Cyndi remembered seeing the hospital building on the hill a few miles away. "You know you could be disrupting a real emergency. So get off the air right now!"

"No, please believe me! I'm not just screwing around. We need help, please! My girlfriend, Cyndi Stevens and I are at Thrill River water park. We're locked in and we've been stabbed! Please send help for God's sake! *Please!*" He practically screamed all this into the radio.

Silence. Johnny almost clicked on the talk button again, but the man cut him off.

"Okay, kid. This better not be a prank. We'll get the police on the phone and have them send someone over. Just sit tight and stay off the radio unless it's absolutely necessary, got it?"

"Yes! Thank you so much! Thank you!" He let go of the talk button and nearly collapsed with joy.

Cyndi threw her arms around Johnny and kissed him flat on the mouth. "You did it!" He tasted the coppery taste of her blood on his lips, but at that moment he couldn't care less. Cyndi hugged him tightly and jumped to her feet. Johnny threw up his fists in triumph, tilted his head back, and howled in the still air. Cyndi jumped up and down in excitement. She looked down at Johnny who was still blessedly alive. She had finally "stuck together" with someone, and it had saved his life.

With a fresh burst of energy, she ran to the stairs and cheered out at the hospital up on the hill. She spun around and ran over to the opening above the middle slide to cheer out there, but a dripping white Smiley mask with oily strings of black hair launched up at her out of the darkness.

Cyndi shrieked and fell back clumsily on the hard wood. Johnny whirled and saw the huge black form of the killer swinging his legs over the edge above the middle slide. One of his heavy boots splashed down into the rushing water of the middle slide a foot behind Johnny.

Johnny let out a guttural scream of shock and terror, and ducked forward as the killer lunged at him. The killer held no weapons. His scarred, fishy fingers hooked into Johnny's shoulders like hard claws. He yanked Johnny up into the air and those long, bony fingers jammed themselves into Johnny's screaming mouth. The killer yanked Johnny's top teeth up with one hand, and his jaw down with the other.

The fingers went down deep enough into Johnny's throat that he began to gag. He felt his jaw crack and stretch agonizingly far. He could taste blood, dirt, and chlorine on the man's hands. He bit down on the killer's dirty fingers, but it only made the man yank his mouth open harder. Above his head, he heard the killer panting and wheezing in coarse, sandpapery breaths.

Cyndi screamed again and backed away from

them. She scrambled to her feet and turned to see the killer holding Johnny's head up to his abdomen. He had his fingers in Johnny's mouth down past the knuckles. Johnny was uttering choked, open-mouthed screams as the killer tried to break his jaw. She could see Johnny's tongue flicking back and forth wildly between the two rough white fingers. Johnny's legs kicked and slid uselessly along the wood while his hands clutched and beat at the man's arms.

Thinking as fast as she could, she turned to those metal pirate swords on the wall and grabbed the handle of one. She tried to yank it down, but it wouldn't budge. Glancing back at Johnny and the killer, she continued to tug at the handle. Turning back to the sword, she saw that it was bolted to the wall. She pulled at it as hard as she could, screaming with desperate effort.

Johnny felt another painful crack way back in his jaw, and his screams became hoarse and panicked, like those of a dying animal.

"JOHNNY!!!" Cyndi cried in agony.

A shot exploded into the night. The killer jerked and fell back a step, instantly letting go of Johnny's mouth. Another ragged hole had opened up in the left shoulder of the killer's tattered jumpsuit and blood sprayed out. Johnny collapsed to the floor, landing in an exhausted heap. Three more shots boomed out and the killer jerked with each shot. He staggered, the rubbery soles of his boots squeaking and sliding in the smooth slide's surface.

Cyndi saw a big man standing in the doorway of the shack. He held a rifle with a smoking barrel in his hands. His long, curly dark brown hair fluttered slightly in the breeze. Cyndi recognized his high tube socks, athletic shoes, red lifeguard shorts, and tight white T-shirt immediately. It was Sheehan.

The killer tottered on his feet, then slipped and fell on his back into the rushing water of the middle slide with a splash. The current carried him backward and he slipped down head first into the darkness. The middle slide had a steep, almost straight-down drop, and a few seconds later, they heard the splash as he hit the water below.

Sheehan lowered the rifle and rushed forward to look down at the end pool. He stepped over Johnny's unconscious body on the way. Sheehan looked down at the body in black floating just under the white, foamy rush of water at the foot of the slide. Cyndi shuddered and wept weakly, looking up at Sheehan. He looked back over his shoulder at Cyndi. His eyes were blazing with terror and adrenaline, he looked directly into her own eyes.

"I told you those three kids were gonna get you into trouble, didn't I?" he said to her.

Cyndi suddenly remembered that day back at Camp Kikawa. He had stopped her outside the mess hall where Stacy, Zack, and Brad were being imprisoned and warned her to stay away from them. He had been right. How much of her life would have been different if she had followed his bitter advice?

Sheehan looked down at the end pool again, then turned and rushed back down the steps.

Cyndi watched him go with a thousand questions on the tip of her tongue, but couldn't bring herself to shout out any of them. The corners of her vision became hazy as she looked down at Johnny. She reached down to shake his shoulder and try to wake him up. Sirens blared off in the distance somewhere. They were the last sounds Cyndi heard before the gray clouds in her vision took over completely and she collapsed next to Johnny.

Chapter Nineteen:

Survivors

Sharp pain in Cyndi's cheek dragged her back to the land of the living. Through bleary, unfocused vision, she looked up into bright white florescent lights and saw three faceless doctors in turquoise scrubs. They were holding her head and poking what felt like sharp needles into her skin.

When they noticed her fluttering eyelids and struggling movements, they pulled their instruments away. She heard an unimportant jumble of words from their mouths, then her head became heavy. She fell back into dark dreams where water came crashing and thundering through greasy black machinery and poured out of the huge mouth of a white grinning face.

*   *   *

Sometime after five in the morning, Cyndi woke up in an unfamiliar bed. She looked around and saw a sterile, unfamiliar room. Everything around her seemed to be either white or dull metal. A medicinal smell hung thick in stale recycled air.

Her right cheek throbbed and before she could reach up to touch it, she noticed that someone else's hand was loosely holding hers. Her mother had fallen asleep in a chair next to Cyndi's hospital bed. She rested her head on the edge of the bed and held Cyndi's hand in her sleep. Cyndi could feel her mother's hand squeezing and jerking as her own feverish nightmares raced through her mind.

The TV bolted high up on the wall in the corner of the room was on, but the sound was turned down so low that she couldn't hear it. Her father sat near the TV, sleeping in a chair with his head down. The morning news was on and a local reporter named Susan Cole with wavy, dark brown hair stood outside Thrill River's closed gates in the dim glow of early dawn. Long ropes of yellow police tape crisscrossed over the wrought iron bars. Behind the reporter, a group of police stood discussing something near a police car with red and blue flashing lights. The news reporter spoke for a while, then the screen cut to a grainy school photo of Brady Johnston with a half scowl on his face. They had taken the picture from the 1982 DeAngelo High School yearbook. Then the TV cut to a shot of paramedics wheeling stretchers with closed black body-bags out to waiting ambulances in early dawn light.

Cyndi pulled her hand away from her mother's, and searched for the remote control to turn the volume up. Her mother suddenly came awake with a jerk. She took only a second to remember that she was in her daughter's hospital room.

"Cyndi!" she said breathlessly. She jumped up stiffly and threw her arms around Cyndi's shoulders. Fresh tears and sobs of relief racked her mother. "Thank God, thank God! Don't you ever do that again. You hear me? Don't you ever!"

Across the room, Cyndi's father came awake with a sharp inhale and gave her his own relieved smile. With one hand he knuckled sleep out of his eye, with the other he picked the remote up off the floor, turned the TV off, and walked over to Cyndi's bed.

"Wait! What was that? Turn that back on. I need to hear what they're saying!"

Her father glanced back at the TV, then over at her mother. "Not right now. How you doin', baby?" he asked softly.

"I'm fine," Cyndi said quickly. "Tell me what happened. How did I get here?" Her mother finally let go and wiped tears out of her eyes. She clutched her husband's arm tightly. She was like a woman who couldn't swim using her family members as life preservers in a churning sea.

"We got a call from the police just after midnight saying that you had been seriously injured and were at the hospital," her father explained.

"You scared the hell out of us!" her mother wailed.

"Why don't *you* tell *us* what happened?" her father said sternly.

Cyndi looked at them gravely for a moment, then said simply, "He came back."

Her mother gasped and clapped a hand over her mouth.

"What'd they say? Is he dead?" Cyndi asked. She unconsciously gripped the hospital bed's comforter with tight, clammy fists.

"On the news they've just started saying he was some kid named, uh, Brady, something. Brady Johnston."

Cyndi let out a startled breath. "Brady? No. It couldn't be him."

"They said that kid was whacked out on drugs

and had a history of violence," her father said.

"They said he got kicked out of school for attacking someone with a knife," her mother added.

Cyndi's mind whirled with the news. She thought back to all of her experiences with Brady and compared them with all of her experiences with the killer, trying to reconcile the two. Brady *could* have been at the dance that night, Brady *could* been at the mall that day, and he *was* there at the water park all day.

But why would he kill his own cousin Jennifer? And why would he have been out in the woods last year?

"No one really knows what happened yet. The police are waiting to talk to you."

"Is Johnny-- What about Johnny?" Cyndi asked.

"I talked with his father earlier. He told me that Johnny lost a lot of blood, but he's gonna pull through." Cyndi let out a long sigh. Her father pointed to the curving cut on her right cheek. "The doctor says that's gonna leave quite a scar. You were in emergency surgery to repair the nerve damage, but they said that your right cheek is never going to move as well as it did. You're gonna have to try to think of it as your *new look.*"

Cyndi tried to smile and the dull throb in her cheek flared. She winced and ran her fingers over the rough black stitches. She thought her own cheek felt like a warm baseball. The skin felt stretched and seemed to throb with every heartbeat.

"Cyndi, what were you thinking? Why did you ask me to take you out there? You knew something was going to happen just as well as I did. You *knew.* Why did you do it?"

"Terri, please," her father said ineffectually. "She needs time to process all of this."

Cyndi honestly considered the question. "Last year when we got to camp, my friend Stacy told me that

306

we had to stick together, but we didn't. I didn't want to make that same mistake again."

Her father felt a surge of quiet pride for Cyndi, but was too worn out to let it show on his face. "Why don't you start at the beginning?"

"I will, but can you wait for the police?" She pointed to her cheek. Reluctantly, they agreed, and less than two hours later she told them everything.

*   *   *

A thin, plainclothes police officer named Harding had returned a few hours after she woke up, and she went through the whole grisly story. Her mother tried to break in with her own part of the story, but after a few of her frantic, disjointed sentences, the officer accurately dismissed her part in the story as irrelevant.

"I'm sorry to interrupt you, Mrs. Stevens, but I'd really like to get *Cyndi's* story if you don't mind," he said in a polite but firm voice. Her mother promptly shut up, and Cyndi gave him a grateful smile.

After her long story came to its sudden end, the officer asked her to describe the killer in as much detail as she could. He asked if she could definitely identify him as Brady Johnston, she replied that she couldn't, but she supposed it could have been him. He asked several more questions about how she knew Brady, and she told him about her few distasteful encounters with him. He asked if Brady seemed particularly interested or attracted to her, she said no. His line of questioning finally seemed to dry up, and he tapped his notepad with the pen in his other hand.

"Can I ask *you* a question?" Cyndi finally asked.

"Shoot," he shrugged.

"Why all this stuff about Brady? I mean...well..." she struggled to find the right words. "I guess I mean why would Brady be after me all this time?"

"I'll tell you what I can about Brady Johnston. He had been expelled from Southwestern University two months ago for assaulting another student with a weapon, a switchblade knife. His manager at Thrill River, the guy that saved you, positively identified his body when we pulled off the mask. He also found a secret spot near one of the rides where Brady had hidden two grams of cocaine, a few ounces of marijuana, and several bottles of alcohol. I'll tell you right now that cocaine is a *nasty* drug, and you better stay from it if you know what's good for you. I've seen dozens of cases where people under the influence of cocaine become wild, irrational, dangerous people. It gives them a sense of power and intense energy, and it makes them want do the craziest things. Some people become extremely violent. We'll have to wait for the autopsy report to come back to see just what was in Brady's system, but I'm pretty sure that's what happened to him." He shook his head shamefully, remembering dozens of encounters with coked up people over the last decade.

"I don't do drugs," Cyndi said solemnly.

"Good for you. Never start. The other piece of evidence we found, let's just keep this between us," he paused and exchanged nods with Cyndi and her parents. "The other evidence was a bit more disturbing. The last thing his manager found was a drawing of you."

"Me?" Cyndi asked.

"Yes, a drawing of your face. It was fairly accurate too. We can't tell for sure if he drew it or not, but it certainly looks like he did. This would indicate that he did have a kind of, uh, fixation on you. An obsession with you."

Cyndi felt sick thinking of anyone drawing her. "Can I see it?"

"Unfortunately, no. It's evidence. There was also a break-in at the Countryside pool the night before last. Were you aware of that?"

Cyndi looked up at him shocked. "What? A break-in at work?"

"Yes. The snack bar where you work was heavily vandalized, and your stereo and tapes were stolen. There was a Smiley-Face drawn in ketchup on the counter window's rolling shutter. We're pretty sure that was him too. He knew you worked there, didn't he?"

Cyndi nodded. The officer gave them a moment of silence to let all the information sink in. Cyndi finally broke it. "I just don't believe it."

"We don't have all the answers yet, we're still investigating. Is there anything else you can think of, anything at all you remember about him or any strange things he ever said to you?" Cyndi only shrugged. "Well, I'll get out of your hair. If you think of anything give me a call." He rose to his feet and handed Cyndi's father his business card. Cyndi smiled politely. The officer thanked them and walked toward the door.

"Wait," Cyndi called, an idea suddenly forming itself in her head. Officer Harding turned around and stood in the doorway. "Can I see his body?"

"Cyndi I don't think that's a good idea," her mother said. Cyndi ignored her.

"As far I know his body is locked away at the County Coroner's office. I don't think you really want to see--"

"Please," Cyndi insisted. "I'd sleep better if I could see it, if I knew for sure that he was really dead."

Officer Harding looked down at the floor thinking for a moment, then gave a slight shrug. "Let me see what I can do." Cyndi gave him one more grateful smile and he left the room.

*   *   *

Cyndi hadn't expected Officer Harding to get back to her so quickly. Less than six hours later, he called her room directly and asked when she would be discharged from the hospital. She explained that the doctor examined her an hour after Harding had left. He had set up an appointment for two weeks from Monday to get her stitches removed, and said she would be free to leave as soon as tomorrow.

"Oh good. Perfect timing. You asked earlier if you could see the remains of Brady Johnston. Well, I called in a few favors with the Coroner's office, and I can get you in. Briefly. But it has to be tomorrow before they turn the remains over to the mortuary."

"Okay," Cyndi said solemnly. She was glad to be granted her request so easily, but she also dreaded being reunited with the killer. In her mind, she saw herself walking down into a cold, dimly lit basement filled with bodies on metal tables covered with stained white sheets. She imagined having them pull the sheet down over Brady's head and seeing that white mask leering up at her from the table.

"Would you be able to meet me at the County Coroner's office at say, eleven tomorrow?" Harding asked. Cyndi's parents only shrugged resignedly, they wanted to put this whole episode behind them. After she hung up the phone with Officer Harding, she wondered if she would have any nightmares about Brady Johnston in the morgue. As it turned out, she slept like a rock.

The next day her parents drove her to the County Coroner's office, a squat little building built in an angled 1950's style. It was less than ten minutes away from the hospital. Officer Harding was waiting for her outside, leaning against one of the diagonal metal columns that supported the flat awning above the glass

310

front door. She gave her parents permission to wait for her in the car, which they refused. The three of them greeted Officer Harding and Cyndi took a deep breath as he led them inside.

Nothing in the office looked the way she expected. Harding led them into a small, cozy little office just near the front door. Cyndi looked around for the stairway leading down into the dark and dingy morgue basement, but there was none. Harding told them to sit down on a clean tweed couch in front of a small television set. A flat wooden coffee table sat in front of them with a white telephone and a box of tissues placed neatly in the middle. Her parents sat down on either side of her just like they always did at home. Cyndi quickly realized that they wouldn't show her the remains in person at all, she would see the body through some sort of closed circuit television system on this TV. In her mind, she half sighed with relief. Seeing something on TV could be bad, but it was nothing compared to real life, she knew that from personal experience.

"Okay, are you ready?" Harding asked. Cyndi nodded, her parents joined her after they saw that she was ready. Harding picked up the headset on the phone and dialed a three-digit extension. Someone on the other line picked up and Cyndi heard Harding mutter, "Yes. Yes. It's Johnston, correct? One moment please." Still holding the phone, he stepped over to the TV, and clicked it on.

On the screen, was a close-up shot of the white sheet covering a head in a brightly lit room. The camera was placed on the right side of the body, looking slightly down at its profile. Cyndi sat glued to the screen, anticipating the grisly reveal. Harding spoke into the phone again, "All right, go ahead." Two gloved hands reached into frame, pulled the white sheet down over

Brady Johnston's face, and stopped just below his chin.

It doesn't even look like him, was her first thought. It was definitely Brady Johnston, but he looked somewhat rubbery, as if this was only some kind of plastic prop designed to look like Brady Johnston. His eyes and mouth were closed, and his skin was a yellowish-gray color. His lips were dry and as pale as the rest of his face.

Cyndi felt her mother and father tense up and squirm on either side of her. Her mother even covered her mouth with her hand and looked down at the floor. Cyndi wanted to see more of the body, make sure it was really him, but at the same time she really didn't want to see any more of this than she already had. Her mind swirled with questions to ask, but they all either seemed irrelevant or wildly inappropriate.

Before she could pick one to ask, Harding asked his own question. "Is it what you wanted to see?" Cyndi tore her eyes away from the television set and looked up at him.

"I-- Yeah I guess," she replied. Harding quickly clicked off the TV, and her mother let out a shuddering sigh of relief.

"Okay, that'll be all. Thank you," Harding spoke into the phone, and hung it up. He saw the perplexed look on Cyndi's face. "Is everything all right, Cyndi. To be perfectly honest, you don't seem very satisfied."

"It's just-- I don't know. I used to have so many nightmares about him. I used to be so afraid, but now he looks--" She shrugged. She couldn't think of the words to describe how lifeless he looked, how all his power seemed to have been stripped away.

"I know what you mean," Harding said. "It may seem anticlimactic, like there should be something more gruesome under that sheet. He terrorized you, and now

312

here he is, just a person. Nothing terrifying about him. Is that it?"

"Yeah, kinda like that," Cyndi agreed.

"You'd actually be surprised how often other people react that way in situations like this. You get a lot of false expectations from the movies and TV, but real life rarely plays out like that. But I hope this has given you some of the closure you're hoping for. You can rest easy now knowing that Brady Johnston is dead. He can't come after you anymore."

Cyndi's parents thanked Officer Harding and he walked them back to their car. She sat quietly with her own thoughts as they drove home.

Maybe he's right. Maybe I've just been expecting some big Hollywood ending. Maybe I've been afraid for so long that I don't know how to recognize a real ending when it finally comes.

*   *   *

Later that afternoon, while Cyndi was upstairs recording the Cyndi Lauper song "Witness" onto a new mix-tape, the doorbell rang. A minute later, Cyndi's mother stood at the bedroom door with a sour look on her face.

"You have a visitor," she said with a bitter tone that Cyndi didn't care for.

They went downstairs into the living room and were greeted once again by Kurt Carver. He looked tall and pale in his dark pin-striped suit. His slicked-back black hair looked even more greasy than it had the first time they met. Cyndi felt dull anger at the sight of his bright, perfect smile.

"Ah, Cyndi!" Carver sighed with relief. "You wouldn't believe how glad I am to see that you're okay."

"Yeah, hi," Cyndi said flatly. He stood up, and

clasped her hand between both of his smooth, long-fingered hands. Cyndi sat down on the couch between her parents just as she had a year ago.

"I am so deeply sorry that we had to meet under such awful circumstances again. This has just been an absolute nightmare for all of us."

"You have no idea," she replied gravely.

"No, I don't. You're right. This is--I just--I'm at a loss for words." He gave a little shudder and sighed. "The important thing is that now we have closure, far more closure than we did last year. We can all sleep comfortably now. That awful Johnston kid is gone for good. Are you healing up nicely?" The wide grin lit up his face again but Cyndi remained cold.

"What can I do for you, Mr. Carver?"

"Cutting right down to the chase. I admire that. My father and I have been very pleased that you honored our little agreement and kept your discretion. You've allowed our company to thrive over the past year without any bad publicity, and for that we are truly grateful. So thank you, Cyndi. And also, Terri, Bill, thank you. I mean it from the bottom of my heart, thank you all." He smiled at her with dripping reverence.

He's so fake, she thought. *Every word he says sounds like a lie.*

"We owe you so much. In addition to the free tuition, we'd like to offer you free counseling for as long as you need. We would also like to provide a free dream vacation every year for the next *ten* years, to Florida where my family owns hundreds of beautiful acres in the Everglades, and luxury beach houses that you wouldn't believe. This applies to you, your family, and the Vesna family if they would like to join you as well. Won't that be nice?" The grin seemed to stretch so tight across his face that Cyndi thought his skull might pop out at any second.

"And what? You have another contract for me to sign?"

Right on cue, he pulled the neatly folded piece of paper and a gorgeous golden pen out of his jacket. "It's really only a slight addendum to the first one."

Cyndi took the contract from him and skimmed it briefly. Her mother and father gave each other a sick, worried glance, neither of them wanted her to sign anything else for this grinning shark of a man.

Finally Cyndi looked directly into Carver's cheerful eyes. "I've kept this all inside me for the last year. It has...eaten away at me. I didn't talk about it with my friends, my boyfriend, my family," she gestured to her parents who both looked down in shame. "No one. I needed to talk about it. I needed to work through it. Why do you need to keep this all so secret?"

"Like I said, I'm trying to protect my company and my employees. You have no idea what damage this kind of publicity could do to my company. It could cost hundreds of people their jobs."

"Yeah, I can see that. That's part of it, but why else?"

Carver looked at her parents and gave them a small shrug. "What do you mean?"

"You know more about all this. What are you hiding?"

Carver watched her cautiously for a moment, then shrugged. "I haven't the faintest idea what you're talking about." She remembered that line clearly. It was the last thing he said to her last year.

"Dozens of people are dead, and all you can think about is your company."

"Cyndi, please. Let's be reasonable here. I do care about--"

She ripped the contract in two. "I don't give a fuck about your company. I'm done keeping your

315

secrets. I'm done keeping quiet. I'll tell the newspapers, I'll tell the radio, I'll tell the TV stations, I'll tell the whole world what happened if I want to."

Cyndi glared at Carver, her eyes blazing. The grin had vanished from his face, leaving his mouth in its more natural state, a grim, sunken sneer.

"And what will they think when I tell them that you refused the counseling I just graciously offered? What will they think when I tell them that during *both* of your admittedly traumatic experiences, you broke in? You trespassed on private property. And what will they think about the fact that you beat up poor Jennifer Johnston hours before her death? I have the incident report with Jennifer Johnston's testimony. What will they think when I tell them that you are a very emotionally disturbed girl?"

Most of the fire disappeared from Cyndi's eyes. He had her right where he wanted her. Every counterpoint he made was valid and legitimately true. They sat there in silence grimly staring at each other.

"Get the hell out of my house," Cyndi said in a small, furious voice.

"Yes, I think it's time for you to leave," her mother spoke up coldly.

"As you wish." Carver flashed that grin of his again, a decidedly more shark-like grin than before. He had won, and he knew it. Without a word, he stood up and made his way out of their house. Cyndi, flanked by her parents, followed him to the door. He walked confidently out of her house toward his parked limousine, then stopped halfway down the front walkway. He turned back, smiling at Cyndi.

"Let me give you a bit of advice, Ms. Stevens," he said coldly, still smiling. "If I were you, I wouldn't make a habit out of making enemies. What happens on the day that you make an enemy that you can't handle?"

"I'll *handle* them," she retorted without missing a beat. "I'm a survivor."

Carver gave a short condescending laugh at that.

"We're *all* survivors, Ms. Stevens. Everyone. But all survivors eventually meet their end."

"Are you *threatening* my daughter?" her father finally spoke up. He sounded furious, and Cyndi's heart was filled with pride and love for him at that moment.

"Not at all," Carver replied. "Just giving a bit of advice from, ah, one *survivor* to another."

Carver flashed his wide toothy smile one last time. He walked down to the limo without looking back. Once he got in, the limo peeled away from their house with a screech of tires on the hot pavement.

Cyndi let go of her tension in a shuddering sigh. She turned and gave her father a warm smile. "Thanks, Dad."

"You bet, hon," he said. "If he ever comes back here, I'll k-- call the police." He changed his sentence at the last second, feeling that in light of recent events, the original wording would have been insensitive and inappropriate. They listened as the sound of the limo dwindled away in the distance, and Cyndi hoped to God that she would never have to see Carver's ugly, sneering grin ever again.

*   *   *

Cyndi was utterly surprised to see Johnny standing with her mother at her bedroom door the next afternoon. She had been reading Judy Blume's *Tiger Eyes* again with the radio on in the background. She expected to hear her mother's voice at the door and didn't look up until she heard Johnny's voice instead.

"Hey, Cyndi." He wore one of his open Hawaiian shirts and athletic shorts over his heavily bandaged right leg. He looked a little tired leaning heavily on one crutch, but he was alive. Cyndi immediately brightened when she saw him.

"They let you out early!" she said, jumping up from her bed and smoothing down her blonde, crimped hair. She hoped it wasn't out of place, and wished she had been able to dress better and put on a little eye-liner for him. Slipping her arm under his crutch, she gave him a long hug.

"I'll leave you two alone," her mother said, and graciously closed the door behind her. She never liked to close the door, but the kids had been through so much that she decided to give in this one time. Once the door was closed, Cyndi grabbed his head in both of her hands and kissed him full on the mouth. After the kiss, they sat down on her bed facing each other. He titled his head to the left and examined her stitches.

"Is that healing up okay?" he asked.

Cyndi shrugged. "I guess so. It still hurts when I eat." Johnny winced and sat there silently for a minute, gathering his thoughts.

"Look, I just wanted to thank you," he finally said. "You saved my life. It feels like such a weird thing to say, but it's true. I owe you my life."

She waved it away. "You don't owe me anything."

"No, I think I do. Over the past few weeks I acted like such a jerk. I wanted to apologize to you in person."

"You don't have to explain it to me."

"Thinking back on it all, it feels like a dream or something. It's like that guy who was drinking, and driving around with that psycho Brady, and smoking pot...that wasn't me."

Cyndi thought back to how she had knocked Jennifer down and slammed his fist into her face. "Yeah,

I know the feeling."

"God, I still can't believe it. All those people, gone. Eddie. He was my best friend. His family is taking it really hard."

"Do you really think Brady did all of it?" she asked. The question had been on her mind for the last few days. Johnny honestly considered the question.

"Yes and no. I knew the guy for years and he never would have done anything like that before. But you didn't see him out there. When he took that cocaine, it was like he was a completely different person. He wanted me to try it, but I told him 'No, that was too far for me.' He looked like he wanted to kill me then, or at least beat the shit out of me. He started throwing rocks and he...he just looked like he'd lost it. He had the craziest look in his eyes. I don't know. I really don't know what to think."

"At least you and Christie are safe. What did she say when you told her?"

Johnny looked uneasy. "My parents actually haven't told her. She was sleeping over at her friend's house when everything happened and they told her to stay there. This guy came to our house and talked to my dad the next day. He offered a full college scholarship if my dad signed this contract thing. So I'm not supposed to tell anyone or talk about it, not even to her. It's such bullshit."

Cyndi sighed angrily through clenched teeth.

"Kurt Carver. He's the reason why I couldn't tell you anything before," she explained. "He came back here again this time, but I ripped his contract up. You said, that guy wasn't you, well, I've kept my mouth shut about everything that happened last year, and I've been all messed up inside. I feel like that girl I've been, that wasn't *me* either. I wanted to tell you everything so bad, but at the same time I just wanted to forget it."

"Are you ready to tell me now?"

"Yeah, I'm ready."

"Thank God. It's like I came an hour late to a movie. I can't make sense out of all this."

"Yeah, well, you better sit back because it's a long story."

"I'm not going anywhere," he said, pointing at his bandaged legs.

Cyndi looked down and thought about how to begin. She walked over to her closet, opened her dresser drawer and brought out two T-shirts. She laid them out carefully on the bed, and Johnny looked down at them puzzled.

"I saved these from last year. They belonged to my friends, some of the best friends I ever had." She felt fresh tears well up in her eyes.

"Hey, Cyndi--" he began.

"It's just not fair, you know?" she interrupted. "It's not fair to have all this stuff taken away. All these friends taken away. All these nights when I can't sleep because I have bad dreams. All this time I've spent thinking about it, that was time I could've spent on other things. We didn't even get to have our first dance." That night at the dance seemed so long ago, so trivial, but it still weighed heavy on her heart. What should have been a magical night had been tainted with terror.

"We can still have a first dance," Johnny said. He stood up. "Let's do it here. Right now."

"Here?" she looked around her room.

"We don't need the gym and the lights. All we need is a good song. Besides, if you haven't noticed, it's not like I'll be dancing as good as Michael Jackson like I usually do."

Cyndi laughed aloud at that. "Don't you want to hear the whole story though?"

"I've waited this long, I can wait a little longer.

320

Pick a slow song."

With a bright smile on her face, she flipped through her records. She had just the song in mind. She pulled out the Cyndi Lauper album and flipped into onto her turntable. She put the needle down near the end of Side A and "Time After Time" began to play.

She walked back across the room and stood in front of Johnny. He smiled that cute crooked smile of his as she stepped forward, wrapping her arms around his waist. He slipped his free crutch-less arm around her waist. They looked into each other's eyes as they swayed to the music. Halfway through the song, she rested her head against his chest, enjoying the smell of him and the feel of his body pressed against hers.

There was no big dance, no nice clothes, and no crowded gym filled with kids, but it was magic all the same. Cyndi reluctantly pulled away from him as the song ended. She walked back to the record player, turned it off, and they sat back down on the bed. Now she had found her words, she had figured out where to begin, and she talked for hours.

Epilogue:

The tall man in the suit pushed the haggard old man in a wheelchair down the hospital corridor as rain poured and thunder boomed outside. It was late, far past visiting hours, but the hospital would make an exception for them. When you were filthy rich, people almost always made exceptions for you.

As they wheeled down the corridor, the old man and the younger man shared identical smiles on their faces. The old man's smile was covered with an oxygen mask but it was still visible through the clear plastic sides. Every few seconds a short hiss of oxygen would fill the mask and he would breath deeply. He sat slumped in his wheelchair, in an expensive white shirt. His long hair had once been thick and black, now it was now thin and white, but he still slicked it back the same as he always had. With his pale translucent skin, slumped, crooked posture, and bony, knotted hands, he looked like was on Death's doorstep.

They turned a corner and a nurse's station came into view. A tall, chunky, red-faced woman in scrubs was seated at the station, she looked up at the two men in surprise.

"How did you get back here? Visiting hours are

over," she said in a commanding voice.

The tall younger man left the wheelchair and walked up to her with that weird smile on his face, his hand sinking into his pocket. She drew back from him, suddenly thinking that he meant to pull out a gun and shoot her. Instead, he pulled out a fresh hundred dollar bill and laid it out neatly in front of her on the counter.

"You look tired," he said in a cool, persuasive voice. "Why don't you go take a break?"

The nurse stared at the man suspiciously for a moment. He gave her a wide-mouthed grin. She looked down at the old man he had been pushing in the wheelchair, and saw the same exact grin on his haggard, spotty face, it spread past the edges of his oxygen mask. Above that grin, the old man's wide, predatory eyes were unnerving. The nurse looked back down at the hundred dollar bill cautiously, picked it up, and examined it. She took one last look at the two grinning men, then made the hundred dollar bill disappear into her pocket. She turned around and walked away without a word.

Satisfied, Kurt and his father, Kent Carver, continued down the hall.

* * *

Kirk Sheehan sighed impatiently for what felt like the hundredth time. He had been told to wait in this dark, quiet hospital room at seven o' clock. The man on the phone had told him to wait until they arrived, no matter how late it was. Now it was after midnight, and he desperately wanted to leave.

On the other side of the curtain, the man in the bed hadn't moved in all that time. Thick bandages wrapped around his entire face and arms like a mummy. Restraints clamped over the man's chest, wrists, and ankles. A neck brace fit tightly around his sprained neck.

323

Sheehan had walked into the room earlier and looked down at this man, thinking he was asleep. A single light behind the bed was on, giving the room a dim, interrogation-room glow that Sheehan didn't care for. He stepped forward to get a closer look at the man and saw two tiny glints of light reflected back from the man's black eyes. He had been watching Sheehan the whole time.

Sheehan had tried to sit down in the chair across the room for about a half hour, but felt those black eyes on him the entire time. So he moved to the other side of the curtain and listened to the storm raging outside. The man wouldn't fall asleep. He just simply lay there silently, and completely still, like a poisonous snake.

Lightning flashed and Sheehan checked his watch again, wondering how long they were going to make him wait with this creepy silent hulk of a man. When he had discovered what had been going on at Thrill River, he had immediately called Kurt Carver. He had been instructed to stop the huge man, but not to kill him. He had found him and shot him on the Falls ride, then had rushed down and pulled this man out of the water. Using what little first aid knowledge he had, he patched up the gunshot wounds that he had inflicted. He called Carver back before calling the police, told him what happened, and was given more instructions. The next day, Sheehan bandaged the man's face and brought him to this hospital room as he'd been directed. He had dropped the man off without being asked any questions, then returned to the park to assist the police. Sheehan had thought about just packing up and leaving so many times in the past, but the Carvers were people you didn't screw around with. If they gave you instructions, you followed them to the letter, or who knew what nasty things might happen to you. The Carvers were a family with a lot of deep, horrible secrets. They didn't have a few skeletons in their closet, they had an entire cemetery full of them.

Sheehan had learned a lot about the Carvers over the past year. They had approached him after the incident at Camp Kikawa. They had known that he was in a weak position, and they had exploited him. It hadn't been the first time he'd had dealings with them.

Finally, the door clicked open, and Sheehan saw the silhouette of Kent Carver roll in, followed by Kurt Carver. Sheehan stood up and walked over to them.

"Hello, Mr. Carver. Mr. Carver," he said politely to first the father, then the son.

"Good evening, Mr. Sheehan. Thank you for waiting with him," Kurt Carver said. He wheeled the old man up to the bandaged mummy in the hospital bed. The old man stared down at the man in the bandages, and his sharky grin seemed to widen. The bandaged man's breathing became a ragged wheeze at the sight of the old geezer in the wheelchair. His chest heaved with every breath, and his fists clenched. He sounded terrified.

Sheehan watched as the old man pulled a small tape player out from under the blanket that covered his frail legs. He set the tape player down on the bed, and with one gnarled, shaky finger he hit the play button. At a low volume, an old rock and roll song started to play. Sheehan recognized it as "Rave On" by Buddy Holly, one of those golden oldies from the fifties.

At the sound of the song, the bandaged hulk began to jerk his body. His arms caught on the thick leather restraints, and his scarred fingers twitched madly. He knew that when the music started to play, you were in big trouble. With the music came the punishment. He had played his own songs and doled out his own punishments over the last year.

"You've been a very naughty boy," the old man rasped slowly, the oxygen mask muffled his voice only a little, making him sound slightly mechanical. The bandaged man's body began to heave and buck in wild terror.

A discolored, bird-claw hand shot out from the old man's waist, and bony old fingers dug painfully deep into the bandaged man's chest where the four gunshot wounds were struggling to heal.

"Lay *down!*" the last word came out as a deep growl, filled with insane rage.

A hand fell on Sheehan's shoulder and he jumped. Kurt Carver stood next to him smiling.

"Let's go outside, Mr. Sheehan," he said amiably. He ushered Sheehan out the door. Sheehan took one last glimpse back and saw the old man pull out a medical bag. He began rummaging through what looked like various sharp chrome dental instruments.

Kurt Carver closed the door, and only the muffled sounds of the old Buddy Holly tune came out.

"You've done well, Mr. Sheehan. It looks like everything will work out," Carver began.

"Look, Mr. Carver," Sheehan said. "With all due respect, I'd really just like to go. I'll sign whatever you want and I promise I won't say a word. But I don't think I can do this anymo--"

"Of course you can, Kirk. You're doin' fine," Carver interrupted. "We can't let you go just yet. You've still got work to do."

"Please, Mr. Carver. I can't...." Sheehan begged. Carver ignored him.

"The situation has changed. There are several loose ends that we'll need to tie up. My father and I do not like loose ends. We'll have to wait for everything to cool down before we can set things right again. So I'm going to need you to stay at Thrill River. You'll have to play chaperone and keep an eye on him for the time being."

Sheehan's mouth dropped open. "What? You can't be serious."

"Don't worry. He won't hurt you. You won't even know he's there most of the time. He can be very quiet."

Sheehan looked sick to his stomach. "For how long?"

"For as long as I tell you."

"Can you at least tell me who he is?"

"Well, the time is rather short tonight, so I can't go into details. He is my brother, at least that's the closest thing that describes my relationship to him."

Sheehan's mind reeled. *Another Carver?*

There was a light rap at the door behind them. Kurt Carver opened it and the old man sat there in his wheelchair.

"All done?" Kurt Carver asked. The old man nodded. The music had stopped and both the tape player and the medical bag had disappeared under the blanket again. Kurt Carver turned back to Sheehan one last time. "Go back to Thrill River and stay there with him. We'll be in touch."

A million questions flew through Sheehan's mind all at once. "What'll I do if he gets out of control again?" he called after them. Both Carvers ignored him. Sheehan watched them walk down the hall, then turned and ran for the side exit. As he ran, he felt damned. *This is what it must feel like,* he thought, *to sell your soul to the devil.*

*   *   *

The head nurse walked up to the empty station just as the Carvers turned around the corner. She caught a glimpse of them.

"Hey," she called out, but they didn't turn back.

327

They were as good as gone and she knew it. She wondered where the hell that new nurse was, she was supposed to be on duty right now. If she caught that new girl out there taking another smoke break again, her head was gonna roll. She had explained over and over: *'You take your breaks when they're scheduled, not whenever the hell you feel like it.'* The stupid bitch probably wouldn't last here very long.

Remembering the two men she had seen just around the corner, she wondered just what the hell they had been doing here. They probably weren't trying to rob the place, one of them was in a wheelchair, but what had they been doing here after midnight? She leaned over the counter and looked down the hall. The door to the room at the end of the hallway was open. Had they been in there?

The head nurse walked down the hall towards the door. The noise of the storm outside became louder as she approached. She saw no medical chart in the little plastic bin in front of the door, but she could have sworn there had been a patient resting in there earlier this evening.

Inside, the room was dark except for one light left on behind the bed closest to the window. The nurse pulled back the curtain and saw an empty unmade bed. The sheets were all rumpled and tossed around, the restraints were gone. Looking more closely, she saw one dark drop of blood on the corner of the pillow.

Lightning flashed again, followed by a loud crack of thunder that made her jump. She noticed that the window was open and rain water was coming in puddling on the floor. Slowly, she walked over to stare out that window at the raging storm. The winds whipped at the trees and thin bushes outside the window. If there had been anyone in this room, they had run off into the night and were long gone now.

Afterword:

Sequels are hard. They are harder than I ever thought possible. I used look at my stack of *Friday the 13th* DVDs and think: *If I ever write a really fun horror story, I'll write nine or ten sequels too. Just keep it going forever, run that baby into the ground.* Probably my favorite slasher sequel is *Child's Play 2*, written by the legendary Don Mancini. I loved how the story took off in a different direction, with Chucky following Andy into the big colorful world of middle-class foster family suburbia. I loved how it was ultimately a lot more fun than the original. I used to watch great sequels like *Child's Play 2* and *Friday the 13th Part 2*, and wonder why so many sequels didn't turn out so well. Wouldn't it be easy to just come up with some slight twist, maybe a new setting or a new character for the killer to face off with? I also used to wonder why Stephen King never chose to write sequels to any of his stories (this was long before *Doctor Sleep*), in my mind a Stephen King sequel would be a slam-dunk.

Then I tried to write *Kill River 2,* and my whole perspective on writing sequels changed. I learned how much of a balancing act writing a sequel really is. I didn't want to write a carbon-copy of the first one, but I also wanted to keep the fun feeling of the first one alive. While writing the first six or seven chapters I found myself missing Camp Kikawa and the out-in-the-woods feel. There were times when I felt very unsure about whether my sequel would live up to the original. But for me, *Kill River* has always been about making a horror story as fun as possible. What gave me confidence to write this story was adding a ton of fun 80s feel to it, like the scenes at the dance, the mall, and the Countryside pool. Once the introductory stuff is over, then it basically becomes a full-on love-letter for my local water park *WaterWorld*, and what it's like to spend a day there. I definitely had some challenging moments writing it, but in the end, I think I may have had more fun writing *Part Two* than I had writing *Part One*, and I hope you had just as much fun reading it. And to add to that, I feel that the soundtrack is easily the best out of all three of my books so far.

Once again, I have to thank my wife, Darla, my dad, and my best friend Tim Taylor for helping me edit this book. Hopefully they won't get tired of editing my stuff any time soon, I don't know what I'd do without them. And I have to thank everyone who has discovered *Kill River* over the past few years and encouraged me to release a sequel. Your kind emails, twitter messages, and conversations with me at conventions really mean the world to me, and keep me going through all the long hours of editing and book-binding. You guys are the best, and I hope this book lived up to your expectations. And as always, feel free to email me or message me on twitter any time. I'd love to talk with you and hear your thoughts on my books, or slasher movies, or superheroes, or anything else.

I apologize if you don't feel entirely satisfied by the way it ended, and I hope you'll stick with me into *Kill River 3*. Unfortunately for Cyndi, a storm is coming, and the three Carvers and their water parks are far from done with her. Also check out my other book, *Disco Deathtrap,* if you haven't already. It spun off from an idea I originally had planned but didn't use for *Kill River 2,* and like the *Kill River* books, it's a ton of '80s slasher fun. So until next time, keep reading, keep watching slasher movies, and keep going to your local water parks. But be sure to get back home before the sun sets, those moonlight beach parties at the wave pool can be killer.

Cameron Roubique
Thornton, Colorado
October 2nd, 2017

Soundtrack:

The following is a list of songs that are either prominently featured in this book or inspired me as appropriate background music in some of the scenes. You really don't have to listen to these songs to enjoy *Kill River 2,* but all of them are excellent and if you're not already familiar with them, I highly recommend checking them out.

Cameron Roubique

1. "The Safety Dance" - Men Without Hats
2. "Money Changes Everything" - Cyndi Lauper
3. "Magic" - The Cars
4. "The Waiting" - Tom Petty and the Heartbreakers
5. "Hot For Teacher" - Van Halen
6. "Hello Again" - The Cars
7. "Don't Worry Baby" - The Beach Boys
8. "Mercenary" - The Go-Go's
9. "Der Kommissar" - After the Fire
10. "All Through the Night" - Cyndi Lauper
11. "Runnin With the Devil" - Van Halen
12. "Time After Time" - Cyndi Lauper
13. "Rave On" - Buddy Holly

About the Author:

Cameron Roubique lives in Thornton,
Colorado, with his wife, Darla, cat, Penny,
and pug Vader. He is an avid 80's slasher
movie, superhero, and water park fan.

You can follow him on his website
at www.killriver.com
on twitter at twitter.com/lil_cam_ron
and on instagram at instagram.com/cameronroubique.

He can also be reached through email at
cameron@killriver.com.